Better Dead

Better Dead

Pamela Kopfler

KENSINGTON PUBLISHING CORP.

http://www.kensingtonbooks.com

KENSINGTON BOOKS are published by

Kensington Publishing Corp.
119 West 40th Street
New York, NY 10018

All Kensington titles, imprints and distributed lines are available at special quantity discounts for bulk purchases for sales promotions, premiums, fund-raising, and educational or institutional use. Special book excerpts or customized printings can also be created to fit specific needs. For details, write or phone the office of the Kensington Special Sales Manager, Kensington Publishing Corp., 119 West 40th Street, New York, NY 10018. Attn. Special Sales Department. Phone: 1-800-221-2647.

Kensington and the K logo Reg. U.S. Pat. & TM Off.

ISBN-13: 978-1-4967-1321-6
ISBN-10: 1-4967-1321-4
First Kensington Mass Market Edition: January 2018

eISBN-13: 978-1-4967-1322-3
eISBN-10: 1-4967-1322-2
First Kensington Electronic Edition: January 2018

10 9 8 7 6 5 4 3 2 1

Printed in the United States of America

ACKNOWLEDGMENTS

Writing is solitary but not lonely. In fact, I dreamed up the plot for *Better Dead* during a writers' retreat at Nottoway Plantation in White Castle, Louisiana. The organizer challenged us to write a ghost story in the spirit of Lord Byron's challenge to Mary Shelley (*Frankenstein*) during an 1816 retreat at the Villa Diodati in France. I will be eternally grateful to the late Nick Genovese for the writing prompt that drove me to see *Better Dead* through to THE END.

Before I wrote the first word of this novel, my dear husband, Joe, believed in me and proved it in deed and spirit. Many thanks to my children, Adam and Caroline, for their cheers and hugs along the way, and to my mother for her tolerance of my tall tales years ago.

Never underestimate the power of a bookseller. Molly Bolden, co-owner of Bent Pages, sat with me one fine day on the front porch of her bookstore after reading my short stories. She leaned back in her rocker and tossed me a simple question. *Why don't you write a novel?* She asked with every confidence that I could. Her question nagged me enough for me to park my caboose in a chair in front of my computer to find out. Thank you,

Molly, for asking the right question, being my friend, and always giving your honest opinion.

Along the way, I had tremendous support and friendship from the Southern Louisiana chapter of Romance Writers of America®, where I met my critique partner extraordinaire, Jaimie Bergeron. I thank her from the bottom of my heart for her commitment and sage critiques from concept to completed novel. Special thanks also go to chapter mates Vicky McHenry, Charlotte Parker, and June Shaw, as well as to my dear friend Emily Rash for beta reading my entire draft and offering insights that enriched the story.

As an RWA® Golden Heart® finalist, I found mentorship and fellowship with the other finalists, which developed into a priceless sisterhood I treasure. Thank you, Firebirds, Dragonflies, and Mermaids.

I owe many thanks to my incredible literary agent, Rachel Brooks (BookEnds Literary Agency) a relentless champion of my work and my savvy guide through the journey to publication.

I can't thank the teams at Kensington Books enough for their dedication to making this book the best it could be. My talented editor, Esi Sogah, and Norma Perez-Hernandez (editorial assistant) offered insights and guidance, which enhanced this novel and my skills as a novelist. I appreciate Rosemary Silva's fine eye for detail in her superb copyedit. Special thanks to art director Louis Malcangi, who rendered a beautiful cover that captured the essence of *Better Dead*.

Finally, dear reader, I must thank you. Writing and publishing a novel is not complete without you. Only through your willingness to open the book can the people between these pages come to life. Then they can take you on an adventure of clues, twists, turns, and laughs to solve a mystery. I hope you enjoy *Better Dead*.

Special note: Two of my characters are named in honor of real people, Mickey and Charlie Lusco. Their generous bid at an auction won them a place between these pages and helped fund their local Kiwanis club in their mission "to improve the world, one child and one community at a time."

CHAPTER 1

Holly Davis wanted a divorce, not a funeral.

The young widow eased her desk drawer open and removed two files. The first held the divorce papers her husband hadn't lived to receive. The second was filled with every reason to divorce him in full-color, glossy prints. She strolled to the fireplace in the parlor of her bed-and-breakfast and dropped both files onto the cold ashes.

Two drops of brut slid between her lips as she tilted her crystal flute. "This requires another glass of champagne," she announced to her Yorkshire terrier.

Rhett's ears perked up.

Holly frowned and shook a finger at him. "Don't you tell me I'm drunk."

As she turned toward the armoire that concealed the bar, she wobbled on her stiletto sandals. "*Lordy.* Good-looking shoes are just like good-looking men. Dangerous."

She kicked off her shoes. One hurled through the air and bounced off the wall, barely missing a portrait of her great-great-grandfather.

Holly returned to the fireplace with a full glass of champagne and a box of matches. She lit the files, then perched on the antique settee in front of the fire. The files curled as the flames consumed them and their secrets. She owed Burl that much.

At least he'd done his philandering out of town. The good people of Delta Ridge, Louisiana, had turned out for his funeral, and they'd poured sympathy her way for the past three months. Holly couldn't make them feel like the fool she was. She'd keep Burl's secret, but she'd accept no more sympathy. Tonight was her last night as a grieving widow. She'd dressed up to celebrate her new life and bid her old one good-bye.

Raising her glass, she made a toast on what would have been their tenth anniversary. "I didn't wish you dead, Burl Davis, but thanks for setting me free."

Smoke curled over the mantel.

"Oh, crapola. I forgot to open the damper." She scrambled to flip the metal catch open as the fire licked her arm. Without thinking, she doused the flames with her champagne.

The fire hissed. Thick billows of smoke swirled and grew. A hazy figure took shape in front of the fireplace.

She gasped and stepped back.

"Is this any way to mourn your dearly departed husband?"

"B-Burl?" She blinked, hoping the image would disappear. Glass shattered as her flute hit the hardwood floor. Her heart jumped from her chest into her throat. Raising her hand to her neck, she took another step back and stared at the silhouette of her dead husband.

The wind howled, sucking the smoke and Burl up the flue. A surviving flame flickered between the logs as silence fell around her.

Holly fingered the Mikimoto pearls Burl had given her last year, on their anniversary, and shook her head. She swallowed hard. She'd buried Burl three months ago. Trying to compose herself, she smoothed her hands over her red silk dress.

Nothing but the wind and her imagination. Guests at her Louisiana bed-and-breakfast often insisted they'd seen the supernatural. Holly didn't believe in ghosts, but visitors expected an antebellum plantation to have a spirit or two roaming around. She played along to boost her business.

She blew out a long sigh. *Guilt and too much champagne.* Both self-inflicted. She didn't have anything to feel guilty about. Burl had crashed his airplane, and she couldn't help it if her life was better without him.

Holly tiptoed around the shards of glass and retrieved one of her stilettos. The room tilted as she tried to balance on one foot to slip on her shoe.

Rhett peeked from under the antique settee.

"Guess I scared you to death when I dropped that glass." She scooped him up and rubbed his head, then sat him down a safe distance from the glass. "You didn't see a thing, did you, boy?"

She scanned the room for her other shoe, then eyed Rhett. "Where is it?"

He wagged his entire backside, as though he had nothing to hide.

"Just like a man."

The opened bottle of brut chilling in the ice bucket was too expensive to waste. She poured another glass of champagne and downed it, hoping for a good night's sleep. Since she had no guests, she'd have the luxury of sleeping until eight o'clock.

Carrying the champagne bucket, she hobbled on

one shoe to the kitchen. Then she armed herself with the Dustbuster and a fire extinguisher to clean up her mess.

Even tipsy, she considered the possibility of the ancient damper closing in the middle of the night, filling the place with smoke or burning down her home and business. Luck had never sided with Holly.

When she returned to the parlor, the logs above the ashes had caught fire. The charcoal scent of the old fireplace floated through the room. Focusing on the tiny shards of glass challenged her alcohol-impaired vision, but she vacuumed, anyway. She didn't want to chance Rhett stepping on a sliver of glass. Besides, the Delta Ridge Bridge Club had rented the parlor for nine o'clock in the morning for their weekly game. She couldn't have broken glass on the floor.

Holly tossed the Dustbuster on the settee, then picked up the fire extinguisher. She couldn't trust the damper to stay open. One spark and the fire could ignite again while she slept.

She'd never used a fire extinguisher before, and reading the label was out of the question tonight. Holly closed one eye and aimed the fire extinguisher toward the flames. Swaying, she squeezed the trigger, and a wide spray of white foam gushed onto the hardwood floor. She tilted the nozzle upward and lost her balance, sending the spray up the fifteen-foot wall to the carved crown molding.

A Casper the Friendly Ghost version of Burl coated in white foam stood before her. She dropped the fire extinguisher and dashed to the kitchen like a peg-legged pirate.

She grabbed the bottle of champagne off the counter and poured it down the drain. "I swear, God, if you'll get Burl out of my parlor, I'll never drink another drop," she said, with as much sincerity as she could pump into her plea to God, since she hadn't talked to Him lately.

She glanced over her shoulder.

Rhett scooted backward into the kitchen and barked all the way.

"What I wouldn't give for a drink right now. And there you go, pouring my best bottle down the drain."

Holly spun around to the powdery face of Burl Davis smiling at her. She strangled the neck of the empty bottle and wagged it at the apparition. "Y-you're not here. Y-you're dead. I buried you three months ago."

"Yeah. I'm dead. You buried me. But I *am* here." He opened his arms, as though she'd rush to hug him.

"No!" She shook her head. "I don't see dead people. Bruce Willis sees dead people. My guests see dead people."

She slammed the bottle into the trash. "I'm just drunk, and you're my pink elephant."

"Afraid not, Blondie." He shrugged. "Besides, Bruce was dead. The kid saw dead people."

Holly rolled her eyes and hiccuped. "Whatever."

She hated it when he called her Blondie. "In the morning, I'll have a hangover, and you'll be gone."

"Not likely."

Stepping from high heel to bare foot in an awkward up-and-down motion that made her dizzy, she backed out of the kitchen.

"Definitely," she said with as much diction as her thick tongue would allow.

He matched her step for step through the entrance hall. "I'm telling you, I'm not going anywhere."

Old anger bubbled up from the pit of her stomach. "You always have to win, don't you?"

"I don't want to argue."

"That's a first." Their entire marriage had been a debate.

Burl laughed. "First time I've been dead."

"That's right. You're dead. Now, get out of my life." She flung her arms, as though shooing him away, and stumbled forward.

He bowed his head and mumbled, "Can't."

She plastered her hands on her hips. "What do you mean, can't?"

"Peter wouldn't let me in."

She leveled her eyes at her dead husband in disbelief. "Do you mean St. Peter, as in the one at Heaven's gate?"

He nodded.

"I'm not surprised," she huffed. "Finally going to hell, huh?"

"Not exactly."

Death hadn't changed him one bit. "Can you just spit out the truth without twisting it into a pretzel?"

"I have some unfinished business." He lifted a shoulder. "Until I make it right, I'm stuck here."

"Here? As in on earth?" She took another backward step into the parlor.

He shook his head and pointed to the floor. "Here, with you, in this house. One step outside and I burn, so I'm stuck here."

"You're not staying here." *I just got my life back.* "You can't."

"Afraid so."

Jealousy from the past pinched her heart. "Go haunt your girlfriend."

She spun around to stomp away and stepped from stiletto to bare foot. In one quick motion, she snatched off her shoe and hurled it at Burl. "Better yet, go to hell!"

The stiletto sailed through him. "It's a possibility."

Holy moly. The first time her aim hit the target and it didn't faze him. "I know the devil will let you in."

"You don't want me to burn for all eternity. Do you?" His pale face drooped.

"I don't care." She glared at him, wishing he'd disappear.

Spots of the powdery foam clung to his outline. Where the foam had flaked off, Burl was transparent.

"You're the only one who can see or hear me."

"Why me?"

"You called to me like I was still alive. You brought me back." He shrugged. "Sort of."

"The toast? That was to say good-bye. Did something get lost in the translation from the real world to the"— she drew quotation marks in the air—"other side?"

Burl grinned. "You called. I came."

"I'm having a nightmare, I'm drunk, or you've finally driven me completely out of my mind." Holly clapped her hands over her ears and squeezed her eyes shut, blocking Burl out of her world. She stood as still as she could, but the floor rolled beneath her feet like the deck of a boat in rough seas. The rocking motion churned her stomach. If she didn't open her eyes, she would either faint or puke. The thought of living with Burl again prompted the same symptoms.

Holly landed on the hardwood floor with a thud but didn't feel the pain she'd expected. She dared to open one eye. A powdery white dust peppered the cypress planks. She pried her other eye open to find the source.

Pieces and parts of the dried foam had flaked off Burl onto the floor. "Are you still here?"

"Barely." He sounded weak.

She closed her eyes. "Good. Maybe you'll be gone when I wake up."

"I have only until midnight on Halloween to make things right, or I'm stuck here forever. You're the only one who can help me." His voice faded.

"No problem, Burl. I have thirty days to get you into heaven and out of my hair. We'll talk about it tomorrow, when I'm sober," she said, waving him off without opening her eyes.

Tomorrow I'll be sober, and Burl will be dead and gone, again.

"Sarcasm doesn't look good on you, Blondie. I have a shot at getting in if you help me."

Holly opened her eyes and looked up at Burl. "Let's see." She lifted her index finger and laid it against her cheek. "You cheated on me, robbed our 401(k), left me in debt for your funeral, and you want my help to get into paradise." She tapped a finger against her cheek, as if she were thinking, then gave a forced laugh. "I don't think so, but what can I do to get you into hell?"

"Very funny. If you don't help, I'm stuck here at Holly Grove for all eternity, and you're stuck with me for life." He raised a brow. "Unless you plan on moving."

Holly had sunk every dime of her inheritance into converting Holly Grove into a B & B three years ago, and Burl knew it. This was the year that Holly Grove was finally supposed to make a profit. She sighed. It had to.

She closed her eyes, and the room spun. Seven generations of her family had held on to Holly Grove through the Civil War, the Depression, and the Great Flood of 1927. Holly Grove and the people who worked there were the closest thing she had to a family. She'd never give up Holly Grove for a ghost or anything else. "What do I have to do?"

He didn't answer.

She opened her eyes. "Burl?"

White powder sprinkled down like salt from a box onto the hardwood floor, and he was gone.

Rhett's yaps pierced Holly's ears and bounced from temple to temple in her aching head.

She cracked one eye open. Sunlight flooded through the floor-to-ceiling windows of the parlor. She squinted and tried to lift her right hand to shield her eyes from the glare. The useless arm tingled and throbbed. No wonder. Her arm was dead asleep from spending the night on the hardwood floor. *Blasted Burl.* She couldn't even toast him good-bye without him causing trouble in her life.

Still groggy with sleep, she remembered what had to be last night's nightmare. Definitely, no more champagne for her.

Shifting her weight and trying to pry herself from the floor to begin her recovery, she noticed Miss Martha Jane Shaw's face, framed by cupped hands, staring at her through the window.

"Y'all. She moved." Miss Martha Jane turned and then crooked her arthritic finger in a motioning gesture toward the other end of the porch.

A cattle clomp of heels tromped across the porch. Oh, no. The Deltas had arrived. All four members of the Delta Ridge Bridge Club pressed their faces against the glass.

Holly dropped her sore head back to the floor. *Just shoot me now.*

Miss Martha Jane rapped on the 150-year-old glass. "Don't move. We've called 911."

Holly opened her mouth to protest as glass shattered. Miss Alice reached through the gaping hole where the windowpane had been and unlocked the window. The ladies heaved open the walk-through window, as Holly struggled to get up with a numb arm and a pounding headache.

Miss Alice Fort stormed to her side, followed by the rest of the club. She pushed Holly's shoulder back to the floor and lunged over her, trapping her under no less than forty pounds of grandmother boobs.

Grabbing Holly's numb wrist, Miss Alice zeroed in on her large-face watch to check Holly's pulse. Miss Alice's husband had been the only full-time doctor in Delta Ridge before dropping dead from a heart attack four years ago. She probably thought she'd earned a medical degree through osmosis in the course of her fifty-year marriage. "Lie still," she commanded.

Holly squirmed. If she wasn't afraid she'd break the old gal's hip, she would've struggled harder.

"Help me hold her down," Miss Alice ordered.

Knees cracking, the other three Deltas scampered to the floor. All four geriatrics pinned her down.

Holly pried her numb wrist free with her good hand. "Miss Alice. I'm fine," she said, dodging a boob.

Miss Alice stared down at her. "How much did you take?"

"What?"

The old lady leaned over Holly, nearly smothering

her. Then Miss Alice swept her hand across the floor. She held her wrinkled fingers, dusted with white powder, in front of Holly's face. "It's cocaine, isn't it?"

Holly remembered showering Burl with the fire extinguisher last night and the white powder that had flaked off him just before she passed out. The fine hair on her neck lifted as she wrapped her mind around the fact that she'd had no nightmare. "Oh, my God. It's Burl."

Miss Alice's eyes widened. "What?"

"That's Burl's dust," Holly blurted.

Miss Martha Jane gasped and covered her mouth.

"She's hallucinating," Miss Alice said to the other biddies.

A wail of sirens drew their attention. Miss Martha Jane rushed to open the front door.

Sandy Wright jogged into the parlor, pushing a gurney. She gave her pants a yank and tilted her chin up. "What happened here?"

"It's an OD," Miss Alice snapped with medical precision.

"No sh—" Sandy covered her mouth. "Sorry, ladies. This is the first OD call I've had since I got my EMT license."

Holly's throbbing head spun back to Miss Alice. "It's not cocaine. It's Burl's dust."

"She's hallucinating, too," Miss Martha Jane added, wringing her hands.

While Miss Alice was distracted, Holly took the opportunity to wiggle out from under her and bolt to her feet. "See. I'm fine. This is just a mis—"

Black and red splotches danced across her vision, and she staggered.

Sandy grabbed Holly's arm and steadied her. "Don't

worry, Holly. Everything is going to be fine. Just lie down here." She helped Holly to the gurney, then strapped her in.

Holly's vision cleared. "No. I just got up too fast."

"You could have a concussion from passing out, too," Sandy said. She gave the straps an extra tug, then eyed the old ladies. "Among other things."

In the distance, Holly heard Burl laughing his tail end off.

"It's not funny," she snapped as she struggled against the straps.

Sandy patted Holly's arm. "No one's laughing. Just try to calm down."

"You don't hear him?" Holly searched the women's faces and met blank stares.

Burl laughed harder and louder. If he weren't dead, Holly would have murdered him on the spot.

Rhett trotted alongside the gurney as Sandy rolled it across the hardwood floor.

Poor Rhett. "You can't go, boy." Holly looked back at the Deltas.

Miss Martha Jane scooped up Rhett. "Don't worry, Holly. I'll take care of him while you're in rehab."

"Rehab? For what? That's fire extinguisher dust."

Miss Alice narrowed her eyes. "You said it was Burl's dust."

"It is. Well, sort of. I meant to spray the fire in the fireplace and sprayed Burl."

"But, honey, Burl has passed on," Miss Martha Jane said.

"A hallucination," Miss Alice said to Sandy, as though Holly wasn't there.

Sandy pushed the gurney out the door. "I'll take good care of her."

Holly's stomach knotted. If the Deltas' version of this story traveled through the gossip circles of Delta Ridge, it could ruin her business.

Dang you to Hades and back, Burl. This is all your fault.

A little prick of an idea loosened the knot in her stomach. Burl owed her, and he needed her to do something big. She had leverage. Her resident poltergeist had better get ready to pay up or burn.

CHAPTER 2

Holly tiptoed on bare feet to her back door after being held for observation most of the day, thanks to a possible concussion and Miss Alice's pull at the clinic. Tugging the aged cypress door open, Holly met the spicy aroma of Nelda's gumbo. Then deep laughter slapped her in the face.

"I don't think it's funny," Holly snapped at her housekeeper. "Where were you when they hauled me off in an ambulance?"

Nelda cleared her throat and rubbed her hands on a white dishcloth. "I was cleaning the guest rooms in the carriage house. You know we got six coming for the weekend. I came running when I heard the siren, but I got there too late. They told me all about it, though." She guffawed again. "I'm sorry, Holly, but I can just see Miss Alice holdin' you down like she was roping a baby calf." She stomped three times, then buried her chubby face in the dishcloth.

Holly glared at Nelda, whom she had known longer than Burl and liked a lot better. Usually.

Nelda held a hand up. "Okay. I won't laugh, but this

is one of the best messes you ever got yourself in. They didn't call you Hurricane Holly for nothin'." She stirred the gumbo with a wooden spoon and shook her head.

Would she never live that name down? One sunken boat, a fire alarm, and a science project gone wrong in middle school had earned her the title of Hurricane Holly, a natural disaster, and it had stuck. "This is different. It's all just a big misunderstanding."

"You know, folks is sayin' everything at Holly Grove is canceled on account of you bein' in rehab and all."

"No." Holly drew the word out with an exasperated breath. She plopped down on an oak bench at the planter's table. The tongue-wagging Deltas hadn't wasted any time. Holly Grove was on the Haunted Pilgrimage Tour of Homes, which brought hundreds of tourists to Delta Ridge every October. She couldn't let a rumor ruin the best moneymaker of the year. Without the money from the tour, she couldn't keep Holly Grove going. What about her staff? Her throat tightened as she looked back at Nelda. She was like family.

"Uh-huh." Nelda adjusted the flame on the 1928 gas stove. "But I told 'em you don't do drugs."

"Unless you're going to scream it from every corner in the South, we're screwed." Holly's stomach pinched.

Nelda lifted the lid on the rice, and steam curled over the pot, reminding Holly of Burl's appearance. "Don't worry. Movie stars go in and out of rehab all the time and don't miss a beat."

Holly looked at her wrinkled red dress and bare feet. She raked a hand through her hair, and it tangled in a snag of blond curls. "But I'm no movie star."

"You're 'bout the closest thing we got in St. Agnes Parish."

"Have you looked at me lately?"

"Sure." Nelda spooned some rice in a bowl. "You done lost 'bout ten pounds and wears lipstick more since Burl passed, God rest his soul. Don't forget you was Sugarcane Queen."

"That hardly counts." She would never have won if the virus she'd had the week before—which knocked several pounds off her—hadn't swept through the competition on pageant day.

"That flu didn't have a thing to do with you winning. Even if folks did call it hurricane flu."

Of course, Mama, Grandma Rose, Nelda, and Jake McCann—the people who loved her—had believed she would have won, anyway. Holly had loved Jake for that back then.

A foolish teenage love for a guy who couldn't wait to get the heck out of Delta Ridge the day he finished high school. Now Jake was probably in some foreign country, living out his dream, and she was in Delta Ridge, living a nightmare. "Well, that was fifteen years and a lot of living ago."

Nelda flooded the bowl with a ladle full of chicken gumbo. "You'd have won Miss Louisiana, too, if you hadn't up and married Burl, God rest his soul."

"Why do you say that every time you talk about Burl?"

"I don't want to call him back." Nelda served another bowl of gumbo. "It's bad luck to talk about the dead and not say something good."

No kidding. Holly glanced around the room for Burl.

Nelda shuffled to the table with the two bowls of hot gumbo. Rhett trailed Nelda, sniffing the air.

"Gumbo's bad for your constitution, boy," Nelda said as she sat across from Holly.

The first spoonful of warm, spicy gumbo hit Holly's empty stomach. "Nelda, don't you dare die without giving me this recipe."

"Humph." Nelda chuckled. "I'll leave it to you in my will. It's gonna be worth somethin' when I win the Haunted Pilgrimage cookin' contest."

"Did you notice that white, powdery stuff the Deltas thought was cocaine?"

"Yeah. I vacuumed it all up after Sheriff Walker said it wasn't dope."

"The sheriff was here, too?" She plunked an elbow on the table and dropped her forehead on the palm of her hand.

"Yeah." Nelda grinned, showing all her bright white teeth. "He laughed harder than me when he found the fire extinguisher rolled up under your desk in the parlor."

Holly blew out a heavy breath. Could this fiasco get any worse?

"Sorry." Nelda's lips strained to cover her grin.

"Wait a minute." Holly jumped up from the table. "I can fix this."

"What you gonna do?"

"The same thing the stars do." Holly framed her face with her hands and flashed what she hoped was a movie star smile. "Damage control."

Holly rushed to her desk. Within a few moments, she'd called and asked the sheriff to e-mail his reports to her. She perched on her straight-back chair and fired up her laptop, which she kept hidden in her rolltop desk. Except for electricity, bathrooms, and a kitchen, Holly had kept the plantation house frozen in 1857. That was what the tourists paid to see.

Nelda poked her head around the door frame. "How 'bout that damage control?"

"I'm going to sweet-talk old Sam into running a feature article on Holly Grove in the *Gazette*, since I can't afford an ad."

"Humph," Nelda grunted.

"So, he's a little tight." Holly lifted her shoulders. "You don't know if you don't ask."

"Tight? He squeezes a penny so tight, he rubs old Abe's beard off." Nelda waved Holly off. "But you go right ahead."

Holly laughed. "I have a backup plan."

"Now I'm all ears." Nelda pulled a chair up beside Holly.

She tapped her laptop screen. "The sheriff and the hospital are going to e-mail my reports to me."

"So what you going to do with the reports? Put them in the paper?"

"No. Better. I'll invite the Deltas to play bridge in the parlor tomorrow for free. I'll show them the reports and explain what happened." *Except the part about Burl.* "The gossip mill started the rumor that I was in rehab, and they can darned well grind it to a halt."

"I don't know about that." Nelda shook her head. "Them Deltas, they got the best of you this mornin'."

Holly straightened and eyed Nelda. "You just make the coffee and dessert. I've got big plans for the Deltas." And if Burl played along, the Deltas were in for a shock that would make Holly Grove the most popular plantation on the Haunted Pilgrimage.

* * *

Holly squirmed in her slightly tight, but most flattering jeans on the leather seat of her Tahoe as she drove into Delta Ridge. Sam's age didn't keep him from looking, and she needed all the help she could get to persuade him to run a nice fluffy piece on Holly Grove.

In ten minutes, the doors of the *Gazette* would be locked for the night. But the gossip mill never stopped. Holly squeezed the steering wheel. She needed an article in the newspaper ASAP to help squelch the rumor she was in rehab. Holly Grove had to pay the bills now, and she couldn't afford bad publicity or another failure.

Holly tilted her head to check her lipstick. Too bright. But Sam had cataracts. It'd work.

She came to the straightaway and sped around a cane-cutting tractor. The white Delta Ridge water tower stood dead center on the horizon, surrounded by a sugarcane field. The faintest outline of a faded pink heart on the tower had bled through the chalky paint again. Her stomach fluttered, as if she'd hit a dip in the road, even though St. Agnes Parish didn't have a single hill.

Every five or so years, the heart bled through. For fifteen years, the whole town had speculated about who had painted the heart on the tower. Only two people knew the truth. Holly and Jake. It was their secret. She'd never told a soul. Jake had left town with his half of the secret and her heart. He'd begged her to go, and she'd begged him to stay, but they had both been stubborn kids back then.

If she'd gone with Jake, would their young love have decayed, the way her marriage had? Now that Burl was gone, she wondered if she'd ever truly loved him or if she'd married him to fill the hole Jake had left in her life.

She drove past the old Bijou Theater, now Joe's Swap and Trade. Bare mannequins stared through the cracked-glass storefront of Delta Style Boutique. She had worked there in high school and had bought it when Miss Darling retired after forty years. A year into the recession, the business had failed. Holly heaved a sigh. Another notch in her list of unlucky ventures. Vacant buildings and a hodgepodge of conversions haunted downtown Delta Ridge from its past. The rural South withered around her, and she hated watching it die.

Holly wheeled into a parking place on the square, then eyed her watch. One minute until Sam locked the doors to the public. She grabbed the quart of gumbo Nelda had donated to the cause. If she couldn't sweet-talk Sam, she would try to reach his heart through his stomach. If Sam said yes, the gumbo was a thank-you gift. If he said no, maybe the old buzzard would feel guilty when he ate it.

The high-heeled boots she hoped made the legs that came with her five-foot-three-inch body look longer hampered her speed. Her heels clicked as she trotted down the street, past Bob's Barbershop. Bob had died years ago, but his daughter, Roberta, stood behind a vintage barber chair, rolling Miss Alice's hair. Holly nearly jerked a crick in her neck to avoid making eye contact. She wasn't ready for Miss Alice yet. That conversation would be best handled over the phone.

Light from inside the *Gazette* shone through the plate-glass window. The breath she didn't realize she'd held rushed from her lungs as she opened the door.

A worn oak counter spanned the reception area. "Hello?" she called in the empty room.

Holly pushed through a swinging panel and strode behind the counter. The panel sprung back in place with a flapping noise as she scurried down the hall to Sam's office.

His wooden door stood ajar. She knocked lightly but hard enough to push it open. "Hello?"

Holding the glass jar of gumbo, she strolled into the room. The stale scent of Sam's pipe tobacco hung in the air. Sam's sailfish covered the wall behind his desk. Piles of newspapers, paperwork, and notes littered his work space. Broad shoulders that didn't belong to Sam inched over the back of Sam's chair, which faced the sailfish.

A keyboard rattled under rapid, heavy strokes. "Yep."

"Sorry. Can you tell me where Sam is?"

The typing stopped.

Massive hands clasped behind a head of short, black hair. The chair creaked as he leaned back. "Vacation."

"Oh." The jar of gumbo felt a little heavier, and her high-heeled boots pinched a bit. She still needed an article in the *Gazette*. Swallowing her disappointment, she asked, "Are you filling in for Sam?"

"Temporarily," he answered with the bland accent of a TV talking head. He leaned forward and hit a few more keys, then spun around in Sam's chair.

Holly faced another ghost. This one from her past. Her heart beat double time and danced her back to her junior year of high school.

Jake McCann's smile still reached deep inside her. Muscles she didn't remember stretched his black knit shirt in all the right places. The tingle she didn't know what to do with back then raced through her. She knew exactly what to do with all six feet of delicious Jake McCann now.

But those days were past for her and for him. She slapped on her polite "Welcome home" smile. "Jake. I can't believe it."

CHAPTER 3

Jake didn't believe Holly was surprised, though she'd done a good job of pretending when she walked in Sam's office. She looked too darned good to be a desperate widow. But there she stood, poured into those jeans, painted up like she needed a man, and packing a jar of food for him.

"Come on, Holly." He winked. "Delta Ridge is too small not to hear I was back in town."

Holly tossed her blond curls and laughed. "I've been too busy for gossip."

"I heard." He stood and extended his hand. She closed the distance between them and took his hand. On tiptoe, she brushed a kiss on his cheek.

Jake sucked in the vanilla aroma of her perfume and, beneath that, the unique scent that was hers. He straightened. The kiss didn't mean anything to her. Women of all ages in southern Louisiana greeted everyone they knew like that. One of the few things he'd missed about the South.

Holly's soft hand clung to his. "And what did you hear?"

Her sweet Southern accent dripped from her words, softening the resolve he needed to be objective.

"You were in rehab." Possibly for sampling the goods.

"And you believed it?" Dropping his hand, she drilled him with a blue-eyed stare.

Jake hadn't believed it, but neither had he dismissed it. "People change." He shrugged. "I haven't talked to you in fifteen years."

Why had the difference in her hit him so hard? Time hadn't stood still, even in Delta Ridge. He'd changed. Why wouldn't she? And he had to admit he liked the improvements.

She lifted her chin and snapped, "You've changed, Jake. You don't even talk like you're from Delta Ridge anymore."

"A necessary change for business." And for survival when Immigration and Customs Enforcement gave him an undercover assignment anywhere above the Mason-Dixon Line.

"That's right. You were bigger than Delta Ridge," she said, then gave a hollow laugh.

His jaw tightened. "Sore subject."

He had dusted the black dirt of Delta Ridge off his shoes after high school graduation and would have never looked back if he'd had a choice. Immigration and Customs Enforcement had a thick file on Burl's drug-smuggling operation. His untimely death had closed the case. Then an upriver ICE agent had tipped them off that the operation might be running again and using Holly Grove as a front. Jake needed this bust to pull his career out of a death spiral, or he would face a life sentence chained to a desk job.

"Guess so, since you're back here at the *Gazette*, where you started."

Ouch. She still had a stinger. "Just doing Sam a favor. It's temporary."

Sam had called Jake in New York about an anonymous tip he'd picked up about suspicious activity at Holly Grove. That call had been Jake's ticket back to undercover work. If he weren't the *only* ICE agent who could fit in as a local boy coming back home to Delta Ridge, he'd be in New York, serving desk time for his major screwup in the field. There his life was nobody's business but his, and Holly was an old memory.

"So, where's Sam?"

"Vacationing in Florida," he said, coloring the truth. Sam had left the *Gazette* as mad as a hornet when Jake wouldn't let him stay for the action.

"Speaking of favors . . ." She gave him a sugar-sweet smile. "That's why I'm here. I was going to ask Sam, but since you're the temporary editor, I guess I'll ask you."

"Shoot." He pointed her to one of the two well-worn oak chairs in front of Sam's desk.

"You heard the rumor." She wiggled her fine little backside onto a chair and balanced the jar on her lap. "Well, it's all a misunderstanding, and it's running like wildfire all over the parish." Her pink-painted fingernails waved through the air. "It won't be long before it spreads further. I need a feature article in the *Gazette* about Holly Grove, so everyone knows we're open and I'm there working." Her hand patted her chest.

Jake didn't remember her having such a nice rack. He shifted in Sam's rickety chair and forced himself to focus.

"But you can't mention the cocaine thing. Just say good things. I've got a copy of my drug test and the sheriff's report, if you don't believe me." Never missing a word, she pulled crumpled pages out of her purse. "The, um, misunderstanding could hurt my Haunted Pilgrimage business, and since Burl died, I depend on Holly Grove to make a living." She stretched over Sam's desk, holding the jar and the papers. "And here's a jar of Nelda's gumbo to show my appreciation for anything you can do."

Holly plunked the jar on top of the papers in the center of Sam's desk. "If I could afford an ad, I'd buy one. I really, really need this favor."

Only a woman could talk that much and not need oxygen. "Burl didn't leave you any money?"

Holly shook her head and groaned. "What money?"

Jake shuffled a few papers to avoid looking at her. "I thought he was a successful businessman." A man who could give her the stable life he couldn't.

"A paper tiger."

More like a cash cow. Burl had operated in cash so the IRS wouldn't notice his success. They hadn't, but ICE had. He looked at Holly. "So sell the business."

"Who'd buy it? Burl *was* Davis Aviation. It looks hopeless on paper."

It had never looked good at all—because it was a front for smuggling. "What are you going to do with it?"

"It's closed except for guests who want to use the landing strip at their own risk. I've got an ad in the classifieds to rent it." She lifted a shoulder. "Only one looker so far."

He studied her face. Could she have lived with Burl and not known he didn't make an honest living? To find out, he needed to get to know her all over again. And that was part of the plan. He just hadn't counted on her walking in and making him remember all sorts of things he'd be better off forgetting.

Holly nibbled on a fingernail and eyed Jake for a long moment before she gathered the courage to ask, "Well, um, do you think you can squeeze an article about Holly Grove in the *Gazette*?" She held her breath, waiting for his answer.

"An article? No."

Jake loved the fact that she wasn't in good financial shape. He'd practically undressed her with his eyes as she had begged for his help. Then he'd had the nerve to say no.

She snatched up her purse and stood. "Thanks for your time."

Spinning on her heel, she turned, then raced to the door. She glanced over her shoulder without slowing down. "I hope you enjoy the gumbo." She bit down on her bottom lip to keep from saying she wished he'd choke on a hunk of chicken.

He jumped up from his seat. "Wait."

She didn't.

His footsteps hit the floor three times before he reached her. He caught her by the elbow and whirled her around to face him. "I wasn't finished."

She yanked her elbow free, then hoisted her purse higher on her shoulder. "Finished looking at my boobs, my butt, or listening to me beg?"

"Answering your question," he said, as though she had the comprehension of a gnat.

"You said no." She jabbed a finger to his chest. "Not

maybe." She jabbed harder. "Or possibly." And jabbed again because it felt good. "I got it."

Jake grabbed her hand and held it in his fist. "Enough with the poking."

His eyes twinkled, and a smile kicked up the left side of his mouth. God, she loved that smile. He pulled her hand across her body, forcing her to turn sideways. Raising a brow, he said, "You look good, Holly. Real good."

A flutter from deep in her belly lightened her anger. It'd been a long time since anyone had said that. A smile crept across her face. "Not bad for a thirty-two-year-old woman, huh?"

He grinned. "So good, you distracted me from fully answering your question." His stare locked with hers.

"Oh," she said.

"You need more than a one-day run to promote the Haunted Pilgrimage." He released her hand.

"Yes, but one article would help," she said, hoping he'd had a change of heart.

"How does a feature article, then an ad, every week for the rest of October sound?"

"Perfect, if you're making a donation."

He stroked his chin. "What if we could work out a trade?"

Did he just look at my boobs again? "Trade?"

"I need a place to stay while I fill in for Sam, and you have a bed-and-breakfast."

"Does this involve getting in *my* bed?"

The corners of his eyes crinkled as he flashed a grin. "Only if you want it to."

"And what if I don't?"

"The offer stands. I'll be a perfect gentleman, and

you'll have an ad and an article every week for the rest of the month in exchange for my rent."

"Perfect," she said as a flash of heat rushed to her cheeks.

Just perfect torture.

CHAPTER 4

What now? What now? The words rattled in Holly's head with each tap of her heels on the aged sidewalk of downtown Delta Ridge. She hadn't been able to say no. She hadn't wanted to say no. What in the world was she going to do with Jake and Burl together at Holly Grove? Nelda was right. Holly was good at getting herself into messes, and this one was knee-deep.

The start of a pounding headache replaced the girlish, giddy feeling that had filled her minutes earlier. She fumbled through her purse for a bottle of aspirin. The childproof lid spun and jiggled as she tried to force it open. Childproof. Unnecessary. Another reminder of what a miserable failure her marriage had been. She bore down on the lid and popped it off.

The door of Bob's Barbershop swung open, bumping Holly's arm. Little pills rained down on the sidewalk.

"Holly Davis." Miss Alice watched the pills bounce on the sidewalk. She drilled Holly with an accusing stare. "You're supposed to be in rehab."

"They're aspirin." Holly jerked the bottle up to eye level so Miss Alice could see the label.

Miss Alice reached for her glasses, which dangled from a beaded chain around her neck. She inspected the bottle. "Humph. You can put anything in an aspirin bottle."

Holly shook the remaining aspirin from the bottle into her palm. "Look. It says aspirin on the pills."

Miss Alice picked up a pill and examined it. She pinched the pill between two fingers and stretched her arm as far from her eyes as she could. With the other arm, she adjusted her glasses. The old woman's mouth formed a tight line. "There isn't any writing on these pills."

"I swear, they're aspirin."

"We'll see." Miss Alice brought the pill to her mouth and licked it. Her penciled brows rose. "It is aspirin."

"That's right. This whole drug thing was a misunderstanding. Since the Deltas didn't get to play bridge yesterday, I'll give the parlor to you rent free tomorrow."

Miss Alice slid the glasses off her nose and let them dangle from the chain. "Free?"

"My compliments, as long as I can explain what happened."

"Nine o'clock sharp." Miss Alice hooked her purse over her arm, then marched over the scattered aspirin without giving Holly a second look.

Holly shook her head and heaved a sigh. That went as well as could be expected, she thought.

Little white pills littered the sidewalk in front of her. A dog or a child might eat the aspirin if she left them on the pavement. She didn't need another incident to revive her Hurricane Holly moniker.

As she kneeled to collect the pills, a smile lifted her cheeks and her spirits. She squeezed the pills in her fist and almost laughed aloud.

This time, she held all the cards and couldn't wait for the game to begin. After she squelched the rehab rumor by showing the Deltas her medical and police reports, she'd throw her trump card on the table, a command performance by the ghost of Burl Davis. He'd said she was the only one who could help him, and she wasn't about to help that lying, cheating excuse for a nearly ex-husband without getting something out of it. He didn't know it yet, but he was going to help her save Holly Grove.

The tongue-wagging circulation of the Deltas declaring that Holly Grove had a resident ghost added up to free publicity. Tourists would come by the busloads to see Burl, and they'd visit downtown, too. She wouldn't have to let Nelda go, and Holly Grove would be safe from her financial crisis.

Holly dropped the aspirin into a trash bin and then dusted her hands together, as though she'd brushed her troubles away. The only card in question was the wild card.

Jake.

Little goose bumps rose on Holly's arms as she entered her dark kitchen. She flipped on a light.

No sign of Burl.

Rhett trotted to her side.

"Seen any ghosts, boy?" she whispered. As she rubbed Rhett's back, she scanned the room. A note propped against the fruit bowl on the planter's table caught her eye.

She crossed the room and picked up the note.

Holly,
   The stove won't light. I ain't gonna blow my head off tryin' to light the fool thing.
   Gas is dangerous. Call somebody to fix it.

                        Nelda

All Holly needed was another repair bill. Every time she got one thing fixed, three others broke.

The last time Nelda couldn't light the stove, it had cost Holly a service call for the repairman to strike a match, but Holly hadn't shared that with Nelda. She would have felt terrible about wasting money.

Holly crossed the room to the stove and dug a match from the matchbox. The stove lit on the first try. There must have been air in the line when Nelda tried to light it. Holly crushed the note and tossed it in the trash can. *Thank goodness for small blessings.*

Walking through the parlor to the entrance hall, she flipped on a light. Then she turned on every light downstairs. "Burl, are you here?"

Only the familiar sounds of the plantation home she'd lived in since she was an infant, answered.

She'd seen him, heard him, and there had been evidence, sort of. Fire extinguisher dust had flaked off him all over the parlor, and she considered that hard proof. She'd heard him just before Sandy put her in the ambulance. And she'd been awake and sober then.

"Burl, where on God's green earth are you?" she shouted.

Rhett tilted his head from side to side and stared at her.

"You think I'm nuts, don't you?"

Rhett yawned.

"I'm beat, too."

Dreaming of a bubble bath and a new day tomorrow, she turned off the lights and then climbed the stairs. Holly shook her head. She'd thought she held all the cards, but she'd forgotten that Lady Luck never sided with her.

Screw luck. She needed a plan.

A few minutes later, Holly stepped into a claw-footed bathtub. Steam rose from the hot water as she immersed herself in the vanilla-scented, foamy bath. If only she could wash away the past two days.

She propped her arms on the sides of the tub and blew out a long, tired sigh. The bubbles rippled away from her with her breath. A foggy steam hung over the water. The jasmine-scented candles she'd placed on the window ledge held a steady flame.

Closing her eyes, she rested her head on the back of the porcelain tub. *Tomorrow will be better.*

When Holly opened her eyes, remnants of bubbles rode little crests coming her way. A cool breeze brushed over her. She glanced at the window. Closed. Another ripple of waves ebbed toward her. Goose bumps raced across her skin with the chilled air that followed.

"I can tell you're excited to see me." A translucent Burl, wearing the black Armani suit that she'd buried him in, materialized as he sat on the edge of the tub. He leaned over and blew into her bubbles.

Holly sank neck deep into what was left of her foamy bath.

Burl stood and crossed his arms. "Aw, you spoiled my view."

"It's not your view anymore." Holly covered her chest with her arms.

A devilish grin slid across Burl's face. "Did you forget you were my wife?"

"Operative word here is *were*." Holly eyed her towel, which hung from a hook on the door, behind Burl. "Till death do we part. And you've parted."

"Death is a matter of opinion, wouldn't you say?" He wiggled his brows like the leading man in an old black-and-white movie.

"What? You think we're still married?" She gathered the small piles of bubbles and strategically placed them for privacy.

"I'm here. You're here. Sure we're married." He cocked his head sideways and peered into her bath-water.

She sank a little deeper into the tub. "I don't think so. Besides, I filed for divorce."

"I didn't sign any papers."

"That's because you died before you were served." And her bubbles were dying, too.

"I may be dead, but I'm not gone, Blondie."

Her temper sparked. That was Burl's code for dumb blonde. Holly raked her cupped hand through the bathwater and splashed Burl.

He jumped back. "Hey, watch it. You'll mess up my aura."

"Aura? What are you? A new age ghost?"

"No, but it's hard work to make myself visible. I don't know if I'm waterproof." He brushed his hand over his trouser legs. "And this is my only suit." He laced his fingers under his lapels and grinned. "Thanks for burying me in my Armani."

"Whatever." He'd always been vain. "Just hand me my towel."

"No can do."

"Then turn around so I can get it."

"And why would I do that?"

"Because I don't want you to look at me."

"Hey, I'm dead. All I can do is look." He nodded and said, "I'm looking."

"Fine." The water sloshed as she stood. She didn't cover herself as she stomped to her towel. It wasn't as if he'd never seen her naked. It was just the principle of it all.

Burl let out a howling whistle.

As Holly glared at him, she snatched the towel off the hook and wrapped it around herself. "Okay, Burl. You've had your fun. We need to talk."

"Not that again." He frowned. "I hate it when you want to have those sappy talks about our relationship."

Holly rolled her eyes. "There is no relationship, and you can't stay here. What's the unfinished business that will get you out of here?"

"Oh, that."

"Yeah, that." Holly folded her arms over her towel and tapped a wet foot.

"Then you're in."

"I didn't say that." Burl always took more than he gave. So far, he was the same Burl, dead or alive.

"So you don't care about my eternal soul?"

"Face it. You haven't led a saintly life. If you want my help getting something you don't deserve, you're going to do something for me first."

"Come on, Blondie. Don't you trust me?"

"Trust you?" Holly hoisted the towel a little higher on her chest as she studied Burl. "Which vow haven't you broken?"

Burl slapped his hand over his heart and gave her the wounded puppy face he'd perfected during their marriage.

"Don't give me that sappy puppy face. I'm immune."

"What do you want me to do?"

"Haunt," she said. "I want you to scare the Deltas tomorrow and my B & B guests when they arrive. Not enough to give them a heart attack, but enough to make them believe Holly Grove is haunted. That way I can draw more business and keep Holly Grove open."

Burl folded his arms over his chest. "And how do you want me to do this?"

"I don't know." She lifted her shoulders. "Moan. Rattle some chains. The usual ghost stuff."

"Blondie, I don't know if you noticed, but no one can see or hear me except you and that rat you call a dog." Burl snatched at her towel.

Holly gasped as his hand faded into the towel and then her chest, where she'd tucked the towel in place. She felt nothing except a chill.

Burl drew his hand back and dropped his gaze to the floor. "As much as I'd like to, I can't even rip that towel off you. So how do you think I can help you?"

Holly's heart sank. Her perfect hand was a bust. He couldn't scare the Deltas. And if she didn't help him, she'd be stuck with a dead husband she couldn't divorce. He'd be her chaperone for life. Her ancestors had sacrificed and died to keep Holly Grove for future generations, and it all ended with her, the unlucky

Holly. She turned away from Burl as tears welled in her eyes.

"I'm sorry," he said in a whisper.

"Sorry?" She wheeled around to face him. "That's it? You weren't satisfied with making me miserable when you were living. You had to come back for more. I hate you, Burl. I hate you!"

Holly ran from the bathroom, then slammed the door behind her. She threw herself on her antique bed and let the sobs rock through her body. He'd won again.

She had no choice but to do whatever Burl asked to get him out of her life.

CHAPTER 5

The thud of the door knocker clattered from downstairs, followed by Rhett's sharp barks. Holly swiped at her tears and looked at the brass face of the Seth Thomas mantel clock. Eight o'clock. She'd forgotten all about Jake. He'd arranged to pick up his room key this evening so he wouldn't have to wake her after the *Gazette* printed at midnight.

Her tears must have vaporized Burl. During their marriage, if she dropped a tear, he dropped out of sight. Same Burl, dead or alive.

Holly slid off the edge of the high bed and then scrambled to the oak armoire that held her clothing. She pulled on a T-shirt and sweatpants, then dashed for the door.

"Coming," she yelled from the stairs.

Rhett bounced as he yapped at the door. He met her at the foot of the stairs, and then he rushed back to the door and barked some more.

"I don't need a doorbell as long as I have you, boy." Holly stopped at the mirror in the entrance hall. Puffy blue eyes stared back from her reflection. *Bless your heart, girl.* The thinning silver on the back of the mirror usually made everyone look better. She wiped at her eyes.

The sharp squawk of hinges in need of TLC grated her ears as she opened the door.

"Sorry about the squeak." A sniffle she couldn't hold back tickled her nose.

Sexy stubble framed Jake's face as he frowned and looked at Holly. "Did I come at a bad time?"

"No. This is just what I look like without the help of professional products."

He winced. "That's not what I meant. It took you a while to get to the door. I can come back later."

"No. I just got out of the tub. Sorry." She opened the door wider, and it squeaked again. "I've got to get that fixed."

"Consider it done," he said and scored points he didn't need. The massive door to the plantation house dwarfed most men. But as Jake strode into the foyer, his broad shoulders and tall frame matched the size of the house.

"Welcome to Holly Grove." She leaned toward him to give him a peck on the cheek, but he stiffened and extended his hand.

"We have an agreement." His eyes danced with mischief, and his dimple deepened with his grin.

"Oh, yeah. You're going to be the perfect gentleman."

Jake nodded, then winked. "So don't tempt me."

She pinched the sides of her sweatpants and stretched them. "Yeah, I wore my most tempting outfit."

"It's not the outfit that's tempting." The stare of Jake's rich brown eyes melted her like the first bite of chocolate after a long diet.

Heat crept across her cheeks. That was a bad sign. Jake had left her heartbroken years ago, and she knew better than to go back for seconds.

Rhett started barking again.

"It's okay, Rhett. Jake's a guest."

Jake patted his knee. "Hey, Rhett."

He jumped back and barked louder.

"Sorry. Rhett doesn't like men."

Jake shrugged. "What happened to man's best friend?"

"Not Rhett. He doesn't trust men."

Jake cocked an eye at Holly. "I've heard dogs' personalities are shaped by their masters."

"I've heard dogs are better able to judge character than people."

"Touché," he said, flashing his killer grin.

She couldn't help but smile back. "Have a seat in the parlor." She motioned toward the open floor-to-ceiling pocket doors. "I'll get your keys and paperwork."

Holly went to the kitchen and whipped up the customary check-in cocktail, a Holly Grove Mint Julep. She poured it in a monogrammed silver mint julep cup and placed the cup on a linen cocktail napkin. As part of their trade, Jake deserved a proper welcome.

Then she checked the reservation list she kept stashed in a kitchen drawer with the room keys. The Grant suite on the third floor or the Huey Long room in the carriage house should be far enough away to keep her hormones in check. Too bad they were rented for the weekend. The room in the boys' tower was available, but the renovations weren't quite complete. She fingered the key. Maybe Jake wouldn't mind.

She pinched the bridge of her nose. He'd agreed to run an ad in the *Gazette* every week and write a feature article on Holly Grove. The least she could do was keep him from having to move rooms throughout the weekend to accommodate previous reservations. The Mark Twain suite was next to her room and shared her balcony. Maybe too cozy for her, but they'd made a deal. She plucked the Mark Twain key, registration card, and a pen from the drawer, then scooped up the mint julep.

When Holly returned to the parlor, she stopped short, paralyzed, as her stare darted from Jake to Burl. They sat side by side on the antique settee like Mutt and Jeff, opposites in every way.

"Who's this big bozo?" Burl said, eyeing Jake.

Beside Jake, Burl appeared paler and less fit. But then again, Burl was a ghost.

Jake didn't flinch.

Holly couldn't move.

Jake's brow creased as he stared at her. "Are you all right?"

"Wait a minute." Burl stood and stepped in front of Jake. "I've seen this guy." Burl snapped his fingers near his head, as if that would rattle loose a memory.

Jake stood and walked right through Burl.

She gasped.

"Holly, what's wrong?" Jake marched to her side.

She couldn't get a single syllable out.

Burl spun around and snapped his fingers one more time. "I've seen his picture."

Jake stretched his arm around her waist.

She couldn't breathe.

Burl held his hands up and poked his thumbs straight across to form a frame with his forefingers. He lined Holly and Jake up in his view. A wry grin spread from ear to ear. "Oh, yeah. He's older, but I remember.

This is the sap you were hung up on when I met you. You turned his picture facedown on the bedside table the first time we—"

"It's not what you think," Holly blurted out. And why did she care what Burl thought? Why did she have a tinge of guilt at having them in the same room? *He's dead, for crying out loud.* It had to be just a leftover habit of thinking of him as her husband for ten years.

Jake frowned. "What are you talking about?"

"Uh," she stammered. "Your room is next to mine, but it's not what you think." *Whew.* She amazed herself at how quickly the lie rolled from her lips. Holly had never been good at lying, but she'd never been in a situation like this, either.

"How cozy," Burl said, all sappy.

Holly looked up at Jake. "I had to put you in the Mark Twain suite, next to mine. The rest of the rooms are rented out for the weekend. This way, you won't have to move to another room until Monday when someone else has the Mark Twain booked."

"I said I'd be a perfect gentleman. Did you think I was going to sneak into your room and seduce you in the middle of the night?" Jake asked with the slightest hint of a smile in his eyes.

In her dreams.

Burl's pale face reddened. "And you're falling for this, Blondie?"

"Of course not," she said, looking at Burl but answering Jake's question. She squeezed the key to the Twain suite in her palm and crumpled the registration card around it. The icy mint julep chilled her hand as she clutched it for dear life.

Burl's translucent image nearly glowed red. "Are you nuts? You're going to put your old flame in the room next to yours, and you don't expect him to think anything about it? And what on earth is he doing here, anyway?"

"Don't you trust me?" Jake asked.

Burl rolled his eyes. "I've used that line a million times. Come on, Blondie. Don't you see what he's doing?"

"I just didn't want to send you the wrong message," she said to Jake. Then she turned and glared at Burl. Would he ruin the rest of her life?

Standing in the parlor between Jake and Burl, Holly realized she had a serious problem.

There stood Jake, a fantasy that could walk off a page of *GQ* right into her bedroom but would never stick around. And there stood Burl, a ghost of his former self and a roadblock in her life that might never go away unless she did something about it.

She knew three Delta Ridge women who'd divorced. Two had moved to a bigger town after about two years of small-town celibacy. The other was taking in cats. Rhett wouldn't tolerate cats, and she could never sell Holly Grove and move away. Unless she wanted to do the big nasty with a widower over sixty or her forty-year-old accountant, who still lived with his mother, Jake was probably her only chance in the Delta Ridge market. Men had flings all the time for the fun of it. But that wasn't her style. She glared at Burl. If she did, she'd be no better than he was. Although she wasn't married, technically, since he *was* a ghost.

Jake pulled her closer. "Are you okay? You were staring at me like you were in a daze."

"Tell the bozo to back off, Blondie. You're a married woman."

She gave Burl a cold stare. He had another thought

coming if he believed he could control her from beyond the grave.

"I'm fine," she said, chancing a look into Jake's deep brown eyes. "I just remembered something." She stretched her arm out, offering Jake the mint julep. "This is for you."

He waved it off. "Thanks, but I don't drink."

She took a gulp of the minty libation to steady her nerves, then turned her back to Jake and faced Burl. She lipped to Burl, "Meet me in the laundry room. Now."

She handed Jake the key, pen, and mangled registration card. "I'm going to get you some fresh towels while you fill out the registration card. Then I'll show you to your room."

Holly needed to set a few ground rules for her not-so-dearly departed. She looked over her shoulder to see if Burl was following her.

Gone again.

A gust of wind rattled the windows of the old house as Jake finished filling out the registration card. He shifted his weight on the flimsy sofa, and it creaked, making him question its ability to hold him. He stood, then paced as he waited for Holly to return.

Patience had never been his strong suit. He scanned the room she'd called the parlor for a chair that could hold his weight. Next to the window, he spotted two curvy chairs with fluffy fabric that looked like Snow White had designed them for the seven dwarfs.

He ambled through the entrance hall, which was as much as he'd seen of Holly Grove back when he'd dated Holly. Her mom had kept Holly on a short leash and him on a shorter one. His skirmishes with the law and having the town drunk for a father had stacked the odds against Jake with most of Delta Ridge and especially with Holly's mother.

The squatty double chair shaped like an *S* caught his attention. He'd sat there and watched Holly float down the stairs like an angel in pink back when he took her to his prom. She and Sam had saved him. They had believed in him when no one else had.

Jake wanted to believe in Holly, but he had a job to do. He had to keep his head on straight. Personal history had no place in an undercover op, except to gain intel. He had to keep the two separate.

By boarding at her B & B, he'd have the freedom to roam the plantation and observe Holly and her guests. This was Jake's one shot to save his career after his royal screwup in New York. Then he'd catch the first flight back to the twenty-first century and life as he liked it. Under the radar.

The old house creaked and moaned with the autumn wind, but with it, Jake thought he'd heard something. He stood still and listened.

As she opened the laundry-room door, it swept through Burl. Too bad she couldn't lock him in the room with the sheets.

"You've got to get rid of that guy," Burl said.

"His name is Jake, and he's filling in for Sam while he's on vacation. And I can't get rid of him." She took another fortifying sip of Jake's mint julep.

"Why not?"

"First, I don't want to. Second, I need some good

publicity for Holly Grove since the whole town thinks I'm in rehab, thanks to you."

"Me?" He pointed to his chest. "I was stone-cold sober."

She didn't have time to explain. "I made a deal with him. A month of ads and articles for a month's free rent. You can't help me, but he can."

"Yeah, I know what kind of help he's going to give you," Burl said, curling his fists at his sides and thrusting his hips forward.

She jammed her hands on her hips. "So what? You're dead! I'm free to do whatever I want." Not that she would.

"Right in front of my eyes?"

"Why not?" She rattled the ice in the mint julep cup. "You did it behind my back."

"But—"

"But nothing. You're the one I need to get rid of. You don't deserve to go to heaven, but I sure as sin don't deserve to be stuck with you, either. Just tell me what your unfinished business is, and don't fade out this time." She drained the silver cup and slammed it on the counter. *Thank you, Jake, for being a teetotaler.*

Burl shrugged and stared at the floor. "I made some bad bets. I took money from our 401(k) thinking I'd win it back, but I lost that, too. I couldn't face you."

"So you screwed a redhead instead." She pasted a sarcastic smile on her face. "That explains everything."

"I'm trying to tell you what happened."

"I don't care what happened. I just want to know what I have to do to get rid of you."

"I'm getting to that."

"Please do." She waved her hand through the air and bowed slightly in mocked reverence.

"After I maxed out at the bank, I borrowed money from a loan shark . . . strong connections. When I couldn't pay, he made me an offer I couldn't refuse, unless I wanted to lose a few digits or worse."

"And I'm supposed to feel sorry for you?" She grabbed a stack of white towels from a closet.

"You should be thankful I paid him off."

"Can you just skip the details?" She unloaded the stack of towels onto the countertop and eyed Burl. "What is this unfinished business?"

"It's complicated." Burl shifted his focus to the toes of his Gucci lace-ups. "All I had to do was meet a barge on the Mississippi riverbank, which is practically in our backyard. Then, a few days later, a contact would stay at the B & B to pick up the goods. With easy access to I-10, running east to west across the country, and a private airstrip on our property, the business boomed."

"What business? What goods?"

"Drug smuggling," he stammered.

Her mind scrambled over images of tattooed drug lords from old movies like *Scarface* and *Pulp Fiction*. She shook her head. Burl might as well have GOOD OLD SOUTHERN BOY tattooed across his chest.

"No way." Holly threw her head back and laughed.

Burl's brows slammed together. "What's so funny?"

"You? A drug lord?"

"I didn't say I was a drug lord."

"Whatever. Now, tell me the truth."

He stuffed his hands in his pockets and sulked. "I did," he said, holding eye contact longer than a lie would allow.

Her stomach quivered at the revelation. Drug smuggling at Holly Grove. "How could you?"

"It's not something I planned. Then the money

started rolling in. I couldn't walk away from the cash, and I couldn't tell you." He shrugged. "I was planning on going straight as soon as I got ahead. Then my plane crashed. I think busting up the smuggling ring at Holly Grove is my unfinished business and my ticket out of here."

Holly's head ached. "It's still going on?"

"We were going to lay low for a few months, because they heard the law was snooping around. Then they planned to make up for it with a huge drop in October."

She paced in front of Burl. "This has got to stop. I'll call the police. They'll send in someone to trap them and, bang, it's done." She eyed Burl. "And you're out of here."

"That's fiction, Blondie."

Holly stopped short. "Stop calling me that, and why on God's green earth shouldn't I call the police?"

"And tell them what? You didn't know a thing about the smuggling your husband was doing, but now you want it stopped. Sure, Blondie. How would you feel about Holly Grove being confiscated in a drug raid?"

"Not happening. I'll call Sheriff Walker. He knows me."

"So does Miss Alice, and you nearly ended up on your way to rehab."

Holly slumped against the dryer. "There's got to be someone I can call."

"You can call them all once you've got proof." He counted on his fingers. "FBI, ICE, the state police, and the sheriff. Call the dogcatcher, for all I care."

Holly folded her arms over her chest. "How do I get this proof?"

"Very quietly. They have ears everywhere. Believe me," Burl said, thumbing his chest. "I learned the hard way. If you blow the whistle too soon, they'll just lay low until it's too late to do me any good. Then they'll start up again, and you'll never know which guest is packing marijuana into his trunk when he leaves here. Can you live with that?"

"No."

He cocked a brow at her. "Can you live with me if I miss my chance?"

"Definitely not." She blew out a long sigh. "What do I have to do?"

"One of your guests will be the contact, and you need to figure out which one."

She launched herself from her perch against the dryer. "Me? Who do you think I am? A Bond girl? You know what the guy looks like."

Burl's image flickered. "Unfortunately, I'm not always available."

"What do you mean? You're stuck here. Where else would you be?"

"Don't worry, Blondie. I've got your back."

"I don't trust you at my back."

He faded a bit.

"We're not near finished here." Holly reached to grab him, as if that'd do any good, and he vaporized.

He's not telling me something. I know it.

A knock at the door nearly made her jump out of her skin.

"I thought I heard voices," Jake said as he pushed the laundry-room door open.

A crease between Holly's brows marred her expression. "I—I must have been muttering to myself." She grabbed the stack of towels, then glanced over her shoulder, as though she'd left something behind. "Sorry to keep you waiting. I had to fold the towels. I'll show you to your room."

Odd. He hadn't been able to make out what she was saying earlier, but it had sounded like an argument, which requires two for most people. "I'll take those."

She handed him the stack of towels and looked over her shoulder again, leaving him certain Holly was hiding something. He wondered if anyone was back there. Maybe she'd been on the phone. Obviously, whatever was going on, she hadn't wanted to say.

"Your room is up here." She led him up a worn cypress staircase.

It felt almost forbidden as he climbed the stairs. "You know, I've never been past the front hall."

"I offer a tour at ten o'clock every morning for guests and day visitors. You can learn more than you ever wanted to know about this house and my ancestors."

They entered a wide hallway. Thick antique Oriental rugs covered most of the cypress planks. She stopped in the middle of the hallway. "There are four bedrooms on this floor, and each shares a balcony."

Jake stood in the middle of the hall, grinning. "You know, I always wanted to come up here. Once I thought about climbing up the balcony and sneaking in your room, but I was afraid your mother would shoot me."

"She would have." Holly chuckled and opened a bedroom door. She stepped into the room and Jake followed her. "This is your room, for now. I'll have to rotate you around reservations. At least, I hope I will, if the rumor hasn't ruined my business."

Holly walked to the corner of the room and opened a short door. "It's small, but it has all you need." She took the towels from Jake and placed them on a shelf in a bathroom.

He stuck his head in the door of the bathroom that was about the right size for Snow White's dwarfs who'd fit in the chairs downstairs. "You sure I'll fit in there?"

A hint of a grin slipped across her lips as she stepped past him and back into the bedroom. "Barely, but yes. I promise I'll upgrade you to a bigger bathroom as soon as I have a room available."

He turned and stared at the bed, with posts as big as his arms. *Now, that's more my size.* "That beats the heck out of sleeping on the sofa in Sam's office."

She gave him a little half grin. "I really appreciate the trade."

Jake put the stack of towels on the bed and followed her onto the balcony. Cypress planks with a worn coat of gray paint slanted toward the banister.

Holly leaned against a white column and folded her arms, facing away from him. Remnants of an autumn sunset, with splashes of deep reds and oranges, hung against an inky sky. "Bet you don't see this sunset in New York City."

"Nope, but the nighttime city skyline is a show, though. Have you ever seen it?"

She shook her head and rubbed her arms against the chill in the air. "When I look at the sky from here, I always think about the generations before me who watched the same sunsets."

He draped his jacket over her shoulders, then stood beside her.

"They had real problems." She pointed to a vacant spot in a row of sprawling oak trees. "There used to be a tree there."

"What happened to it?"

"My great-great-great-great-grandfather was hanged from that tree by renegade Yankees after the war." She turned to face Jake. "After the Yankees left, his wife and three daughters cut the rope from around his neck and buried him. That same day, the women sawed down the tree. The oaks were much smaller then, but big enough for a hangin', as Grandma Rose used to say."

"That's quite a story."

"I know all the stories that come with this house. They were passed down from generation to generation, just like Holly Grove."

"You come from tough stock."

"That's right, and I'm not going to be the weak link that breaks the chain." She swept the grounds of the plantation with her gaze. "It's the stories I tell that keep Holly Grove and my family alive." Pride filled the smile that seemed to come straight from her heart. "Holly Grove means everything to me."

Jake knew that. The question was, would she do anything to keep Holly Grove? Would she allow herself to become involved in smuggling? Drug running?

Murder?

CHAPTER 6

A scream ripped through the house, jarring Holly from a deep sleep. She leaped from her bed and ran for the door. Footsteps thundered in the hallway, and when Holly flung her door open, she nearly smacked into Nelda.

Nelda wrenched her neck as she turned toward the room next door and pointed. "There's a necked man in there."

With his dark hair slicked back and dripping water, Jake strode through the open bedroom door. Rivulets glided down his neck and combed through a patch of coarse hair on his chest before traveling over the tight cords of tanned muscle to the towel wrapped around his hips.

Both women froze.

Jake took a step toward the women. "I didn't mean to frighten you," he said to Nelda.

Holly pried her stare away from Jake and turned to Nelda. "What happened?"

"I was gonna air out the musty old house smell 'fore the guests got here this evenin'. After I opened the windows, I turned around, and there was a necked man. I screamed 'cause I ain't used to seeing necked men just show up out of the blue."

"Nelda." Holly held her voice steady and firm. "This is Jake McCann. He's a guest."

Nelda looked back at Jake, then to Holly. Bunching her brows together, she whispered, "Your Jake from high school?"

Holly nodded.

Nelda huffed. "If you'd told me we had a guest, I wouldn't have busted up in his room," she said loud enough for Jake to hear.

"Last minute reservation," Holly said.

Nelda squeezed Holly's arm and whispered, "That guest needs to be in your room, not next door." She winked and nodded. "Believe me."

Heat rose to Holly's face like a pink plague.

Nelda sashayed over to Jake and held her hand out. "I'm Nelda. Sorry for bustin' in on you like that."

Jake held his towel with one hand and shook Nelda's hand with the other. "No harm done."

"How long you stayin'?" Nelda continued, like Jake wasn't standing there mostly nude.

"Nelda, let's let Jake get dressed," Holly said, still standing in her doorway and wearing an old sleep shirt and sweats.

Nelda shoved a hand on her hip and eyed Holly. "I already seen him necked. I just want to know how long he's stayin' so I can make him some pralines to make up for bustin' up in his room."

"No rush on the pralines, Nelda. I'll be here all month," Jake said, propping a shoulder on the door frame.

Nelda cocked an eye at Holly, then looked back at

Jake. "You got a wife or girlfriend comin' to stay with us, too?"

"Nelda!" Holly marched toward her housekeeper.

She grinned at Holly. "I need to know how many pralines to make."

Holly grabbed Nelda by the arm and ushered her down the stairs. "Let's go make some coffee and breakfast for our guest."

"Nice seein' ya, Jake," Nelda hollered over her shoulder.

Jake let out a low chuckle, but Holly didn't dare look back.

"What were you thinking?" Holly said as she towed Nelda into the kitchen. "Nice to see ya." Holly shook her head. "You don't say that after you accidentally see a man naked, especially our guest."

"Ya do if it was nice. And it was *real* nice."

Holly rolled her eyes. "If it was so nice, why'd you scream?"

"The scream came out when I didn't expect to see a necked man in the room. The nice came after I was runnin' down the hall, thinking about how nice—"

Holly held up her hand in a halting motion. "Nelda."

"I know Burl ain't been dead long, God rest his soul, but you're still livin', last I checked."

"This has nothing to do with Burl." Holly opened the glass canister of French roast coffee. The aroma wafted through her senses, promising needed high-octane caffeine.

Nelda had never been known to think before she opened her mouth, and instructing her in the fine art of tact was a waste of time Holly didn't have. She filled the vintage drip coffeepot with water, then scooped the grounds into the basket. "The pot is ready. Just put it on when you get the stove lit. I have to dress before the Deltas catch me in my sweats. They'll be here at nine."

"If they're gonna want a cake, like usual, we got a problem. Remember, the stove's broke. Y'all gonna have to eat cereal for breakfast, too."

Holly huffed. "It's fine. I lit it last night. There must have been air in the line."

"If I get blowed sky-high, you gonna have to live with it," Nelda grumbled as she ambled to the stove.

Caffeine deficient, Holly plopped the pot on the stove. "I'll live with it."

"Who peed in your soup?" Nelda asked as Holly padded across the kitchen.

"Nobody."

"Uh-huh," Nelda said in her "Yeah, right" tone.

"I just need coffee." Holly pushed through the kitchen door, and it flapped behind her.

"You need more than coffee if that man didn't wake you up," Nelda called from the kitchen.

Holly pretended she hadn't heard her. She didn't need that part of her to wake up. Not by Jake. Not now.

Ten minutes later, Holly dashed down the stairs. She wore a black skirt, a white blouse, and practical flats for the long day ahead preparing for the Deltas and the weekend guests.

Rhett's yaps rang out from the kitchen as Holly padded through the entrance hall.

Nelda's voice carried through the door. "Hush up, Rhett. I can't feed you till I make breakfast. And I can't make breakfast till I light this contrary old stove. I told Holly it was broke, but she's got more broke stuff around here than money. So I'm gonna light this stove if I have to strike every last one of these matches. That girl needs a break, and you just got to wait."

Holly slowed her pace. Nelda might not censor her words, but she didn't censor her heart, either. As exasperating as Nelda could be, she was the one person Holly counted on. It'd been tough to pay her lately, but she couldn't let Nelda down, because Nelda never let her down.

When Holly entered the kitchen, Nelda was tossing a burnt match on the counter with a dozen more. She struck another match, turned a knob, and then held the match to the burner.

A translucent image came into focus. As soon as the burner caught, Burl leaned over the stove and blew the flame and the match out. He covered his mouth, and his shoulders shook in a silent laugh. While Nelda flipped the gas off and pulled another match from the box, Burl wiggled his leg at Rhett, causing a barrage of shrill yaps.

Burl jerked to attention when he saw Holly. He rubbed the grin off his face and cleared his throat. "Just having a little fun with Nelda and Rhett."

Holly folded her arms over her chest and glared at Burl.

"If this contraption don't blow me up, I'm gonna light it," Nelda said, striking another match.

Glowering at Burl, Holly marched to the stove. She grabbed the matchbox from Nelda and lit the burner. "The stove isn't broken. It's haunted."

"What you talkin' 'bout?" Nelda said, taking three backward steps, the lit match glowing between her fingers.

"All that God blessing you did didn't help. Burl is

back, and he's blowing the flame out on the stove every time you light it." Holly plunked the coffeepot on the lit burner.

Nelda cocked her head to the side and opened her mouth, but nothing came out. A flash of pain leapt to her face, and she shook the match until the flame died.

"Remember, Blondie, she can't see me," Burl said.

"Just because she can't see you doesn't mean I'm going to let you mess with her." Holly scooped Rhett into her arms. She wagged a finger at Burl. "And leave my dog alone, too."

"Can't a guy have a little fun?"

Holly's brain slammed into overdrive, and her heart pumped with anger. "Burl, you're a lying, cheating pile of—"

"Hey. Don't get personal."

"You said you couldn't haunt. You lied. Again." She pointed to the stove. "You just haunted my stove."

"Uh-uh. You ain't talking to a ghost," Nelda said, wide eyed, her backside hugging the kitchen cabinet and her hands curled in a death grip over the edge of the countertop.

"I'm talking to the sorriest excuse for a husband that ever lived and an even sorrier ghost."

"Come on, Blondie. Lighten up."

A blur of arms, legs, and a printed caftan raced to the back door.

"Nelda, wait," Holly called.

Heavy footsteps clattered across the porch. The whop of the screen door followed close behind.

Holly spun around to face Burl. "Look what you've done."

The squeal of burning rubber and an engine pushed to its limit rang out.

Holly wagged her finger at Burl. "Nelda didn't deserve to be scared like that."

Burl took a step back.

"What's she ever done to you? All she's trying to do is her job." Holly slapped her forehead. "Lordy. I've got the Deltas coming in less than an hour and six guests checking in for the weekend, and you just ran off my housekeeper." And the only person she'd thought she could count on.

"Me? If you hadn't opened your mouth, she would have just thought the stove was broken."

"You said you couldn't haunt."

"I can't." He lifted his shoulders. "I can blow a little."

"You're going to blow a lot. I'm going to light every candle I own." She pointed a finger at Burl. "And you're going to blow them out on cue. Got it?"

"Will that make you forgive me?"

"No."

"But if I do it, you'll help me." He rubbed his hands together. "We're partners. Right?"

"You'd better get ready to pucker up and blow if you want to see the pearly gates." Holly pasted a sardonic smile on her face.

"I don't think I like your attitude."

Holly lifted her chin and stood tall. "I don't think I care."

She sat Rhett on the floor. "If you'll excuse me, I have my work and Nelda's, too, because you had to have a little fun at her expense."

Rhett snorted as he trotted past Burl and out of the kitchen.

"Excuse you?" Burl said, with his eyes bugging out, like she'd said something he didn't understand. "I know this routine. You act all polite, then give me the silent treatment for a week. Come on, Holly. I don't have a week to waste."

"You've got eternity to waste. I'm on the line here."

"I'm not wasting my ectoplasm to get the silent treatment."

Before she could open her mouth, he vanished.

She turned a full circle in the kitchen and yelled, "On cue, Burl. We have a deal. You hear me?"

The flame under the coffeepot flickered, then sputtered out. He'd heard her.

Holly rushed to turn the gas off. *Lord help me. If I don't get him out of my house, he may blow the place off the map.*

Talk about backfiring. She hadn't counted on Burl scaring off Nelda. The ghost was supposed to save Holly Grove and everyone's job. Holly winced. And Nelda couldn't compete in the gumbo contest if she wasn't working at a tour plantation. She had to get Nelda back somehow.

On a larger scale, the haunting would work. But she had to appear sane while Burl haunted, Jake tempted, and she figured out who the smuggler was.

CHAPTER 7

Jake, dressed in khakis and a black shirt, strolled into the kitchen. Nelda's "real nice" popped into Holly's head, and her cheeks heated.

She poured coffee into a porcelain cup and pretended she barely noticed him. "You take anything in your coffee?"

"Straight up." He closed the distance between them, and the air filled with essence of clean man.

The cup rattled against the saucer as she handed him his coffee. She gave a nervous laugh. "Too much caffeine."

He didn't attempt to run his finger through the dainty handle. His hand swallowed the delicate cup as he sipped the coffee. "Where's Nelda?"

Holly heaved a sigh. She didn't think Jake would peel rubber and run, but she had to keep her distance from Burl's antics to appear sane and sober. She freshened her coffee to avoid looking at Jake while she lied. "She had an emergency."

"Is she okay?"

"Oh, yeah. Nothing major." She waved a hand through the air. "She'll be back."

Holly *had* to get Nelda back. Guests expected breakfast at a bed-and-breakfast. The Deltas expected fresh homemade cake or pie for their bridge game. But another cook wouldn't do. Nelda was more than a cook. She was family and couldn't be replaced.

Now Holly, whose homemade lemon pie could be used to remove varnish, was forced to cook something edible for her guests until she could coax Nelda back.

Jake sniffed the air. "Do I smell something burning?"

A thin ribbon of smoke snaked from the oven door. Holly grabbed pot holders, then threw the oven door open. More smoke funneled out of the oven. "My biscuits!"

Jake grabbed a kitchen towel and fanned the air. "Well, you didn't set off any fire alarms this time."

A Hurricane Holly flashback to a home skills class that had ended with a fire alarm and a school evacuation raced through her mind and, evidently, his.

Holly slid a baking sheet out of the oven and then dropped it on top of the stove. Crusty brown meteors smoked on the baking sheet. She used her spatula to chisel under a burned biscuit. "Maybe the insides are okay."

"Sweetheart, I'm not sure the Jaws of Life could get to the insides of those biscuits."

"Don't worry. I've made scrambled eggs and grits, too."

Jake lifted the lid on an iron skillet on the stove. "Are these the eggs or the grits?"

Holly peered into the skillet at unappetizing lumps and clumps of grits, which could pass for scrambled eggs.

He cocked an eye at her. "You don't cook, but you run a B & B."

The statement speared her confidence. "Okay, cooking isn't my strong suit." She took the lid from Jake and hid her attempt at grits. "Nelda is the breakfast part of B & B here." She tilted her chin up and squared her shoulders. "Just because I'm not a cook doesn't mean I don't run a darned good B & B."

He invaded her space. "What is your strong suit?"

Screwing up. Bad luck. Marrying trouble. Pick one. And Jake could be just the kind of trouble she didn't need. She yanked a cabinet door open and then shook a box of cereal. "Cheerios."

"Seriously. You didn't have any guests last night, except me, and I'm not exactly forking over cash. How do you manage to keep this place going?"

"I manage." But she couldn't manage much longer, according to her bank statements. She grabbed a bowl from the cabinet, then poured Cheerios into it. "I'd give breakfast another shot, but I have to burn a cake for the Deltas now."

"The Deltas?"

"The bridge group that rents the parlor every week for their bridge game." She aimed a look at Jake. "One of the ways I manage."

He eyed the burned biscuits. "And you need cake."

"Or pie."

A grin that made her hungry for more than breakfast slipped across his face. "I'll take care of that."

And Mr. Real Nice can cook, too. Lordy, it's getting warm in this kitchen.

He smiled and headed to the back door.

"Where are you going? I thought you were going to bake a cake."

"Real men don't bake cakes, sweetheart." He winked. "They buy them."

"But Delta Ridge doesn't have a bakery."

"Don't burn anything while I'm gone," he said, then closed the door behind him.

She eyed the smoldering biscuits. *No problem.*

A clap of thunder rattled the house. Holly smiled as she poured coffee into a carafe. Thunder and a ghost. At least Mother Nature was on her side. Maybe luck. Holly couldn't afford to have her plan backfire this time.

The tick of the kitchen clock punctuated the silence as Holly set out her mom's Blue Willow china plates, silver dessert forks, and embroidered linen luncheon napkins for the Deltas. She eyed the crystal compotes. If Jake didn't come in with a dessert soon, she'd have to chisel into the half gallon of vanilla ice cream she'd found in the bottom of the freezer. If she doused enough crème de menthe on it, the Deltas might not notice the taint of freezer burn.

She'd manage. She always had.

The Deltas tittered in the parlor while they played bridge. She had produced the sheriff's report and deserved an Academy nod for her performance, especially the part about how she had been overwhelmed with grief and had drunk too much champagne on what would have been her anniversary. Three of the four women had eaten it up. Miss Alice had suggested Alcoholics Anonymous.

Everything was going as planned, except dessert and Burl's parlor tricks. So far, Burl was a no-show for his command performance. No surprise.

"Burl, where are you?" she whispered, glancing around the kitchen. "It's showtime."

All she wanted to do was rouse the Deltas' curiosity. The mystery of a few candles going out and some well-placed suspicions should do the trick. She didn't have to prove she had a ghost. All she needed was a rumor, and the Deltas could start a rumor better than anyone in St. Agnes Parish. Once the gossip started, Holly Grove would have its ghost even after she ushered Burl into heaven.

She grabbed the carafe of hot coffee and walked into the parlor. Rain pelted windows darkened by the storm. A dozen little flames flickered from the antique silver candelabra on the mantel. Jasmine-scented tea lights danced in every corner of the room. To explain lighting candles in mid-morning to a group of women who referenced *Amy Vanderbilt's Complete Book of Etiquette* like it was a social bible, she'd confessed to burning the biscuits and using candles to cover the smell. Not exactly a lie. Not exactly the truth. She could live with that.

The four Deltas perched around a mahogany game table under the chandelier Grandma Rose had called an electrified gasolier. It had been converted from gas lighting to electric lightbulbs when she was a little girl. Rhett, curled in a ball under the table, snoozed as the women chatted with the ease of a lifetime of friendship.

Miss Cora Beth held her cards six inches from her Coke-bottle glasses, studying her hand. Her gray brows bunched together in concentration. She'd been the parish librarian until she retired at age seventy-five for health reasons she'd never made clear. She'd also taken the place of Holly's grandmother in the Delta Bridge Club after her death three years ago. Looking at Cora Beth leached sadness from hidden places in Holly's heart. She couldn't help but wish Grandma Rose sat in the chair instead of Cora Beth.

Burl appeared behind Cora Beth. "If she were playing poker, the old lady would have a winner." He looked at Holly and lifted a shoulder. "But I don't play bridge."

She couldn't talk to Burl in front of the Deltas. If she did, they'd have her committed this time. Holly gave a subtle nod toward the candles on the mantel.

He whistled as he sauntered to the fireplace. Burl propped an elbow on the mantel. "Ready when you are, Blondie."

Holly added fresh coffee to the Deltas' cups and gave Burl another nod. Burl blew out a candle and took a bow like he'd earned applause. Holly rolled her eyes.

The Deltas didn't notice that one less candle burned. Holly tilted her head toward the candles as a signal to Burl to blow out more.

Threads of smoke tangled around the extinguished candles as Burl blew out every flame in the room, but the ladies didn't seem to notice anything except their game.

"Hey, I told you I couldn't haunt." He folded his arms over his chest. "Now what, Blondie the mastermind?"

Anger pricked her neck. *Think, Holly. Think.*

"Did y'all blow out my candles?" she said to draw attention to Burl's handiwork.

Miss Alice pushed her glasses down her nose and scanned the room. "You must have let your wicks drown in wax. You have to keep the wicks trimmed and freeze your candles to make them last." She slid her glasses back in place, then picked up a pencil and jotted down a score.

Holly opened her mouth to protest, then closed it. Instead, she plastered a smile on her face. "Good idea. I'll do that next time."

Next time, she'd plant the candles right in front of their old eyes.

Burl frowned. "What the heck is she talking about? Candles are simple. Nothing complicated about firing up a candle." He winked at Holly. "Kinda like a man."

Maybe I should have frozen him and trimmed his wick when we were married. Ignoring Burl, she said, "I'll have your refreshments ready in a few minutes."

Miss Alice snatched her glasses from the bridge of her nose and let them dangle from a beaded chain as she stared at Holly. "You're not serving us some microwave concoction, since Nelda isn't here, are you?"

"Don't worry. I've got something very special for you ladies," Holly said over her shoulder as she ambled to the kitchen. *Something worth talking about.*

As soon as she was out of sight, she scurried to the back of the laundry room, then opened the breaker box. Holly looked toward heaven and waited a few beats for a clap of thunder. So much for Mother Nature's cooperation. Holly flipped the main power switch, anyway. The hum of the refrigerator ceased, and the house fell silent. She dashed back to the kitchen as Miss Alice called from the parlor.

"Coming." Holly rushed through the entrance hall to the parlor.

Without the light from the chandelier, shadows streaked the room and the Deltas' faces.

Miss Alice stood at the doorway, flipping the light switch on and off. "The power is off," she snapped.

Miss Martha Jane fingered the lace on her blouse. "Oh dear, I hope we don't have to quit in the middle of a game. We've never done that. How would we tally?"

"Don't be ridiculous, Martha Jane." Miss Alice peered over her glasses. "It's just the storm. The electricity will be on shortly."

Holly grabbed the candelabra from the mantel. "You ladies relax. I'll serve dessert by candlelight." She placed the candelabra in the center of the game table and then lit all twelve candles. "It'll be fun."

Miss Martha Jane smiled and patted her chest as Holly lit the candles. "Oh my, I haven't eaten by candlelight since my Marvin passed on."

"Quite charming, my dear, but I fear I won't know what I'm eating," Cora Beth said, clipping her words in a singsongy English accent. She'd never lost her native accent, even though she'd lived in the South for forty-five years. She'd married the town lawyer, Leo Perkins, when he was stationed in England after the Korean conflict.

"Y'all excuse me. I've got to go to the ladies' room," Penny said as she stood. Standing made her round body only inches taller.

"I don't know why you keep putting off that bladder suspension surgery," Miss Alice said as she tromped back to the bridge table. "I'm glad we aren't paying for the parlor this week." Miss Alice huffed and jabbed her hands toward the chandelier. "No lights."

Holly gave Burl a nod.

He saluted Holly and sauntered to the bridge table, rubbing his hands together. "They'll notice me this time." He blew the top candle out, then stood back and grinned.

Rhett growled under the table.

"My, but this old house is drafty today," Miss Martha Jane said, looking at the extinguished candle.

He sucked in a big breath and blew out all of the candles in rapid succession. "Draft, my butt," he said, panting.

"Get up, girls," Miss Alice said. "Let's move to the dining room, out of this draft, before we catch pneumonia. Holly, bring the candelabra."

"It ain't no draft. That's a ghost what blew them candles out," Nelda said, charging into the room. Wide eyed, she wielded a silver cross in one hand like a gun, flashing it from side to side. In the other hand, she clutched red rosary beads. "He's been up in my kitchen, hauntin', and he's gotta go."

Father Martinez followed one step behind her. Lightning cracked, and he crossed himself. Fresh out of seminary and new to America, his first parish was St. Agnes Catholic. He wore a large gold crucifix and held a vial of holy water, the Bible and, from the look on his face, his bowels.

The Deltas froze, mouths open.

Dang! Why didn't I think of calling a priest to get rid of Burl? Holly smiled at Nelda.

"I got reinforcements," Nelda said. "We gonna evict that ghost."

Rhett tore from under the table, yapping and snapping at Burl.

Sidestepping Rhett, Burl looked from Nelda to Father Martinez to Holly. "What in blue blazes is going on?"

Father Martinez inched in front of Nelda. His gaze shifted around the room, and then, with shaking hands, he pulled the crucifix to his lips and kissed it. In a thick Spanish accent, he said, "I can't make exorcism without the bishop's permission, but I will bless this house." He opened the Bible and started speaking Spanish, or was it Latin?

"Speak English, so I know what you're saying," Miss Alice snapped.

"Forgive me." Father Martinez bowed slightly. "When I get nervous, I sometimes forget my English. I asked the Lord to be with me, as I have never witnessed a ghost, and I asked for His help with the blessing. I'll need your help, too."

Miss Alice grabbed Miss Martha Jane's hand as they scurried toward the priest, with Cora Beth at their heels. The candelabra teetered in the center of the table, then toppled over in the wake of their escape.

Father Martinez said, "The Lord be with you."

"And also with you," the Deltas chimed as they huddled behind the priest.

Pacing the room, Father Martinez held the Bible in one hand and splashed holy water from side to side with the other. The old ladies shuffled behind him, chanting at his prompt.

Burl puffed his chest out, squared his shoulders, and looked at Holly. "Now you owe me." He folded his arms over his chest. "My work here is done."

As Father Martinez walked by, sprinkling holy water, his blessing reverted to Spanish again. Holy water splattered across Burl's face.

Burl slapped his hands over his face and fell to the floor, writhing in pain. He moaned as holy water splashed across his back.

Holly gasped. She had wanted Burl out of her life and had thought she wanted revenge, but she couldn't bear to see him in pain.

"Stop. You're hurting him," she screamed, snatching the vial of holy water from Father Martinez.

Holly fell to her knees at Burl's side as tears stung her eyes. What kind of monster was she? She wouldn't let an animal suffer like that. "I'm sorry. I didn't know they'd hurt you."

Burl faded before her.

She'd wanted him gone. She'd wished him dead. And she'd used him just like he'd used her. Worse, she was relieved he was gone. She was no better than Burl and would probably join him in Hades for what she'd done.

Through tear-filled eyes, Holly looked at Nelda, the priest, and the Deltas. They had their backs glued to the wall, their mouths open, and their stares fixed on her like she was possessed. Her world slowed to a frame-by-frame motion picture as she remembered they couldn't see Burl.

Miss Martha Jane wrung her hands. "Do y'all think she's hallucinating again?"

"Perhaps not." Miss Cora Beth tilted her head to the side. "I've read quite a bit about the supernatural. One of my ancestors was burned at the stake for witchcraft." She arched a brow. "My mum said they burned her because she talked to the dead."

Miss Martha Jane's fingers fluttered to her neck. "You think Holly has the gift?"

The chalky red lipstick Miss Alice wore nearly disappeared as her lips tightened into a flat line. She folded her arms under her grandmother boobs and eyed Holly. "Gift, my foot."

Holly's stomach tightened. She'd done exactly what she knew would make everyone in Delta Ridge think she had lost what little mind she had left. Her name would be added to every prayer list in town because she'd proven she was nuts. Instead of gaining business with a ghost, she'd ruined her chances of saving Holly Grove. Who would want to stay at a bed-and-breakfast run by a crazy woman? She might as well change the name of the place to the Bates Motel.

"Is he gone?" Nelda asked, taking a tentative step toward Holly.

"Yes," Holly whispered as she rose to her feet. She swept her hair from her face.

Lordy. What could she say to get out of this? *Just kidding?*

"Who wants pie?" Jake's voice rang from the entrance hall. He strode into the parlor, balancing a coconut meringue pie in one hand and a chocolate pie in the other. His smile faded as his brows smashed together. He stared at the carnage from the bridge game like he had walked in on the first line of a bad joke and had no clue what the punch line could possibly be.

Cool air brushed Holly's neck.

"Gotcha, Blondie."

CHAPTER 8

Holly slammed her bedroom door, then locked it behind her. She leaned her back against the door and slid down onto the hardwood floor where she clutched her knees against her chest. The Deltas had to think she was certifiable. How could she face anyone ever again? Tears burned her eyes. Burl wasn't worth it. He never was. She swiped at her tears, then pushed to her feet.

She met Burl eye to eye. In one quick motion, she launched a blow to his face and caught nothing but air. Fury ripped through her. She'd needed to make contact, give him the physical pain he'd faked.

Burl stepped back. "Whoa, slugger. You're going to throw your arm out."

"Why did you do that?" She shoved her hands on her hips.

"You mean the holy water?" Burl laughed. "Why did you fall for it?"

"I thought you were in pain."

"I could have drunk that stuff. Don't you realize that peon of a priest is at the bottom of the food chain?

St. Peter sent me here, for Christ's sake." He looked heavenward. "Sorry, God. Just making a point for Blondie here."

"Leave God out of this. The point is now the Deltas just think I'm nuts. The whole plan was to show them the house is haunted."

"Ah, but you missed the second act. After you got all pissy and ran upstairs, I blew a pencil across the table and flipped some cards over a few times. All with perfect timing for effect, mind you." He aimed a look at her. "I'm good," he said, puffing out his chest. "It looked like the Senior Olympics when the old ladies cleared out of there."

"What about Jake?"

"If that loser had seen the whole show, he'd have hightailed it, too."

"You mean the Deltas think the place is haunted, after all?"

"Not the one with the big hooters."

"Eeew. She's an old lady. You shouldn't say that."

He cocked his head. "You knew who I was talking about, didn't you?"

Holly groaned.

"She may give you trouble, but the others are coming around." He opened his arms to her and grinned. "Now, don't you feel bad about trying to slug me?"

"Not one bit."

"Come on. I know you still love me. I saw you cry."

"We've been over this. You and I are history. This is a business deal. You haunt, and I bust the smuggling ring, and *then* you get your ticket out of here. End of story." She pointed a finger at Burl. "But get this and get it good. I will not talk to you in front of anyone ever again. I don't care if your hair is on fire."

* * *

Holly jumped when a knock sounded on her bedroom door.

"Holly," Jake said from the other side of the door. "Can I come in?"

She rested her hand on the doorknob. What could she say?

Burl frowned. "Tell what's-his-name to go away."

She wished she could. Holly glared at Burl. "No. You go away."

"I was here first."

"You sound like a second grader," she whispered.

Burl's face swelled into a sulk.

She gave Burl a "butt out" look and opened the door.

Jake handed her a card and cocked an eyebrow. "Nelda left this for you. She said if you wanted her back to call this woman."

Holly glanced at Claireese, the psychic's card. She blew out a sigh and stuffed the card in her pocket. *What the hell could it hurt?* She'd call her tomorrow, since the pope wasn't available to exorcise Burl. A psychic probably couldn't get rid of Burl, but she'd try one for Nelda.

Jake looked down at Holly. "Is there something you want to tell me?"

"Not really," she said, with a downward glance. Thanks to Burl, the whole town would think she was nuts after the Deltas told their tale. She'd rather not confirm it to Jake.

"Mind if I come in?" Jake asked.

Holly lifted a shoulder and stepped back as he strode into her room.

Burl sat on her bed and pounded his fist in his hand. "If I could land a punch, I'd knock this guy out. He's just worming his way into your life." Burl looked around the room. "And your bedroom. I don't like this, and I'm not sticking around to watch."

"Nelda and the bridge ladies think you saw a ghost. You want to explain?" Jake asked.

Woman up, Holly. Think of something. She forced a lighthearted tone into her voice. "You know the Deltas. They're easily excited. They're the ones who thought I was on drugs."

"Uh-huh."

"The whole thing was bizarre." She waved her fingers through the air. "The lights went out, and the candles kept blowing out. Then Nelda came in with a priest. I got caught up in it all and thought I saw something."

"Uh-huh."

"I'm so embarrassed."

"How do you suppose the electricity went out and the candles blew out? And why is Nelda so convinced there was a ghost down there?"

Holly shrugged. "I don't know," she said, avoiding eye contact.

"I think you do." He grabbed her by the hand, and she trotted behind him down the stairs to the parlor.

"You see that window?" he asked with a nod to the broken windowpane.

She slammed a palm against her head. "I've got to get that fixed."

"You don't suppose the wind from the storm blew through that window and blew out the candles, do you?"

"I suppose it could have."

"And you don't suppose someone pulled the main power switch, do you?"

Holly chewed a nail, wondering if he'd checked the power switch. "I suppose someone could have done that."

"Someone did." He directed an accusing stare at her.

"You don't believe I saw a ghost?"

"Nope."

"You think I'm crazy?"

"Nope. I think you rigged a haunting."

Rigged? Okay, she'd go with that. She huffed and stuffed her hands on her hips. "Okay, okay. You got me."

"What I want to know is why."

She gave a sheepish look and lifted a shoulder. "I need a ghost."

CHAPTER 9

Jake parked himself at the counter at Dottie's Diner and combed a hand through his hair, resisting the urge to yank it out by the roots.

A ghost. That'd sound great on his report. He could hear his whole department laughing now. After they stopped laughing, he'd be yanked from this dead-end assignment.

He rolled his neck, which seemed to get stiffer by the minute. She'd said she needed a ghost for business. And ICE had considered Holly capable of running drugs out of Holly Grove. Jake rubbed his hand over his mouth to discourage a grin.

As he slid a greasy Dottie's Diner menu from behind a chrome napkin dispenser, he tipped over a saltshaker. Dot snatched the saltshaker from Jake's hand and shook it over his shoulder.

"I don't want any bad luck sitting in my diner," she said, then thumbed toward a box of a room in the corner. "I got video poker machines in there."

"Don't worry." He winked at Dot. "I was born lucky."

"Nah. You were born good looking." She winked

back and sat the shaker on the red Formica counter. "Lucky too. You got your looks from your mama instead of your daddy."

"So I hear." He wouldn't know. His mother had left before he started school. His dad had burned all her pictures and drowned the memories in Jack Daniel's.

"She was something." Dot pulled a towel off her shoulder, then wiped up a few drops of coffee from the counter. "Yeah, Marcella blew into town, married Mackie, and you came along in short order." Dot flipped the towel over her shoulder. "Blew out of here just as fast." She shook her head. "Mackie ain't been the same since."

"No one's fault but his own." Jake set his mug down harder than he intended, and coffee sloshed in the mug.

"I used to think so, but now I think he's gone too far to help himself." Dot looked past Jake to the diners behind him, probably to see if they needed anything. Their conversations and the clinking of silverware blended into a white noise. In New York he'd be part of the white noise. Here Dot wouldn't allow it.

Jake sipped his coffee. "I do my part." The hiss of the grill and the smell of fried bacon wafted from the kitchen. "Which reminds me . . . What do I owe for his meals this week?" He straightened a leg and reached for his wallet.

"Nothing." Dot topped off his coffee. "He hasn't darkened my door lately."

Jake shrugged. "He'll come around when he's sober enough to realize he's hungry."

"You're probably right, but he's got high mileage. He can't keep on like he has. He won't last."

Fifteen years ago, Jake had made the choice to stop trying to save his dad the only way he could. He stopped by bailing out of Delta Ridge for good. He couldn't save him then, and he couldn't save him now. "His choice."

"Guess so, but it's a waste. He's the best carpenter in town when he's sober." She reached under the counter and pulled out a stack of messages. "You see these? Every widow woman in town is waiting for him to do some sort of chore."

Jake took the messages and thumbed through them. "How long this time?"

"A couple of weeks or more." She pulled the towel from its perch on her shoulder and rubbed a smudge on the counter. "Mrs. Martha Jane Shaw calls nearly every day. She thinks Mackie is the only person on the planet who can replace the rotten gingerbread on her Victorian."

"He may be." Jake handed the stack of messages back to Dot.

"You could. You used to come get his messages and do his jobs." She stuffed the slips of paper in her apron pocket. "You'd make up some excuse about his back, but we all knew he'd fallen off the wagon again."

"It's called enabling. People have to pay for their mistakes, or they don't change." His voice came out firmer than he'd intended. "Sorry, Dot."

She waved his apology off like it wasn't needed. "Well, between you and me, at least we know he won't starve if he doesn't see the error of his ways. He still thinks he won free lunches for life as a door prize. I can't believe you sucked me into that scam."

"You know if I gave him the money, he'd drink it." Jake didn't owe his father respect, but duty had nothing to do with respect. Usually, he paid his dad's tab at the diner by mail, but this time he'd wanted to pay in person and show Dot some appreciation.

"Why don't you and Mackie make up? How long has it been?"

"It'll be long enough when he stops drinking." Jake's jaw tensed around the words he lived by.

"You don't get to choose your kinfolks, but he's the only daddy the good Lord gave you."

"I hear you, but it is what it is."

The bell over the door jingled, and Jake turned. He stiffened as Sheriff Walker and a deputy walked in.

"You're both hardheaded." Dot pulled out her order pad and moved down to the end the of counter where Sheriff Walker and his deputy had claimed two bar stools.

The last time Jake had talked to the sheriff, he'd opened the parish jail door and instructed Jake to stay out of trouble, or he'd end up like Mackie. Jake had been arrested for driving underage with an open container of alcohol in the truck. It was Mackie's whiskey, and Jake was driving so his dad wouldn't get another DUI. None of that mattered to by-the-book Sheriff Walker.

Dot took the sheriff's order, then hollered over her shoulder, "BLT, extra mayo."

The bell over the door clanged as more diners came in for lunch, and Jake scanned the menu. He'd better load up, because if Holly was cooking tonight, it might not be edible.

"I hear you're staying at Holly Grove," Dottie said, parking herself in front of him again.

"Yep."

She leaned into Jake. "See any ghosts?"

"Nope."

"I don't believe in that malarkey, either, but if it gets tourists to Holly Grove, they'll venture into town, too, and be hungry." Dot straightened and scratched her head with her pencil. "Weren't you and Holly sweet on each other in high school?"

"Yep."

"Now, that's a nice girl. She could use a good man."

"Who says she's looking?"

Dot cackled and slapped Jake on the shoulder. "Honey, every single woman is looking."

"She hasn't been a widow long."

"Well, she's been a widow longer than she knows. Burl was carrying on with a redhead over in the next parish." She propped her elbows on the counter and eyed Jake. "I heard she used to be a stripper."

Jake raised a brow. "Holly know he was cheating?"

"Don't think so. Now, with him dead and all, who wants to tell that? Might as well let her think he was better than he was. Ignorance is bliss, you know." She flipped to a fresh sheet on her order pad. "Now, what you having?"

The bell jingled again. At least business was good for Dot.

"I'll take a blue plate." If Holly hadn't known her husband was cheating, it was likely he'd hidden the smuggling from her, too.

"I'll have eight of those to go," Holly said, leaning against the counter next to Jake. She brushed a Southern hello on his cheek. His gaze lingered on her as she settled on the stool beside him. He was 99 percent sure she didn't have anything to do with Burl's operation and

100 percent certain he'd do something he'd regret if he didn't blow this town soon.

Holly's body temperature spiked as she brushed a peck on Jake's cheek.

Dot hollered over her shoulder, "Eight blue plates to go."

Jake spun on his stool and flashed a teasing smile at Holly. "Hungry, huh?"

"I noticed the pies you bought for the Deltas came from Dottie's, so I figured I'd cook like a man." She cast a smile at Jake. "I don't want to poison paying guests with my cooking."

Dot pointed her pencil at Jake. "Jake here is special. I'd bake him a pie anytime."

Lordy. His charisma even crossed age barriers.

Jake gestured to an empty booth. "Come on." He brushed his hand across the small of her back, sending warm shivers through her. "I'm cooking."

Lunch did sound good. Holly slid across the Naugahyde bench.

Two of the Deltas, Miss Martha Jane and Miss Penny, huddled in a corner. The sheriff and a deputy perched on stools at the counter. Holly knew nearly everyone in the diner, but she hadn't noticed anyone except Jake when she'd come in.

Forks scraped ironstone plates as diners whispered back and forth between each other and some looked her way.

"You think they've heard about my ghost?" she asked.

"No doubt."

Unless they all thought she was nuts or an addict. "Good. Publicity is what I wanted."

His look turned serious. "Anyone who would fabricate a ghost to draw business has got to be desperate."

"Look, Jake, I know you're trying to help, but it's this simple. Burl spent everything we had before he died. End of story."

Jake eyed Holly as though he knew there was more. Dot rescued her by interrupting to take their lunch order, but he jumped back on topic as soon as Dot left.

"Any idea why?" Jake asked.

Holly shook her head. She wasn't about to tell the editor of the local newspaper Burl had been smuggling drugs through Holly Grove to pay gambling debts.

"Didn't you and Burl discuss your finances?"

"I know. I know. I should have been more involved." Holly ran her finger around the rim of her water glass. "I was so focused on Holly Grove, I didn't pay attention to Burl's business, until it was too late. We didn't really talk that much in the end."

Jake nodded. "So you and Burl weren't happily married?"

"Is there such a thing?"

"I wouldn't know. Never bit that bullet."

"Why not?"

"Never found the idea of settling down in one place with one woman appealing."

Proof positive. He was trouble. "I can't imagine living anywhere except here." She lowered her gaze. "I had thought Burl was my happily ever after, but I should have known better. Women in my family have a history of marrying trouble. But they all held on to Holly Grove. That's why she's so important to me. I can count on her to be there, always." *Unlike money or men.*

Dot slid two burger baskets on the table. "Can I get y'all anything else?"

"Are you still taking messages for Mackie?" Holly asked.

"Yep." Dot fished a stack of messages from her apron. "Get in line, girl."

"I was hoping he could fix my window and some other things." Holly eyed the stack. "He's pretty backed up, huh?"

"Most of the messages are a few weeks old. He could be off on another tear. It wouldn't be the first time, you know." Dot turned and headed to the next table.

Holly looked back at Jake. "He cleaned up Burl's hangar last month so I could rent it out. He was sober and didn't even look hung over then. I thought he was doing better. Have you talked to him?"

"Nope," Jake said.

"He's your dad, Jake."

"Don't you start, too." He nodded toward Dot. "She's already lectured me." He leaned on his elbows and drilled Holly with a stare. "And I'm not going to look him up now, because he doesn't feel like working."

"But, Jake. What if he's sick?"

"He's not sick. He's drunk." His eyes told her the conversation was over, but she couldn't let it go. She'd love to see her mother or her grandmother in any state just once more.

"I think we should go check on him."

"We? Look, you don't have a pony in this race, and I'm not betting on Mackie ever again." He leaned back and folded his arms. "Let it go."

"I do have a pony in this race. I need my window fixed."

"I'll fix it."

"You've got free room and board. What will this cost me?"

"Don't mention him again."

"Fine. I'll check on Mackie myself."

CHAPTER 10

Mackie wasn't Holly's business, but they weren't so different. Neither of them had close family around, and the town looked after them. Granted, people in Delta Ridge stuck their noses where they shouldn't, but she'd never felt alone. Now she was doing what she should to look out for one of her own, whether Jake liked it or not. If Mackie was drunk, so be it. But he could be ill or injured.

As Holly drove down River Road, she strained to see the overgrown turnrow that served as a dirt road to Mackie's place. She turned off the blacktop onto the dirt road lined with twelve-foot-high sugarcane. Her Tahoe sank into ruts from tractors that had cultivated the field. Take-out blue plates slid across the passenger seat when she hit a deep rut. The road didn't look like it had been traveled in months.

The turnrow widened at the back of the field. A stand of oak trees and thick undergrowth marked the old McCann homeplace at the base of the levee. She parked her Tahoe and looked at the shack that had once been an overseer's cottage, never a fine home.

But now it was uninhabitable. A trailer covered with a coat of green algae stood nearby, with Mackie's rusted-out truck parked beside it.

Holly grabbed one of the blue-plate lunches then climbed out of her Tahoe. If Jake was right and Mackie was drunk, a hearty meal might help sober him up. A deep layer of oak leaves crunched under her feet, releasing the musky smell of fall. She trudged past the dilapidated cottage and toward the trailer. From the coat of dust on the old truck's windshield, she suspected that Mackie hadn't gone anywhere in weeks.

A deep, low growl came from under the truck.

Her breath caught as the ugliest dog she'd ever seen crawled out from under the truck. He looked like a cross between a wolf and a shar-pei and probably answered to Killer.

"Nice dog," she said in the most calming voice she could muster, considering her words might be her last.

The mutt's lip curled in a snarl.

Her mouth went dry.

The animal held his back left leg off the ground, and it dangled there as though it was paralyzed. Dried scabs dotted his hip.

No wonder he's so grouchy. He's hurt.

She took a slow step in the dog's direction. The hair on the mutt's back rose, and he shot in her direction with a three-legged gait that would easily overcome her two-legged run. She snatched open the blue-plate box and hurled a piece of roast at him. His three legs skidded as he slid to the spot where the roast had landed in the dirt.

Holly glanced over her shoulder at her truck and then at Mackie's camper to see which was closer. Sure as sin the camper was closer.

Lordy. Don't show fear. Dogs can smell it, and this mutt may eat it.

"Want some more, boy?" She tried to control her shaky voice and tossed another piece of roast to him.

The mutt caught the meat in midair. He swallowed without chewing, then settled on his haunches and licked his lips.

"That's right, boy. We're making friends." She reached for another piece of beef. *Oh, crapola. No more beef.* She dangled a green bean from her fingertips. "Want this?" She flung the bean across the yard.

The dog took off in a three-legged trot and sniffed out the bean.

A few green beans later, she and the dog had an understanding. She gave him food, and he let her live as she made her way to Mackie's trailer.

She pitched the Styrofoam container, with the remaining mashed potatoes, gravy, and banana pudding, toward the old truck. As soon as the dog sank his nose in the grub, she yanked the doorknob on the trailer door. Relieved to find the door unlocked, she stepped inside.

The trailer smelled of whiskey, stale cigarettes, and dirty laundry.

"Mackie?" She sniffed the rank air as she turned a full circle in the room, which served as a kitchen, dining room, and den. A metallic ping pulsed through the room as a steady drip of water hit a pot crusted with something unidentifiable. The plaid sofa against the wall held piles of dingy laundry, and a lamp lay overturned near a worn-out recliner.

The door at the rear of the kitchen stood ajar. She

took a deep breath. Mackie could be sick or worse back there.

"Mackie. It's Holly Davis. You back there?"

Holly slid the pocket door open to a dark room. She rubbed her hand over the wall until she found the light switch. A dusty fixture cast a dim light on an unmade, empty bed surrounded by hundreds of books. Everyone, including her, saved their old paperbacks for him, but she hadn't realized he never passed them on. She relaxed a bit. An empty bed was a good thing.

At least he wasn't dead. Maybe he was off on a drunk, like Jake had said. Unless he'd collapsed in the bathroom. She navigated through the stacks of books to double pocket doors, then slid both doors open at once. On one side, bare hangers dangled like skeletons between well-worn shirts. On the other stood an empty compact bathroom.

Mackie had left dishes in the sink, laundry everywhere, and his lamp tipped over. Maybe he'd left in a hurry. But why?

Holly walked back into the living area. Jake had grown up in this place. Was it any wonder the only way he wanted to see Delta Ridge was in his rearview mirror?

Aside from the squalor, something was terribly wrong. If he was out on a drunk, Mackie might leave dishes in the sink and laundry on the sofa, but he wouldn't have left his dog to fend for himself. Not the Mackie she knew. Not if he could help it.

She dug her cell phone out of her purse and called the *Gazette*.

Miss Penny, one of the Deltas, answered and put her through to Jake.

"I'm at your dad's place. You've got to get out here."

Jake blew a hard breath into the phone. "Is he passed out?"

"No." She paced across the kitchen. "He's not here. The place is a wreck. I think something happened to him."

"Something happened, all right," Jake said. "He got plastered somewhere and hasn't sobered up yet."

"No. This is serious."

"Look, Holly. I appreciate your concern for Mackie, but I'm busy here. He'll come back when he dries out. I promise."

"If you don't come, I'm calling Sheriff Walker."

After a long pause, Jake said, "Mackie wouldn't appreciate that."

"So you'll come?"

"Nope."

"There's something else."

"What?"

She hesitated. "I can't leave."

"Why not?"

Holly bent a yellowed mini-blind and looked out at the dog, who appeared to be guarding the door. "Mackie's dog won't let me out of the trailer."

Jake could have lived his entire life without ever setting foot on this place again. Nothing had changed. Mackie's twenty-year-old Dodge Ram truck and raggedy trailer looked just like they had when Jake escaped from Delta Ridge.

A knot tightened in his stomach as he glanced at the house next door. Mackie had locked that door and moved into the trailer after Jake's mother left. He'd shipped Jake off to his grandmother, but they had visited Mackie. The last visit became permanent, because his grandmother got sick and died when Jake was twelve. For years, Jake could see every detail of the house in his mind, but not now.

He opened the car door and stepped out. A puff of gray dust scattered around his shoes. In Louisiana, if you stepped on bare ground, you hit either a dust bowl or a mud hole, depending on the time of year. It might as well have been a cow patty. Jake didn't want to be here. And wouldn't be if not for Holly meddling in his business.

"Jake," Holly yelled. "Watch out for the dog."

He looked up to find her waving from a crank-out window in the trailer.

A scruffy oversize mutt stood at attention, staring him down from the front of the trailer. Jake slid two fingers in his mouth and let out a piercing whistle. The mongrel's ears perked.

"Come, Dog," Jake said as he slapped his thigh.

Tail wagging, the mutt trotted to Jake's side.

Holly opened the door and leaned out. "How'd you do that?"

Jake held his hand out for Dog to sniff, then rubbed his head. "It helps to know his name."

"Dog?"

"Mackie has called every dog he's had Dog. It makes remembering its name under the influence easier." Jake eyed Dog's lame leg and then reached to inspect the mutt's haunches.

Dog growled.

Jake pulled his hand back. "Hurts, huh?"

Wielding a Louisville Slugger in a death grip, Holly

stepped from the trailer. Her cheeks flushed as wisps of curls blew across her face. Normally, a woman packing a baseball bat wouldn't be a turn-on, but nothing had been normal when it came to Holly.

"Were you going to save me from this vicious dog?" he asked.

As if on cue, Dog licked Jake's hand.

"What are you? A dog whisperer?" she asked. "And what are you grinning about?"

He rubbed his hand across his mouth. "You." Jake crossed the distance between them. He took the bat from her. "Come on. Let's go."

She pulled back. "Not until you come inside and see what I'm talking about."

"We don't have any business in Mackie's trailer."

"Just come inside. If you don't think something is wrong, I'll go." She grabbed him by the hand and squeezed it. "I promise."

Why was it so hard to tell her no? He mounted the steps and entered the trailer. If King Kong had picked up the place and shook the thing, it wouldn't have looked worse. Jake shrugged. "Same old Mackie. Let's go."

"Wait." She motioned toward the toppled lamp. "What about this?"

"He knocked it over and was too drunk to pick it up. Look around, Holly. You think he cares if a lamp tips over?" Jake scanned the cluttered room, and something unusual caught his eye.

On the floor next to the recliner, that he'd watched his father pass out in too many times, was a near-full bottle of whiskey and a half-empty glass. Never had he known Mackie to leave a drop of whiskey in a glass.

Holly touched his arm. "I'm worried."

He crossed the room, then squatted beside the bottle and peered into the glass. Ants floated on top of the whiskey, and a few clung to the sticky sides where the booze had evaporated. Mackie hadn't been home in a long time.

"What is it?"

"Nothing." Jake rubbed his hands over his thighs. He couldn't use logic to figure out why a drunk had left a bottle of booze untouched. But he couldn't shake the feeling that maybe something wasn't right, even for Mackie.

Holly knew something was wrong. She walked to where Jake squatted beside the recliner.

His brow creased with worry as he fingered a half-empty whiskey glass on the floor.

"You think something happened to Mackie, too. Don't you?" she asked.

Jake looked up. It was as though he'd put on an expressionless mask. "I doubt it."

She trailed behind him as he left the trailer, but stopped short when he marched past Dog. The mutt gave her an eye, as if to say, "Stay put, or else," and then he fell in step behind Jake. They both disappeared behind the trailer.

Holly ventured down the steps and peeked under the trailer. Empty whiskey bottles littered the black dirt. Beyond those, she saw Jake's feet and Dog's paws near a dripping water faucet and a crumpled sack of dog food that looked like it'd been licked clean. That explained Dog's appetite.

Jake kicked the empty sack and muttered under his

breath, then tromped back around the trailer. Holly jumped back up to the top step as Jake and Dog approached.

Jake's eyes flashed with anger. "I'm done here."

"What about Mackie?"

"He's fine," he said, as though the words were toxic.

"Why are you so mad?"

"Because he went off on a drunk and left his dog here to starve."

"He wouldn't do something like that."

"You don't know Mackie. He keeps a bicycle chained to the faucet on the other side of the trailer. It's gone, which means he left and planned to be too drunk to drive home, or he was drunk when he left."

"But that doesn't explain where he is now."

"You can't explain a drunk. All I know is when he's drunk, he forgets about everything." He squatted and rubbed Dog's head.

"But, Jake, what if Mackie isn't off on a drunk? What if someone came and took him?"

Jake blew out a heavy breath. "Why? Who'd want Mackie?"

"I don't know. I just can't imagine him leaving his dog without any food or anything."

"Why not? He left his own kid home alone to go on a drunk plenty."

Her stomach knotted around the thought of Jake as a boy, left alone and scared.

Jake gave Dog another pat, then stood. "Mackie always left a sack of dog food under the trailer. Dog just ate it too fast, then went looking for something to eat and got hit by a car."

Holly looked at the baseball bat, which he'd leaned against the trailer door. "Or a baseball bat."

"Now, *that* Mackie wouldn't do."

"What if Dog got hurt trying to protect Mackie from whoever took him?"

"Your imagination is working too hard. Mackie probably doesn't have more than twenty bucks in his pocket on his best day and doesn't owe a dime to anyone. Besides, his bike is gone."

Holly lifted her hands in the air. "Okay, maybe he wasn't abducted, but I'm still worried about him."

"You've got a good heart, but you're worrying about nothing. This is how Mackie rolls." He reached for Holly's hand. "Let Dog sniff your hand so you can make friends."

She pulled her hands in close to her chest.

"If you don't make friends with Dog, it's going to be hard for you to get to your car."

She chewed her bottom lip. "I'd rather keep my distance."

"Suit yourself." He scooped her into his arms as if he was carrying her over a threshold. "We'll do it the hard way."

She squirmed. "Put me down."

"You sure? What about Dog?"

She eyed the mutt over Jake's shoulder, then looked back at Jake. Dog might take her leg off, but he wouldn't break her heart.

CHAPTER 11

An hour later and minus Dog, Jake walked into the *Gazette*. He had stayed at the River Run Animal clinic until the vet put Dog under to patch his hip. Jake would pick him up in a couple of days, if Mackie didn't surface. And if he could last a couple more days around Holly.

He hadn't been in town a week, and already he was cleaning up after Mackie and couldn't keep his mind off Holly. Nothing had changed in Delta Ridge.

"Good afternoon, Jake," said Penny, Sam's plump assistant who had probably been eligible for retirement twenty years ago. After surviving the encounter she and the other bridge club ladies had with Holly's fabricated ghost, he was certain Penny would pass an EKG easily.

"I've had better." He flipped through the old-fashioned paper messages Sam preferred. "No new messages."

"None today."

He dug a chocolate Kiss out of the glass jar on her desk. "What does Sam do around here, anyway?"

She chuckled. "Not much."

"Now that the paper is out, what do I do the rest of the week?"

She shrugged. "Sam sniffs out stories and tells me to write them."

He popped the chocolate in his mouth, then strolled back to Sam's office. The chocolate melted as he plunked himself down in Sam's chair and propped up his feet.

All he had to do was make a token appearance, but he'd enjoyed putting the paper together on Friday night. It reminded him of when he'd worked nights with Sam in high school and the pride they'd taken in making the *Gazette* the best it could be. He picked up the latest edition, then thumbed through the paper and smiled.

"Don't get too comfortable, you little turd." Sam's gruff voice jerked Jake's feet off the desk, like he'd been caught loafing on the job.

"What are you doing here? You're supposed to be on vacation."

"I can see if I'd stayed gone much longer, I wouldn't have a paper to come back to."

"Bull. This thing practically prints itself."

"Not quite." He took off his sunglasses.

Jake nearly choked on his chocolate. Sam had a perfect replica of his sunglasses branded over his eyes in lily white.

Sam's woolly brows bunched over fiery blue eyes. "What in Sam Hill is so funny?"

"Have you looked in the mirror?"

"Oh. Too much vacation." He stuffed his sunglasses in his shirt pocket and pulled a pair of reading glasses from another pocket.

"You saved me a phone call. I was going to call you back to work."

"You catch the smugglers?"

"Sorry, Sam. This assignment is a bust."

Sam adjusted his glasses and peered over them. "You didn't find anything strange going on at Holly Grove?"

"Strange, yeah." He grabbed the *Gazette* and gave it to Sam. "Page three. Holly thinks she has a ghost, or she wants one. I'm not sure which. Nelda is on strike because of said ghost. And the Deltas sent Holly to the hospital for an overdose that wasn't. I'd say everything going on out there is strange but not illegal."

"You need to stay, Jake."

"What for?"

"Because I'm asking." Sam looked over his glasses at Jake. "Give it a few more days, Jake. Call it an old reporter's hunch, but there's more going on at Holly Grove."

Holly pulled the burlap covering off the coffin. It'd been tough to get it on the four-wheeler trailer and then to the front steps, but she'd managed.

She ran her fingers over the rough pine box Mackie had built the first year Holly Grove opened for business. Since then she'd decorated the house for mourning every October to honor the Holly Grove generations who'd passed on. And Mackie had helped her haul the coffin from the barn into the house.

Jake didn't seem to be worried about Mackie, but she couldn't shake her concern. And she couldn't understand how Jake could cut all ties with his father, though she had a harder time judging Jake after seeing how he'd grown up. No wonder he'd kept her away from his place when they were teenagers.

Mackie did have a drinking problem, but he was a good person, and he'd mellowed through the years. Of course, Jake hadn't been around to see that.

Holly eyed the eight feet of brick steps that led to the front door. To lighten the load, she lifted the life-size dummy dressed in period costume from the coffin. Eudora's plain broad face, smeared with make-up, looked at Holly. A smile played at her lips. She'd ordered the doll head online. When it arrived, Nelda had said, "You got the name wrong on this doll. She ought to be You Ugly instead of Eudora."

Holly sucked in a breath and wished for Nelda's help and her sense of humor.

"I can do this," Holly said, as though saying it out loud would make it so.

She pulled one end of the coffin from the rack of her four-wheeler onto the third step, which was parallel to the rack. She stood on the fourth step and dragged the coffin up the steps until it was at a forty-five-degree angle. Sweat beaded on her brow as she gave it her best, but the coffin didn't budge more than a few inches. Maybe pushing it would be easier than pulling, but she couldn't let go to get to the other end.

Gravel crunched under tires as Jake's rental car pulled in the driveway. He unfolded from the car as though it was a bad fit. He gave her a dimpled grin, and she tried to tamp down the schoolgirl excitement that rushed through her.

Then Dog bounded out behind Jake.

Oh, crapola. Holly's heart thudded as she forced herself to hang on to the coffin rather than run.

A white cone framed Dog's mug, and a bald patch

the size of a pot holder marked his shaggy hindquarter, but he now trotted on all four legs. Either the vet did wonders or the dog had good drugs.

"Why'd you bring him here?" Holly yelled, struggling to hold on to the pine box.

"I'm stuck with the mutt until Mackie shows up." Jake slammed the car door shut.

Dog shook himself from the tip of his snout to the end of his tail and then fell in step behind Jake.

He jabbed a thumb toward the coffin. "Is that for your ghost?"

"No, but if that dog comes one step closer, I'm going to drop it, and it'll be kindling."

The cone around Dog's neck became her cone of uncertainty as his black eyes zeroed in on her. He sniffed the air, then loped toward her.

Holly shot up, and the coffin slid down the brick steps.

Jake blocked the coffin's fall with one hand.

She froze. "Jake," she said in a shaky voice. "The dog."

"I told you that you needed to make friends with Dog. Where were you going with this, anyway?"

"Inside, on the long table."

Jake hefted the coffin over his shoulder and hauled it up the stairs. Ignoring Holly, Dog followed Jake. When he opened the door, Rhett shot out like a pit bull ready to fight and snapped at Dog's heels.

Dog lowered his head and swiped Rhett out of the way with his cone. Rhett spun across the porch planks like a dust mop.

A primal mothering instinct kicked in. Holly snatched Dog by the collar. *Now what?* If she let go, Dog would take a bite out of her and have Rhett for dessert. She wrapped her hands around his collar in a death grip. Rhett scooted under Dog and between Holly's legs. Holly lost her balance and her grip when Dog took off after Rhett, heading down the steps and into the yard.

As Holly skidded across the porch on her stomach, Dog closed in on Rhett. She hid her eyes in the crook of her arm. *Poor Rhett.*

There were barks and growls, then silence.

Laughter rang out from behind her. Holly spun onto her back and glared at Jake.

He bent down and grabbed her hands, then pulled her to her feet. His body shook with laughter as he steadied her with an arm around her waist.

She shoved him away. "What's so freaking funny?"

He pointed his head behind her and made a half-hearted attempt to cover his smile. She turned. Dog lay on the grass, with a glassy look in his eyes and a bent cone around his neck. Rhett straddled Dog, humping his leg at double time.

"Looks like Dog is a girl." The dimple in Jake's cheek deepened with mischief.

"Okay, enough with the animal science." She blocked her view of the doggy foreplay with her hand. "Can you do something here?"

He walked over and grabbed Dog by the collar. Holly picked up Rhett and held him at arm's length as she climbed the brick steps at a brisk pace.

"Where can I put Dog?"

She stopped. "What do you mean, 'put Dog'?"

"Dog has to stay with me until Mackie shows up. If she's alone too long, she'll chew her stitches out."

"I thought that cone kept her from doing that."

"It's a deterrent. Not a guarantee."

"I made a deal for you to stay. Not Dog." Holly opened

the front door and plopped Rhett inside, then closed the door on him.

"I'll sweeten the pot," he said, flashing a grin as he released the mutt.

"How?"

Jake thumbed toward the broken windowpane. "I'll fix that and a few other things that need repair around here, until Mackie gets back."

Holly thawed a bit. Jake was still covering for his dad like he had in high school, whenever Mackie fell off the wagon. And she did need the help. "I'm not using the chicken coop. She'll be fine there, but she can't run loose. I thought she was going to take off one of my legs when I met her, and I'm a dog person. She may scare my guests."

"Fair enough. She does have to warm up to most people."

A low growl and the sound of cloth ripping came from the front yard. Eudora's legs and arms flailed through the air as Dog shook her from side to side.

"Dog!" Jake shouted.

Dog jerked her cone in Jake's direction, then bounced like a puppy with a chew toy.

Jake eased down the steps with his hands extended. "Give it here, Dog."

Dog's tail twitched back and forth. Jake snatched the dummy, and Dog dug her feet into the grass and pulled. A resounding rip tore through the air. Dog shook her half of Eudora as she pranced around the yard like the victor.

"I'll fix this, too," Jake said, lifting what was left of Eudora's head and upper body. Plastic bags dropped with a clump of moss stuffing to the ground.

Holly covered her mouth and sucked in her breath.

She'd watched enough CSI to guess that the white powdery stuff was cocaine and the grassy stuff was marijuana. "Burl."

She bit down on a string of curse words Grandma Rose would have washed from her mouth. If anyone deserved to roast for all eternity, it was him. *And I'm supposed to help him get into heaven? Lord, help me.*

Jake's brows framed accusing eyes aimed at her.

She rushed down the steps as more bags dropped from the dummy. "Jake, you've got to believe me. I don't know how that got in there."

He squatted beside the bags and she knelt beside him. When she reached for a bag, he caught her by the wrist.

"Don't touch it," he said. "It's evidence."

"Evidence? I can't report this. Things just settled down from the Deltas thinking I'd overdosed. The tour. Holly Grove." Her heart hammered. If she called the police, the smuggler would be anywhere but here. She had to put a face and a name with the drugs to put them away, or she'd never get rid of Burl.

Dog ran past them, dropping Eudora's lower body. The hair rose on her back as she barked.

Miss Alice's light blue Cadillac Fleetwood crept up the gravel driveway.

"Crapola." She looked back at Jake. "Miss Alice can't see this." Holly tried to twist free from Jake's grasp so she could hide the bags. "Please, Jake."

He held tight.

Chapter 12

"Why did you say Burl's name when you saw the cocaine?" Jake clamped down on her wrists and drilled her with a hard stare. "What do you know about this?"

"Nothing you'd believe."

"Try me."

A car door slammed in the distance, and Miss Alice walked to the back of her Fleetwood.

Holly pointed her head toward the Delta. "She has more circulation than the *Gazette*. If she sees this, my business is ruined."

A little muscle twitched in Jake's jaw, as though he was holding back something. "Which one?"

"Holly Grove. The only one I have. Please, Jake. You can't possibly think . . ." Her voice cracked and her eyes stung, but she held his stare, as if she had nothing to hide and everything to lose. "I believed in you once, when no one else did. You've got to believe me."

His eyes softened before that little muscle relaxed.

"I'll explain later. I swear," she pleaded.

"You will or else, and I better not be aiding and

abetting." He released her wrist and nodded toward Miss Alice. "Distract her."

Holly scrambled to her feet and trotted toward the Fleetwood. *Aiding and abetting?* The last thing Holly wanted to do was get Jake sucked into this mess, but she couldn't think about that now. She had to rush to meet Miss Alice at her car. Whatever she wanted, she wasn't getting today. Holly met Miss Alice as she opened her trunk. An ancient Samsonite wedged between a doctor's bag and a basket of knitting hinted at why she'd shown up.

"I'm getting the floors refinished in my house, and I can't stand the smell," Miss Alice said. "I'm renting a room until they're finished. Now, get your man over here to carry my luggage."

"But, Miss Alice, you don't have a reservation."

"I called, but I got a recording, and I don't talk to machines." Miss Alice looked over her glasses. "Is there any reason you don't want me to stay here?"

"My ghost?" Holly blurted.

Miss Alice waved Holly off. "I know more dead people than live ones. I am not afraid of a ghost." She turned toward Jake. "Young man," she called.

Holly's stomach knotted as Jake continued to stuff Eudora's illegal filling into her torso.

Miss Alice glanced back at Holly and huffed. "Is he deaf?" She picked up her basket of knitting, then hooked it over her arm. "Never mind. I'll get him myself."

"Wait. The dog. She's vicious," Holly said, stepping in front of Miss Alice.

"Vicious? She looks ridiculous. What's that thing on her head?"

"She had a little surgery. The cone keeps her from chewing out her stitches."

Miss Alice squinted. "What is your man doing, anyway? Is that—"

"It's stuffing," Holly said, keeping an eye on Jake as she grabbed Miss Alice's arm and towed her toward the back of the house.

Jake glanced over his shoulder as he sped-fed moss stuffing and bags of dope into Eudora.

"I'm talking about the dog. She looks like Mackie's dog."

"That's because she is."

Miss Alice wheeled around and picked up her pace. "Did the vet give you instructions on how to care for her wound?"

"No, but—"

"Infection can be fatal, you know."

Holly wrapped her arm around Miss Alice's to guide her toward the back entrance again. "She'll be fine."

Miss Alice stopped short. "I am perfectly capable of walking on my own, and I'm going to check on Mackie's dog."

Other than tackling the old gal, there was nothing Holly could do as Miss Alice marched toward Jake and the evidence that could ruin everything.

Jake's body blocked their view, but Holly knew he was shoveling cocaine bags in Eudora.

Miss Alice marched toward him like a staff sergeant on inspection. She ignored Jake and the dummy and headed for Dog. If Jake hadn't dropped Eudora and yanked Dog back, her paws would have landed on Miss Alice's shoulders. She bent to inspect Dog's stitches.

A soft sigh slipped from Holly's mouth as she studied the dummy that concealed the dope. She turned to Jake and mouthed, "Thank you."

"The vet did a good job, but this wound will need care." Miss Alice shook her head. "Mackie needs a dog like he needs a hole in his head." She glanced at what was left of Eudora. "What happened here?"

Holly blocked Miss Alice's view and then steered her toward the house. "That's the dummy I use for the haunted tour. Dog mistook her for a chew toy."

"No discipline in the owner means no discipline in the pet." Miss Alice looked over at Jake. "My husband's doctor's bag is in my trunk. Would you bring it when you get my luggage?"

"Miss Alice, Jake doesn't work here. He's a guest," Holly said.

"I'm sure he is a gentleman, too."

"We haven't officially met." Jake stepped up to Miss Alice. "I'm Jake McCann."

Miss Alice shook his hand and eyed him up and down. "I met you the day my husband delivered you, and I know the location of every stitch on you."

"Nurse Fort?" He rubbed the back of his head.

"Retired." She hefted her knitting basket a little higher. "About twelve stitches from hitting your head on the monkey bars. It took two to hold you down."

"Yeah, well . . . I hear you know everything that goes on in the parish. I'm filling in for Sam at the *Gazette* and looking for stories, so keep me in mind." He shrugged. "You never know. There could be a story right under your nose, if you keep your eyes open."

Jake cast a sharp glance at Holly, which hit home. She had some explaining to do, but how?

Fifteen minutes later, Jake opened the front door and strode in with a suitcase in one hand, a doctor's bag in the other, and Eudora tucked under his arm like a life-size rag doll.

She couldn't chance a moment alone with Jake until she got answers from Burl. The tiny lie she'd told Miss Alice about washing her sheets guaranteed she'd park herself downstairs for at least an hour or two. That would give Holly protection from the interrogation she expected from Jake.

Holly stood on a ladder and out of reach as she busied herself decorating the entrance hall for the Haunted Pilgrimage. Part of the decorating included dressing the house for a ritual mourning by covering all the mirrors, including the eight-foot-tall pier mirror in front of her.

Jake glanced from Miss Alice, sitting nearby, to Holly. "Where do you want the dummy?" he asked.

"Lay her in the coffin," Holly said. "How'd you put her back together?"

He lifted Eudora's dress. A six-inch band of duct tape, with curls of Spanish moss stuck to it, cinched the dummy's waist. "Duct tape will fix anything." He cocked a brow at Holly. "Some of her stuffing had gone bad, though." His eyes locked with hers.

"What did you do with it?"

He laid Eudora out in the coffin. "I'll decide later."

Great. Now he had the dope. If she couldn't explain

it, would he call the police? What if Burl hadn't put it there? Would whoever had come looking for it?

Miss Alice looked up from her knitting. "You should burn the moss. You know that stuff carries mites." She eyed the hand she'd used to shake Jake's earlier. "I'm going to wash my hands."

Holly couldn't be alone with Jake for even a minute. "Wait," Holly said as she backed down the ladder.

Miss Alice disappeared around the corner.

Holly missed her step and teetered on the edge of a fall.

"Careful there," Jake said, catching her in his arms.

"I'm fine." She slid down the length of him. Jeez, was there any other way she could get down? By the time her legs reached the cypress floor, they might as well have been pudding.

"What were you doing up there, anyway?"

"Huh? Oh," she stammered. *Just keep talking. Don't give him a chance to ask questions.* "It's part of dressing the house for mourning." She looked into the massive pier mirror at Jake. "There's a superstition that if you don't cover the mirrors with a black cloth, the spirits of the recently departed will get trapped in the mirrors."

Jake squinted and stared into the mirror. "What's that?"

Holly spun around, expecting to see Burl behind her. Nothing.

Jake whispered in her ear, "You've been drinking your own Kool-Aid, sweetheart."

Every sharp comeback melted from her mind.

"First a ghost and now . . . this. There's something going on here, and you've got some serious explaining to do."

"I will, but it's not something I can explain in a few minutes."

Miss Alice walked back in the room. *Thank goodness.*

He leaned in and whispered, "Something's come up at the *Gazette*, but tonight, when we're alone, you'll tell me everything. Or tomorrow there'll be a special edition of the paper."

Chapter 13

It wasn't like Holly could ring a dead person up on a cell phone when she needed to talk to him.

She shoved a plate filled with the last of Dot's blue-plate specials into the microwave hidden away in the butler's pantry, then hit the button to nuke dinner. As soon as the guests retired for the night, Jake would expect answers she didn't have. But Burl did.

"If you can't hear me, Burl, I hope you're in hell, and I hope you stay there."

The microwave dinged, and she jumped.

"I knew you missed me," Burl said from behind her.

She whirled around. "Where have you been?"

"Heck if I know." He shrugged. "One minute I'm here, and then I'm in that black hole where time stops. Being dead is weird, but I'm getting used to it."

"I didn't ask for a dissertation," she said, taking the plate from the microwave.

"Fine. I'll go back."

"Wait!"

"See?" Burl flashed his patented "I am the greatest," cock-and-bull smile. "You can't get enough of me."

"Oh, I've had plenty of you. Unfortunately, you're the only one who can tell me why Eudora had bags of dope stuffed inside her."

"Eudora?"

"The dummy." She fisted the plastic wrap from the blue-plate and bunched it into a ball. "Don't pretend you don't know what I'm talking about."

"Why on earth would you go digging inside a dummy?"

"I didn't. Dog tore her in half, and it fell out."

"Rhett?"

"No. A real dog. A big one." Holly blew out an exasperated breath. "It doesn't matter. Eudora was full of drugs. Did you leave dope in Eudora?"

"You didn't call the police, did you?"

"No, but if I don't have a good story, Jake will."

Burl's brows shot up. "You told that hack?"

"No. He saw it fall out. If I can't explain, he'll call the cops and put the story in the paper."

"Where's the dope?"

"I don't know. Jake hid it."

"Are you crazy? Do you know how much that stuff is worth? He may be in Mexico by now."

Holly jabbed a hand on her hip. "He's in the dining room, along with three couples who are old enough to be my grandparents. I'm as sure as sin they didn't stuff Eudora, so that leaves you."

"Me? What about your freeloading guest, Jack, or whatever his name is?"

"He was just as shocked as I was when the dope fell out. I know Jake." Holly leveled a stare at Burl's pale face. "He'd never get mixed up in something like this. That leaves you."

Burl stubbed a Gucci-clad toe across the floor. "I was

waiting for a good time to tell you this, but you've been a little testy lately."

"Imagine that."

"I had your interest at heart when I skimmed from the loads. I was planning on making a transaction that would have solved all our financial problems." He lifted a shoulder. "Then I crashed, and I never got around to telling you about my stash. I knew you'd be ticked, and I've been trying to get on your good side."

"So you left Lord knows how many dollars' worth of cocaine and marijuana in Eudora for me to haul in the house and put on display."

"How was I supposed to know I was going to crash? Besides, that load was supposed to be in my storage container." Burl looked toward heaven. "I swear to God. I didn't put it in Eudora. And I wouldn't chance lying to Him right now, if you know what I mean."

"But if *you* didn't put it there, who did?"

"I don't know, but they'll be back for it. I'd bet my life on it, if I had one." Burl's image faded a bit.

"How did someone get your stash?"

"How would I know? I've been dead," he said as his translucent body melted before her.

"Great. Just great." She never could finish a conversation with him when he was alive, either. Now what was she going to tell Jake?

Jake had worked undercover in some of the most dangerous cartels in the world and had suffered less. He forked a bite from the slab of chocolate pie as the conversation at the dinner table groaned on.

The three old couples had come to town for their sixtieth class reunion. Miss Alice knew them from high school, though she'd been quick to point out she'd been a freshman when they graduated.

Miss Alice dished juicy town gossip, catching the out-of-towners up on the locals.

Holly sat at the head of the table, directly across from him. She nodded sympathetically to Mrs. Bell, who was yammering on about her gall bladder surgery. So far, Jake had counted four surgeries for Mrs. Bell and three for her husband. The conversation turned to prescription drug coverage, and Jake yawned.

Every time he looked at Holly, her interest shifted to another guest, as though their laundry list of health issues had captured her attention. She'd avoided him since he'd come back from the *Gazette*, but he darned well would get answers soon.

He'd been shipped down to a speck in the road to bust a drug ring and save what was left of his career. Three days ago he'd almost called his boss to tell him there wasn't anything here. Today the angel at the other end of the table had knocked a few dents in her halo when the dope fell out of the dummy.

His gut told him she wasn't in on Burl's smuggling ring. But that same gut feeling had blown his cover and his bust back in New York. If he'd followed the rules, he wouldn't have been cast out to Delta Ridge. If he didn't prove himself in the field this time, this snore-fest would be exciting compared to the cubical life at ICE.

This time he'd follow the rules. He'd secured the drugs and filed a report. Telling Holly he'd hidden the drugs gave him power over her for now, but what he needed was her trust. Until then, he'd use power to get answers—for her own good.

The sooner he made this bust, the sooner he'd be

out of Delta Ridge. And the more distance he put between Holly and himself, the sooner he could relegate her to a memory. Or he could try.

"If y'all will excuse me, I'm going to go for a walk to settle my dinner." Miss Alice stood and patted her stomach. "Exercise keeps me healthy."

"I'll help you clean up here, Holly," Jake said, to give him the opportunity to talk to her alone.

"George, did you hear that? I've waited forty years to hear those words from you," Mrs. Bell said to her husband.

"If you looked like Holly, I might offer," he said as he winked at Jake.

Mrs. Bell gave her husband's arm a backhanded slap. "George Bell. You old goat. You never offered when I was young and shapely, either."

Mr. Bell moaned. "Jake, you're making us old guys look bad."

Jake strode to the other end of the table. He picked up Holly's iced tea glass and plates. "It's an investment, if you know what I mean." Jake winked at Holly.

Her lips parted as though she would speak; then her face flushed.

As Jake pushed through the swinging kitchen door, Mrs. Harper said, "Holly, you're lucky. Your husband is so helpful." She paused. "And good looking, too."

He'd been mistaken for good looking before but never for husband material. A shiver ran down his spine.

"Oh, he's not my husband," Holly said.

"Well, honey, don't let that one get away," Mrs. Bell said.

Jake set the dishes on the ceramic counter, then held Holly's glass by the stem and rotated it in the light. Her fingerprints—the best way to clear her of any involvement—dotted the crystal. He slipped a napkin over the glass, then put it on top of the refrigerator and pushed it all the way back to the wall. Holly was too short to notice it there. He'd put it in his bag and take it with him early in the morning.

Holly entered the kitchen with a stack of plates.

"Let me help you," Jake said as he crossed the room to her.

"Cut the act. You've got them fooled, but not me." She strutted to the sink and unloaded the dishes.

"Let's both cut the act. You've had all day to come up with something to cover your, uh, assets, but I suggest the truth."

Holly turned the faucet on, then opened a bottom cabinet that hid a dishwasher. Without looking at him, she said, "What do I have to tell you to keep this quiet?"

"Everything." He moved to her side and leaned against the counter.

"You're going to have to be more specific than that," she said as she ran water over the dirty plates.

"Start with what you know about the dope that fell out of the dummy."

She whirled around at him with her finger to her lips. "Shh. I don't want my guests to hear you."

Holly glared at him as she grabbed a dish towel and wiped her hands. She stomped across the room, then eased the door open. She turned back to him and blew out a breath. "They're gone."

He pulled the *Gazette* from his back pocket and plopped it on the counter. "Here's today's ad, but your guests will be the least of your worries if my special edition prints tonight. I can see the headline now." He tracked his hand from left to right, as though he were reading an invisible banner. "Holly Grove Plantation owner linked to drug trafficking."

Holly stared at Jake like a wide-eyed doe. "You wouldn't?"

"Right after I call the sheriff."

"Jake, you know me."

"Correction. Knew you. When I knew you, you didn't have dope stuffed in your dollies."

"Do you think I would have taken Eudora out of the barn and put her on display if I thought she was stuffed with dope? You know I wouldn't get mixed up in something like this. I'm the same person you left behind fifteen years ago."

He pointed to his chest. "I left *you* behind? You told me it was over. What'd you expect me to do?"

"Exactly what you did. Leave."

"Did I miss something here? You're the one who had a boyfriend as soon as my dust cleared."

Miss Alice burst through the swinging door. "There's someone out in your barn with a flashlight." Gasping for air, she held her chest. "When I called to him, he ran."

CHAPTER 14

Holly followed Jake as he charged out the front door of Holly Grove. In the distance, a light flashed near the tree line. He sprinted ahead of her, past the carriage house and the barn, after the intruder.

Gasping for air, she lagged farther and farther behind. She had run track in high school and still had her speed but not her lungs.

By the time he reached the tree line, the light had disappeared. He bent and rested his hands on his knees.

"Did you see him?" she said between pants as she caught up with him.

"No." He glanced over his shoulder at her. "By the time I got out here, he was in the woods." Jake stood up straight and turned toward her. "You know what he was after, don't you?"

"Yeah," she said, rubbing her side and wishing she were in a bad dream. Drugs at Holly Grove sounded impossible.

"He won't find it. But he'll be back." A deep line creased his brow as he stepped through the shadows to her. His eyes darkened to a dangerous black. "You're going to tell me now exactly what is going on."

That look told her that if she didn't tell him something, there would be consequences she couldn't talk her way out of. She swallowed hard and stared at the decaying sycamore leaves beneath her feet. Should she trust him?

"I didn't do anything. Trouble found me this time." She blew out a sigh. "That stuff was Burl's. He was using Holly Grove as a front for smuggling."

"And you didn't know a thing about it?" He stared at her a beat too long, as if he was trying to detect a lie.

"I swear." She crossed her heart, as though she were twelve, but meant it.

"So how did you find out about his operation?"

"I have a source that felt the need to come clean after Burl crashed." *Or risk burning for all eternity.* She lifted a shoulder, then cast a downward glance. "Guilty conscience, I guess."

"Who's your source?"

She rubbed her arms against the chill and turned to head back to Holly Grove. "You're a newspaper guy. You understand the privacy of a source, don't you?"

"I'll give you that." He paused. "For now." Moonlight lit the grassy path as they walked. "Let's say I believe you didn't know. Why don't you want to call the police?"

She stopped short and grabbed his sleeve. "I can't. My source says the big boss behind the smugglers has ears everywhere, even with the police. I've got to catch them in the act."

"And do what?"

"Then I call everyone with a badge."

"It's still going on?"

She nodded. "Apparently, Burl would meet a barge

on the riverbank. He'd off-load a shipment, then store the goods. Later, a contact would stay at Holly Grove and pick up the drop from Burl. My source says to expect a shipment in October so . . ."

"Is the dope in the dummy a shipment?"

"Nope. Just another loose end Burl left behind."

"Any idea who was after it?"

"None."

Jake nodded. "So you're expecting a shipment any day?"

"Or a contact to arrive. That's why I want you to give me the bags of dope back."

Holly stood firm as Jake stared her down like she'd asked for his firstborn child. The hoot of an owl broke the silence of the night. She'd stand in the clearing till sunrise before she backed down.

"You want me to give you the narcotics?" Jake repeated.

"Yes." Could she say she was afraid he'd take them and run? That the seed of doubt Burl had planted refused to die? Hardly.

His expression hardened. "Not happening."

"They're not yours."

"Are you saying they're yours?"

"No, but what if the guy who put them in Eudora comes back for them?"

"You want to give them back to him?"

"No, b-but I might make a deal," she stammered, trying to think of a good reason why she had to have the bags of dope. "I could take Burl's place."

Jake tilted his head and frowned, as though he hadn't heard her right.

"Well, not really, but I could act like I was stepping in for Burl."

"You want to go undercover?" Jake rubbed his hand over his forehead, like the idea gave him a headache. "On your own?"

"Yes. Why not?" she said, though she thought the idea was a bad one, and she'd never really do it. She had to say something to get Jake to give her the bags.

A smart-aleck smile slid across his face. "You're joking, right?"

"I've never been more serious." She shot a searing stare his way. He had to believe her to make this work.

"Okay." He lifted his hands in the surrender position. "Have you thought about what would happen if a bust came down while you were pretending to take Burl's place? How would you feel about spending the next twenty or so years in prison?"

"But I'd explain—"

"How? Why would they believe you? I'm going to hold on to Burl's packages for your own safety, but I'll make you a deal."

Holly folded her arms. "What now?"

"This is a hell of a story, and you could use some help. Right?"

"Maybe." Definitely. But did she want to chance getting Jake mixed up in this more than he was? "It's too dangerous."

"More dangerous than a tour of duty in Iraq? I've had a few stints as an investigative reporter, and I'm good. I can help you."

"I don't want you involved."

"Too late. What I want is exclusive rights to the story. Sam would die a happy man if the AP picked up this one, and it'd give my career a boost."

"But I don't want this story in the paper."

Jake shrugged. "If not me, it'll be someone else when the bust is made."

She gnawed on her bottom lip. "Can I trust you to make me and Holly Grove look innocent in your article?"

He took her hand, and they walked toward Holly Grove. "You can trust me, period, if you've told me everything. All I ask is that you don't do anything without talking to me first." He cocked an eye at her. "Agreed?"

The porch light at Holly Grove flashed.

"Holly," Miss Alice called. "Can y'all hear me?"

Jake pulled Holly behind an oak tree and pinned her there. "Don't answer her. Tell me you won't do anything stupid."

She should push him away. She shouldn't trust him. But she did. She wet her lips and tried to speak, but the words didn't come. How could she swear to drag him deeper into a dangerous situation? She closed her eyes and gave the slightest nod to pacify him.

He leaned in closer, but she dared not show her lying eyes.

Holly woke to an empty bed. She rubbed her hand across the pillow beside her. It had taken all her strength to pull herself away from Jake last night, but she'd managed to use good judgment, for once— with Miss Alice's help. If she hadn't come looking for them . . .

Holly sat up in bed and sniffed. Bacon? Was Nelda back? Holly kicked off her covers and grabbed her robe. She ran her arms through the sleeves as she raced down the stairs.

Rhett met her at the kitchen door, prancing from

foot to foot. She pushed the door open, and Rhett ran ahead of her, sniffing the air. Red, dusty footprints trailed behind him as he trotted to a glass bowl in the middle of the room. A pentagram drawn in what looked like charcoal framed the bowl.

What on God's green earth . . . ?

Holly stepped over the red dust that lined the threshold. Sand gritted under her feet as she entered the room. She squatted and touched the sand, then rubbed it between her fingers. *Salt?* White candles flickered in the four corners of the kitchen, and bacon sizzled in Nelda's favorite iron skillet. She shook her head and stood. *Just when I thought things couldn't get any stranger, they do.*

The screen door squeaked, and Holly turned toward the sound. Nelda backed into the room as she poured salt from a box.

"Nelda! What in the world are you doing?"

Nelda screamed and waved her arms in the air as she danced around like a grown woman about to pee herself. Salt spewed from the box in swirls around her head, then peppered the floor.

"Good Gawd." Nelda held her hand over her chest. "I almost caught a heart attack." She shook the box of salt at Holly. "I thought you was that ghost."

"Oh, Nelda. You're back." Holly rushed to her. When she squeezed Nelda in a hug, the strong scent of garlic pushed Holly back.

Two strings of garlic swayed around Nelda's neck and tangled around a large silver cross. Her lips broke into an ear-to-ear grin. "Told you I'd be back." She glanced around the room. "I fixed up the kitchen with some voodoo to keep that ghost out, too."

Holly pointed to Nelda's necklaces. "Garlic and a cross? Isn't that for vampires?"

"If it keeps away them bloodsuckers"—her brow flattened, and she set her jaw—"probably works on ghosts, too."

Rhett lapped water from the bowl in the middle of the kitchen floor.

"Acht," Nelda shouted, shooing Rhett away. "That's my holy water, and I don't got none to spare."

Rhett slunk over to the floor-to-ceiling window near the table and sat.

"Holy water?" Holly asked.

"It was the best Father Martinez could do. He said the bishop couldn't do the exorcism for months." She shuffled to the stove and flipped the bacon over. "You know, Catholics don't do nothin' in a hurry." Nelda pointed the spatula at Holly. "You remember when your mama tried to get that annulment? Humph." She turned back to the bacon. "She died waiting on it. God rest her soul."

Holly's throat tightened at the mention of her mother. "I remember." The aroma of the bacon settled into Holly's senses and somehow made her feel everything was going to be better now that Nelda was back.

"Anyway, this holy water ought to hold back the ghost," Nelda said.

"Did you do all this to the kitchen by yourself?"

Nelda laid the strips of bacon on a paper towel. "Sure did. The voodoo priestess, she called it cleansing rites. That ghost can have the rest of the house"—she thumbed her chest—"but the kitchen is mine."

Holly snatched a piece of bacon and scanned the room. "I could hug you again, garlic and all. You think it'll work?" She'd never believed in hocus-pocus things, but she'd never believed in ghosts, either.

"Sure do. I got a cousin in New Orleans. That's where I was. My cousin, Della, works in a voodoo shop and hooked me up with the priestess. She knew just what to do." Nelda put her hands on her generous hips and nodded with approval at her handiwork. "I ain't seen hide nor hair of Burl's ghost since I voodooed up the kitchen."

Nelda pointed her spatula at the collection of six-inch iron skillets on the wall. "I gotta cook here to win the big skillet. Ain't no ghost gonna come between me and first prize this year."

"And I thought you came back because of me," Holly said, beaming at Nelda.

A hint of a smile curled Nelda's lips, but she quickly hid it by turning to poke at the bacon sizzling in the skillet. "That too."

"I'm glad you're back. I missed you."

"Oh, I almost forgot." Nelda slipped a garlic necklace over her head, then draped it around Holly's neck. "I made one for you, too."

The strong odor would, no doubt, keep away humans. But if it'd send Burl to another dimension, Holly was willing to reek. "Thanks."

Nelda nodded, then turned back to tending the bacon.

"Well, well, well. My favorite housekeeper is back." Burl strolled across the room.

Speak of the devil. So much for voodoo magic. Burl needed a bell or something, so she'd know he was popping in. Holly dared not acknowledge him in front of Nelda.

He fingered a candle on the counter. "She thinks this voodoo smoodo will keep me away?"

Holly ran a finger across her throat, signaling Burl to cut it out. Instead, he leaned forward and blew. All four candles sputtered out like magic.

Jeez. He's getting better at haunting.

Nelda froze with the spatula in midair. "You see that?" She turned and faced Holly.

Holly grimaced and nodded.

Nelda bolted toward the back door, but Holly caught her by the arm and dug her heels in the floor. Nelda outweighed her by at least fifty pounds, but she wasn't getting out the door, even if Holly had to tackle her.

"Wait," Holly pleaded.

Nelda's eyes bugged as her stare darted around the room. "Where is he?" She lifted her cross and held it like a shield.

"I'm here on higher power," Burl said as he hunkered over the bowl of holy water.

"Um, Burl says he can't touch you," Holly said to Nelda, then shot a "Shut up" stare at Burl.

"She can't hear me," he grumbled.

"He's talkin', ain't he?"

"Don't worry about Burl. He's all talk," Holly said.

"Let me show you my new trick, Blondie." Burl stirred the holy water with his finger until it swirled like water going down a drain. "I may not be able to touch her, but I can give her hell." He winked at Holly. "And I will."

"Why?" Holly snapped.

Nelda pointed the cross in the direction Holly spoke. "What's he doin' now?"

"Nothing. I think the voodoo is working."

"You told me to haunt, didn't you?" He blew at the tip of his finger as if it were a smoking gun. "I'm going pro, Blondie."

Nelda fingered the garlic around her neck. "You sure he can't touch me?"

"He says your magic keeps you safe."

"Good one, Blondie."

The whites of Nelda's eyes widened, and she pointed to the bowl of holy water, "Look at my holy water."

Holly cut her eyes at Burl. "It must be working against the evil spirit."

Nelda slapped her hands together. "That's what I'm talkin' about." She strutted around the bowl of holy water and right through Burl.

Burl shivered and jumped back. "I never wanted to be that close to Nelda."

"Look at my holy water workin' it." Nelda slapped her hands together again. "Praise God."

"Come on. Give me a little credit," Burl said, lifting his arms in disbelief.

Holly folded her arms over her chest and smiled at Nelda. "Gotta give credit where credit is due."

Burl stomped around the room. "What *do* women want? You want me to haunt. I haunt. Now you're pissed, and I don't get any credit."

A grin sliced across Nelda's face like the sun breaking through a storm cloud. She grabbed Holly by the hands and danced her around the kitchen floor. Laughter Holly almost didn't recognize as her own bubbled through the room until it forced happy tears from her eyes. How long had it been since she'd laughed so hard?

"No sorry ghost gonna hold us back," Nelda said, then let loose a deep cackle.

"Y'all, don't mind me. I'll just make myself comfortable here," Burl said, inspecting his nails. "Forever."

Holly stopped dancing.

"What's wrong?" Nelda asked. "That ghost opening his big mouth again?"

"If I don't get him to heaven by Halloween, he's stuck here with us forever."

Nelda fingered her garlic necklace. "I ain't wearing garlic forever. How you gonna get that cheat into heaven?"

"Cheat?" Holly let go of Nelda's hands. "You knew?"

"Everybody knew, girl."

"Why didn't anyone tell me?"

"By the time I found out, he'd gone and killed himself in that plane. No use trashing the dead." She shook her head. "That's how everybody felt."

"This town is too freaking nosy." Burl shook a transparent finger at Nelda. "And I didn't kill myself. I'm an ace pilot."

"No, you're an ace screwup, Burl. You screwed up my life, and you even screwed up dying." Holly turned to Nelda. "He has unfinished business here, and I've got to finish it, or I'm stuck with him for life."

"Let's finish it and get him outta here," Nelda said, giving Holly's shoulder a quick squeeze.

As grateful as she was, Holly couldn't chance involving Nelda in the drug-smuggling thing. "It's not that simple."

Burl groaned. "It'd be simple, Blondie, if you did what I told you to."

"It'd be simpler if you'd stayed dead," Holly snapped.

Burl looked over Holly's shoulder. "What's that redneck doing here? Don't tell him anything."

"Ahem," came a man's voice from behind her, and she wheeled around.

Sheriff Walker stood at the screen door with the *Gazette*, whacking it across his palm like a baseball player fidgeting before he goes on deck.

Holly's legs melted under her weight. The picture Jake had painted last night of the *Gazette*'s front page headline being about drugs found at Holly Grove came into focus in her imagination. She stared at the newspaper in the sheriff's hand.

Could Jake have called her bluff and printed the story?

Chapter 15

Sheriff Walker opened the screen door and walked in the kitchen. "I see y'all made the *Gazette*."

Holly opened her mouth to speak, but nothing came out. Had Jake followed through on his threat to put everything in the *Gazette*? How could she explain it to Sheriff Walker? Point at Burl and say he did it?

She rushed across the kitchen to meet the sheriff at the door. "I can explain everything, I swear. It's not what you think."

Sheriff Walker cut his eyes around the room. "What you do in your own place isn't police business unless you break the law." He pulled his hat off and scratched his head. "I saw something like this last fall in a pasture. Y'all ain't planning on killing any cows, are you?"

Tension melted away as she realized the sheriff hadn't come about the drugs. "Um, cows. No."

Nelda piped up. "This ain't no devil worship. It's a voodoo cleansing. We got a ghost up in here."

Holly cringed. She had to get the sheriff out of her kitchen and quick. He already thought she was nuts after the fire extinguisher incident.

"I heard about that." The sheriff handed the *Gazette* and a few pieces of mail to Holly. "Page three." He looked over his belly at the red dust.

"That's brick dust," Nelda said as she poured a cup of dark roast coffee. "Ain't no ghost can walk over that. But you can, Sheriff. Want some coffee? It's fresh," Nelda said, as though the kitchen didn't look like a scene from an occult movie.

"I don't like the SOB," Burl said.

Holly glanced from Burl to the sheriff. What was Burl's problem? She'd known the sheriff her entire life, and Delta Ridge had voted him in for the past twenty years. Of course, she wasn't a drug smuggler.

Nelda handed Sheriff Walker the cup of coffee. "You take anything in your coffee?"

"Cream, if you've got it."

Holly's fingers stumbled as she pulled the pages of the *Gazette* apart. "Oh, my God. I forgot one of the Deltas wrote the senior column."

"Best column Miss Cora Beth ever wrote." Sheriff Walker nodded. "Got the whole town talking."

"Let me see," Nelda said, peeking over Holly's shoulder.

Burl read over the other shoulder. "Man, oh, man, I'm good. You've got a bona fide ghost, according to this rag. I'm doing my part, Blondie. It's up to you now."

"And look here." Nelda pointed to the bottom of the page. "Jake put the ad in, just like he said he would."

You are cordially invited
to
the Holly Grove Plantation Home
for
the Haunted Pilgrimage Tour
October 1 through 31
Hayrides, cane-field maze, historical tours,
pumpkin patch, and possible ghost sightings.
Sample Nelda's famous gumbo
and
Vote for the best gumbo
on the Haunted Pilgrimage.

Nelda read the ad aloud, then tapped the page and grinned. "That's my name in the paper."

"I may have to taste that gumbo," the sheriff said.

"You just get yourself back here at lunch and taste it." Nelda pointed a finger at Sheriff Walker. "Then vote."

"The sheriff can't be driving all the way out here for lunch. I'm sure he has important police business to take care of, Nelda," Holly said.

"As a matter of fact, that's why I'm here."

Holly's brain skittered over his words before they made sense. "Police business?"

"Yep. Jake here?"

Oh, crapola. Jake did call the sheriff. "I'll get him." Holly pushed through the swinging door to the entrance hall and ran into one hundred eighty pounds of man.

* * *

"What's your hurry?" Jake said, holding her where she'd landed, in his arms. He sniffed the air. "And what's that smell?"

Her eyes sparked as she fisted his shirt. "You said I could trust you," she whispered.

"You can."

"Sheriff Walker is here to see you. He said it's police business." She tightened her grip on his shirt. "I thought we had an agreement."

"I didn't call him." Jake peeled her hands off his shirt, then led her into the kitchen. He took in the voodoo in the tricked-out room. "What's going on in here?" He fanned the air. "And what's that smell?"

"That's me." Holly lifted her garlic necklace. "Did you notice Nelda was back?" Holly said in what sounded like a fake cheery voice. She waved her hand through the air. "This is a voodoo cleansing rite. She did it herself."

"I see." Nonplussed, Jake tromped over the pentagram. "You wanted to see me, Sheriff?" His tone was more abrupt than he'd intended. He had noticed the sheriff at Dottie's but hadn't wasted his breath to speak to the old codger, and the feeling was probably mutual.

The sheriff extended his hand. "It's been a long time, Jake."

Not long enough. Jake gave a passing glance at the man's hand but didn't take it. The last time Jake had spoken to Sheriff Walker was when he'd collected his belongings from the parish jail. "About fifteen years."

"Staying out of trouble, I hear," Sheriff Walker said, awkwardly rubbing the hand he'd offered across his hip.

"Valid driver's license and no arrests, if that's what you mean." The sheriff had been hell-bent to arrest one of them that night. Jake had taken the wheel at thirteen because Mackie had been too drunk to drive them home from Jake's football game. That arrest and a few other skirmishes had likely cost Jake a football scholarship. "What can I do for you?"

"It's about your dad."

"What about him?" Jake said, seeing no need to keep the edge off his voice.

"The widow women in Delta Ridge have been calling the jail, offering to bail out Mackie."

"Drunk and disorderly?" Jake asked, but not surprised Mackie would turn up in jail.

"Nope. He's not in jail." The sheriff settled at the planter's table, across from Nelda. "This morning I was having breakfast at Dot's, and Doc Stratton told me you'd brought in Mackie's dog to get him patched up. I thought you might know where he was."

"Did you check his trailer?"

"Yep."

"Under his trailer?"

The sheriff grinned. "Not there this time. I gotta tell these widow women something." He slurped his coffee. "They're wearing on my deputy's nerves."

"Tell them he's on a drunk. They'll understand," Jake said.

"You don't know these women." He set his empty coffee cup on the table. "Since you're next of kin and all, I thought you'd fill out a missing person's report. That way, I can circulate it to the nearby parishes."

Jake crossed the room to the coffeepot and poured himself a cup. "He'll come back when he sobers up."

"Can I file the report?" Holly said.

Jake gave her a hard look, but it couldn't match her hard head. When was she going to get it? He couldn't fix Mackie, and neither could she.

Holly stood in the middle of the pentagram, arms folded over her chest, and matched his stare.

Sheriff Walker pushed his hat back on his head and eyed Holly. "Well, I don't guess it has to be family." He looked at Jake. "But it usually is."

"Then you don't need me." Jake had sworn he'd never pull Mackie out of another one of his drunk-induced jams, and by God, he wouldn't.

He stormed out of the kitchen and let the screen door flap behind him.

Jake had left before he said anything he'd regret. He stood on the back porch and sipped his coffee alone. A blue jay dive-bombed a squirrel as it hauled butt across the lawn. The squirrel scratched its way up a massive oak in a spiral path, then barked from a fork in the gnarled limbs. The blue jay circled overhead in wait.

Pecking order. There was a pecking order to everything, and in small-town life, it started with your daddy, which put Jake just above pond scum in Delta Ridge.

Aren't you Mackie's boy? He'd heard that too many times since he came back to town. Just like the blue jays, someone in Delta Ridge was always ready to peck him on the head to remind him his daddy was the town drunk.

Mackie had Jake's cell number and instructions to call him anytime. Sober. He hadn't called in fifteen years. If Holly thought she could guilt Jake into looking for someone who didn't want to be found, she had another thought coming.

He pitched the coffee over the porch rail, then headed to the *Gazette* before he could change his mind and start looking for Mackie.

"I don't think you scored any points with your old beau," Nelda said as she slid two plates of scrambled eggs, grits, bacon, and hot buttered biscuits onto the planter's table.

Rhett took his begging position at the end of the table.

The bench scraped the floor as Nelda pulled it out and sat across from Holly, then gave her the eye. That look meant Nelda expected a response, even though she hadn't asked a question.

Holly glanced at Rhett. His puppy eyes had questions, too, but more likely about the bacon. She tossed him a crumb of bacon and looked back at Nelda, who would be harder to please.

"I'm not trying to score points." Holly slid a spoonful of muscadine jelly into her biscuit. "Someone needs to look after Mackie, and if Jake won't, I will."

"You could've just slipped down to the sheriff's office and filled out the papers on the sly." Nelda took a swig of coffee. "Just sayin'."

"Like I said, I'm not trying to score points." Holly nibbled on a piece of crispy bacon and shuffled through the mail. "I've got other things to worry about than Jake's guilty conscience." She pointed her bacon at Nelda. "That's what had him ticked, even if he didn't know it."

"Suit yourself, but a good man with a good j-o-b is hard to find." Nelda polished off her grits.

"Not interested." Holly still had a ghost of a man she didn't want. She lifted an envelope off the stack. The sheriff's office. She read the fine print on the bottom right of the envelope. *Property tax information.* "Oh, boy. Tax time already." She ripped it open and gasped.

Nelda set her fork down. "How bad?"

"This can't be right." Holly picked up her cell phone and called the assessor's office. After a few transfers and the necessary niceties, she reached the assessor, who had been her high school math teacher before he retired and went into politics.

"Mr. Fremeaux, I'm afraid there must be an error in my assessment this year."

"Let me pull up your file, dear," he said. She heard clicking on a keyboard in the background. "I've been reading about Holly Grove in the *Gazette.* You always did have an active imagination. Though I'm not sure a ghost is your best marketing plan, I hope you've finally found a business in which you can have success, my dear."

He might as well have substituted "Miss Hurricane Holly" for "my dear."

"I have, Mr. Fremeaux." Or Mr. Freako, as he was known by the students. Holly hadn't forgotten his nickname in high school, either.

"Everything looks accurate here," he said.

"But it can't be." She stood and paced across the kitchen with Rhett at her heels, hoping for another crumb.

"My dear, last year Holly Grove was assessed as a residence. This year it was assessed as a business."

"For twice as much?"

"The value was slightly more, but the assessment rate

was significantly more. It's the rate voted on by the good people of St. Agnes Parish, my dear, and due in full by the end of the calendar year. Will that be a problem?"

A huge one. "What if I'm a little late?"

"The rules are clear. Delinquent property taxes are auctioned for tax due within six months of default."

"I see."

"If you can't raise the money, you may need to consider a mortgage or a quick sale. Of course, I hope it doesn't come to that, but I know someone who would be very interested in buying Holly Grove for the right price."

"That won't be necessary."

"Are you sure, my dear?"

"Yes, sir." She ended the call, then plopped down at the planter's table and stared at the bill. When would she ever get a break? On top of everything else, she had to come up with thousands of dollars more than she'd expected. She looked up at Nelda. "How am I going to pay this?"

"Like I said before, a good man with a good j-o-b."

"Are you seriously telling me to get a man to pay my bills?"

"Nope. I'm saying get a good man with a j-o-b and paying your bills will be a whole lot easier. You know, a little insurance for your future. Just in case . . ."

"In case what? I fail again?" She drew quotation marks in the air. "Hurricane Holly strikes."

"Now, Holly." Nelda's mouth turned down at the corners, and she shook her head. "I didn't say that."

"Why not? The whole town thinks it." She'd thought she could count on Nelda to believe in her.

"You know I want you to fly as high as a bird, but it'd be nice to have a net until you get your wings flappin' just right."

"There is no net, Nelda. If I've learned anything from my many calamities, I've learned to never give up."

"You better not sleep, either, girl. I'll do all I can to help, but you got more than you can do. I'll be praying for you."

"I hope you have a main line and the good Lord is listening."

CHAPTER 16

Burl floated into the foyer like autumn fog as the guests gathered for the ten o'clock morning tour. "Looks like my haunting is bringing in the masses," he said.

Unwilling to acknowledge Burl, Holly smiled, greeted the guests, and collected tickets at the door. She kept an eye out for Jake, but he was nowhere to be seen. He'd said he'd take in a tour for research on the articles he was writing about Holly Grove. She hadn't talked to him since he stormed out of her kitchen earlier this morning. Maybe he was still bent out of shape about her filing the missing person report, but he'd have to get over it. She'd done the right thing.

She'd collected twenty tickets so far. Hardly a mass, but twenty bucks a head added up to four hundred more dollars than she'd had an hour ago. Every dollar helped, but money couldn't get Burl out of Holly Grove. She scanned the crowd. Any one of the guests could be the smuggler, and Burl was the only one who could point him out.

Holly's petticoats rustled under her black mourning dress as she gathered more tickets from the guests. The period costume always reminded her of the women before her who had walked these grounds and buried loved ones. She pulled her shawl over her shoulders to block the October breeze that whipped in with the guests.

The tennis shoe–clad feet of tourists shuffled into the foyer and then around the coffin, but no Jake. She told herself he'd probably gotten tied up at the *Gazette*. But a tightness in her stomach, which had nothing to do with the cinched waist of her costume, grabbed her. The seed of doubt Burl had planted about Jake encroached on her trust like a weed. He had pounds of dope, likely worth more than Holly Grove. What if Burl was right and Jake was long gone with the goods?

Holly pushed the thought out of her head. She'd meddled in his business by signing a missing person report on Mackie, and he hadn't hidden how he felt about it. Maybe he was cooling off.

Forcing a smile, she dipped in a modest curtsy for her guests. "Welcome to Holly Grove."

Burl rubbed his hands together. "This is going to be fun."

As far as Holly was concerned, he could have all the fun he wanted as long as he picked out the smuggler. Lately, it seemed Burl would rather move on to his favorite new sport, haunting.

She had to admit most of the guests didn't look like smugglers to her. But Burl had seen the contacts before and would be able to recognize them if they were among the guests.

Gray hair dominated the crowd, until a late group squeezed into the room. Pale-faced teenagers dressed in drab colors and sporting nose and brow piercings stood in the back.

Teenagers? She'd never had teenagers on the tour, unless their parents had forced them to tag along.

Burl weaved in and out of the guests. "Where do these people come from?" He shook his head. "The only lineup they belong in is a Sunday school line. Nobody in this group could be smuggling."

Holly wasn't surprised. So far, eliminating suspects had been a no-brainer even for her.

"Is it true you have a ghost?" The teen's voice cracked from a manly pitch to a hoarse screech. The lanky teen had long, dark hair, a knit cap pulled down low on his head, and leather bands on his wrists.

She looked him right in the eye and didn't blink. "Yes."

There. She'd said it. The sooner she embraced the idea, the sooner the news would spread. But she had to be careful not to look like a fool again. Burl had to make this work.

"You've seen it?" The teen tossed his hair out of his eyes.

Holly glanced at Burl. "He's here right now."

Blue-haired old couples, families, and lovebirds exchanged glances.

"Prove it," the teen said, then looked to his buddies. Their eyes shone with admiration for their obvious leader.

Burl sauntered over to the teen. "Ask him his name."

"What's your name?" Holly asked.

"Matt." He jutted his chin out. "Why?"

Holly smiled. "My ghost wants to know."

"Yeah, right." He elbowed the guy next to him, and they snickered.

Burl's lips flattened into a line. "I'm going to show that little punk a thing or two."

"Be careful. You're upsetting my ghost," Holly said as she winked at her guests.

"Ooh." Matt shook his hands in the air. "I'm shaking." He motioned to his pals. "Come on. I told you guys this was bogus."

Burl sucked in air like the Big Bad Wolf, then blew. The front door slammed shut just before Matt and his friends reached it. The crowd collectively gasped.

"Whoa." Matt spun around to Holly. "How'd you do that?"

Holly could hardly contain her laugh. She raised her hands in innocence. "I didn't do a thing." She smiled at the crowd. "Just the wind." Holly looked over her shoulder at Matt. "Or maybe the ghost. Now, if you'll follow me into the parlor."

Matt's thumbs tapped out a text on his cell phone.

Holly positioned her hoop skirt to avoid bumping the pocket door as she stepped into the parlor. She stood in front of a pier mirror situated between two floor-to-ceiling windows. "Notice the black cloth." She pulled the fabric aside to reveal a sliver of the mirror behind it. "The superstition of antebellum days was that if you didn't cover the mirrors, the spirits of the dead would be trapped in the mirrors and would be unable to pass on to the other side." She let the black drape fall over the mirror.

"How'd the spiwits get out?" asked a little girl with strawberry-blond hair and trouble pronouncing *r*'s.

"They couldn't." Holly stole a glance at Burl. "They'd be stuck here forever."

Holly led the group through the rest of the tour and back to the entrance hall that ran the depth of Holly Grove. She opened the back door and motioned toward the back balcony. "Please step out on the veranda for a taste of Nelda's famous gumbo and a sip of iced tea."

With a smile that nearly sang, Nelda ladled steaming hot chicken and sausage gumbo over rice in a plastic bowl for the first in line. "Y'all don't forget to vote for the best gumbo, and the best is Nelda's." She stomped and wiggled as she served the next guest. "This is 'slap yo' mama' good."

As she checked out the crowd one more time, Holly noticed that the tall teen, Matt, was missing. And so was Burl. Holly walked up to the other teens. "Where's Matt?"

A stocky, rosy-cheeked teen scraped the bottom of his gumbo bowl and shrugged. The other two shoveled gumbo into their mouths, probably to avoid answering.

Holly slipped back into the house to look for Matt. She found him in the parlor, in front of the pier mirror. She looked around for Burl, but he'd obviously gone wherever he went when he wasn't around.

Matt flipped the black cloth that covered the mirror over the edge of the frame, and jumped back. Holly folded her arms and watched. Her cheeks tightened around a smile. Burl was missing a golden opportunity. She slipped her shoes off and tiptoed across the room toward Matt, but she was careful not to allow herself to be seen in the mirror.

Matt dug his cell phone out of his pocket and backed a few more feet away from the mirror. He aimed the cell phone at the mirror, and a little red light glowed on his phone. Was he taking a video of the mirror?

Holly eased closer and covered her mouth with her hand to suppress a giggle. As soon as she got close enough, she was going to yell boo and watch the little delinquent run. Burl couldn't have all the fun.

"Whoa," Matt whispered.

A round spot of condensation the size of a dinner plate had formed on the mirror. Matt stepped back a little farther but kept the camera on the mirror. A handprint appeared in the condensation.

"Whoa. Just freaking whoa," Matt whispered, still stepping backward, until he bumped into Holly. He screamed in the pitch of a soprano.

Burl walked right out of the mirror. "Told you I'd get the little punk."

Matt fumbled with his cell phone, then pointed it back at the handprint on the mirror. He wheeled the cell phone camera back at Holly. "D-d-did you see that?"

Holly smiled and folded her arms over her chest. "Told you I had a ghost."

"Awesome." Matt backed out of the room with his cell phone camera rolling. "This place rocks."

"Thanks, Matt. Come back anytime," Holly called to him as he left. Twenty bucks was twenty bucks. "Hey, bring a friend."

Burl lifted his hand in a high five. Holly swiped her hand through his, and a chill went through her.

His brows slumped into commas. He shoved his hands into the pockets of his Armani. "Sorry. Occupational hazard."

"Yeah. Well, as soon as you point out the contact, you'll be on your way out of here."

"I've been meaning to talk to you about that."

"Did you figure out who he is?"

"Not exactly."

"Exactly what, then?"

"You must have misunderstood me. I never said I could recognize the guy."

* * *

Jake slammed the door to Sam's office when he walked in.

Newspapers rattled as Sam startled on the sofa. He pushed the newspapers off his face and stared at Jake with sleepy eyes. "What in tarnation?"

"Tough job, huh, Sam?"

"I'm on vacation, remember?" Sam stretched, then eased off the sofa to meet Jake at the door. "I couldn't sleep a wink last night."

"Don't let me interrupt your beauty rest," Jake said as he pulled his laptop out of his bag, then put it on Sam's desk. At least he could finish checking out Holly's guest list before he went back to Holly Grove. He'd bailed on the 10:00 a.m. tour, so he had plenty of time until the afternoon tour.

"All right, son. This is serious."

Jake looked at Sam. Red lines trailed across his old eyes like a web of misery. "Man. You look rough. What's up?"

"I'm going to have to do something a good reporter never does."

"You're the best newspaperman I know." Jake parked himself on the chair at Sam's desk. "If you're doing it, then it's the right thing to do."

"I'm going to have to give up my source, but you're not going to like it."

"Tell me, anyway."

Sam cleared his throat. "Remember when I called you up in New York and I said I got a tip about smuggling at Holly Grove?"

"Yeah."

"The guy took me to the river, and I watched Burl

off-load something from a barge. Less than a week later, Burl was dead." Sam looked over his glasses at Jake. "My guy called again a few weeks back. Said he was working on something. He was supposed to call me three days ago." Sam shook his head. "Nothing. Now I'm worried. That's why I came back to check on him."

"Who's your guy?"

"That's the part you're not going to like." Sam pointed an aged stare, but one no less powerful, at Jake. "It's Mackie, and I think he's in trouble."

"What?" Jake shot from his chair. What had Mackie gotten himself into now, and how was Jake going to get him out of it this time? Fear doused Jake. This wasn't a bar fight or a DUI. This could be life or death for Mackie.

Sam shook his head. "It's not good."

"I thought he was on a drunk."

"Any other time I'd agree, but here's the kicker. Mackie was drunk the first time he called me. I blew him off." Sam rubbed an age-spotted hand across his forehead. "The next time he called, he was stone-cold sober. Same when I met him at the river and when I talked to him a couple of weeks ago."

"Sober?"

Sam nodded. "And, Jake, he wanted to know if I'd called you."

"What'd you tell him?"

"The truth."

"So Mackie was sober for a couple of phone calls and once when you saw him. That doesn't make him a credible source." He must be Holly's source, too. Why else would she be so determined to find him?

Sam thumbed his chest. "I'm a credible source, and

he put me onto the drop. When he called me the last time, I asked him if he'd given up drinking."

"And?"

"He asked if you'd come."

"What the . . . ?"

Sam lifted a shoulder. "I thought the same. All I know is he's been right so far *and* sober. And now he's missing."

Two hours of silent treatment later, Burl trailed after Holly like a puppy as she cleaned the Longfellow suite. "Come on, Blondie. Speak to me. You just assumed I could pick out the smuggler. I never said I could."

Duh. He'd been in the smuggling ring for months. Sure she thought he'd know the people. How was she supposed to know they sent a new contact every time? Holly stretched the clean white sheet over the four-poster bed. Her anger simmered under her resolve to block Burl from her life. He'd lied. Again.

"You're all I've got. You can't do this to me."

Watch me. This was what she should have done from the beginning. If she ignored him long enough, maybe he'd shut up. She tossed a pillow on the bed, and it slammed through Burl.

He grabbed at his stomach where the pillow had passed. A stupid grin inched across his face. "Good! At least you threw something at me. That's progress."

Progress, my foot. Burl couldn't even guess who the contact was. Jake had offered to help, but where was he now? In fact, she was a little worried. Maybe he'd found his dad, and Mackie was hurt or sick or worse.

Or maybe Jake was seriously ticked off that she'd filed that missing person report.

"Okay. I know you're mad. You don't have to talk, but I know you're listening."

Lordy, he'll never shut up. She punched the pillow into a fluffy pad, releasing a bit of tension but not nearly enough.

"I'm good at haunting. Right?"

Thanks to Burl, she did have more business, but at what cost? She glanced at him out of the corner of her eye. Was having him around worth it? How was she going to bust the smugglers if Burl couldn't pick them out? And how was she ever going to have a chance with Jake, or any man, with her dead husband haunting the place?

"I've been thinking."

She sidestepped Burl and picked up the wad of dirty sheets. "Don't hurt yourself."

"Very funny, Blondie."

Holly kept walking. "Look, Einstein. You're a waste of time. If you can't recognize the contact, you're no help." She stopped and looked over her shoulder at Burl. "In fact, you need to just get out of our way."

Burl appeared in front of her. "Our way?"

"Yes." Holly sucked in an exasperated breath and walked around him. "Jake is going to help me."

If he was still willing.

Burl's brows pinched together. "You told Jack about the smuggling?"

"His name is Jake."

"So what'd you tell him?" Burl trotted beside her.

"I told him a friend confided in me about your illegal activities, and why I couldn't go to the law."

"So you and what's-his-name think you can figure this out all by yourselves."

"Like you've been any help whatsoever." Holly sidestepped Burl again and kept walking.

"Well, he's not in his room, and neither is his bag. Bet the stash is gone, too. Looks like Jakey wimped out on you."

Her stomach dropped like a rock. It couldn't be true. Jake would never do that. Never. Holly dropped the sheets and ran to Jake's room. She fished the master key out of her pocket and opened the door. The bed was made. She flung open the armoire. Empty. It was as though no one had been in the room.

She pounded down the stairs. Jake couldn't have left. He wouldn't. She flew through the kitchen and passed Nelda.

"Lord, have mercy. Is the house on fire?" Nelda asked.

"Have you seen Jake?"

"I ain't seen him since he stomped out the kitchen this mornin'."

Holly flung the back door open, then bounded down the steps. Her stride faltered, and she stopped. The gate on the chicken coop stood ajar. Dog was gone. And so was Jake's rental. Her legs weakened, and she leaned against the coop for support. There had to be an explanation.

She peeled her cell phone out of her pocket and dialed the *Gazette*. "Penny, this is Holly. Is Jake in?"

"No. Would you like to speak to Sam?"

"I thought Sam was on vacation."

"He's back now."

Holly's heart sank. If Sam was back, there was no need for Jake to stay in Delta Ridge.

Jake had left her, again. Only this time he'd taken more than her heart. Jake had cheated her, just like Burl.

"You smell like a brewery." Sam stretched and sat up on the sofa in his office. He'd been napping since Jake came in the back door at the *Gazette*.

"Some drunk spilled a beer on me." Jake looked up from his DIY fingerprint operation. "I've been to every bar within a thirty-mile radius. Jails, hospitals, and morgues, too."

"Any sign of Mackie?"

Jake leveled an eye at Sam. "What do you think?"

"From your attitude, I think you should have had a drink."

"I don't drink."

"Well, I do." Sam checked his watch. "Five o'clock." He crossed the room to the file cabinet, then fished out a pint of bourbon and a shot glass.

Jake leaned back in his chair and clasped his hands behind his head. His back hurt from hunching over the desk, dusting for fingerprints. "Nobody's seen him in at least a week or so."

"I knew I should have come back sooner." Sam splashed some bourbon in the glass and downed it.

"It's not your fault. For all we know, he may show up tomorrow, hung over." Jake hoped so, anyway. He lifted Holly's iced tea glass to the light and used a soft paintbrush to apply more carbon. Among the slate-colored smudges, the distinct pattern of two finger-prints stood out.

Sam's bushy brows lifted. "What in Sam Hill are you doing? Arts and crap?"

"Nope." Jake lifted the glass as if he were toasting Sam. "Checking fingerprints." And totally rogue on his part, which might cost him. He had to know if Holly's prints were on those bags. Tech could dust the half dozen other bags he'd locked in Sam's safe soon enough.

"Whose?"

"Holly's and some prints I found on a bag of cocaine."

"Don't you need a lab or something for that?"

"Google. DIY fingerprinting." He carefully placed a piece of clear tape over the fingerprints that stood out on the glass, then pulled it off. "I'm no pro, but I can eliminate a match if it's obvious. I'm sending the prints to the techs, but that'll take a while." He lifted a few good prints from one of the bags of cocaine he'd stored in Sam's safe until he could get it to ICE. He swung Sam's lighted magnifying glass over the lifted finger-prints.

"Where'd you find the dope?"

"Holly Grove."

"Son of a gun. Mackie was right." Sam peered over Jake's shoulder. "Well?" Sam said with an edge of im-patience. "Do they match her print?"

"Too close to call on some of them." Jake rolled his chair back from the desk. He'd wanted to put his mind at ease, anything to crush the pebble of doubt that rubbed away at his willingness to believe Holly's story.

Sam adjusted his reading glasses and nearly pressed his nose to the magnifying glass. He pointed to the prints on the plastic bag. "That one has a scar clear across the thumbprint."

"I'm guessing that's Burl's print or another smuggler's. The lab will run them for a match. Let's hope Burl's prints are in the database."

Sam stepped back from the desk and rubbed a leathery hand across his jaw. "You going to arrest her?"

"Nope."

"Why not? You found dope at her place. What else do you need? Live footage?"

"I'm here to bring down the organization, not a small-time player. It's a game, Sam, and I know how to play."

"This isn't any game, son. For all you know, she's the reason no one can find Mackie."

"Why are you so against Holly?"

"Because you don't think straight when it comes to that girl." Sam poured another shot of bourbon. "Remember, I was the one that had to call you and tell you she'd married Burl."

"History, Sam. Get over it. I did." Or had he?

CHAPTER 17

"You think Burl scared Jake off?" Nelda asked as she entered the barn. She handed Holly a thermos of hot chocolate.

Holly took the thermos and sat on a hay bale. "Jake doesn't believe I have a ghost. I can run off a man without Burl's help."

Nelda lifted a shoulder. "It don't seem like he'd just up and leave town without sayin' good-bye, unless he was runnin' from the law or somethin'."

Yeah, or something. The Jake she'd known would never jump town with a load of dope, no matter how much it was worth. But it sure looked like he had.

He had been broke all through high school and had never done a dishonest thing. Why now? But where were the bags of dope? Hidden away? Destroyed? If he'd turned them over to the police, they'd have been here by now. There had to be an explanation.

Nothing was going as Holly had expected, but what did she expect?

Hello? Nothing was normal at Holly Grove anymore.

"I got to check on my roast. See ya at supper." Nelda turned and walked back toward the house.

Holly loaded another bale of hay on the trailer attached to her four-wheeler, then eyed the cloudy sky. Another unexpected problem. The cane maze would be a mud trap without a bedding of hay, and by the time the student council gathered a crew to help, it would be too late. If she worked hard, she'd have the hay spread before dark and some of her frustrations worked out.

For the past three years, the student council had collected the gate money for the maze. She'd donated the money to the restoration fund for their one-hundred-year-old school. She couldn't bear to see another local landmark decay. Though this year she couldn't really afford the donation, but she'd keep her commitment.

She swiped her brow, then pulled off her gloves. The hay bales teetered in a stack three high and eight long. Holly stuffed her gloves in the back pocket of her jeans, then dusted off her hands. Nelda had told her she needed a man, but she'd managed just fine. Nelda was wrong.

She heaved a sigh and swung a leg over the four-wheeler. Problem was she fell for trouble in a male package. Burl had lost all their money, had screwed a redhead, and had the nerve to come back asking for favors. Big ones!

She'd given her heart to Jake once years ago, and he'd given it right back to her, tattooed with THANKS, BUT NO THANKS across it. That faded pink heart on the water tower had nothing on the mark Jake had left on her heart. What he'd done this time was criminal, and she couldn't even report it. How could she be so gullible?

Holly groaned at her stupidity and started the four-wheeler. As it thundered to life, she hoped it'd drown out her thoughts. She pointed the four-wheeler toward the cane maze. Thunder rumbled in the distance.

She pulled her cell out of her pocket and dialed Holly Grove as she drove deep into the maze.

"Holly Grove Plantation. Nelda speakin'."

"I'm out back, in the cane field. You may have to start supper without me," Holly shouted over the motor. "Any more guests check in?"

"If you're talkin' about that good-lookin' one that left this mornin'—"

The four-wheeler lurched as a trailer wheel hit a hole she hadn't noticed. Holly bounced and dropped her phone. She turned to check the load as bales tumbled from the trailer.

"Crapola." She put the four-wheeler in park and killed the motor. Pursing her lips, she blew air out, as though that would keep her from exploding. "What else can go wrong?" She looked up at the cloudy skies. "Lordy mercy. When all the big things are going wrong, you're supposed to let the little things slide." She climbed off the four-wheeler.

Nelda's voice came from the phone, which was under the trailer. "Holly. You there?"

At least she hadn't rolled over the phone. She stretched out on the grass and looked under the trailer. The screen of her phone glowed at just about center. She crawled under the trailer and felt around. When she touched the slick surface of the phone, she wrapped her fingers around it. Inching out backward, she rocked to her knees but kept her head down to keep from bumping it on the underbelly of the trailer.

"Beautiful view tonight."

Holly nearly whacked her head on the trailer. *Jake?*

From under the hay trailer, Holly looked between her legs at Jake. Perfectly beautiful crinkles framed Jake's eyes. She'd never been so glad to see a man in her life.

He tilted his head and stroked his chin. "Not that I mind the, um, view, but what are you doing under there?"

Holly shimmied out from under the trailer and jumped to her feet. "You're back!" She launched herself at him and landed with her arms around his neck.

"Yeah," Jake croaked in a husky voice as his body tensed against hers. "I didn't expect this kind of greeting."

"I thought you were gone for good, just like last time." Only worse. She'd thought he was a criminal.

Jake gave her a quizzical look. "Why?"

She realized she still had her arms around his neck. Heat rushed her cheeks as she took an awkward step back.

"When I saw your bag was gone, I called the *Gazette*. They said you weren't there but Sam was." She folded her arms and then tried to make them look natural by swinging them to her sides. "You know, two plus two."

And never mind that she'd let Burl convince her Jake had taken off with the dope.

"I don't have control over Sam." He leaned against the hay trailer and grinned. "My bag was at Wash 'n' Dry."

"And Dog was gone." She grabbed a hay bale and started spreading hay to have something to do besides sound like a babbling fool. It had all made sense at the time.

"At the vet." He stuck a piece of hay between his teeth and shook his head. "Getting her stitches out."

"Well . . ." She stood a little straighter. "I thought . . . maybe—"

"I jumped town with your stash?"

"Of course not."

A smile slid across his lips. "That just leaves one other reason you'd be so glad to see me."

CHAPTER 18

"I promised you an upgrade to a bigger bathroom," Holly said as she pushed the screen door open.

Jake followed her outside and looked up at the stars. "I know I'm back in the South and all, but I wasn't talking about a bathroom as big as all outdoors. Just one big enough to stand up in."

A weak smile lifted her cheeks. She seemed down, maybe distant. "All the rooms have indoor plumbing except one, and it has an outhouse."

He cocked his head to the side. "You're not serious."

"Oh, yeah." She pointed to a cabin in the distance. "Abe's cabin, as I call it, has an outhouse and no air-conditioning or heating. No electricity, period."

"People pay money to stay there?" He looked from the cabin to her. There was something about her affect that felt off.

"I offer it as a cabin in the woods on my Web site. Every once in a while, I get a tree hugger or a history junkie who wants to see what it was like back then, instead of the fantasy."

"I wouldn't call that an upgrade."

Holly laughed, but it seemed tense. "Come on. I'll show you your upgrade. I'm moving you to the garçonnière."

He slung his duffel bag over his shoulder and fell in step beside her. "Sounds fancy. What's the garçonnière?"

"It's French for 'bachelor's apartment.'" She climbed a narrow staircase on the exterior of the house. "It's a small attachment to the upstairs balcony. The garçonnière was used as a dormitory for adolescent boys or for travelers. That's why it has a separate entrance."

Jake pointed to the hollow patches on the steps as he followed her up the staircase. "Do you want me to replace these steps while I'm here?"

"God, no. That's history. These steps were worn down by people who've been dead over a hundred years."

"Can you get into the house from the garçonnière without going outside?"

"No," she said as they reached the top of the stairs, which ended at the front balcony shared by his previous suite and Holly's bedroom. "Back then, there weren't any hotels. Sometimes the traveler would have a letter from an acquaintance but would otherwise be unknown to the plantation owner. These near strangers weren't given the keys to the house."

He cocked his head to the side. "What about guests like me?"

"Sorry. None of my guests get keys to the outside doors. After ten at night, there'll be no access to the main house without ringing the bell."

"So this is where they kept the strangers and teenagers." And others not to be trusted, like him. Two iron brackets framed the door to the guest room, and a wooden bar rested across the door. "What's this?"

She lifted the bar. "The travelers were locked in at night since the family didn't know them very well."

"They locked the teenagers in, too?"

"Boys." She smiled. "They didn't trust them around the girls."

"Do you think I'm dangerous?"

Holly fidgeted with the room key and avoided eye contact. "I know you're dangerous, but I'm not locking you in." She opened the door and handed him his key. "It's just historical, so I left the bar in place."

As Jake followed her into the guest room, he made a mental note to remove the bar so he wouldn't be locked in for the night. Something just wasn't right about this move.

Bleached hardwood striped the floors of the large room. Moonlight from the four twelve-pane windows cast the room in shadow.

Jake fumbled for the light switch and flipped it on. One bare bulb dangled from the beaded ceiling.

"Sorry," she said. "This room is still in the renovation stage, but as you can see, it has the biggest bathroom." She gave a *Price Is Right* wave to the copper tub in front of the bare window. Candles of every size lined a matching copper tray on the floor in front of the tub. A four-poster bed covered with a white quilt sat between two tall windows.

He walked across the room and dropped his duffel bag on the bed. "You didn't mention the bathroom was the bedroom. Where's the, um, rest of the bathroom?"

She pointed to a door in the corner of the room where a wall had been built at an angle. "Since there are so many windows in here, adding a bathroom was a challenge. The rest of it is behind that door and under a twelve-foot ceiling. The upgrade."

"As much as I appreciate this upgrade, I don't want you in the house by yourself. The guy who came after the dope in the dummy may come back."

"It's not there, anyway. Besides, your old room is rented. I have a house full of guests to look out for. Everything is locked up tight, and I probably won't sleep much, anyway. I'll be fine."

Holly ambled to the door. She paused with her hand on the doorknob as though she had something to say. She didn't look back as she said, "Goodnight," then left, closing the door behind her.

He couldn't even access the rest of the house without walking down the stairs and outside to the front door or going through one of the upstairs balcony doors, which were all locked. Was she trying to put some distance between them, literally? Or was she hiding something?

Holly had been acting strange ever since he saw her in the cane maze.

Jake bathed, then shrugged into jeans and a shirt. He shoved his hands in his pockets and studied the room she'd called the garçonnière. She'd explained that the design was a safety measure back in antebellum days, but he was convinced she was using it to keep him at a distance, and he needed to know why.

Jake slipped on his jacket and headed to Holly's balcony door. He had his knuckles positioned to rap on her door when he heard footsteps below on the downstairs balcony. He checked his watch. Eleven o'clock. Way past the bedtime of Holly's geriatric guests.

Jake froze on the balcony to focus on the sound. Footsteps padded across the downstairs balcony below him. He heard the metallic sound of the release of a lock, then the squeak of the front door as someone opened it. He'd expected whoever had snooped around in the barn to return for the drugs, but not tonight. He hadn't expected them to have a key, either.

Jake took light, quick steps across the balcony to the exterior stairs, then raced on tiptoe down the steps. As he rounded the house, a flashlight beam slashed across a window from inside. A guest wouldn't use a flashlight. His heart pumped with the familiar rush he had before every bust. He steadied his breathing. But this wasn't just any bust.

He crept across the porch with easy, slow steps until he reached the front door. Moonlight flooded the porch between patches of darkness as clouds blocked the moon. Jake wrapped his hand around the door handle. With any luck, the perp had left the door unlocked for a quick escape. Jake silently cursed himself for not getting around to oiling the hinges. The darned squeak might as well be an alarm.

Jake reached under his jacket for his gun out of habit, only to pat down his empty side. He winced, remembering he'd put the gun in his bag before he headed to Holly's room. As he opened the door, he told himself the perp wouldn't know he was anything more than a guest who had no idea what he was looking for and no reason to accost him. The guy had run when Miss Alice spotted him the last time. He'd run again, but this time Jake would be closer and faster.

The squeak echoed through the empty foyer as Jake opened the door. Moonlight dappled the room, and a shadowy figure hunkering over the coffin jerked to attention, his face concealed in darkness. He snatched the dummy out of the coffin and bolted for the back door.

Jake pounded across the wood floor, then lunged for the guy. A passing cloud snuffed out the moonlight. The room plunged into blackness, except for the retreating flashlight.

Groping in the dark, Jake caught what he thought was a leg before he hit the floor. The perp's body slammed onto the floor and coughed up a winded grunt. The flashlight skittered across the floor and landed with the beam wedged in a corner as moonlight sliced through the room.

Jake crawled across the floor to the crumpled body gasping for breath. Hand over hand, Jake dragged himself on top of the perp, then grabbed him by the shirt. When Jake stood, he jerked the guy to his feet with him. The moonlight gave way to darkness again.

CHAPTER 19

Holly shuffled in fuzzy slippers to the planter's table and plopped down in the dark with a hunk of Nelda's chocolate pie. After a few satisfying bites, she looked out the window. Moonlight flickered between the branches of the oak trees, casting long shadows on the lawn. All was quiet. She'd left Rhett having doggy dreams in her bed. No Burl. No guests. No Jake to distract her. Just Holly Grove and her for a blissful moment.

Everything was riding on catching the smugglers and making Holly Grove a success. Time was running out, and she was one calamity away from losing everything.

A crash sounded from the foyer, and Holly jumped to her feet. She scurried to the kitchen door and peeked into the foyer. As her eyes adjusted to the darkness, two figures came into view. A man stood holding someone or maybe something by the shirt. *Eudora?*

Holly's heart beat against her ribs. The smuggler had come back for the cocaine and marijuana he thought was still in Eudora. This was her chance to catch the smuggler and get Burl out of her life for good.

She eased the door closed. What could she use from the kitchen as a weapon? The thought of a knife sent shivers through her. She couldn't stab anyone. Too bloody. Besides, she needed the guy alive so he'd squeal on his boss. Holly spied Nelda's second-prize six-inch skillet on the wall. She lifted it from the nail, then squeezed both hands around the handle.

On tiptoe, she entered the foyer. What little moonlight had lit the room had evaporated into shadows. Trying to calculate how hard to hit the man, Holly hefted the skillet and tested its weight. Too hard and she could kill him. If she didn't hit him hard enough, he could turn on her.

Rhett's yaps rang from the top of the stairs as she whacked the smuggler on the head.

He dropped to his knees and swayed a bit before he fell.

But Eudora didn't fall.

Holly blinked as the shadowy figure turned and scooped up something on the floor, then dashed for the door, with Rhett yapping at his heels.

She scampered to the light switch, then flicked it on.

A scream welled in her throat. "Jake!" The skillet slipped from her grip and clunked to the floor.

Oh, no. She might have cracked his skull.

She rushed over to Jake and knelt at his side. Her hands shook. She wished she'd paid attention to Mr. Moses in freshman first aid rather than staring at the back of Jake's head. "Lordy, mercy me. What have I done?"

Rhett scampered back from his smuggler chase like

the beast of the manor. He gave her and Jake a good sniff and pranced off like all was well. She wasn't so sure.

Footsteps clattered on the stairs.

Holly looked up at her guests. "I—I thought he was a p-prowler."

Miss Alice pushed her way through the other guests. "What happened here?" she asked, tying her chenille robe under her grandmother boobs.

"I hit Jake on the head with Nelda's skillet."

"Good grief. You may have fractured his skull."

"I didn't hit him as hard as I could have. I didn't want to kill him. Just knock him out," Holly said, realizing she was blubbering like an idiot.

Miss Alice padded down the steps in her orthopedic slippers. She crossed the room to Jake, then creaked as she knelt beside him.

"Please tell me I didn't kill him," Holly whispered.

Miss Alice pressed her wrinkly fingertips to his neck. "Nope. He's got a good pulse."

"Thank God," Holly said.

The rest of the guests hovered around in a hushed circle.

"Stand back and give him some air," Miss Alice ordered. She rubbed her aged hands over his scalp, then shook her head. "He's got quite a lump, but that's a good thing."

"Good?" Holly questioned.

"It means the swelling is pushing out and probably not pushing on his brain."

"So I didn't hit him too hard."

"Hard enough to knock him out cold." Miss Alice pried two fingers between each of his eyelids. She leaned into him, then pulled away, squinting her eyes. "My glasses are upstairs. Are his pupils the same size?"

Holly looked from one dark eye to the next. "I think so. That's good. Right?"

"We'll see when he comes around. Go get a glass of water and a bag of frozen peas to ice the bump."

Holly fetched a glass of water and a bag of frozen peas. She handed the peas to Miss Alice, and she pressed the icy bag to Jake's head.

He didn't flinch.

Holly kneeled beside Jake and Miss Alice, then handed the glass of water to her.

Miss Alice frowned. "Why are you giving it to me?"

"You asked for it."

"Unless you have smelling salts, he may be out awhile. It's best we bring him around."

"You're not going to throw water on him?"

"You knocked him out." Miss Alice pointed a finger at Jake. "You bring him to."

Holly's skin itched with the creepy feeling of guilt. She wasn't looking forward to telling Jake what she'd done.

Jake gasped as he bolted forward. His head throbbed with every beat of his heart. Cold water dripped down his face and chest.

What the . . . ? A blur of faces huddled around him. *A dream?*

"How many fingers am I holding up?" said a haze of pink hovering over him.

He rubbed his eyes and blinked. "Huh?"

Miss Alice leaned over him. "How many fingers?"

Her image looked like the view from a camera lens when adjusting the focus from fuzzy to clear. "Three?"

"Good. What month is it?"

"October. Why?"

"Checking for brain damage," Miss Alice said.

"Brain damage?"

Holly set the empty glass down. She rubbed her hand over his arm. "Uh, I—"

"She hit you over the head with an iron skillet," Miss Alice said.

"Why?" Jake looked back at Holly. His head throbbed as he recalled the struggle and the blow that had brought him to his knees. Jake rubbed the goose egg–sized bump on his head. "Last time I checked, we were on friendly terms."

Holly wrung her hands and stammered. "I-it was an accident. I—I didn't know it was you." She picked up the bag of peas beside Jake, then pressed the icy bag against the back of his head.

"Ouch."

Holly winced. "Sorry."

"So why'd you nearly bust my skull?"

"It was dark. I heard a noise and saw someone beside Eudora's coffin. I thought he was going to steal something." She squeezed his hand. "You know." Holly held his stare, as though she needed to know he understood.

He squeezed back to show he got it. She'd obviously thought that he was the smuggler and that he'd come back for the goods in the dummy. The guy had scored the dummy but not what he'd come for.

Holly curled her fingers around his. "I'm so sorry." Her brow creased as her eyes pleaded for under-standing.

"It wasn't good enough for you to knock me out." Jake forced a smile to relieve her tension. He pulled his wet shirt away from his chest with two fingers. "You had to try to drown me, too."

"I'm not sorry for that." She gave a weak smile. "At least I woke you up."

He attempted to stand. Pain shot from the lump on the back of his head to his temples.

"Where do you think you're going?" Miss Alice pushed one of his shoulders, and Holly pushed the other.

Surprisingly, Jake found it difficult to get past them. Rather than chance getting put down by two women, he said, "I think I'll sit a minute."

"Good thinking." Miss Alice nodded.

The guests whispered among themselves. Some pointed to Holly. This couldn't be good for Holly's business, and she'd had enough trouble.

Jake gave a thumbs-up. "I'm okay. Y'all can go back to bed. It was my mistake for milling around in the dark. Believe me, you're safe with Holly on patrol."

After several minutes of grumbles and reassurance, Miss Alice and the rest of the guests filed to their rooms.

"Thanks," Holly whispered as they departed.

Jake held his hand up to Holly. "Give me a pull."

"You sure you're ready?"

"I'm sure I'd be more comfortable in a chair."

As Holly helped him to his feet, a dull pain radiated across his skull. Jake closed his eyes. Jumbled flashes of memory tumbled in his head. The footsteps on the porch. The flashlight through the windows. A squeak. A shadowy figure.

"Jake." Holly's voice sounded muffled and far away. "Jake," she said again, pulling on his shirt. "Please don't pass out on me."

He opened his eyes. "Did you get a good look at him?"

Holly shook her head. "Too dark. If I'd seen the guy's face, I would've hit him instead."

Holly steadied herself under Jake's weight as she helped him to the courting chair. It was the closest chair to him but probably the most uncomfortable seat at Holly Grove. When she was a kid, she'd called the courting chair the crazy S chair, because of its shape. One person sat in each curve of the chair. Jake barely fit in his portion of the S, and he stretched his arm over the low chair back so that it encroached on the other portion. She'd have to move him as soon as he could walk on his own.

"Can I get you anything?" Holly asked. She'd do almost anything to make up for knocking him out. She'd thought she was saving the day, getting the bad guy and all that. Instead, she'd nearly killed Jake, her only potential ally in the whole mess. She sighed. *Hurricane Holly strikes again.*

He shook his head and grimaced.

"Let me do something. I feel awful about this. A bowl of gumbo? A slice of pie? A praline? A pillow? Iced tea?"

He waved her off.

Holly pressed the frozen peas to the back of his head again.

"Too cold." Jake grabbed the bag of peas. "That's giving me a headache."

"The swelling is giving you the headache," Miss Alice said as she gripped the banister on her way back down the stairs. In the crook of her free arm, she carried a basket. Strands of colorful yarn trailed from the basket, which was filled with balls of yarn impaled with knitting needles. A paperback novel teetered between the balls of yarn.

"Miss Alice, I thought you'd gone to bed with the others," Holly said.

"Nonsense. I have a patient." As she crossed the foyer to Jake, her glasses bounced on a chain against her chenille robe. Miss Alice frowned and snatched the frozen peas from Jake. She put them back on his bump, then grabbed his hand and directed it to the peas. "Hold the cold compress in place for at least twenty minutes."

"Yes, ma'am."

"You need constant observation and absolutely cannot go to sleep for at least four hours," Miss Alice said, pouring herself into the other side of the courting chair, beside Jake.

Jake curled his arm across his chest and shifted his weight to make room for Miss Alice.

Holly held her lips in a tight line to hide her amusement. Courting chairs were called that for a reason. The two seats, separated by an upholstered curve, were designed to prevent unwed couples from cuddling and engaging in other nineteenth-century taboos. In this instance, the S shape very nearly failed to live up to its purpose, though the two before her were more of an odd couple than a pair.

"Thanks for everything, Miss Alice, but it'd take more than a bump on the head to keep me down," Jake said, leaning back as far from Miss Alice as he could.

"I'll not have a death or a serious complication on my conscience." Miss Alice balanced the basket on her knees as she slipped her glasses on her face. "You go to bed, Holly. I'll take care of the patient." She flipped open her paperback. "This story will keep me up all night."

Holly tilted her head sideways to read the title. *Silence of the Lamps*. Holly sighed. She could easily title tonight's escapade *Lights Out*.

Miss Alice looked up from her book at Holly. "Why are you still standing here?"

"I, uh—"

"Holly was telling me earlier she'd do anything to make up for nearly killing me."

Miss Alice snapped her book closed. "Well, she should. If she'd hit you any harder, you'd have a minimum of several stitches and probably a skull fracture."

"But I didn't hit him that hard. You said—"

"Yep." Jake held the peas to the back of his head. "A little harder hit, and we could all be at the hospital right now, praying for me to pull through."

Holly pointed a finger at Jake. "But—"

Jake lifted a hand in a halting position. "Now, don't apologize again, Holly."

"But—"

He leaned in to Miss Alice and said, "She won't leave my side," as though Holly wasn't in the room. "There's no need for both of you to lose a night's sleep." He looked back at Holly. "Especially a paying guest. Right?"

Jake had baited Holly and had set the hook like a seasoned pro. What could she say that wouldn't make her look like a throw-back trash fish?

Chapter 20

Holly had watched the perfect gentleman sleep in his room, while she sat in a chair at his bedside—until she decided he'd live. At dawn, she sat on the balcony outside her bedroom as she sipped a much-needed cup of coffee and watched the sun rise over the levee.

Jake strode from his room in the garçonnière across the balcony and joined her. "Thanks for helping me to my room and saving me from Miss Alice last night. Sorry I conked out on you."

"It was the least I could do. How's your head?"

"Lumpy." He rubbed the back of his head and Holly cringed.

"I'm really sorry," she said.

Jake leaned against the balcony railing. "I've got to check out a couple of things I remembered about the guy I had by the throat last night."

"Like what?"

"He had a flashlight. I knocked it out of his hand, and it landed in a corner of the room. If it's still there, it'll have fingerprints on it." He slipped his shoes on. "And the guy had a key."

She tilted her head to the side. "That's impossible."

"You lock the outside doors after ten p.m., right?"

"Every night." She took another sip of coffee. "It's not like I can afford a rent-a-cop on patrol."

"You didn't give me a key to the exterior doors." He lifted a shoulder. "But maybe you didn't trust me enough with one. How about the other guests?"

"No one gets a front-door key. It keeps security simple. Historical locks are irreplaceable. If a guest loses or forgets to return a key, I'm screwed. If a guest stays out after ten at night, they have to call my cell or ring the doorbell."

"I was on the balcony when I heard footsteps on the porch below, then the click of a lock and the squeak. So who has keys to Holly Grove besides you?"

"Nelda and Burl each have a set." *And Burl can't do anything but blow so far.*

"Well, it sure wasn't Burl, and I think I would have known if I'd tackled a woman." He crossed his arms over his chest. "Anyone else?"

"Oh, yeah. Mackie."

"Why Mackie?"

"He fixes everything that breaks around here. He's had keys for years. You don't think Mackie could have—"

"Mackie's got his problems, but drugs aren't one of them. He thinks drugs ruined the country."

"He'd never use his keys, unless I asked him to come in and fix something." She hesitated. "But, Jake, he's missing. Someone trashed his trailer. Maybe they took his keys. I'm worried about him."

"To tell you the truth, I'm worried, too. Everything keeps pointing to Mackie. I'll go back to his trailer and see if I can find his keys. If I don't, either Mackie used them or someone took them from him. Where are Burl's keys?"

"Somewhere at the hangar."

"Can you trust me with a key to the hangar, or do I need to wait until you get dressed?"

"There's a set of keys to everything hidden outside for an emergency. It's in an old film canister under the twelfth brick in the flower-bed border."

"Anyone know about that one?"

"Just Mama and me—and she's not telling."

Jake lifted a brow. "And you told me. Does this mean you're starting to trust me, sweetheart?"

Holly's gaze fell to the floor. "You won't be around to use them, anyway. I trust you won't be using my keys from fourteen hundred miles away."

Holly pushed through the kitchen door for a second cup of coffee. Boy, did she need it.

Nelda jumped and threw her hand over her heart. "I thought you was that ghost."

"No, but I feel like death." She scanned the room for Burl. He'd been scarce since he threw his hissy fit because he was jealous of Jake. *Well, he can just get over it. I've got enough to deal with right now.*

"How 'bout some fresh coffee?"

"Got an IV?"

Nelda filled Holly's Blue Willow cup. "I know you wasn't in your room at six, 'cause I came up there to tell you Eudora was sittin' on the porch steps."

Holly nearly spewed her coffee. "Is she still there?"

"I put her back in her coffin." Nelda shook her head. "I don't even want to know how she got out."

Holly rushed to the coffin to open it.

Eudora looked a little thinner and had a few dirty spots on her period outfit, but other than that she was fine. Holly lifted Eudora's skirt. More duct tape circled her waist. The smuggler hadn't found what he was looking for, because Jake had the dope hidden away, but why would he tape Eudora together and return her? It didn't make any sense.

Nelda peeked around the kitchen door. "You think Burl put Eudora on the steps?"

"I know he didn't. Burl can't lift a sheet."

"I'm working on that." Burl leaned against Eudora's coffin. "But I did see who took the dummy."

Holly's mouth dropped open. "Who?"

"What's in it for me if I tell you?"

"Eternal peace."

"You talkin' to Burl again?" Nelda crossed herself. "God rest his soul."

"Don't worry, Nelda. He's not staying for breakfast." Holly glared at Burl.

"You tell him to stay out of my kitchen." Nelda pulled the swinging door closed behind her, then yelled, "If he comes up in here, I got holy water locked and loaded."

Burl swaggered toward the kitchen.

"You've had enough fun." Holly stepped in front of Burl. "Who was it?"

"Your boyfriend's drunk papa."

"Mackie?"

"Yep. And I bet what's-his-name is in on it, too. You've been duped, Blondie."

"I don't believe it. You're making this up to make Jake look bad."

"Suit yourself. I saw what I saw."

CHAPTER 21

Burl hovered over Holly's shoulder, and she ignored him. As long as she didn't talk to him, Nelda could stay on task.

While Nelda cooked breakfast, Holly booted up her laptop at the planter's table. She hadn't had time to check her Web site for hits or inquiries about vacancies since yesterday morning. All her guests would check out at 10:00 a.m. today, and only three new guests had reserved rooms for the weekend. Holly sighed. She could use a stimulus package.

The laptop hummed to life; then she clicked to her site. "Unavailable," she read aloud. She tried again. *Unavailable?*

"How do you expect to run a business when your Web site is down, Blondie?"

Holly rolled her eyes at Burl, then shot an e-mail to her Web host. When she'd signed up with them, they'd guaranteed service 24-7. *Fat chance.*

"How many tickets have we sold for the tour today?" Holly asked Nelda.

Nelda scooped up curls of crispy bacon with a spatula. "We got two tour buses for sure. Praise God."

Burl rubbed his hands together. "Stick with me, Blondie. When I finish with those tourists, Holly Grove is going to be famous."

At least he wasn't giving up haunting. Holly stood and crossed the kitchen, then opened a cabinet. She grabbed a sterling silver pitcher engraved with an *H* and as old as the oak trees out front. Grandma Rose had bought the heirloom back from an antique dealer in New Orleans when she recognized it as the missing part in the Holly Grove silver service. It belonged here. Just like Holly.

After Holly filled the pitcher with freshly squeezed orange juice, Burl shadowed her into the dining room. When she stopped short, the chill of his body touched hers. She took a deep breath, refusing to acknowledge him.

"I'm not going away," Burl said.

Nelda carried the beginning of the buffet parade into the kitchen. She slid a pile of bacon in the chafing dish on the sideboard. Holly poured the freshly squeezed orange juice from the silver pitcher into her mother's crystal goblets at each place setting. She set the footed pitcher on the tablecloth Grandma Rose had custom made to fit the formal dining table. Everything at Holly Grove gave her comfort.

Burl sniffed the air. "Mmm. Bacon." He floated to the sideboard, then cupped the air over the chafing dish and fanned it to his face. "This is man candy, you know."

Everything gave her comfort, except Burl.

Nelda returned with a pot of garlic-cheese grits. She poured the grits into a silver chafing dish on the sideboard. "Would you look at that? Not a lump in the batch."

Within a few minutes, Holly and Nelda had the buffet stocked with crispy bacon, grits, sausage, fluffy scrambled eggs, mayhaw jelly, real butter, and slap-yo'-mama biscuits, as Nelda liked to call them.

Holly looked at her watch. Eight o'clock. "Perfect timing."

"You want me to let 'em in?"

"Go ahead. I'll be back in a minute. I need to see if my Web site is up yet."

"Make it fast. My grits ain't as good after they set up and get that skin on top."

Holly rushed back to her laptop and clicked on her Web site again. Nothing. Holly could feel Burl's chill behind her. "You mind?"

"Hey, I'm invested."

She gave him a "drop dead" look, as though it'd do any good. "Yeah. Right."

"Haven't you ever heard of sweat equity?"

She clicked on her e-mail to see if her webmaster had responded. "Wow! That was fast."

Ms. Davis,

Your site crashed due to an overload of traffic.
We will resolve the problem shortly.

Sincerely,

Joe Smith

Webmaster

"You see that?" Burl tapped the screen. "Mrs. Davis."

Holly groaned. "Ms. It doesn't say Mrs. Get over it, Burl." She shook her head. "This must be some automated message. I've never had more than a dozen hits in a day."

As Holly stood there, the familiar click of new mail caught her attention. Her webmaster's address popped up in her in-box. They were really true to their 24-7 promise. She clicked on this second e-mail from her webmaster and sat down.

Ms. Davis,

You had 47,371 hits in less than twenty-four hours, which we did not anticipate for your account. I have adjusted the settings on your site to accommodate higher traffic.

Sincerely,

Joe Smith

Webmaster

Holly frowned. "No way could I have had enough hits to crash my site."

"Unless it was hijacked, and there's only one kind of site that gets that kind of traffic."

Holly held her hand over her shoulder like a stop sign. "Don't say it. I'll never get you into heaven."

She clicked to her Web site and froze. There were 460 comments and 160,823 hits. "What on God's green earth?"

She scrolled through the comments.

Awesome ghost. Gigme4209.

"He's got that right," Burl said.

Holly squinted at the message. "Huh? Who's gigme4209, and how does he know Holly Grove has a ghost? The *Gazette* doesn't circulate on the World Wide Web. Even the Deltas don't spread the word to cyberspace."

She read the next comment.

> Amateur hour. You can put anything up on YouTube. Runwithit8921.

"You do YouTube?" Burl asked.

"No. I mean, I watch, but I've never uploaded a video."

Holly did a YouTube search for ghosts. At eight on the list was "Ghost in the Grove." She hit PLAY. A shaky cell phone video of the parlor at Holly Grove spread across the computer screen. The camera was focused on the pier mirror draped in black. A hand with a beaded leather wristband pulled at the cloth.

Holly pointed at the screen. "That's the teenager from the tour."

"Yeah. Matt," Burl said. "I got him good."

On the screen, a fog-filled circle appeared on the pier mirror. "Whoa," Matt's voice whispered through the speakers. Then a handprint melted through the hazy circle. The camera shook as the same voice said, "Whoa. Just freaking whoa."

A loud scream blared through the speakers, and the video jerked around the room, until it settled on Holly's face, but way too close. The camera zoomed out to a full-body view of her.

"D-d-did you see that?" Matt said from behind the camera.

Holly's voice came through the computer. "Told you I had a ghost."

"Awesome," Matt said, his voice cracking. "This place rocks."

The view spun in a blur, until Holly's face filled the screen. "Thanks, Matt. Come back anytime." Her image became smaller as the camera wobbled away. "Hey, bring a friend."

Then the screen went black.

Holly stared at the computer screen with her mouth open. She turned to Burl. "Do you know what this means?"

Burl's powdery face split in a smile. "This means you can't afford to get rid of me."

Burl had a point, financially speaking, but Holly wasn't willing to pay the high price of his constant company for the haunting.

"We had a deal." The planter's bench scraped the wooden planks as she stood to face Burl.

"I told you I changed my mind." He folded his arms over his chest. "I'm not ready to leave."

Holly clenched her teeth as she tried to tamp down her frustration. She'd never won a fight with Burl. She had to outsmart him, for once. "You're right. You're a valuable asset to Holly Grove."

"You've got that right." Burl pointed to the laptop. "The pencil-pusher you're giving free room and board to can't get you worldwide living-color promotion like that."

"No, but I made a deal, and I stick by my word." She picked up her empty coffee cup. "But I understand the sacrifice you're making." She turned and crossed the room to get more coffee and to avoid looking at Burl—to manipulate the master manipulator.

"Sacrifice?"

"Well, yes." She topped her cup off with dark roast. "I mean, you are a ghost." She chanced a glance at Burl.

He pulled his shoulders back. "I'm a grade A ghost, baby. And don't you forget it."

She sipped the hot brew and looked over the rim of her cup at Burl. "I'm sure you'll get used to smelling bacon instead of tasting it again, ever."

Burl whiffed the air. "I can exist without bacon."

"No coffee in the morning, and no cocktail at the end of a hard day."

"I'll drink vicariously."

She rubbed her finger around the rim of her cup, then lifted a shoulder. "Watching me drink champagne is almost as good as drinking it, I'm sure." She set her cup on the counter. "But no wife in a physical sense, and no redheads and no—"

"Wait a minute. I know what you're doing." Burl marched over to her and pointed a finger in her face.

"Me?" Holly patted her chest and tried to look innocent. "I'm just trying to understand why you'd give up heaven for me."

Burl raised his finger higher and opened his mouth to speak but didn't. He relaxed his hand and reached toward her face, as though he would stroke her cheek; then he pulled back. He stuffed his hands in his pockets and stared at the floor. "Because I love you more than I ever realized I did when I was alive."

"If only you had loved me like this before." She hesitated. "Before our marriage died. Before you died. It's too late, Burl."

He raised his head. His brows slanted downward over a sadness in his eyes she'd never seen, and his image faded away.

* * *

Jake bounced down the dusty road to Mackie's trailer in his rental car. Mackie seemed to have disappeared, but that was something he did well if he wanted to. Jake blew out a heavy breath. He was no longer sure if Mackie had wanted to disappear or had to.

Finding Mackie's set of keys to Holly Grove would prove Mackie could have used the keys, not that he actually had. If the keys were missing along with Mackie, it would be hard to deny Mackie hadn't used them.

Dog paced across the backseat and punctuated her steps with short barks.

Everything looked the same at Mackie's trailer, except for the thicker coat of dust. Jake parked, then opened the door. He grumbled as Dog bounded over the backseat and him.

"Hold on, Dog."

Dog wagged her entire backside like she'd never seen a better sight than Mackie's place. No matter how humble, this was home to Dog. And it'd been Jake's home once. He wished he could see past the dirt and the years of disappointment to be as happy to see Mackie as Dog would be. Jake would settle for relief.

Fresh handprints in the dust around the toolbox on Mackie's truck caught Jake's attention. A padlock secured the tools, which, Jake knew, were perfectly organized inside. He eyed the trailer for signs that Mackie was home.

Dog planted her front paws on the doorstep and let out a sharp yap.

Jake crossed the yard to the trailer. "Let's see if he's home, girl."

Dog whined and shifted from paw to paw.

Jake rapped his knuckles on the metal door but didn't wait for an answer. He stepped inside. The air in the trailer had marinated into a stale funk. "Anybody home?"

Nothing had changed since Holly and he had been there. Jake scanned the room for the keys mixed in the clutter. He opened drawers, cabinets, and closets and poked through their contents. No keys.

He leaned his backside against the kitchen counter and surveyed the kitchen, dining room, and den combo. It'd take hours to look through all this junk. He spotted a coatrack loaded with assorted jackets and shirts. A vision of Mackie rifling through pockets, looking for lost keys, flashed through Jake's mind.

He crossed the room to the coatrack. As he fumbled through the pockets, the coatrack tumbled to the floor. Jake groaned. When he righted the coatrack, he noticed a crude wooden key rack on the wall that had been hidden by the mountain of coats. The key rack held a collection of keys dangling from brass cup hooks that had been randomly screwed into a square piece of oak. At the back of each cup hook, a paper tag identified the key. As he flipped through the tags, his chest tightened. On a tag at the bottom of the rack, scrawled in faded black paint, were the letters *D, A, D.* He'd stopped calling Mackie Dad back in junior high.

Jake had been eight or nine when he'd made the key rack as a Father's Day present. He'd collected wood scraps from Mackie's truck and stolen the brass cup hooks from his box of screws. He had almost been finished when he got caught stealing a piece of copper wire to use as a hanger.

Back then, Jake had tried to tell Mackie he was

stealing for a good reason, but Mackie had said there wasn't a reason for stealing that was good enough. That night, after Mackie had gone to bed, Jake threw the key rack in the trash can outside. He never saw it again. Until now.

Jake swallowed down emotion that was more than he could chew. Mackie had never been the sentimental type. Yet he'd kept the gift Jake never got to give him.

He thumbed a dangling key. Would it have been too much for the stubborn old coot to admit he appreciated his own kid making him a gift? Hell would freeze over before Mackie backed down from one of his platitudes.

Jake shoved his fists on his hips and blew out a long breath. *Let it go.*

Right now, all he needed to do was find out if Mackie's Holly Grove keys were here.

The last tag Jake flipped over had the initials H.G. on it, but the keys were missing. He rubbed the tag between his thumb and finger.

Mackie was missing.

Someone could have taken Mackie's keys, like Holly said. Or Mackie could have used them last night to get into Holly Grove. Jake's guts churned. As tough as Mackie was, he'd never laid a hand on Jake, and the prowler looking for the dope hadn't so much as thrown a punch.

CHAPTER 22

Holly jumped at the sound of the screen door slamming and turned to find Jake walking into the kitchen. His face looked like a road map to misery. He lumbered to the coffeepot without as much as a sideways glance at her.

"Who peed in your gumbo?" Holly asked.

"Sorry," he mumbled as he turned to her and did a double take.

She probably looked like she'd stepped out of a Civil War time warp. The big black bell skirt swayed as she looked down at her period costume. It covered every inch of her except her head.

"Southern belle gone gothic?" he asked.

"Tour day." She curtsied, holding the sides of her skirt with her fingertips and spreading it wider. "Ten o'clock."

Jake rolled his neck. "That video you sent me is going to draw half the screwballs in the country to see a ghost you needed so bad you fabricated him."

"Fabricated?" If she were going to fabricate a ghost,

it wouldn't be Burl. She looked over her shoulder. Where was her poltergeist of an ex when she needed him? She jabbed a thumb toward her laptop. "You saw the proof on YouTube."

"I've seen three-headed cats on YouTube." Jake raked through his hair as though he wanted to yank it out by the roots. "I just watched a promotion gimmick."

"You don't believe in ghosts." She rolled her eyes. "Fine. What's the big deal?"

Jake stepped closer and towered over her. "I think you and that video just made finding the smuggler one hundred times harder."

She planted her hands on her hips and met Jake's stare, not willing to allow his size or his opinion to intimidate her. "I think . . ." She stood a little taller. "Correction. I *know* that video just saved my home and my business. If I don't pay my debts, the smuggler can buy Holly Grove from the bank after she's repossessed."

"Holly Grove is a house, not a person."

"I know that."

He leaned in closer, and his breath brushed her face. "You said she."

"Yes, I did." Holly broke her stare with Jake to sweep the kitchen, the heart of Holly Grove, with a glance. "This place is more than brick and wood." She sighed and looked down at the cypress planks. "These were new and shiny one hundred fifty years ago. Now they're etched with the patina of the lives of everyone I've ever loved. They all loved Holly Grove, too." She looked back at Jake. "She keeps us together."

"How do you feel about her moonlighting as a front for drug smuggling?"

"That's a ridiculous question. I just told you she's everything to me."

"What do you want, Holly? A ghost story or a real story, as in front-page news about the end of a drug ring?"

"Is that what this is about? You're mad because I made getting your story harder?"

"My story? I'm going to sleep like a baby when I get back to New York. Will you be able to sleep at night, knowing your very profitable B & B is a front for a drug-smuggling organization? Yeah, it's my story, but it's your problem, sweetheart. I'm here to help, but you don't make it easy."

"I never asked you for anything except free publicity, which I traded for, anyway, and I don't need that anymore."

"Are you suggesting I move out?" His jaw twitched as he stared her down.

She'd begged him to stay once, and she'd never do that again. "I—I didn't say that."

The house phone blared for the tenth time that morning, and she'd made a reservation with each call. Was Jake right? Had she sacrificed Holly Grove for money?

Jake collapsed on the sofa in Sam's office at the *Gazette*. Holly drove him nuts. He'd used every ounce of restraint he could muster to keep from exploding. Why couldn't she see how the kind of publicity she'd garnered was a problem?

She wanted Holly Grove to be successful so badly, she'd do anything. He was sure of that now. His gut told him she wasn't involved in the smuggling, but should he trust his instincts when she was doing everything possible to make it more difficult to catch the smugglers?

Jake groaned. The only solution was to do what he was paid to do, no matter how difficult. The sooner he caught the scumbags, the sooner Holly would be cleared of any suspicion.

"What's with the long face?" Sam barked from behind his desk as he shuffled through a stack of mail.

"Women."

"Say no more."

Jake rubbed the knot on the back of his head. "Toss me that bottle of aspirin you keep in your drawer."

"She gives you a headache, huh?"

"I'll say. Holly hit me over the head with a skillet." Not to mention, she'd orchestrated a circus at Holly Grove, with a ghost as the ringmaster.

"You probably deserved it." Sam pitched Jake the bottle.

"She thought she was hitting a burglar." He popped two pills in his mouth and plopped down in the oak chair across from Sam's desk.

"And why would she think that?" Sam asked as he settled back in his chair.

"I was milling around in the dark. My fault." Sam didn't need to know everything.

Jake's phone buzzed with an e-mail alert. He fished his phone out of his pocket. ICE had sent the finger-print results. He sat up straight to read the fingerprint report. "Burl's prints were on the bags."

"No surprise there."

"Holly's prints matched the third set of prints on the bags."

"Not to say, 'I told you so,' but I told you so, son."

"I'd expected that. Since then, I've watched her hand plastic bags to Nelda to bag her pralines. Burl could have asked for a few plastic bags, and she would have put her prints on any empty bags she gave him."

"Will ICE buy that?"

"If I do my job, they will."

He continued reading the report. The other print, the one with the scar across the thumb, matched Mackie's thumbprint from a DUI arrest twenty years ago. The coffee in Jake's stomach felt like acid. How did Mackie's print get on that bag if Burl left the dope there before he died? How did Mackie know it was there?

"Well?" Sam said, peering over his glasses. "What about the other prints?"

Jake blew out a sigh. "Any idea how Mackie's prints got on the bags?"

"That old fool. I don't have a clue why he'd be fingering that stuff. Why wouldn't he just call me and tell me where it was?"

Jake grunted. "Whiskey makes a man do strange things."

He read on to find Mackie's military records. Jake's throat tightened as he flipped through page after page of commendations, including a Purple Heart. Mackie had been a Navy SEAL in Vietnam, and he'd never mentioned any of this. Jake had assumed Mackie had been a grunt in the army and had done just enough to get by. A loser. That was how Jake had known his dad.

Jake told Sam about what he'd learned about Mackie, then asked, "Did you know about this?"

Sam scratched his head like that'd make the facts

sink in. "He never said a word about it. If he had, I'd have put it in the paper."

The guy Jake had struggled with last night hadn't fought back. Even a sixty-eight-year-old former Navy SEAL would remember how to pack a punch, but he hadn't thrown one.

Chapter 23

"Looking for something?" Jake asked, standing in the doorway of his room.

Holly jumped, whirled around, and faced him with her mouth open and her hand at her neck. She wore jeans and a T-shirt with DOMESTIC DIVA printed in pink across the front and stood in front of the open armoire in his room. "No."

"Jumpy much?" He had no doubt she was looking for something. With her nose for trouble, that wasn't a good thing. He strode across the room to her.

"I—I came in to clean." She glanced around the room. "But it looks like Nelda beat me to it."

"I told Nelda not to clean my room."

"Housekeeping is part of our deal." She plucked a feather duster from her cleaning basket on the floor and waved it in the air. "It comes with the room."

"You both have enough to do."

She pointed to his bag. "You didn't unpack."

"Nope." Luckily, he'd taken his gun with him when he left. "And you were snooping."

"But you'll be here all month." She stared at the bag, zipped tight and ready to go. Just like Jake liked it.

He shrugged. "It never occurred to me to unpack."

"Of course, it wouldn't. . . ." She picked up her cleaning basket and hooked it over her arm. "And you don't want us to clean your room, because you don't want us snooping around. Is that true?"

"Nope. Nothing to hide. You saw everything because you snooped, right?"

"Fine. Clean your own room, and while you're at it, clean up your attitude. I got enough of that this morning."

He blew out a heavy breath. "About this morning . . . I was having a bad day."

More like a bad month. It'd been too long since he'd lived as himself in his own skin. He didn't like lying to Holly. It turned him inside out.

"I know what you mean. I've had a few of those." Holly gave a halfhearted grin. "Or maybe a hundred."

"I shouldn't have taken my history with Mackie out on you. I went back to his trailer. It didn't look like he'd been there. The keys to Holly Grove weren't there, either."

"His place was a mess. Maybe you just couldn't find them."

"Trust me, they're not there." And worse, he couldn't tell her ICE had found Mackie's prints on the goods. "Did you find Burl's keys?"

"Yes, and I don't think anyone could have used them. The hangar was locked. His office was locked, and the desk drawer where I found the keys was locked. Oh, and I had to disable the alarm to get into the hangar. Evidently, a man smuggling drugs needs serious security."

"So no one used Burl's keys"—Jake cocked a brow—"unless Burl made copies and gave them to someone."

She shook her head. "They haven't made the master key for the historic lock I have here for nearly a hundred years. I couldn't get a copy if I wanted one without removing the lock and sending it away to an antique lock specialist."

That left Mackie's keys. *Great.* "Okay, that means the guy I pinned last night has Mackie's keys." Jake replayed the struggle over and over in his mind, hoping for a glimpse of the guy. Nothing. The only thing that stood out was the smuggler's lack of aggression. It had to be Mackie.

"Do you think Mackie could have used the keys last night?" she asked, as though she'd read his thoughts.

"The only way to find out is to find dear old Dad."

"So you don't think he's just off on a drunk anymore?"

"I wouldn't count that out, but I've already been to every bar within a thirty-mile radius."

"Have you checked the hospitals?"

Jake nodded. "The morgue, too. The sheriff has a missing persons bulletin out on him, and every woman in Delta Ridge in need of a handyman is looking for him."

Holly sighed. "If the Deltas can't find him, he's not in St. Agnes Parish."

"I'll put a full-page ad in the next *Gazette*, offering a reward for finding him. Someone has to know something."

"The last time I saw him, he'd cleaned out Burl's

hangar and storage container. He looked better than usual."

"You mean sober."

"No, but—"

"How long ago was this?"

"A month. Maybe less. I can check my calendar. Mackie cleaned the hangar a few days before I posted an online ad to lease the place."

"You may have been the last person to see him. I'd like to take a look around Burl's hangar. There may be a connection between Burl and Mackie there."

"Sure. I've got to meet guests at the airstrip at four. You can look around then." Holly nibbled on her bottom lip and eyed Jake. "I still can't help but wonder if someone came to his trailer and got him. What if something really bad happened to him?"

"Not Mackie. He's too tough," Jake said with bravado, because he couldn't go there. "He doesn't want to be found, and I want to know why."

According to Burl, the drug drop had to be in October, and there were only a couple of weeks left in the month. Holly punched in the security code, 1001, to enter the side door of the hangar so Jake could look around.

"Pretty easy code for a drug smuggler's lair," Jake said as he brushed the small of her back.

"Ten-oh-one, October first." She slid the key in the lock and opened the door. "It was our anniversary. Burl forgot it one year, so I set the code as a reminder."

Jake winced. "That had to hurt."

Holly forced a self-conscious laugh to hide the

sting of the memory. "Just history. He still forgot my birthday."

Jake followed her into the massive metal building. "August twelfth." His voice echoed off the vacant walls like a blast from the past.

Holly caught her lip between her teeth. "I can't believe you remember my birthday."

Jake tapped his temple and grinned. "Steel trap, sweetheart." His footsteps sounded through the empty room. "Wow. This place is big enough for a couple of birds."

"Yeah. I wish I could rent it. I've had only two bites. The environmental guys from New Orleans never called back, but the sheriff may lease it if he can get the parish to spring for a helicopter." Holly plopped her purse down on a counter. "I'm not holding my breath."

"Do you have the name of the environmental company?"

"Yeah. I have a card somewhere." She dug through her purse. "What if they were shopping the hangar for smuggling? I do have a nice airstrip and lots of storage."

"Don't get carried away. They didn't rent the hangar."

Holly handed him the card. "Yet."

"I'll check them out. If you hear from them, let me know."

"If they're not smugglers, the hangar is still for rent." She pushed a button on the wall in the cavernous space, and chains rattled as the huge hangar door cranked open.

A plane buzzed in the distance. Jake jacked a thumb skyward. "Your guests?"

Holly tilted her head upward. "Our suspects."

"Two of thousands."

"Okay. I got carried away, but these folks had reservations before the 'Ghost in the Grove' video hit the Web."

"And who else had pre-ghost-mania reservations?"

"Very funny." Holly folded her arms over her chest. "A couple honeymooning and a guy by the name of Dunbar. I only have six rooms to rent, so three may have been attracted to the ghost, but that's a good thing."

"How do you figure?"

"We can eliminate them."

"But you can't be sure."

"Well, no, but it hasn't been that hard to figure out who's on the up-and-up." She shrugged. "I mean really. Did you think the group in for their sixty-year class reunion was here to pick up drugs?"

Jake chuckled. "Painkillers, maybe. I see your point, but it's not going to be as easy as you think."

"We'll see." She handed Jake a set of keys. "These will open anything around here."

"I'll lock up and walk back to Holly Grove to meet the suspects." He winked at Holly.

"Good luck."

When Holly stepped out of the hangar, Dog growled. She jumped, even though she knew Jake had tied her to a fence post on the side of the building. "Jeez, Dog. I'm not the bad guy."

A small plane banked overhead as it positioned for landing. She shielded her eyes from the sun and watched the plane touch down on the far end of the runway, then taxi toward her.

Heart drumming with anticipation, she walked across the field to stand beside her Tahoe. If she were running a drug-smuggling ring, she'd use a plane. Lord knows, organized crime could afford a plane. The reservations were under the names Toni Bolla and Duke Fontana. Mob names, if she'd ever heard them.

The plane rolled to a stop as the engines throttled down. The propellers spun in a blur before slowing to a clip, revealing a red ring of paint on each blade. The plane wasn't new but had been pimped out with black and red pinstripes and a logo that would look at home on Hugh Hefner's plane. Perched on the plane's tail fin, the black silhouette of a well-endowed woman with her hair perpetually caught in the wind caught Holly's eye. Under the silhouette was the plane's name, *Fly Baby.*

Mercy, could it get any sleazier?

A woman with a head full of Bergdorf blond hair and wearing four-inch pink stilettos stepped out of the plane. She looked about twenty-five, wore skintight jeans, and had legs that stretched nearly up to her armpits. Miss Legs carried a purple alligator purse and a pink train case, filled with make-up, no doubt.

As soon as her heels hit the concrete, she pulled a long pencil-thin cigarette from her purse. "Oh, my God. You can't smoke anywhere anymore."

"Toni?" Holly said, guessing.

"Toni Bolla." She extended a hand with pink, sparkly nails. "I hope I can smoke at Holly Grove."

"Outside, on the balcony."

Toni flicked a silver lighter over the tip of the cigarette, then blew a funnel cloud of smoke. "That's okay. Duke won't let me smoke in the room, anyway.

Doc made him quit." She thumped an ash. "Now he hates it."

A guy at least twice Toni's age stooped as he exited the plane. Man fur curled around the collar of his extra-large Hawaiian shirt. He held a bottle of champagne in each hand. "You want I should bring some bubbly, fly baby?"

Fly baby? Oh, my. Was Toni the logo model?

"We can drink in the room, right?" she said to Holly.

"Sure," Holly said.

Duke tucked a bottle under his arm and shook Holly's hand. "Are you the lady I talked to on the phone?"

"Holly Davis. Welcome to Holly Grove." She knew she was blabbering, but that was what she did when she didn't know what to say. What could she say? *Do you have a suitcase of money on board? Dope? Or are you just a sleazy kind of guy?*

"Glad you've got a truck. Fly baby can't pack light." He eyed Toni.

Holly called over her shoulder as she headed to her Tahoe, "I'll back up to the luggage compartment."

The Tahoe shook as Duke loaded it down with suitcases. Holly got out and walked around to the back of the Tahoe to help load the luggage.

Toni stood back and sucked on her cigarette. She didn't look like the kind of woman who'd risk breaking a nail.

The stainless-steel briefcase with a combination lock on it caught Holly's eye. Was it filled with money? Could she tell by lifting it? She reached in the airplane's hold for the case.

Duke covered her hand with his. "I'll get that."

"Mixing a little business with vacation time?" Holly asked, trying to be nonchalant.

He pulled the case from Holly's grip. "Look at Toni over there. She don't lift a finger. You could learn somethin' from her."

Holly wanted to learn something, all right. She wanted to learn what was in that locked briefcase.

CHAPTER 24

Car doors slammed across the grassy field, and Jake watched Holly drive away in her Tahoe. He couldn't see her guests through the darkened back windows, but the plane looked like money.

Dog jerked on her leash and barked at the Tahoe, as if she'd like to chew a wheel off.

Jake rubbed Dog's head, then untied her leash from around the fence post. "She's one of the good guys."

I think.

If he could find Mackie, could he explain how his prints got on those bags? Could he clear Holly? This assignment blew four ways to the wind.

Shielding his eyes from the glare, he studied the plane. When his gaze landed on the tail section, he did a double take. *Wowzer.* The playmate on the tail fin would make the plane's description easy. He squinted to make out the call numbers, then keyed them into his phone. He'd run a search later on the numbers and the guests.

Jake flipped Holly's key ring around on his finger. He'd found a lock for every key except one, a dull Yale padlock key. He had rummaged through file cabinets, desk drawers, and closets but hadn't found anything to link Burl or Holly Grove to smuggling, or Mackie, for that matter. ICE knew there were operations along the Mississippi River, but until Sam called in his tip, that was like catching the fifty-pound catfish everyone heard about but no one landed.

If the dope hadn't fallen out of the dummy, Jake wouldn't have jack as far as this investigation went. And the hard evidence he had was marked with his father's and Holly's fingerprints. He needed something to point him in another direction, because the leads he had couldn't be right.

Walking Dog around the metal building, he spotted a small railroad container, covered in vines and barely visible, butted up to the fence line. Tall grass whipped around his jeans as he approached the container. A Yale padlock dangled from a rusty metal eye. He fingered the padlock key. "Be the match, baby."

Dog sniffed around the container and tugged against her leash as Jake tried to insert the key.

"Dog. Be still." Jake needed two hands to get the key in the lock. He towed Dog to a nearby sapling, then tied her to it.

Dog whined and pulled against her leash.

"You don't know how lucky you are. You could still be under Mackie's trailer, chewing on an empty sack of dog food."

Sunlight glinted off the shiny lock next to the rusty metal eye on the container. New lock. From the invasion of the vines, it was clear that the container had been parked there for years. Why a new lock? Jake eyed the dull key, then shoved it in the lock, anyway. It didn't budge, but that didn't surprise him. One more reason there was something inside that he needed to see.

Jake fished his cell phone out of his pocket and dialed Holly. "Hey, the padlock key doesn't work. It looks like the lock is new. Do you have a newer key?"

"Oh, I forgot. After Burl died, I was going through his stuff out there and his key wouldn't open the container. I got Mackie to cut the old lock off and replace it."

"What's in the container?"

"Mackie cleaned it out. He said it was a bunch of junk."

Mackie again. "Why would Burl keep junk hidden away under lock and key?"

"Who knows why Burl did anything? I'll bring you the key as soon as I check in the guests."

"See you in a few." Jake shoved his phone in his pocket and walked around the container. *Junk. Yeah, right.*

The container was built like a brick outhouse and was anchored on a concrete slab. If he hadn't been looking for an outbuilding with a padlock, he would have never noticed it. No way that it wasn't short-term storage for narcotics, and unless Mackie had steam-cleaned the place, there would be trace evidence.

Dog let out a sharp bark and wagged her tail. Footsteps crunched on the dry grass behind Jake.

"Yoo-hoo."

He looked over his shoulder to find Miss Alice tromping through the weeds, wearing white tennis shoes and a black jogging suit.

"There you are," she said. "Here's the key. Holly got tied up."

Jake took the key. "Thanks. You didn't have to walk all the way out here."

"Nelda told me you didn't eat breakfast this morning."

"Uh . . . no." And why would Nelda or Miss Alice notice or care?

Dog broke free of the sapling and bolted for Miss Alice. Jake lunged for Dog's leash but missed.

"Dog!"

"Sit," Miss Alice shouted with the command of a drill sergeant.

Dog skidded to a stop.

Miss Alice patted her on the head. "Good, Dog."

"How did you do that?"

"Bacon. She'll do anything for bacon."

"You trained her."

"Stay," she said to Dog. "She needed social skills, since your father didn't teach her any." She looked Jake up and down. "I'm not surprised."

One more peck on the head. "Social skills are over-rated. Dog is supposed to be a watchdog."

"A watchdog won't bite the hand that feeds her, and I give her bacon every morning." Miss Alice marched up to Jake and felt his forehead. "Were you having nausea?"

"No. Why?"

"Dizziness?"

"No."

"More swelling?"

He rubbed the back of his head. "Oh, the bump."

"Let me see." She pulled his head down to take a look.

"You hiked all the way out here to check a bump on my head," he said, looking at his knees as he stooped.

"You didn't eat." She released his head. "You'll live, no thanks to Holly. That girl is a train wreck. The whole town knows it."

"And why is it the whole town's business?"

"You ought to know. Who do you think watched out for you when your daddy couldn't?"

"I watched out for myself."

"You think Sam gave you that job at the paper because he needed help? You needed to be kept off the streets for your own good."

"Look, Miss Alice, I appreciate Sam giving me a job back then, but I earned every penny I squeezed out of him. He paid me a salary that probably wouldn't come to minimum wage during the Depression for all the hours I worked."

"You think your B average got you a college scholarship? Sam knew better than to give a kid like you too much money. He invested the rest of your wages and added his own money for your so-called scholarship."

Jake's stomach pinched in a gotcha grip. The job. The scholarship. Not only had Sam believed in Jake, but he'd also invested in him. Sam had told Jake he wanted him to come back and run the paper one day.

"There's nothing I don't know that happens in this town, and contrary to gossip, I can keep a secret."

Jake looked at the key in the palm of his hand, then back at Miss Alice.

Miss Alice narrowed her eyes at Jake. "And what are you doing, snooping around Burl's hangar, anyway?"

Rhett yapped as Holly answered the front door. For once, it didn't squeak. Jake must have fixed it.

A couple tangled in a passionate kiss, oblivious to her presence, stood on the porch. Holly gawked, not knowing what to do and thinking they'd come up for air any minute.

They didn't.

Wondering why Rhett had stopped barking, she glanced down at him.

Rhett tilted his head from side to side, then sat and watched. *Jeez.*

The guy wore a black baseball cap, and the young woman wore a white baseball cap. Both caps were on backward, to optimize kissing, Holly supposed. *How sweet . . .*

"We used to be like that," Burl said over Holly's shoulder.

His words iced her warm thoughts. She'd thought she loved Burl once, and look what that got her.

Rhett sniffed at Burl's pants leg, then snorted and pranced away. Holly wished she could walk away from Burl every time he ruined a moment.

"Ahem," she said, opening the door a little wider.

Burl folded his arms over his chest. "Spoilsport."

The couple startled and turned to Holly. The woman flipped her white cap around and adjusted her long, brown ponytail. The word *bride*, blazing in gold glitter, decorated the front of her cap.

"Sorry." She wrapped her hands around the man's arm. "We just got married."

Holly pointed to the cap. "I see. Congratulations."

The man tipped his matching groom's hat. "Mr. and Mrs. Charlie Lusco," he announced, beaming at his bride.

"Mickey Lusco," the bride said as she waved a pale hand. She wore a silver wedding band.

"We have reservations." Charlie leaned into his bride and planted a quick peck on her lips, as though he couldn't get enough of her.

"Enjoy the honeymoon. It's the best part of marriage." Burl cut his look to Holly.

She ignored Burl. Opening the door all the way, Holly said, "I've been expecting you. Welcome to Holly Grove."

They didn't look like drug smugglers, which would give her more time to concentrate on Toni and Duke.

Mickey sauntered into the foyer, with Charlie behind her, carrying their suitcases. She stopped short in front of Eudora's coffin. Pressing her hand over her mouth, as though suppressing a gasp, she turned to her husband. He stood motionless, staring at the coffin. The two exchanged a look that struck Holly as odd, maybe suspicious.

Burl propped his elbow on Eudora's coffin. "Guess the lovebirds weren't expecting a coffin in their love nest."

Holly brushed her suspicions aside as she joined the couple near the coffin. "Maybe you didn't realize it, but you've come to Holly Grove during the Haunted Pilgrimage," Holly said to break the odd silence. "As part of the tour, we dress Holly Grove for mourning."

"Mourning? You mean, like, death?" Mickey said, crinkling her turned-up little nose.

"Well, not real death." Holly lifted the coffin lid. "Eudora is a dummy. See?"

The honeymooners exchanged another odd glance.

Charlie set the suitcases on the floor. He pointed to the coffin. "You do this every year?"

"Every October." Holly grabbed a Holly Grove newsletter from a stack on an Empire table. She handed it to Mickey. "We have lots of activities that go along with the Haunted Pilgrimage."

"Look, honey." Mickey held the newsletter in front

of her husband and pointed. "They have a psychic coming on Saturday. We can see our future."

"Um, we may be busy." He winked at Mickey and slid his arm around her waist. "I know our future, baby cakes."

Standing behind the honeymooners, Burl's brows shot up. "You better get this guy a room quick."

"I'll be right back with your room key and complimentary mint juleps." Holly walked to the kitchen. She gathered the registration card and pen, then plucked the key with the honeymoon tag from the drawer.

"Why are you putting them out there?" Burl said, trailing behind Holly as she made her way to the kitchen.

She rolled her eyes and blew out an exasperated breath. "Jeez, Burl. Honeymooners."

"You know I can't go out there."

"So?" Holly poured julep mix into two silver cups lined with mulled mint and crushed ice.

"Hey, I've been the entertainment all month. After the herd of geriatrics you've had sleeping in here, I deserve a little entertainment."

Holly's mouth dropped open. "Ew."

"What?" Burl said, holding his hands palms up, as if she should explain.

Holly shook her head. "You're hopeless."

With Burl at her heels, two mint juleps in hand, and guests registration cards in her pocket, she marched to the entrance hall. The honeymooners were kissing again. Holly stepped back around the corner and into the kitchen to give them a moment of privacy. Burl floated on into the entrance hall like the sleaze he was.

She placed the icy juleps on the counter and leaned a hip against the wall. They were going to be busy, all right. Too busy to smuggle drugs? Maybe she was overly suspicious.

But Burl was right. They needed a room and quick. A smile teased Holly's lips. They'd love the honeymoon treatment she'd given the room earlier. Rose petals on the bed. Massage oil. Bubble bath. Chilled champagne. She might never have another honeymoon, but at least she could do her part to make sure her honeymooners had the best.

Holly peeked around the door to see if it was safe to go into the foyer.

They weren't there.

Burl pointed to the coffin. "Check this out. I think we've found a winner."

Charlie and Mickey stood hidden, except for their legs, behind the open coffin.

Hearing whispers, Holly tiptoed around the coffin. Holly blinked, as though that would clear her vision. Bent over the coffin, the honeymooners were peeking under Eudora's dress as they whispered to each other.

Holly widened her stance and squared her shoulders. "Looking for something?"

CHAPTER 25

The fight-or-flight mechanism roared to life in Holly. She'd just confronted smugglers, and she was alone in the house.

Looking for something? What was she thinking? Okay, she was thinking about getting rid of Burl, but she should have kept quiet until Jake got back. *Dumb. Dumb. Dumb.*

The honeymooners straightened from looking in the coffin and stared at Holly, then looked at each other.

"Just checking out the dummy in the coffin," Charlie said.

Holly pointed a shaky finger at Eudora. "Under her skirt?"

The front door opened, and Jake strode into the foyer like a white knight.

Burl groaned. "You give him a little attention, and the bozo doesn't even knock."

Holly rushed to Jake's side. "They were looking under Eudora's dress," she said, pointing to Charlie and Mickey.

Jake's brows slammed together; then he eyed the honeymooners. "You want to tell me what's going on?"

"Look, man." Charlie held his hands up. "It's nothing."

Mickey straightened Eudora's dress. "This is embarrassing."

"We made a little bet." Charlie draped an arm over Mickey's shoulder and grinned.

Mickey gave a sheepish look. "He bet me the dummy wasn't wearing panties."

"And I won, didn't I, baby cakes?" Charlie said, giving Mickey a squeeze.

"We didn't know we weren't supposed to touch," Mickey said.

Jake wiped his hand over his face, but Holly saw a shadow of a grin.

He's buying this. I can't believe it.

Burl spewed laughter and pointed at Holly. "Gotcha, again, Blondie."

"That's just wrong," Holly blurted to Burl without thinking. "A lifetime isn't a long enough curse for you. A thousand years wouldn't be enough."

Mickey buried her face in Charlie's shirt.

"Now look what you've done on our wedding night!" Charlie said, patting his sobbing bride.

"A thousand-year curse for touching a dummy." Jake paced across the front porch as the honeymooners walked to their cottage. Miss Alice was right. Holly was a train wreck, and she'd wreck this bust or get herself killed if he didn't control her. "What were you thinking?"

Holly perched on the edge of a wicker sofa and swung

a crossed leg, bouncing her hoop skirt up and down. "I don't know." She lifted a shoulder. "It was the first thing that popped into my head."

Jake blew out an exasperated breath.

"I told them I was kidding," she said, fidgeting with the buttons on her dress.

"Charlie wasn't laughing. Mickey evidently believes in ghosts and curses and all that mumbo jumbo."

"What was I supposed to say? 'Gee. I thought you were looking for your stash. Sorry.'"

Jake leaned against the porch rail and folded his arms. "You weren't supposed to say or do anything without talking to me."

"But—"

"But nothing." Jake paced again.

"What was I supposed to think when I saw them peeking under Eudora's skirt?"

"Think this. You're not a cop or Nancy Drew."

Holly stood and marched over to Jake. "Think this." She wagged a finger in his face. "I'm in the best position to figure out who the smuggler is. I clean the guests' rooms every day. I eat with them. We talk. And I see them come and go. If I see something suspicious, I'm doing something about it."

"What you're doing is complicating things, and it may get you hurt or worse."

"But—"

"The whole idea is to figure out who the smuggler is without them knowing, so we can catch them in the act."

Holly plastered her hands on her hips. "Stop interrupting me."

"Then say something I want to hear."

She lifted her chin. "I think I know who the smuggler is."

"Not Mickey and Charlie?"

"I may have gotten a little off track with them," she said as she pushed a curl behind her ear.

"May have?"

"Okay. I messed up, but I really think I have something this time. Do you know how to pick a lock?"

"Maybe. Why?"

Her eyes sparked with excitement. "You haven't met the guests I picked up at the airstrip yet. Just wait till you see them."

"I saw the plane."

"Have you ever seen anything like it?" she said, as she settled in the swing at the end of the porch.

"Can't say I have."

"They match the plane, if you know what I mean." She pushed off with her foot. "Toni Bolla—she's not a guy, by the way—and Duke Fontana."

"Let's not jump to any conclusions this time."

She raised a finger. "They had a stainless-steel briefcase with a lock on it."

"Most briefcases have a lock."

"Yeah, but he wouldn't let me touch it. I bet it's filled with cash to make the transaction. We've got to get in there."

An unlawful search and seizure could blow his chances of making a bust stick. Not to mention that he could be breaking into an innocent person's private property. "You know about surveillance, don't you?"

"Sure. I watch detective shows."

"No drama. Just watch and report. No breaking into

briefcases or confronting a guest if they do something that you think is suspicious. Watch and report to me. That's all. Can you do it?"

She put her foot down and stopped the swing. "But—"

"No buts. I don't want anything to happen to you."

Her look said it all. She couldn't be trusted to follow directions or stay out of trouble.

"You think the undertaker puts drawers on folks 'fore he buries 'em?" Nelda asked as she helped Holly wrangle a pair of pantaloons on Eudora. "Ain't nobody gonna see 'em."

"I'd never thought about it until the honeymooners decided to take a peek under Eudora's skirt." And Burl had made her look like an idiot in front of Jake and the honeymooners. Now Jake thought her imagination was in overdrive, and he didn't trust her judgment or her suspicions. *A locked stainless-steel briefcase. Come on. Who wouldn't be suspicious?*

Nelda shook her head, and her garlic necklace swung. "All folks care about is what shows on the outside, anyhow."

Holly tugged Eudora's stuffed leg through a pantaloon leg. "You're right about that."

If Jake didn't want her to do anything, fine. What he didn't know or couldn't see wouldn't hurt him.

"So why we tusslin' with Eudora to put pantaloons on her?"

"Because now I know she needs them, even if no one else can see them."

"Humph. Guess you shoulda buried Burl in starched shorts." Nelda slapped her hands together. "Heavy starch to give him a rash till kingdom come, 'cause he deserves it."

Holly giggled. "No. Flaming red jockeys, three sizes too small."

"You right." Nelda stomped and covered her mouth as she laughed. "That'd cramp his style." She stopped short, then jerked her head to look over her shoulder. "He ain't up in here right now, is he?"

Holly shook her head. "Thank God."

"Amen to that. I done had enough of that ghost."

"Me too." Whatever it took, she was catching the smugglers. She needed to get Burl a one-way pass through the pearly gates, whether he deserved it or not and whether she did it Jake's way or not.

Nelda pulled Eudora's other leg through the pantaloons. "Maybe we can get Eudora some glass feet for next year and some shoes."

"If we keep getting reservations and tour buses, we'll get Eudora a whole new outfit for next year." Holly pulled Eudora's dress in place, then turned to Nelda. "And a big raise for you."

Nelda's face cracked into a toothy grin. "Thanks to boob tube."

"YouTube." Holly laid Eudora out in the coffin for viewing, then closed the lid and gave it a little pat.

"I don't care what you call it." Nelda picked up a dust cloth and passed it across the coffin. "I was startin' to think Holly Grove wasn't gonna make it long enough for me to win my big skillet, especially since that tax bill came. Then boob tube got 'em callin'."

"I told you plantations with ghosts draw a bigger crowd. Even the small ones, like Holly Grove."

"But you don't want Burl round forever. What if you get rid of your ghost? Then what?"

"It doesn't matter. Once a plantation is known as haunted, it will always be considered haunted."

"That's what I call job security." Nelda tossed the dust cloth over her shoulder.

Holly caught a whiff of garlic and stepped back.

"I was feeling a little worried 'bout makin' you get that psychic and wonderin' if I'd done the right thing. I mean, she might be able to get Burl outta here."

"I never really believed in that stuff." Holly lifted a shoulder. "But then again, I never believed in ghosts until Burl came back."

"Humph." Nelda picked up her bucket of cleaning supplies and ambled toward the kitchen. "I believe it. I believe it all."

"Are you coming back for the séance tomorrow night?"

"You ain't got a raise big enough for me to come back up in here for some lady to call up ghosts," Nelda said, never breaking her pace.

"Nelda," Holly called.

Nelda turned around and bumped the swinging door open with her generous backside.

"Thanks for staying with me." Holly fidgeted with her hands, trying to say the right thing. "I know the ghost thing is difficult for you."

"You ask that psychic if I'm gonna win my big skillet." She turned, then jerked back, grinning. "And how big my raise is gonna be."

The kitchen door flapped closed behind Nelda and muffled her laugh.

Holly sucked in a deep breath. She couldn't manage without Nelda, and if the business kept growing, they'd need more help. She hated to admit it, but Jake had been right about the publicity. It was hard enough to keep the guests fed, their rooms clean, and to run tours every morning and afternoon, much less pick out a smuggler. Much more business and she'd be too successful to sleep. But that was a good thing. The only thing better would be if she could nail the smugglers and get Burl out of her hair.

The low ring of the house phone sounded from the kitchen, followed by Nelda's voice. Moments later, she busted through the kitchen door and thundered up to Holly. The whites of Nelda's eyes bulged around her black pupils. "You ain't gonna believe it."

CHAPTER 26

Nelda opened her mouth, but nothing came out. Holly had known her all her life and had never known her to be speechless. Nelda nodded her head toward the kitchen. She looked like she'd seen a ghost.

Ghost. Ire inched up Holly's back. If Burl was tormenting Nelda again, she'd, she'd . . . *Crapola.* She couldn't do squat to him. "Did Burl do something to you?"

She shook her head.

Holly remembered Nelda had answered the phone. Visions of accidents, death, and disaster whirled through her mind. "What is it, then?"

"S-she's on the phone."

"Who?"

Nelda's face melted from shock to awe. "Sylvia Martin." She said the name like it should mean something important. Her lips spread in a smile.

Holly searched her mind for a Sylvia Martin. "Who's that?"

Nelda released Holly's hands and blew out a breath

like Holly didn't know who the president was. "That lady from *Inquiring Minds.*"

"*Inquiring Minds?*"

"You know. Sunday nights."

"What about Sunday nights?"

"*Inquiring Minds.*"

Holly felt like she was trapped in *Groundhog Day.* "Okay. Slow down and start from the beginning. Is anyone hurt or dead?"

"No, but last week on *Inquiring Minds,* there was this man who could drive nails in his hands, and it didn't hurt," she said, as though Holly should be impressed.

"Huh?"

"And the week before that, there was a man who got sucked up in a spaceship and lived to tell it." Nelda shoved her hands on her hips. "She seen our ghost on boob tube and wants to do a story on Holly Grove." Nelda yanked Holly's arm. "Hurry up. She's a TV star, and she called all the way from New York City. She ain't got time to wait on you to get yourself to the phone."

Holly followed Nelda into the kitchen and picked up the landline. "Hello."

"Ms. Davis," a pitch-perfect voice purred on the other end. "I'm so glad I caught you. My producer has been e-mailing you all day. I guess you've been out of touch."

"Busy." Holly propped herself against the ceramic counter and twirled the cord of the outdated phone around her finger. "I haven't had a chance to check my e-mail since this morning." *Or change clothes or eat.*

"I'd love to do a show on the ghost in the grove. We'll need three rooms for this weekend."

"I'm sorry. I don't have three rooms available." Which was a welcome first.

"I'll make it worth your while."

"It's not that. The rooms are all reserved. With the Haunted Pilgrimage and the YouTube video, I've been swamped."

"Surely you have something. Do you realize the publicity this will generate for your B & B?"

Holly paced, tethered by the phone cord. YouTube had stirred up business, but not everyone surfed the Internet. Everyone watched TV. "Well, I do have one room with a loft. It's a bit rustic, though."

"I realize Holly Grove isn't a five-star hotel."

Holly brushed off the sting of Sylvia's comment. "I don't think you understand."

"My producer will handle the details. I'm thrilled you want to be on *Inquiring Minds*. See you on the thirtieth."

The phone clicked.

"Hello?" Holly pulled the phone away from her ear and stared at it. "She hung up."

"She comin'?"

"Looks like she'll be here on Halloween weekend. We'll have to clean up Abe's cabin for her."

Nelda gawked at Holly. "You puttin' a TV star in that place?"

"I tried to tell her it wasn't our luxury suite."

Nelda trotted to the pantry. "What am I gonna cook? I ain't never cooked for a TV star before."

"Don't worry about that. She probably weighs ninety pounds and is a vegan."

"Vegan?"

"They don't eat meat."

"Humph. She ain't had my fried chicken."

"Since you're going to be so busy with the gumbo competition and cooking for a full house, I'll clean the rooms outside the main house, too." That would give Holly every opportunity to investigate all her guests' personal belongings for anything suspicious.

"Fine by me. I'd rather cook than clean any day."

"Are you coming to the séance now?"

"Not on your life."

"But you said you watch *Inquiring Minds* all the time."

"I ain't never heard of nobody reachin' through a TV and gettin' somebody. I'll be watchin' from my La-Z-Boy, where it's nice and safe."

"I think we should keep our new guest a secret until she arrives." Smugglers probably wouldn't be too keen on TV cameras if they knew they were coming.

"Why?"

"I want it to be a big surprise. Everyone loves surprises." Except Jake. He wouldn't like this one bit.

"I know you said you didn't want to go to heaven, but you're going if I have to escort you myself," Holly said as Burl floated through the bedroom door of the Longfellow suite.

The lights on the brass gasolier flickered. Burl looked up and grinned like he'd invented electricity. "Damn. I'm getting good."

"You flickered lights." Holly snatched the black fabric cross of mourning from the canopy bed. "Big deal."

"You bet your sassy little heinie it's a big deal. I blinked the lights every time the tour group entered a different room."

"Okay." She folded the fabric in a tight square. "So you've got the tourists whipped into a frenzy."

"It's what you wanted. Right?"

Holly stuffed the cloth in a hidden compartment of the fireplace mantel. "Yes, but I need you to spy on my guests. You can see things I can't. Like inside a locked stainless-steel briefcase."

"Blondie, I told you. I'm not ready to go to heaven," he said, trailing behind her.

Holly snatched the shammed pillows from the bed and smashed them under her arm. "I told you, you can't stay here."

"Do you realize I'm getting closer and closer to being whole? I can turn lights on and off, not just blow out candles. I put my handprint on a mirror, for crying out loud. If I stay long enough, I'll figure this out. And I'll be whole again."

Holly just stared at him. "No one can see you, Burl."

He cast a glance down his body, then poured a pleading look over her. "You can."

She smashed the extra pillows in an armoire. "And I don't want to."

Holly marched past Burl to the basket of pralines on the marble-topped bedside table. Holly placed one of Nelda's pralines in a crisp waxed-paper sleeve on the feather pillow on the bed.

Burl floated to her side. "You loved me once."

"And look what it got me." She picked up the basket of pralines and hooked it over her arm.

"Give me a chance, Blondie," he said, following her like a lovesick puppy around the bed.

"You had your chance. Now I'm on my own."

"I'm here for you."

Holly walked to the door, then turned to Burl. "I

have six more turndowns to do tonight. Can you do that?"

Burl squirreled his mouth to the side and looked away.

"I didn't think so." She grabbed the antique brass doorknob. "I have a business to run, and thanks to you, one of my guests is a criminal."

She flapped her free arm against her side. "Mr. Dunbar requested a room with a view of the river. That's why he's here in the Longfellow suite." She gestured toward the window. "Is he watching for a barge to push up onshore for a drop, or is he just like every other tourist enamored with the Mississippi?" Holly shrugged her shoulders. "I don't know. I can't see what he's doing in here, but you can."

Burl sliced his palm through the air in a flourish. "You think I'm just roving around this house all the time?"

"Where else can you go?"

"Hell if I know, but when I'm not here, it's like I don't exist. When I show up again, it's in a room with you or Nelda. I can't just drop in wherever I want to."

"You're telling me you can't take a peek in the rooms anytime you want?"

"Not exactly."

"What's not exactly?" She patted her foot. "And don't you dare bend, shade, or twist the truth one iota."

"I'm not lying. I swear to God." He cast a look upward. "And He's listening. I've been thinking about this. I know I have more energy when you're in the house and when people believe I'm here. Like Nelda. Or the people on the tours. They believe."

"Energy?"

"Yeah. When you leave the house or sleep, I lose my energy after a while, and *poof*"—he snapped both fingers—"I'm in that weird timeless hole until you come back."

"Surely you're not saying I give you energy."

Burl lifted a shoulder. "Maybe."

"That's ridiculous. Why do you fade out when I'm right here?"

"Good question." Burl fingered his chin. "How can I put this, Blondie?" He cocked a brow. "It's kind of like when a lucky guy kicks his boots under his best girl's bed."

Holly rolled her eyes, then yanked the door open. Everything was like bedroom rodeo to him. She huffed as she stomped down the stairs.

Burl trailed behind her. "It's like this. You may turn me on, but I'm good for only so long. And I can never predict how long."

"This is so like you. It has nothing to do with any of that stuff, and I have nothing to do with you being here. Period."

"Hey, you turn me on." He winked. "Always have."

"You screwed up your life single-handedly. Correction. You and the redhead screwed. The rest, you just screwed up solo."

"Let me make it up to you in this life."

"What life? You're a ghost. Besides, you couldn't make it up to me in ten lives."

"That's why I'm staying. I messed us up in my lifetime, but I have the rest of yours to make it right."

Chapter 27

No way would Holly give Burl the rest of her life. She'd do anything to get rid of him. Even hire a psychic. She groaned inwardly as Angel Dupree swept into the foyer. Her silky black hair floated across her shoulders as she turned to Holly.

"The spirit is with us," Angel whispered through crimson lips.

Holly blinked and looked at Burl. Maybe Angel *was* a real psychic. Excitement tingled through her. Could Angel get rid of Burl?

"Who the devil is this?" Burl asked, circling Angel. "And why is she whispering? I'm dead, not deaf."

"Can you see him?" Holly whispered, only because Angel had.

"No." Angel spun in the foyer. "I feel his presence."

"Bull," Burl said.

"The spirit is restless." Angel closed her eyes and tilted her flawless porcelain face upward. She lifted her hands, palms up. "Oh, spirit guide, come to me."

Burl looked from side to side and smirked. "Who's the spirit guide? I could use that dude."

Holly inched closer to Angel. "Do you think you can help me?"

Angel opened an eye. "Shh. I must take in the energy of the spirit to tap my psychic powers."

Holly tilted her head. *There's that energy thing again.*

"Help you?" Burl asked. "What's she talking about?"

Eyes closed, Angel lowered her head and clasped her hands together. "He's not yet accustomed to death."

Burl's lip curled into a sarcastic smirk. "Who gets used to death?"

"He feels alone." Angel opened her eyes. "Forgotten."

"I'll show her forgotten." Burl squinted as he stared at the 150-year-old gasolier. The lights flickered.

Angel smiled. "I have his attention." She turned to Holly. "Did Aunt Claireese tell you our fee?"

"Blondie, tell me you're not paying this sideshow to talk to me. You've got a direct line. What is she? A psychic marriage counselor?"

Angel touched Holly's arm. "Spirit chatter makes it hard to concentrate, doesn't it?"

Holly sucked in a sharp breath. "Can you hear him?"

"No. I sense his frustration, but I'll soon be able to connect on a higher level."

"Yeah. When she gets the money. She's playing you like a gambler with two deuces. Call her bluff, Blondie."

"How soon will you be able to hear him?" Holly asked.

"At the séance. Did Aunt Claireese explain our fee?"

Holly scrunched her brows together. "Aunt Claireese?"

"You spoke to her on the phone," Angel said as she meandered around the foyer.

"Oh," Holly mumbled. "I thought I'd spoken to you."

Angel ran a finger down the length of Eudora's coffin. "I'm Aunt Claireese's student."

Holly caught her lip between her teeth. "Is that like a psychic in training?"

"More like a con artist in training," Burl said.

"You could say that," Angel said as her gaze trailed up the staircase and lingered at the top.

"What's Elvira looking at?" Burl said, following her gaze.

Angel looked back at Holly. "I've had the power all my life, but Aunt Claireese is helping me connect with the spirits in a more controlled way."

"Is there an uncontrolled way?" Holly asked.

"Unfortunately, yes." A small sigh slipped from Angel's red lips. "Instead of me seeking out the spirits, they sought me." She shook her head. "Very troubling. They showed up whenever and wherever they wanted, and always wanted me to do something for them. They were ruining my life."

Holly had only one ghost. She couldn't imagine how wrecked her life would be with several. "So ghosts talk to you?"

"All the time, if they want something. Well, they did until Aunt Claireese taught me how to control my ability. It's like the real world. It's all about boundaries."

"So have you ever been able to, uh—"

"Help a ghost pass to the other side?" Angel finished Holly's sentence.

A little chill pricked the hairs on Holly's neck. Had Angel just read her mind?

"Yes, but sometimes it takes many contacts with the spirit to help them understand their destiny."

"And does each contact cost three hundred dollars?" Holly asked.

Angel's red lips smiled. "In advance."

"Aha," Burl blurted.

Holly's excitement flattened. "Any money-back guarantees?"

"Only that if I get your ghost to the other side, he won't come back."

If Angel was just a con artist, Holly wasn't going to be her unlucky sucker. "I'll give you your check before the séance. You've got one shot at Burl."

"Aunt Claireese said the room was complimentary."

"Yes," Holly said.

Burl shook his head. "Sucker."

Holly had no doubt Burl wasn't a mind reader, and neither was Angel.

Angel lifted a perfectly shaped dark brow. "And not in the main house."

"You'll be staying in the carriage house."

"Good. I wouldn't get a wink of sleep with all the spirits in this house."

"I have only one ghost."

"You only have one ghost who can communicate with you. I sense the presence of others."

"More than one ghost," Holly mumbled under her breath as she descended the exterior carriage house stairs. And she'd given the counterfeit psychic a complimentary room on top of three hundred hard-earned bucks. *I might as well have* LOSER *tattooed on my forehead.*

She looked up at the massive canopy of oak trees framed by a brilliant orange sky. Perfect for Halloween. Maybe Angel wasn't the real deal, but she'd put on a good Halloween show for the guests with Burl's help. And it was worth three hundred dollars to settle Nelda's nerves. Too bad it wasn't going to get her what she needed: Burl gone for good.

Holly blew out a sigh. She had work to do, if she was going to catch the smugglers. As crisp leaves tumbled with the wind across the side yard, Holly followed the brick path to the main house at Holly Grove.

Burl was convinced a shipment of drugs would arrive at Holly Grove during the thirty-day window of opportunity St. Peter had given him. And time was running out.

Heaviness settled in her heart. In only a week, Jake would leave.

When Holly neared the back of the main house, Nelda stepped onto the porch, with her purse on her shoulder. "What you think 'bout that psychic?"

"Not much."

"My cousin says Claireese cleared out a whole family of ghosts in a house in New Orleans."

"Claireese didn't come. She sent her niece, Angel."

"Maybe 'cause we only got one ghost."

"Maybe so," Holly said. She wasn't about to tell Nelda that Angel believed they had more than one.

A car door slammed, and Holly and Nelda turned toward the sound.

Holly's heart did a little two-step as Jake folded out of his rental car. He had the swagger of quiet confidence and wore jeans, boots, and a well-fitting black T-shirt. Nothing fancy, but he didn't need fancy.

"Mmm, mmm, mmm, that's one fine man," Nelda said, leaning in to Holly.

Holly swallowed. She hated to admit it, but she was going to miss way more than Jake's looks when he left.

He strode up the back steps and met them on the porch. He slipped his arm around Holly's waist and planted a quick peck on her cheek as naturally as though he'd been doing it for years.

Nelda patted her cheek and tilted it up to Jake. "You outta be kissin' me. I cooked your favorite tonight. Smothered chicken, field peas, corn bread, rice and gravy. Homemade chocolate pie, too."

Jake kissed Nelda on the cheek. "You're a woman after my heart."

"You somethin'." Nelda held a hand to her cheek and grinned. "It'll be good, if Holly don't burn it while she's heatin' it up."

"I'll supervise," Jake said, winking a dark eye at Holly.

"You do that." Nelda dug her car keys out of her purse. "See y'all tomorrow." She'd taken two steps before she turned around and looked at Holly. "I almost forgot. They's a man waitin' on the front porch for you. Said he called for a room for him and his wife and they was all rented out."

"Mr. Fletcher?"

"That's him. He brought his own room. Called it a motor coach. Says he wants to pay to plug it in. I think he's one of them ghost hunters."

Or a smuggler who didn't book before the boom at Holly Grove.

"You've talked to this guy?" Jake eyed Holly as Nelda ambled to her car.

"Yeah. He wanted a room this weekend. When I told him we were booked, he asked if I could put him on the waiting list." Holly almost giggled. If business stayed good, she could renovate the other rooms over the carriage house. "Waiting list. Can you believe I have a waiting list?"

"I can believe it. I told you the YouTube video would bring in the nuts."

"I'm not sorry about the video. I'm booked through Christmas because of it." She fidgeted with her nails to keep from facing Jake. "But I thought it would be much easier to spot the smugglers." And it would have been if Burl could pick them out. "I don't need any more guests as suspects, so I guess you were partially right."

"It's not about who's right." He stepped closer. "I know how much this place means to you, but it's only bricks and mortar. This isn't a game of Clue. I'm going to look out for your safety whether you like it or not."

"I can look out for myself. I need help figuring out who the smuggler is. If you want to do that, go for it." Holly turned and walked across the porch and entered the house through the kitchen. Jake followed her through the house to the front door.

He put his hand on the door. "What are you going to say to him?"

"Mr. Fletcher is mighty determined. What if he didn't expect all the rooms to be rented and is getting creative to—"

"Pick up the drop."

Holly nodded. "Looks like I have another pair of potential smugglers."

"Or paying guests." Jake opened the front door, and they stepped onto the porch.

A middle-aged man wearing a polo shirt and khakis stood waiting. He walked with a slight limp as he crossed the porch to Holly. He extended his hand. "Tom Fletcher. We talked on the phone."

Holly shook his hand, then turned to Jake. "This is Jake McCann. He's a guest here."

Jake shook Mr. Fletcher's hand.

"What can I do for you, Mr. Fletcher?" Holly said.

"Call me Tom, please." He took his Falcons baseball cap off, revealing a shock of salt-and-pepper hair.

Everything about the man screamed middle-class suburbs. She shot a look at Jake.

"Falcons fan, huh?" Jake said.

Tom turned the cap around to look at the dirty bird on the front. "You bet."

"We'll forgive you since you're just passing through Saints territory," Holly said, with a teasing smile.

"You from Atlanta?" Jake asked.

"There about." He pointed to the motor coach. "We've been driving across the South for a couple of weeks. The grandma is keeping the boys, so it's just us for a change." He slipped his cap on his head. "Anyway, we've been cooped up in that motor coach, and we'd hoped to spend the night in a plantation home while we were passing through. Since you're booked, I thought we'd do the next best thing and stay on the grounds. I'll be glad to pay a hookup fee."

"I don't have a hookup," Holly said. "But you can park on the grounds. Do you think sixty dollars is fair?"

"Is the tour included?" he said, reaching for his wallet.

"Sure."

Tom handed Holly three twenties. "Where do you want us to park?"

Holly pointed toward the carriage house. "On the other side of that building." She looked back at the motor coach. "You have a very nice motor coach there, but it doesn't exactly fit the time period."

"No problem."

"Just curious," Holly said. "Why did you want to stay here instead of the other plantations on the Haunted Pilgrimage?"

"My wife found this place on YouTube. Lately, she's been interested in the afterlife."

CHAPTER 28

Jake leaned back in the only chair at Holly Grove that he felt confident could hold his weight and assessed the guests around the dining-room table. According to a tip from an undercover agent upriver, 1.2 million dollars' worth of marijuana would be dropped off a barge after dark somewhere on the Mississippi within the next two days. There were 2,340 miles of Mississippi riverbank. The agent couldn't be sure where the drop would be, but Jake was betting his reputation on his faulty gut feeling that it would be on the riverbank at Holly Grove.

He sliced off a bite of his pork chop and put it in his mouth. Chewing slowly, he savored its taste. The mix of crunch and tender meat sent a comfort signal to his mind. Dinner was served from six to seven thirty, and he wanted to linger long enough to meet all the guests. Thanks to Nelda's good cooking, that wouldn't be a problem.

Holly popped in and out of the dining room to check the buffet and make introductions, which distracted the hell out of him. Her sweet Southern voice seeped into his consciousness like a lullaby.

Since he'd been focusing on the guests, Jake hadn't said much. He'd caught bits and pieces of conversations. Miss Alice had proved an unlikely ally by asking all the mundane questions as different guests joined them in the dining room.

He'd learned Mr. Dunbar was originally from New Orleans, but he'd been vague about what he did for a living and equally vague about why he was here. Jake didn't like the way he'd looked down at his plate every time he answered a question, either.

Angel was from a small bayou town south of New Orleans and near the coast. She could speak Cajun French and thought she could communicate with the dead better than the living. Though Jake didn't believe a word of it, Angel seemed to believe herself.

Tom and his wife, Kate, were from the Atlanta area, and he was a retired factory worker, though he seemed a bit young for retirement. Kate didn't do much of the talking. Sadness etched her face, until Miss Alice asked if she had children. Kate flashed pictures of boys dressed in Little League uniforms.

Charlie walked into the dining room like he'd been ridden hard and put up wet, looking the part of a man on his honeymoon.

"Would it be okay if I got our dinner to go?" Charlie asked Holly as she added another pan of hot corn bread to the buffet.

"How about room service?" Holly tucked a pot holder under her arm. "Just let me take care of a few things here."

Charlie scratched his head. "Nah. Mickey isn't, um . . . I'll just take ours on paper plates."

Holly's cheeks paled, as if Charlie had committed blasphemy. "It's your honeymoon." She wadded the pot holders up in her hand. "It's no trouble. I'll put your dinner on a nice tray, and then I'll set it at your door, knock, and leave. You won't see me, and I won't see you or Mickey."

"Okay, okay," Charlie mumbled.

"I'll knock with dinner in about fifteen minutes," she said, then marched into the kitchen.

Toni Bolla wiggled into the chair next to Jake and across from Miss Alice. "Are you saving this seat for me?" she asked, not waiting for the answer.

Jake half stood. He couldn't be sure, but Toni looked familiar. He'd seen her somewhere, though he couldn't recall meeting her—and she'd be memorable. She wore a hot pink dress that looked like she'd been melted into it. "Toni, right?"

"Toni with an *i*. That's me."

Jake waited for her to sit before he did.

Toni batted lashes too long to be real. "Aren't you the gentleman?"

Duke turned from the buffet. "Are you flirting again?"

"Who? Me?" Toni patted her chest.

Duke loaded a second pork chop on his plate. "Are you breathing?" He lumbered to the table with a plateful of food and a briefcase built like a small tank.

"Yeah. What about it?" Toni said.

"If you're breathing, you're flirting." Duke slid the briefcase between the chairs, then wedged himself in the seat next to Toni. He tilted his chin up in a macho nod to Jake.

"Don't be so jealous." She picked up her napkin and put it on her lap. "Relax. We're on vacation."

As if on cue, Miss Alice ground out her usual questions.

"He's from Jersey," Toni said, tilting her head toward Duke. "And I'm from Vegas. I'm in show business, and Dukie, he's—"

"Sales." Duke pointed a "shut up" look at Toni. He shoveled peas in his mouth, then sucked down some iced tea.

Holly hovered over Duke's shoulder, holding a pitcher of tea. She cast a pointed stare at the briefcase. Duke put the half-empty glass down, then cut into his pork chop. Holly filled Duke's glass with tea. She moved behind Toni to top off her tea, and Toni placed her hand over her glass.

"Honey, do you have anything stronger? Champagne maybe?" she said.

"Sorry," Holly said. "I don't have any champagne."

Toni circled a fingertip around the rim of her glass. "What about BYOB?"

"Sure."

"We'll make it a party." Toni clapped her hands together. "Dukie, baby, would you go get a couple of bottles?"

"Anything for you, fly baby."

That was it. Jake remembered the centerfold he'd seen pinned up in a gas station bathroom. She'd worn a flight captain's hat and brass wings dangling from a chain around her neck and nothing else. A dead ringer for Toni.

Duke stood and picked up his briefcase.

"I can put that in my safe, if you'd like," Holly said.

"No offense, but it's safer with me," Duke said.

Toni fluttered her pink nails through the air. "It's his security blanket."

"What do you have in there? Fort Knox?" Miss Alice asked.

Duke patted his briefcase. "Better."

Jake had given Holly a sisterly kiss good night and had told her she needed rest. She was exhausted, but that had nothing to do with what she needed.

Besides, how could she sleep, knowing any one of her guests could be at the river right now, unloading some sort of drugs? And, darn it, she wanted to know what was in Duke's briefcase.

Holly looked out over the levee from her second-floor balcony and pulled the patchwork quilt a little higher around her shoulders. She gave the glider swing another push with her bare foot.

The swing glided back and forth, and she folded her legs on the seat under her. Occasionally, the distant horn from a tugboat downriver punctuated the crickets' constant chorus.

Her eyes had adjusted to the darkness, allowing her to see the silhouettes of oak trees around Holly Grove and the path that led to the river. She couldn't stay up all night, but it made her feel she had some sense of control to stand watch as long as she could.

Jake had said that he was a light sleeper and that Dog would bark if anyone milled about in the yard. Holly rubbed Rhett's ears. "You do your part in the house, too. Don't you, boy?"

Rhett yawned.

Holly stretched and yawned. She shook her head. Yawns were contagious, even from dogs at midnight.

Rhett's ears perked. A low growl rumbled in his throat as he set a bead toward the path to the river.

Movement at the tree line caught her attention, and she placed her foot on the floor to stop the swing. A thudding in her ears drowned out the crickets. She laid her hand over her heart. Holly squinted. A form came into focus. Her heartbeat slowed. An animal. She leaned forward and blinked a few times for a better look. *Dog?*

She gathered Rhett in her arms and stood, then walked to the balcony railing. Why was she running loose? Dog darted back into the woods. Holly held Rhett tightly as he whined and squirmed to get down.

Had Jake let Dog free to roam as a guard dog? What if a guest forgot something in his or her car? Dog would do what she did best, scare the bejesus out of people.

Another shadow emerged with Dog from the woods. Holly shrank behind a massive brick column. Peeking around the corner, she watched a man pet Dog. Mackie? The only other man who could pet Dog was Jake, but what was he doing at the river at midnight?

Holly opened the door to her room and put Rhett inside. She hurried to the balcony rail and scanned the grounds below. Nothing moved. Holly slid her hand over the railing and kept a lookout below as she padded across the balcony toward the garçonnière. When she reached Jake's door, she tapped on it.

No answer.

She knocked again. Still no answer. *Okay. Either Jake isn't the light sleeper he thinks he is or he's definitely the one with Dog.*

Dog let out a bark, and Holly turned in the direction of the sound. Had Jake and Dog happened upon someone? What if the guy Jake had tackled in the entrance hall was back? She pushed aside her anxiety about facing Dog and dashed down the exterior stairs to the yard to help Jake.

She jogged past the chicken coop, the carriage house, and the honeymoon cottage, then toward where she'd seen Jake and Dog at the tree line. Every shadow morphed into a possible man or a dog. She looked back at the darkened house in the distance. If she screamed, would anyone hear her? What was she thinking, running out here alone?

"Jake?" she whispered.

A sweet, earthy scent laced the air. *Cigar? Pipe?* A long-forgotten memory of a wild party in college popped into her head. She sniffed the air. *Marijuana?* She sniffed again and followed the scent. As she passed the honeymoon cottage, the odor grew stronger. She eased into the shadow of an oak tree and leaned against its trunk and peeked around it.

A hand cupped her mouth from behind, snuffing her scream. "Shh," a voice whispered in her ear. "It's me." Jake released her, and she turned to face him.

"You scared the living daylight out of me. What are you doing out here?"

"Patrol." He cocked an eye at Holly. "Why aren't you in bed?"

"I couldn't sleep. Where's Dog?" she asked, checking for the mutt, who would just as soon chew her leg off as look at her.

He motioned to the left with his head. "Dog. Come."

Holly slipped behind Jake. She grabbed a fistful of his jacket and prepared to climb up his back if necessary. Dog trotted from the shadows to Jake's side and sat, as if Holly wasn't there. She blinked. Maybe Dog's indifference was progress. At least, she hoped so.

Holly positioned herself on Jake's opposite side and leaned in to sniff him.

"It's not me. I smelled it, too. I was trying to figure out where it was coming from when you showed up."

"Is that smell what I think it is?"

"Yep."

They both lifted their noses and inched forward.

"It's this way," Holly said, turning toward the carriage house. "You think Angel is smoking pot?"

"I wouldn't be surprised if a psychic was into recreational drugs. She may think it heightens her awareness of the spiritual world."

"Where'd that come from?" Holly said, surprised by his thinking. "I thought you weren't into that mumbo jumbo, as you call it."

He lifted a shoulder. "I wrote an article about shaman journeys once."

"Oh." Holly looked at the darkened carriage house. "What are we going to do if we catch her smoking pot?"

"Nothing. Remember. You're observing and gathering evidence so the authorities can make a bust. A small-time user isn't who we're after."

"So why do we want to see if she's smoking?"

"The more we know about your guests, the better."

They climbed the exterior stairs of the carriage house and stepped onto the balcony. Jake sniffed the air. "The scent would be stronger up here if she'd smoked here." He walked to the far end of the balcony, then leaned over the side. "The Fletchers' RV is parked around back."

"Oh yeah." Holly turned and headed down the stairs, with Jake and Dog following. Holly stopped at the corner of the carriage house. The scent grew stronger.

Jake put his hands on her waist. "Wait here," he whispered. He eased around the corner of the carriage house to the back of the RV.

I don't think so. Holly followed several feet behind Jake. A dim glow, maybe from a candle, cast a flickering light that spilled around the edges of the RV. Muffled voices came from the other side. The Fletchers.

Jake leaned against the RV, and Dog sat beside him. He looked back at Holly and motioned for her to go back. She tiptoed to Jake's side. The unmistakable scent of marijuana wafted to her nose.

Holly leaned down and looked under the RV. She positioned herself on all fours for a better look and found herself eye to eye with Dog. She froze. Dog sniffed Holly's face. She prayed Dog didn't think she smelled good enough to take a bite out of her nose. Dog swiped her wet tongue across Holly's cheek and then lay beside her.

She'd heard dogs didn't smile, but she could have sworn Dog smiled at her. Holly smiled back. If she'd won Dog over, maybe her luck was changing. Maybe she *could* stop the smuggling and get Burl out of her life.

From her view under the RV, everything looked cropped. Lawn chair legs, half an ice chest, the fat end of a Louisville Slugger, a man's hairy ankles above well-worn Sperrys, and a pair of sensible women's shoes on feet at least two sizes smaller than Holly's.

Jake stood a couple feet away, peeking around the corner of the RV.

"This is the last time I'm going to Houston," Kate said, her voice unsteady. "I can't do this anymore."

Houston. A big city on I-10. Easy route from Holly Grove, just like Burl had said. Holly inched her way over to Jake, then tugged on his pants leg.

"Shh," Jake whispered.

"You can, and you will," Tom said, more like an order to his wife than a statement.

Was he forcing her to run drugs with him? Holly strained to hear every word.

"I'm tired of living like this," Kate said, sounding as weary as her words. And there was something else in her voice. Anger? Resentment? How long had he forced her into a life of crime?

After a long silence, he said, "You can't quit on me." The edge in his voice was gone. "I need you," he said, almost pleading.

"The risk isn't worth the money," Kate said in an odd nasal voice.

The ice chest skidded a few inches as Tom rattled the ice and pulled out a beer. He said something, but Holly couldn't make it out over the clatter. The lid dropped in place with a solid slap. "Don't worry about the money end. That's my job."

Holly jerked on Jake's pants leg again. "They're the smugglers. My contact said Houston was a distribution point."

"Who's there?" Tom called out.

Oh, crapola. Holly looked under the RV. The Louisville Slugger inched out of her view, and the Sperrys rocked in place. A cat landed on the grass in front of the Sperrys, which were on the move.

Dog let out a grunt.

Holly latched on to Dog's collar as the cat leaped onto a fold-down step and into the RV, Holly hoped.

Dog dragged Holly under the RV and banged against every pipe, until Jake yanked them both back. No way could they sneak away now.

"Follow my lead," Jake whispered as he grabbed Dog by the collar. They stepped from behind the RV.

CHAPTER 29

Kate, with every hair still in place at midnight and wearing the same outfit she'd worn at dinner, sat in a folding chair. She looked like a soccer mom, except for the smoke that curled around her from the marijuana in the ashtray.

Tom stood in front of a folding chair, with a baseball bat in one hand and a longneck beer in the other. He took a protective step in front of his wife. "Come in the light, where I can see you."

Clutching Dog's collar, Jake stepped under the RV canopy, and Holly followed. Dog growled, and the hair on her back stood on end.

"If I were you, I'd put the bat down and not move too fast," Jake said.

Recognition flashed across Tom's face. "What are y'all doing out here so late?" He leaned the bat against the folding chair.

Jake looked at Holly, then back to Tom. "We smelled the weed. I thought I might be able to buy some off you." He shrugged. "That's all."

"It's not for sale," Tom said, easing back into his chair.

"Most doctors tell you to stop smoking," Kate said, reaching for the reefer. "Unless you're dying, anyway."

"You're not going to die." Tom slammed his beer on the folding table. "Do you hear me?"

His wife shot a laser stare his way. "You don't hear *me*!" Kate grabbed a handful of shiny brown hair and snapped a wig from her head. The wig of perfect hair dangled from her fingers. Patches of brown and gray stubble dotted a mostly bald head. Tears rimmed her big brown eyes as they flashed with anger. "The treatment is going to kill me before the disease gets a chance!"

A lump too big to swallow wedged in Holly's throat. Houston. MD Anderson Cancer Center. Tears stung her eyes as she remembered the pictures of the two young boys Kate had shown off at dinner. Holly's mom had lost the same battle, but Holly had been grown when it happened. Holly wished she could evaporate into thin air like Burl. She shouldn't be here. What the Fletchers were going through was painful enough without witnesses.

Jake cleared his throat. "I'm sorry. We didn't know."

"How could you know? My husband bought this wig for me. He thinks if I don't look like I have cancer, it'll go away." She threw the wig to the ground. "It won't."

"The Fletchers didn't come to breakfast or go on the tour. After last night, they're probably embarrassed," Holly said as she and Nelda stood in the kitchen loading a wicker basket with pralines.

"I'd smoke them funny cigarettes, too, if I had cancer." Nelda shook her head. "She's got young'ns at home, too. Humph, humph, humph. I'm gonna say a prayer for that lady and light some candles, too." Nelda folded a white linen napkin over the basket. "Hope these pralines make her feel better."

"Thanks. At least I won't knock on their door empty handed."

"You don't got nothin' to apologize for. How could you know?"

"It's not that. We were listening in on their private conversation." Holly took the pralines. "A painful one."

"Maybe God wanted you to hear. Maybe you can help."

"Me?" Holly could barely help herself.

"You never know when God might call on you. This may be it."

"If God is calling on me, we're all in trouble," Holly said, walking out the door. At least she could eliminate the Fletchers as suspects. They were in the fight of their lives, and running drugs just didn't make sense.

A light mist drifted through the air as Holly ambled to the RV. She looked at the gray skies, which threatened to burst open. The tour would have a light turnout today, but that was okay. She didn't need any more innocent people to suspect.

When she reached the RV, Jake was easing down the folding step. Kate followed him with her arm on his shoulder. She wore a pink scarf tied over her head, no make-up, and another soccer mom outfit. She wrapped her arms around Jake's neck and said something, but Holly couldn't hear what. Tom stepped out of the RV and shook Jake's hand; then he wrapped his arm around Kate's waist.

A heavy ache settled over Holly. She couldn't imagine

how difficult life was for them right now. And she'd made it worse last night.

Jake lifted his hand and waved at Holly as she approached the RV. "Good morning, sweetheart." He plucked a praline out of the basket before Holly could present them to Kate. "Got to run." He planted a peck on her cheek. "Sam's expecting me."

Kate wiped a tear from her eye, but her smile seemed to bubble from deep inside. A genuine smile. And it was pointed at Jake. She patted him on the arm. "I can't thank you enough."

Holly tilted her head, wondering what Jake had done but unwilling to ask in front of the Fletchers. She'd intruded enough last night. Besides, she could ask Jake later.

"We missed you at breakfast." She held the basket out to the Fletchers. "Nelda made a batch of pralines for you." She glanced at Jake as he strode across the lawn. "Minus one," she said, smiling. "Jake loves them."

"Mmm. I think I should sample these," Tom said, pulling a praline out of the basket.

"He's one special man." Kate's gaze darted to Holly's left hand. "Boyfriend?"

Holly stumbled over what to say. She'd loved telling anyone who'd listen Jake was her boyfriend in high school. Now? What was Jake to her? "Uh, an old friend. I mean . . ."

"I know what you mean."

"You do?"

"Sure. You love him but don't want to put yourself out there."

A shiver threatened to dance up her spine. She'd thought she loved Burl. Look what that had got her. "Oh, no. It's not like that."

"Are you sure? He seemed crazy about you. Couldn't say enough good things about you."

"Y'all were talking about me?"

"Some. Mostly, he made me see something I hadn't thought about." Her eyes watered. "It made all the difference in the world."

"What did he say?"

"You probably know," Kate said. "His mom ran off and left him when he was about the age of my boys. He said he could have stood losing his mom if she hadn't run away. He is a grown man and can't forgive her for leaving him. I was running away and didn't know it. If I lose this fight, my boys are going to know I did everything I could to stay with them. They can forgive me for being taken, but not for leaving."

Tom squeezed his wife to his side. "He gave my wife her fight back."

And gave Holly one more reason it would be harder not to fall for Jake again.

Holly had never so much as opened a suitcase when she cleaned her guests' rooms, until now. Maybe she should feel guilty about snooping around in their private belongings, but she couldn't. Nothing was more important than finding the smuggler, and if it took a little snooping, so be it.

Guilt niggled at her, anyway. Most of the guests had to be legit, but she had to search all the rooms to know who wasn't.

She lugged a basket filled with fresh towels and her cleaning basket, which teetered on top of the towels, as she climbed the stairs. Her flip-flops flapped with each step in the quiet house. Everyone was in the sugarcane maze or having their fortunes told by Angel, which gave Holly time to search the rooms.

One of the four upstairs rooms had a DO NOT DISTURB sign hanging from the antique brass knob. *Crapola*. Not only did she have to peruse their stuff, but she also had to do it with a written request not to enter plastered on the door. *Double crapola*. Holly sighed, then looked both ways. She flipped the sign off the knob onto the worn Oriental rug. *Oops*. Must have fallen off.

Pushing her guilt aside and telling herself the means justified the end, she tapped on Mr. Dunbar's door with the master key. "Housekeeping."

No answer.

She inserted the master key and then opened the door. She called again, "Housekeeping."

Holly stepped inside the suite and placed the basket of fresh towels and the cleaning basket on the floor, then closed the door. The sheets were folded back and the praline was on the pillow, just as she'd left the room last night, during turndown service. She shifted her weight and cocked her head to the side. If Mr. Dunbar didn't sleep in his bed, where did he sleep? She eyed the straight chair in the corner by the floor-to-ceiling window facing the river. The 1860s walnut commode, which she had converted to a side table, had been snuggled up to the chair as if it were a foot-stool. Had he slept there? *Surely not.*

A small notebook in a red binder lay on the commode. Holly picked up the notebook and opened it. She ran her finger over the LCD screen that she'd expected to be a paper notebook. *Cool gizmo*. It lit up and filled with text. *A novel?* The words *Final Target* were written across the top of the page. Had the novel kept him up all night? And why didn't he read in bed?

She looked out the window. A sliver of the river showed through the trees. At night there would only be darkness at that distance. But tugboats had lights. Was he on watch? She closed the notebook and carefully placed it on the commode in the same cocked position. With a techie gadget like that, wouldn't he have a smartphone or some way to communicate if he were waiting for a barge with drugs on board? Why would he watch?

She wandered into the bathroom, where she found wet towels and washcloths draped over the side of the tub. Well, at least he'd bathed here.

Turning back to face the antique bed, she scanned the suite for his suitcase. She crossed the room and opened the double mahogany doors of the armoire. On the bottom shelf, a suitcase sat open, with undershirts and underwear folded neatly in it. His clothes hung above the suitcase. The scent of cedar drifted to her nose as she filed through his hanging clothes, checking each pocket. Something hard and smooth slipped through her fingers. *A ring?* She fished it out of the pocket and then held the gold wedding band to the light. A date was engraved on the inside, *10-22 . . .*

Twenty years ago tomorrow.

She looked back at the bed he hadn't slept in. Who comes to a B & B alone on his anniversary, then doesn't sleep in his bed, and why?

Holly gnawed her bottom lip. This didn't have anything to do with smuggling. She'd invaded Mr. Dunbar's privacy, just as she'd invaded the Fletchers' last night. She stuffed the ring back in his coat pocket, then rubbed her hands down her jeans, as though that would rub off the nosy deed she'd done.

"Lots of men carry their wedding ring, instead of wearing it, when they're not with the old ball and chain," Burl said.

Holly turned to find Burl propped on one elbow and stretched out on the antique bed.

"Ball and chain." She scrunched up her face. "Is that really how men think about their wives?"

"Face it. Men aren't meant to be monogamous."

"Some men."

"Most men."

"Whatever." She picked up her basket of towels and cleaning basket, then marched into the hall. "Every man isn't like you."

Burl bounced off the bed and followed her to the next room. "You're right about that." He thumbed his chest. "I'm one of a kind, huh?"

He was truly a legend in his own mind, and once upon a time, she'd been young and naive enough to believe everything that came out of his mouth. No wonder he thought she was a dumb blonde.

Was. Not anymore. She saw Burl for who he was. A scared, insecure man.

She plopped the basket of towels and cleaning basket down in front of Duke and Toni's room, pulled the master key from her pocket.

He lifted his hands, palms up, as though he could coax words from her. "What?"

Holly shook her head. "Nothing."

He had about a snowball's chance in a Louisiana summer of getting into heaven on his own. No wonder he'd decided he didn't want to go. Somehow she was going to wedge his sorry self in, if it took snooping through the pope's luggage.

She tapped on Toni and Duke's door with her key,

even though she knew they were in town, having lunch at Dottie's Diner. "Housekeeping."

"You think your bozo is different?" He leaned against the door frame. "We're all alike."

Holly slipped the key in the lock. "You have nothing in common with him."

"Stripped down to the bones, you wouldn't know us apart. I guarantee it."

"Housekeeping," she called again and opened the door, then grabbed her baskets of supplies.

Burl let out a long whistle.

She stood in the doorway for a moment. Her gaze followed a trail of clothes from the door to the bed. A knotted red silk scarf dangled from each of the four posts of the ransacked bed.

"Okeydokey." Holly set the baskets down inside the room and closed the door. She retrieved her rubber gloves from the cleaning basket, then shook her head as she slipped on the gloves. "You'd think they'd have the DO NOT DISTURB sign on their door so housekeeping wouldn't see this."

"Check this out." Burl pointed to a stainless-steel briefcase hanging from a metal cord around a bedpost.

"That's what I was looking for." Holly rushed around the bed. "Duke has guarded that thing like it has the crown jewels in it."

"Double locked, too," Burl said.

Holly fingered the padlock on the metal cord. "This one needs a key, but I don't need to remove the briefcase to see what's in it. All I need to do is open the combination lock on the briefcase."

"Got the combo, Sherlock?"

Holly fished a piece of paper out of her pocket. "I've got their birthdays and driver's license numbers from their registration card. I'm hoping one of them is the combination to the case." She keyed in the first six numbers of Duke's driver's license number. No go. She tried the last six, and it didn't budge. "It's got to be a birthday."

"It could be anything," Burl said. "You're wasting your time."

"If you'd help me out by doing a little spying, I wouldn't need the combo. You could just tell me what's in it."

"If I could materialize anytime and anywhere I wanted, I'd have been in here watching this show."

Holly blew out an exasperated breath. She tried Duke's birthday, then Toni's. "Crapola."

"There's a million possible combinations. You'll never get it right."

Holly added the five years most women like Toni shave from their age, then rolled the cylinders. The latch clicked open. "Ta-dah."

CHAPTER 30

Wiggling her fingers over the briefcase, Holly hesitated before she lifted the lid. So far, every time she invaded someone else's privacy, she'd been sorry, but a locked briefcase had to contain something important. Jake wasn't going to like her doing this, either, but she had to find out what was inside.

If it was a pile of cash, she'd know who the smuggler was for sure. If it was something else, she'd just close the case and forget it. At least she could eliminate Toni and Duke from suspicion.

Burl's translucent body waded through the bed and the briefcase. Burl spun his finger in a circle at the side of the briefcase. "Come on, Blondie. Get it over with. Open it."

She pulled back. "What if it's booby-trapped?"

Burl rolled his eyes. "You'd be dead already. Open it."

Holly eased the case open, then blinked a few times, as though her eyes were lying. The inside of the case was lined in blue Pacific Silvercloth and was heavily padded. In the middle of the case, secured by what had to be a custom-made form, sat a—

"What the devil is that?" Burl leaned over the case.

"It looks like a . . ." Holly pointed to the shiny gold resemblance of man parts in full erection mode. "Is that a plug?"

"Yep."

Holly leaned a little closer to read something written across the, um, base of it. "Gold Member?"

He hummed a verse from the classic James Bond movie *Goldfinger*.

"Shut up," she said. "Why would anyone keep a gold dildo in a locked stainless-steel case?"

"Maybe it's real gold," Burl said.

"Okay. Why would anyone make a statue of that out of gold? Unless"—she paused—"they were trying to make it look like an adult toy and it really is gold."

"With the dollar down, gold could be what the Colombians want now. If it's just for show, it won't work. Plug it in and see what happens."

Holly pulled her rubber gloves on, then removed Gold Member from the case. She tested the weight, but how heavy was gold, anyway? She'd never lifted more than a bracelet or a ring made of gold. "It's not that heavy."

Burl rubbed his chin. "Is it hollow?"

Holly tipped it over. "It has some sort of packing material in here. Gel pack maybe." The plug teetered from the balls for a second, then fell out. "Crapola. I've broken it."

"Unless the cord was detachable."

"Only one way to find out." She held Gold Member in one hand and the plug in the other. As she tried to plug the cord back into Gold Member, her thumb brushed over a button. Gold Member hummed to life.

"Eek!" She dropped it on the bed.

"Cordless. Good move," Burl said.

Gold Member crawled across the bed like Thing from the old black-and-white reruns of *The Addams Family*. Holly resisted an urge to swat it like a fly.

"Holly, are you in there?" Miss Alice's voice came from the other side of the door.

Mercy. That woman might as well wear a trench coat and glasses. She's on my tail all the time.

"There's a Sylvia Martin on the phone downstairs for you," Miss Alice said as she pushed the door open a crack.

Holly dashed across the room to the door as Gold Member neared the edge of the bed. She peeked around the door to Miss Alice in the hall, and a thud sounded from inside the room.

Miss Alice put her glasses on her nose and attempted to lean around Holly. "What was that?"

"Oh, I—I leaned the broom against the bed when you knocked. It must have fallen," Holly lied, hoping Gold Member had survived the plunge.

A faint buzz came from the bedroom.

"What's that sound?" Miss Alice stretched her neck, trying to see around Holly.

"Electric broom." Holly stepped into the hall, then eased the door closed. "Great for allergies."

Miss Alice lifted a finger and wagged it at Holly. "Always prop the broom in a corner, and that won't happen."

"I'll remember that."

"She says she has a reservation, but I know you're full."

"Thanks. Tell her I'll call her right back," Holly said, opening the door only enough to slip inside the bedroom. She closed the door and locked it. Holly leaned against the door and blew out a breath.

Another knock came at the door. Holly nearly jumped out of her shoes.

"You're full." Miss Alice called from the other side. "Where are you going to put her?"

"Abe's cabin," Holly answered as she ran to the side of the bed where Gold Member had taken his fall.

The thing wasn't there, but she heard a low buzzing sound. *Lordy.* Gold Member must have vibrated across the wood floor.

Miss Alice's retreating footsteps sounded, and Holly dropped to her knees to look for Gold Member. She spotted the thing under the bed as it gyrated out from under the bed skirt on the opposite side.

Holly scrambled to her feet and looked at Burl on the other side of the bed. "Do you see it?"

Burl looked down at the floor. "Afraid so." He'd faded a bit, and if a ghost could look sick, he did.

Holly scurried around the bed. Gold Member buzzed and crabbed across the floor, but one of its balls trailed behind it, hanging by a wire.

"Blondie, you've turned into a real ballbuster." He shook his head. "I don't have the stomach for this." He faded into a fine mist, then disappeared.

Just craptastic.

How am I going to fix Gold Member before Toni and Duke get back? She checked her watch. Eleven o'clock. They'd said they were going to town for lunch.

Jake could fix anything, just like his dad. No matter

how she rolled it around in her mind, she couldn't find a way to tell Jake he needed to repair a pair of balls because she'd broken them.

Jeez. Ballbuster.

She wasn't looking forward to explaining this.

Jake scrolled over the profiles and substance reports ICE headquarters had e-mailed to his laptop. Leaning back in Sam's creaking chair, he shook his head. None of Holly's guests were exactly as they had presented themselves. But who was?

He sipped what Sam called coffee. It tasted more like tar. Jake spun the ancient swivel chair to face his old friend. "When did you make this sludge?"

"Three or four hours ago," Sam said from the oak chair across the desk from Jake. "Waste not, want not." Sam took a sip from a chipped brown mug. "Ah. A man needs a little bite in his coffee."

"It's got teeth, all right." Jake could almost scrape the brew off his tongue. It'd keep him alert, for darned sure.

"Anything interesting?"

"Privileged information," Jake said as he scanned the brief, knowing he'd tell Sam, anyway. Ever since Miss Alice had told him about Sam's generosity, Jake had been thinking of a way to pay him back without Sam knowing. And the old coot wasn't easy to fool.

"Privileged, my hindquarters." Sam's wiry gray eyebrows matted like two sparring caterpillars. He paced across the cheap tile floor like an army general. "Only reason ICE knows about this operation is because of me."

Jake rubbed a hand across his jaw to suppress his grin. He enjoyed riling Sam. It brought out the old spunk that had earned Sam Jake's respect when he worked for him in high school. There were two things he knew about Sam. He could squeeze a dollar until George broke wind, and he could keep a secret.

"This can't be printed," Jake said, because he needed to say it, not because he didn't trust Sam.

Sam stood a little taller. "Hell, no. All I want is first dibs on the story when you make the bust. You can even write the thing, as long as the story breaks in my paper." Sam took another sip of coffee and looked into the distance, as though he could see something there. "If I get the AP to pick up a *Delta Ridge Gazette* story before I leave this world, I'll die a happy man."

"When I was looking around Burl's hangar, I found a railroad container out back. It was covered with vines and locked up as tight as a drum. Mackie lopped off the lock after Burl died and put a new one on it because Holly couldn't find Burl's key. She sent the new key over by Miss Alice." Jake raised a brow. "I found a few seeds on the floor and some powder traces. Sent those off for analysis."

"And?"

Jake tapped the screen. "Confirmed. Marijuana and cocaine."

"A railroad container full of dope." Sam whistled. "How much do you think that would be worth? And how did he move it?"

"I'm guessing in small batches. He probably flew some of it out. Holly said Burl's contacts would stay as guests at the B & B and then haul out the rest in their suitcases."

Sam pulled his pipe out of his coat pocket. He stuck it in his mouth but didn't light it. "What's the computer say about the guests? I bet it's that quiet fella staying by himself. What's his name?"

"Dunbar. He just got out of prison with early parole. He was sentenced to twenty years and served ten. Money laundering."

"Told you." The pipe hung from Sam's mouth like a pacifier. At least he'd quit smoking it, a relief from the fog of smoke Jake had tolerated from him years ago.

"He was a model prisoner." Jake leaned back in his chair and laced his hands behind his neck as he reviewed his file on the computer. "Taught GED classes behind bars. His wife divorced him three years into his sentence. He has a job teaching English at a trade school in a little town in St. Charles Parish and volunteers for a literacy foundation. I talked to his parole officer. Dunbar is trying to get back with his wife. Had to ask permission to come here to meet her on their anniversary. On paper, he looks rehabilitated."

"Once a crook, always a crook."

"Maybe, maybe not. His wife is a no-show." Jake shrugged. "Can't bust the guy because he has a record."

Sam poured enough sugar in his coffee to make a mudpie.

"So that's how you can drink that stuff you call coffee."

"That's how I stay so sweet, you little tenderfoot." Sam took a swig. "Ah. Now what about Miss Centerfold and her bodyguard?"

"Miss Centerfold, aka fly baby and Toni Bolla, is an aspiring actress, a model, and a semiretired Vegas dancer. No record, but her ex-boyfriend is in San Quentin for racketeering. She and Duke have been seeing each other for about six months. Duke has a string of adult video stores in New Jersey that are close to going belly up. He hired a patent attorney recently and invested fifty thousand dollars he didn't have in prototype and startup costs for his invention. Looks like he took out a private loan to finance it. No bank records."

"Just 'cause the guy is kinky and on the skids financially doesn't mean he's a crook."

"Depends on who he borrowed the money from. He runs in some shady circles. Maybe he promised a big favor for the loan, or drug running is how he plans to pay it off." Jake put his feet on Sam's desk and got the eye from him. He groaned and eased his feet off the desk.

"Who else do you have the skinny on in there?" Sam motioned with his pipe toward the computer, then stuck his pipe back in his mouth.

Jake opened another file. "The Fletchers are on their way to Houston. Kate has cancer."

"Cancer is expensive." Sam shook his head. "I've seen it ruin people financially. They may be desperate."

"Yeah. Breaking bad."

"Huh?"

"Never mind." Jake wasn't even sure Sam had a TV. "I thought they may have needed the money, but Tom got a good-sized settlement a few years ago from an on-the-job injury. Nearly lost his leg. Had to retire early."

Sam shook his head. "Might as well be in purgatory as retire before your time."

"Anyway, they paid off their home and could easily get a mortgage on it if they were in serious financial trouble. They haven't. And they seem to be the kind of parents who wouldn't chance jail time for themselves and foster care for their boys."

"Scratch them, then." Sam rubbed his hand across

the gray stubble on his chin. "Who else is staying at the
B & B besides Alice? I know darned well that old battle-ax
isn't smuggling drugs."

"She's not a suspect, but something is fishy. She told
Holly she needed to stay at Holly Grove because her
floors were being refinished. I drove by her house, and
the floors are not being refinished." Jake lifted a shoulder. "Why she lied, I can't be sure."

"Because she's a nosy old bat." Sam looked over his
glasses at Jake. "I'd bet my best hat on that."

The intercom buzzed on Sam's desk.

Sam crossed to the phone and pushed a button.
"Yeah, Penny?"

"Sheriff Walker is here to see Jake," she said.

"Send him on back." Sam released the button. "The
sheriff doesn't make social calls. This is probably about
Mackie."

Jake's spine tensed. Had the sheriff found him
drunk or worse? A dread settled over Jake like a dead
chill. For once in his life, he'd like to see Mackie drunk.
He'd allowed years to pass without talking to his
father. Why? Pride? Stubbornness? Would he get a
chance to make peace with Mackie? Or would he be
saddled with guilt the rest of his life because he
couldn't accept his dad for who he was?

Sheriff Walker rapped on the door as he swung it
open. He nodded to Sam, then turned to Jake. The
sheriff didn't hold eye contact for more than a second
before he took off his hat. Looking down, he fingered
his hat and shifted his weight from left to right.

Jake curled his hands around the smooth worn
wood of the old desk chair. This couldn't be good.

Chapter 31

Sheriff Walker stood rubbing the back of his neck and looking out of place in the middle of Sam's office. He jerked his head up and squared his body, as though he needed fortitude to say what he needed to say. "Jake, some teenagers were squirrel hunting this morning at the edge of the river. They found something." He rubbed a hand around the brim of his hat. "It don't look good."

Jake clamped down on the arms of his chair and prepared to hear the worst.

The sheriff shook his head but didn't look Jake or Sam in the eye. "The boys found Mackie's bike right at the river's edge."

The muscles in Jake's neck relaxed as he wrapped his mind around the news. "Bicycle?" *That's it. No body.*

"Yeah. The boys didn't shoot any squirrels, but they were bragging about shooting up an old bike pretty good, and their dad overheard. He'd heard Mackie was missing and knew he rode an old bike sometimes, so he called me."

Jake stood and crossed the room. "I want to see it," he said, snatching his jacket from a coatrack.

"Figured you would," Sheriff Walker said.

Ten minutes later, Jake squatted on his haunches, studying the ground around Mackie's bike on the bank of the Mississippi. Something about the whole scene felt off. "Are you sure the boys didn't move the bike?"

"Yep," Sheriff Walker said, leaning against a cottonwood tree.

Jake swiped his finger through the thin coat of green moss that mottled the old bike. Mackie had been missing for a few weeks. Plenty of time for moss to grow in this humidity. Plenty of time for a body to show up downriver.

Sheriff Walker flipped a small pocketknife open, then raked it under his nails. "You know he rode his bike down the levee to his place when he was drunk, don't you?"

"Yeah," Jake said. "Better than a DUI, right, Sheriff?"

"I gave him three before he quit driving drunk. Looks like he may have veered off the levee and landed in the river," the sheriff said, pointing the tip of his pocketknife from the levee to the river.

Jake looked over his shoulder at the massive levee. Hardwoods, saplings, and underbrush covered a good sixty yards of the flatland at the base of the levee. Mackie rode on the top of the levee, which was at least twenty feet wide and was mowed regularly. "Even drunk, it'd be hard to run off the levee road on a bicycle, and there isn't exactly a bike trail down here."

The sheriff wiped his knife on his pants leg. "Maybe he had to take a leak and pushed to the river."

"Maybe." But why would a drunk man climb down a forty-foot levee and through the woods to take a whiz? And why was Sheriff Walker so determined to convince him that Mackie had landed in the river?

The sheriff flipped his knife closed and strode toward Jake. "The fact is nobody's seen Mackie in weeks, and his bike is on the edge of the Big Muddy." He stopped and shoved his knife in his pocket. "You might ought to get prepared to identify a body, son."

"The name is Jake," he said, pushing to his feet. If Mackie didn't have a Purple Heart and a Navy Cross tucked away somewhere in the rubble at his trailer, Jake might believe Mackie had drowned in the river. "I don't think you'll find a body."

"It's only a matter of time before the Old Muddy coughs him up."

"What makes you so sure Mackie is in that river?"

"Evidence." He pointed to the bike. "And common sense."

That was just it. Too easy. Someone wanted it to look like Mackie had landed in the Mississippi. Jake turned to the river. Sunlight bounced off the ripples and swirls as it pushed its way southward. No one questioned the power beneath the calm. Mackie knew the river better than anyone. He knew no one would question his fate with the evidence on the bank. Jake's gut told him Mackie was alive and well. Or alive and drunk at least. But why didn't he want to be found?

"You broke what?" Jake said into his cell phone. Leaves crunched under his feet as he hiked back to Holly Grove from the river. Did Holly say she had busted Duke's balls? "My signal must be bad."

"Gold Member. I need you to fix it," Holly said.

"Fix what?" Jake stopped. Maybe he could hear better if he wasn't tromping through the leaves.

"Never mind. Where are you?"

"I'm walking back from the river. Why?"

"I've got it with me. Meet me at the hangar." The phone clicked.

Jake held the phone away from his ear and looked at it as though it could interpret what she'd said. He rolled his neck in a circle. Par for the course at the circus she called Holly Grove. At least she wasn't wigging out about a ghost this time.

Whatever she'd broken, he could fix it. He only wished fixing the trouble at Holly Grove would be as easy.

By the time he arrived, Holly was inside the hangar. She wore the tight little jeans she'd worn the first day he saw her and a T-shirt with DOMESTIC DIVA emblazoned across the front. She paced back and forth across the concrete floor, beside a workbench.

"Hey, diva. What's up?"

Her curls bounced when she spun in his direction. "Diva?"

Jake gave the hem of her T-shirt a playful jerk.

She pinched her shirt and pulled it out on the sides. "This is what I wear when I clean the guests' rooms." Her smile faded into an apologetic plea. "And that's how I broke Duke's, um, um . . ." Holly turned to the workbench and reached in a backpack, then pulled out two pairs of rubber gloves. She handed him a pair and put on the other pair.

"Messy job, huh?" Jake said as he took the gloves.

She blew out a heavy sigh. "You have no idea."

"Don't worry, sweetheart. If it can be fixed, I'll fix it."

"This was really, really an accident." She folded her

gloved hands, as though she were ready to say a prayer. "I would never do this on purpose."

"Okay." Jake shrugged. "Let's see what you've got."

She reached into the backpack. "I broke this," she said, holding something gold and tubular.

What the . . . ? Jake eyed what looked like a gold johnson and its one detached ball. His stomach rolled. "I see."

"It's called Gold Member, and it was in Duke's locked briefcase. He's definitely kinky, but not a smuggler." She cocked a crystal-blue eye at him. "I figured out the code without your help."

"I see," he said, suppressing a laugh.

Two cute creases lined Holly's brow. "What's so funny?"

"I'm sorry. It's really not funny, but I did some research on Duke today. I found out he applied for a patent recently. And—"

"Oh, my." She stared at Gold Member. "This is it."

"Yeah, but that's not all. He took out a fifty-thousand-dollar private loan to fund his, um"—Jake eyed Gold Member—"project."

Her mouth gaped open. "I'm holding a fifty-thousand-dollar . . ." She gulped. "And I broke it."

"Yep."

"You've got to fix it." Holly thrust Gold Member and its dangling part in Jake's direction.

Jake took a step back. "Not my area of expertise."

"But you've got to."

"How about I put a new roof on Holly Grove instead?"

"Duke and Toni will be back from lunch soon, and this has to be back in its case."

"I hate to ask, but how did you break it?"

"I didn't technically break it. I put it on the bed, and it crawled off."

"Hold on a minute." Jake shook his head. "Crawled off?"

"This thing does tricks. I swear."

"For fifty thousand dollars, it should, but how do you know?" He cocked a brow. "Did you give it a test drive?"

Pink patches stained her cheeks. "Lordy, no. I was checking to see if it was real gold that could be traded for drugs, and I accidentally turned it on. When it started moving, I dropped it." She eased Gold Member onto the workbench like it was nitro, then took a step back. "Then Miss Alice knocked on the door. By the time I got rid of her, it had walked off the bed and busted."

Jake laughed. "It walked?"

Holly held a finger up. "Watch this."

She pushed a button, and it started squirming, then inched across the workbench, dragging a nut.

Watching the thing struggle sent a shiver down his back. "Okay. Can you turn it off now?"

She pushed a button, ending Gold Member's torture and his. "You've got to fix it."

Jake stuffed his hands in his pockets. "When I said I could fix anything, I had no idea what I was getting into."

"But you'll fix it. Won't you?"

He hesitated. It wasn't that he wasn't comfortable with his own equipment, but the idea of handling a replica with superpowers creeped him out.

"Come on, Jake. I don't have fifty thousand dollars to replace it."

"All right." He grimaced. "You hold it down, and I'll operate."

"Guess I owe you one."

"And Duke could be in debt to some shady characters who expect him to pay them back by doing them a favor."

Holly's eyes widened. "Like picking up drugs in his plane."

CHAPTER 32

Holly's fingers might as well have been crawfish claws as she tried to fit the repaired Gold Member in its case. She sat on the bed to get a better angle on the case. It would be easier if the stupid thing weren't latched around a bedpost.

A car door slammed outside, jarring Holly to her feet. Then a second door slammed. She scampered to the balcony window of Duke and Toni's room. Her heart hammered as Toni and Duke walked away from their red convertible rental in the driveway below. *Oh, Lordy.*

She looked at her watch. Twelve o'clock. *What happened to their lunch in town?*

Holly rushed back to the case to finish packing Gold Member into it. Finally, she clicked the latch in place. Holly hurried to the door and propped it open with a pile of towels. Nelda always said an honest housekeeper worked with the door open. At least Holly could look honest.

And look busy. She snatched the sheets off the bed

and rolled them in a ball, then threw them on the floor.

Footsteps padded up the stairway. "You're paranoid. You know that?" Toni said.

"I don't trust nobody." Duke's deep voice came from the stairwell.

"It's in a steel case locked to the freaking bed, for Christ's sake," Toni said.

Holly pulled a fresh set of sheets from the armoire. She grabbed the end of a sheet and popped it into the air as Duke darkened the doorway.

Duke gave her a hard glance. He didn't smile, nod, or even grunt at her but marched straight for the briefcase. He unlocked it from the bedpost, then eyed her again. She looked away and tucked the sheet around the mattress before he could see the guilt in her eyes.

He carried the briefcase into the bathroom and slammed the door. Holly's legs trembled under her, and she did her best to keep her hands from shaking as she finished making the bed. If he noticed anything had happened to Gold Member, she didn't want to think about what would happen to her.

"Don't let him get to you." Toni propped a hip on the dressing table.

Mercy. She must have noticed my hands shaking.

"He never lets that box out of his sight." She dug a cigarette from her purse. "We'd just sat down at Dottie's Diner to order a burger, and he realized he'd left the box. Then *boom*. We had to split."

Toni shoved off the dressing table and waved her unlit cigarette through the air as she sashayed to the balcony door, flung it open, and stepped outside. "I need a smoke. Duke drives me nuts sometimes."

Holly sucked in a little secondhand smoke that

drifted in with a cool breeze from the balcony. If her stress level didn't drop, she might have to take up the habit.

Duke opened the bathroom door.

Holly froze. Did Jake's repair work? Could Duke tell Gold Member had been broken?

"Where's Toni?" Duke said, looking the room over.

"She stepped outside for a smoke," Holly said.

"*Toni*," he called, pitching his voice like the late pitch master Billy Mays.

"Give me a minute," she yelled back. "And you need to apologize to Holly."

"For what?" he asked.

"You acted like a barbarian," Toni said between puffs.

"What?" he yelled back.

"You're paranoid, that's what." She leaned into the room and held her cigarette behind her. "You gave her the Terminator eye because she was in the room with you-know-what. The poor girl was shaking."

Duke looked at Holly. He held the briefcase up. "It's not like I think you're dishonest or nothing, but I got a lot riding on what's in here."

"Oh." Holly shook her head. "I'd never tamper with any of my guests' personal possessions." *Under normal circumstances*, she wished she could add. She tucked the coverlet around the mattress, then smoothed over the wrinkles, keeping her lying eyes focused on her task.

"Yeah, but I ain't taking no chances," Duke said.

"You're a barbarian," Toni yelled as she stormed through the open French doors. She stood nose-to-nose with Duke. "That's not an apology."

"What? You want me to write her a letter?" Duke asked.

"Yeah, peel about twenty of them out of your wallet and leave them for a tip."

"Just because you used to be a maid don't mean you got to be the union boss for the maids of America."

Holly jerked to attention. "For your information, I own this place. I clean the rooms because it's part of running a B & B." She looked at Toni. "Not that being a maid isn't an honorable thing to do."

Toni crossed the room and stood beside Holly. "It doesn't matter. Dukie needs a lesson in how to treat women, and he's going to apologize." She shot a look at Duke. "Or else."

"Or else what?"

"You know what." Toni folded her arms over her chest.

Duke's deep chuckle startled Holly. He dug in his pocket and pulled out a wad of bills, then peeled off a hundred-dollar bill. "You know I love it when you get all huffy, don't you, fly baby?" He pitched the bill on the bed. "Big enough apology?"

Holly looked at the bill. "I can't accept this."

Toni snatched the bill from the bed. "Oh, yes you can." She stuffed the bill in Holly's hand. "If you don't take this, you're letting him get away with being a barbarian, and I'm trying to make him a gentleman."

Holly slid the bill in her pocket. "Apology accepted."

If she didn't take the money, she'd never get out of there. She gathered her cleaning supplies and watched Toni slink to Duke's side. Holly eased out of the room and closed the door behind her, but she heard Toni's voice and leaned in to the door.

"You need to get a grip and be a gentleman. Do you remember why we're here?"

Holly pressed her ear to the door.

Duke didn't answer.

"Romance, Dukie. Do you see me acting all paranoid about that thing you keep locked in a box? No. Because I bought insurance."

"That's my million-dollar idea in there, and someone could steal it. You can't buy insurance on an idea," Duke said, his voice grew louder.

"No, but technically, Gold Member is mine until you pay my fifty grand back. Isn't that right, Dukie?"

Holly gulped. Toni was the mystery financial backer?

"That's right, fly baby, and I'll pay back every penny as soon as the orders start rolling in."

"So can we get back to the romance?" Toni practically purred.

Holly stepped away from the door. She'd heard enough.

Toni and Duke might be a bit on the sleazy side, but they weren't doing anything illegal.

Nelda stood over the stove, stirring her gumbo. "Taste this," she said, holding a spoon toward Holly.

She'd had so much of Nelda's gumbo in the past two weeks, she really didn't want to taste it, but refusing wouldn't go over well with Nelda, and Holly needed a favor. She crossed the kitchen to Nelda and took the spoon. The taste that invaded her mouth was not what Holly had expected. Spicier, but not in a hot way. Fresh. Unique. "Something is different."

"They's good different, and they's bad different."

Nelda shoved a hand on her hip. "Which one is it? You be honest, now."

"Good different. Really good."

"I thought so, but I done tasted gumbo so much, I lost my taster." Nelda picked up a wooden spoon from the spoon rest, then stirred the gumbo. "Glad you still got yours."

Holly smacked her lips. "If I can't cook, the least I can do is taste. What did you add?"

"Secret weapon." Nelda rapped her wooden spoon on the side of the gumbo pot, then set it on the spoon rest. "I heard Estelle over at Goutreaux Plantation had the jump on me yesterday in the cookin' contest. I needed to kick it up a notch, like Emeril says."

Holly dropped her spoon and a mixing bowl in the dishwater, which sloshed on her DOMESTIC DIVA T-shirt. *Well, crapola.*

Miss Alice pushed through the kitchen door, like she did countless times a day. It was as though she had a sixth sense about where Holly was at all times. Miss Alice pointed a wrinkled finger at Holly. "What happened to your shirt?"

Holly looked down at her wet right boob. "Dish-washing mishap."

"Don't you own an apron?" Miss Alice shook her head. She pushed the swinging door back toward the foyer, then stuck her head out. "Come on in. I found her."

Nelda grabbed her chest. "Kingdom come. It's her."

In walked Angelina Jolie—or she could be. The model-perfect woman stood nearly six feet tall, had Miss Clairol dark waves, and wore shoes that probably cost ten times more than Holly's entire domestic diva outfit. The woman's pink lips parted in a fake TV smile as she extended her French-manicured hand. "Sylvia Martin. *Inquiring Minds.*"

"Welcome to Holly Grove." Holly wiped her wet hand over her jeans and then shook Sylvia's cool hand. Holly had to look up to make eye contact and wished she'd worn heels, not that it would make her equal to Sylvia in any way.

Sylvia didn't attempt eye contact. Her gaze darted from the pentagram to the candles and to Nelda. Holly had gotten used to the voodoo decor Nelda had added to armor the kitchen, but it had Sylvia's attention.

Sylvia's high-dollar heels clicked as she walked along the edges of the pentagram and studied its form. "Great visual. My producer will love this."

Nelda wiped her hands on her apron and crossed the pentagram to Sylvia. "I watch your show every Sunday night," she gushed with an ear-to-ear smile, then shook Sylvia's hand with too much gusto. "You look just like you do on TV, 'cept skinnier in person."

"Thank you," she said, never quite looking at Nelda

If she were any skinnier, she'd be invisible. Holly didn't like Sylvia, and it wasn't because she was too pretty, though that didn't help. She spoke to Nelda and her like they weren't really there or, worse, as if they were part of the "great visual."

"By the time you leave, I could put five pounds on you," Nelda said, eyeing Sylvia up and down.

Sylvia actually looked at Nelda. "Pardon me?"

"You like fried chicken? Everybody loves my fried chicken," Nelda said.

Sylvia stood in front of the bowl of holy water. "I'm vegan."

Nelda waved a hand through the air. "That's okay. I got a friend who's Muslim. She loves my fried chicken."

"I don't eat meat," Sylvia said, bending to touch the bowl of holy water in the center of the pentagram.

Nelda tilted her head to the side and eyed Sylvia. "Your God told you not to eat meat?"

Sylvia looked at Nelda as though she were a bug.

"Nelda, Miss Martin's religious beliefs aren't our business," Holly said. No need in embarrassing Nelda by defining *vegan* in front of Sylvia and rubbing Nelda's nose in her mistake.

"It is if I got to cook for a vegan, and I don't know what that vegan God lets 'em eat," Nelda said.

"I eat vegetables, as long as they aren't cooked with animal fat."

"Butter count?" Nelda said.

Sylvia stood and leveled her eyes at Nelda. "Yes."

"Humph. That's why you ain't got no meat on your bones."

"We always accommodate our guests' special dietary needs," Holly said, giving Nelda a look she hoped would shut her up.

"We aim to please," Nelda said, with a touch of sarcasm in her voice.

"Sylvia, if you'll just have a seat in the foyer, I'll have your room ready shortly," Holly said.

Nelda huffed back to the stove, then turned down the gas. "She still ain't got nothin' to eat if I don't know what to feed her."

A digital version of "New York, New York" blared on a cell phone.

Sylvia flipped open her handbag and took a sleek phone from a side pocket. "Where are you?" She tapped a well-heeled foot. "Lost? You're driving to the end of the world and you didn't rent a car with a GPS? Hold on."

She reached in her purse and pulled out a car key, then extended it to Holly. "It's the red Lexus. Tell the bellman I need all the bags in the trunk and the one on the passenger's seat." Sylvia walked out of the kitchen into the foyer as she ranted into the phone.

Holly looked at the key in her hand and turned to Nelda. "I don't like her."

"Bless her heart. She just don't know no better," Nelda said.

"Well, she needs an education." Holly slapped the car key on the counter near Nelda. "When she gets back, tell her we don't have a bellman and to meet me at Abe's cabin with her luggage."

"TV stars ain't used to carrying their own suitcases," Nelda said as she picked up the key. "I hear millions of folks watch *Inquiring Minds.*" She took Holly's hand and placed the key in it. "If I was you, I'd pack that pride away and tote them suitcases in."

CHAPTER 33

Jake had taken a chance that one part of Dog's mutt mix was bloodhound, and walked him to Mackie's bike at the riverbank. The scent was old, but he had to give it a try. No way in hell could Jake believe that Mackie had fallen in the Mississippi or that anyone would be stupid enough to throw him in and leave his bike to mark the spot.

He clipped a leash on Dog's collar in case she caught the scent. Then he pulled one of Mackie's dirty work shirts out of a plastic bag and held the shirt to Dog's nose.

"Find Mackie," Jake said, like the mutt was a pedigreed tracking hound. "Mackie might not be much of a master *or* a father, but he's the best we've got."

Dog whiffed the shirt, and her tail thumped the bare ground.

"You smell him, don't you, Dog?" Jake said, stuffing the shirt back into the plastic bag.

She circled the bike and sniffed the ground. She lifted her dirt-crusted snout and whiffed the air. Passing her nose over the ground, Dog padded to the bank.

Her front paws sank into the mud, and she looked across the river and sniffed. She snorted, then sniffed again and sat.

Jake's hope deflated. He rubbed Dog's ear. "You tried, girl, but I can't believe he's in there."

Dog turned her snout downriver and took three quick whiffs. She lunged ahead, pulling Jake behind her through the dense underbrush at the edge of the Mississippi. Mud caked Jake's boots as Dog led him on a slow jog along the riverbank and over fallen logs, washed-up ice chests, and debris left from the last high watermark.

After fifteen minutes at a steady pace, Dog stopped at the river's edge, then doubled back to a bent-over cottonwood. The branches dipped into the river like long, strong arms. Dog snorted and rubbed her snout in the ground as she turned in a circle at the slanted tree trunk. A perfect snag in the river for Mackie to pull himself out of the current.

The leash jerked against Jake's wrist, and Dog made a sharp turn away from the river, then picked up speed. Jake dodged saplings and low limbs. He gave Dog slack on the leash to run. Dog zigzagged, with her nose to the ground, up the slow grade to the levee base, and then she shot up the steep side. At the top of the levee, she stopped and whiffed the air, as though she had a better scent from that elevation. Nose to the ground, she trotted down the other side of the levee.

When Dog reached the foot of the levee, she bolted, ears pinned back and in a full-out gait, over a grassy patch to a sugarcane field. Jake sprinted behind her in the valley of a cane row. He wrapped the leash around his wrist twice to keep a firm grip. Blades of cane whipped across his face and stung his cheeks. Jake lifted a hand to block the blades but didn't slow down. In a blind run through twelve-foot-high cane, Jake trusted Dog to lead the way like he'd never trusted a human, much less a female.

They burst through the cane into a narrow clearing. *The maze.*

Dog stopped and pressed her nose to the path. She sniffed, plowing her snout over the ground, and then trotted a few steps. Dog kept her nose down, sniffing and snorting, as she took nervous steps in one direction, then another.

Giggles came from nearby, probably from another path in the maze. How many people had tromped through the maze this week? A hundred? Two hundred?

Jake let out a ragged breath and rubbed Dog behind the ear. Too many scents for a dog that was one-fifty-seventh bloodhound. At least Dog had validated Jake's hunch that Mackie hadn't drowned in the river, no matter how drunk he might have been. He'd made his way to Holly Grove. But why here? Why hadn't he gone home?

"Come on, Dog." Jake tugged on Dog's leash. "I'll take it from here."

Dog didn't give up. She sniffed and snorted as they meandered through the maze.

Jake had no doubt Mackie had abandoned his bike. He'd either jumped or been pushed into the river. Then he'd grabbed on to the low-lying cottonwood limb to pull himself out downriver. If he'd jumped, who could have been chasing Mackie? Who was more dangerous than a swim in the most treacherous river in America? And why would they want Mackie?

It all came back to the drug smuggling. If he was pushed, why would they leave the bike on the bank to be found? Unless, they wanted it found. But why did they want it to look like Mackie had drowned? No body. No crime. Mackie could be alive or dead.

Dead. Jake shook the thought out of his head. If he let that thought in, he'd have to face the guilt that came with it. Jake kicked a black dirt clod.

Why was I too hardheaded to be concerned when Mackie went MIA, until now?

Mackie had always said he wasn't worth killing, or he'd have been dead a long time ago. Jake sucked in a breath. Mackie was in trouble, the kind that made him worth killing.

Jake looked ahead as the path widened at the entrance of the maze. Holly Grove stood about fifty yards away.

The drugs Burl had packed through Holly Grove could get a man killed. Or a woman.

Jake quickened his pace. He couldn't allow Holly to risk getting caught snooping around the rooms. If Mackie's disappearance and the smuggling at Holly Grove were connected, he had to cut her out of all aspects of this investigation, whether she liked it or not.

Dog buried her nose in the grass and yanked Jake on a parallel path to Holly Grove along the edge of an old fence line overgrown with trees. Dog's tail wagged double time.

"You've got his scent again, don't you, Dog?" Jake looked down the fence line. Abe's cabin stood in the distance.

Dog bolted ahead with a bead on Mackie's scent.

Mackie had always been crafty when he needed to be. He would know the cabin was rarely rented and it'd be a safe place to hide. If the smugglers were staying at Holly Grove, they wouldn't think to look there for him. They'd expect him to go as far away from them as possible.

Jake charged toward the cabin.

"Bellman, my big toe," Holly muttered under her breath as she pushed a cart loaded with Italian-leather suitcases down the brick path.

Nelda was right. Holly would have to suck it up to get the publicity she needed for Holly Grove's future, but she didn't have to like it or Sylvia.

The smallest of the suitcases teetered on the top of the pile.

Why would anyone pack this many suitcases for two nights?

She secured the bag on top of the other five and sighed.

Because real divas don't have to carry them.

When she reached Abe's cabin, a toppled potted plant cluttered the path to the door. Holly stepped over the pansy remains. *Mercy. If the raccoons could open the door, they'd move in.* She made a mental note to come back with a broom to clean the mess as she slipped the key in the door.

Abe's cabin smelled of cypress and spent fires. She'd loved the scents when she'd played house in the cabin as a child.

Holly placed the suitcases on the floor. Four chairs with deerskin bottoms surrounded the table. She picked up the water bucket from the center of the table and sat it on the potbellied woodstove as a reminder to

orient the guests to 1850s life. She'd have to show
Sylvia where the well was and how to light the stove.

Holly unfolded the thin moss-stuffed mattresses
onto the rope-bottom beds on each side of the room.
She dressed the beds in fresh cotton sheets and patchwork quilts, then surveyed the cabin. *Habitable.*

She climbed the ladder to the loft and peeked into
the dark room. As her eyes adjusted, she noticed the
mattress lay flat on the bed and the sheets were mussed,
as though someone had slept there. A chill danced
across her arms. She'd removed the sheets and rolled
up the mattress when she and Nelda cleaned the cabin.
Raccoons sure as sin hadn't slept in that bed.

What if the smuggler was camping out here? Holly
frowned. Not logical. The moocher was more likely a
vagrant or teenagers, like Matt and his friends. But the
door had been locked. Holly groaned, remembering
the broken window latch Mackie had never gotten
around to fixing.

The sharp click of heels on the front porch sounded,
and Holly jerked toward the noise below. Sylvia gin-
gerly stepped over the uprooted pansies. Her lip curled
as she looked from the pansies across the room.

"Sorry about the mess," Holly called down from the
ladder. "Raccoons. I'll clean that up as soon as I finish
here."

"Are you telling me raccoons just wander around
here?"

"Only at night."

"And this is your suite for three?"

"It will be as soon as I get it ready," Holly said, forcing more cheer into her voice than she thought she
could.

"This isn't acceptable."

"Pardon me?"

"This isn't a suite."

"It does sleep three. I thought you knew it was rustic. I told your producer all about Abe's cabin and sent her the Web link so she could check it out. She made the reservation." Holly lifted a shoulder. "Besides, it's all I have available."

"I'll just rent a room in town. Have the bellman put my luggage back in the car."

"The bellman is gone for the day, and there isn't a hotel within thirty miles. I'm it."

"Great." Sylvia looked up at Holly. "What are you doing on a ladder, anyway?"

"Getting your room ready."

"Up there?"

"It's called a loft. It's more private, but if you'd like to sleep in one of the beds downstairs, that's fine with me."

Not waiting for an answer, Holly crawled into the loft. She scrambled to the bed and snatched the dirty sheets off of it. A paperback tumbled out of the sheets. *Silence of the Lamps.* She opened the novel to find Miss Alice's name inside. Holly eyed the ladder. No way had Miss Alice climbed up here. She stuffed the paperback in the wad of dirty sheets, then grabbed a fresh set of sheets from the nook beside the bed.

"Where are you?" Sylvia's voice carried to the loft as she spoke on her cell phone and Holly changed the sheets. "Finally. Follow the brick sidewalk, only go left, away from the house, and look for a shack."

Shack? "Well, la-di-da," Holly whispered to herself as she finished changing the sheets. If she didn't need the publicity, she'd evict Sylvia from the shack. Holly

tamped down her ire as she backed down the ladder
with the basket of soiled sheets. Two days. That's all she
had to endure of Sylvia, and millions would see Holly
Grove on her show. More reservations. Cash to pay
taxes, bills, Nelda . . . Holly stepped onto the cypress
planks and turned to find Sylvia waiting, arms crossed.

"We're going to shoot everything tonight, during
the séance. I won't be staying tomorrow night."

Good. The sooner she leaves, the better. "Aw, I'm so sorry
to hear that. Abe's cabin isn't for everyone, but some
people appreciate it."

"Who? Survivalists?"

Holly nearly laughed, but Sylvia's face posted a
"no-fun zone" look. "Let me show you around," she
said.

Sylvia looked left to right and smirked. "I believe I
can see it all from here, except the loft. Unless you
have a sauna and a feather bed up there, I'm guessing
it's the same."

"All true to the period." Holly straightened her
spine to address the prima donna. "You may not know
it, but this place is on the National Register of Historic
Places."

"Well, I live in the twenty-first century and like it
that way."

"Well," Holly said, mocking Sylvia and not too
subtly, "in that case, there are a few things you need to
know about the nineteenth century and the historical
accuracy of the cabin."

A clatter came from across the room, and a young
woman, loaded down with equipment bags, stumbled
through the door. Her auburn hair was swept into a
ponytail, which whipped around as she dumped the

bags on the floor. She wore khaki pants, a pocketed vest, and not a bit of makeup.

Sylvia let out a groan. "This is my backpacking-naturalist producer, Liz. Holly owns this place, and her husband is the ghost."

"Technically, he's not my husband anymore. You know, until death do we part and all that."

Liz's green eyes narrowed as she looked the room over. "Is this place what I think it is . . . or was?"

Holly nodded.

"If walls could talk," Liz said.

"They'd probably cry." Holly sighed. "Most of the slave quarters have been torn down at the antebellum homes that survived the Civil War. Places like this are a reminder of an ugly part of history, but one that is important to remember. I restored the only one left standing here as accurately as I could."

"I see," Sylvia said and turned to Liz. "Where's Bob?"

"He's setting up the equipment to get some exterior shots before dark," Liz answered.

Holly checked her watch. "I've got a tour in thirty minutes, so I better show you a few things that may prove useful before morning."

She walked to the fireplace and took a box of matches from the mantel. She shook the matches. "We're expecting a cold front tonight. Just light the newspaper under the kindling if you get cold."

"You have that, Liz?" Sylvia said.

"No problem."

Holly crossed the room to the potbellied stove and took the water bucket off the top. "If you want hot water to bathe, light the wood in the stove the same way."

"No hot water?" Sylvia glanced around the room. "Where's the bathroom?"

"I'm getting to that." Holly grabbed the bucket and walked to the back door.

Sylvia's mouth hung open. "You've got to be kidding."

Holly opened the door and pointed to the outhouse. "It's all part of the authentic eighteen-fifties experience."

Sylvia clutched her chest. "You're serious."

"Cool," Liz said. "I've never used an outhouse before."

Holly automatically liked Liz.

"And I never will," Sylvia added as they followed Holly out the back door.

"There's a guests' bathroom downstairs at Holly Grove, if you want to make the walk, but there's no tub. The well is over here." Holly turned toward the well and saw Jake, led by Dog, fast approaching.

Jake jogged across the grass like a pro football player in game-day shape. She could have sworn she heard a collective sigh from the other two women.

Sylvia shielded her eyes from the sun and squinted. A smile inched across her lips as Jake came closer.

"Mmm. Is he a guest here?" she said, never taking her stare off Jake.

Who could blame her?

"That's Jake." Holly smiled and waved at Jake as he jogged closer to them. "We're old friends," she said, but it didn't sound quite right. Heat pricked her cheeks.

Sylvia looked down at Holly and smirked. "Old friends, huh?"

"If he's staying here, she'll be camping out here as long as he does," Liz said, rolling her eyes at Holly.

Crapola. Holly knew the woman was trouble, but not that kind.

CHAPTER 34

The chill of the fall air bit through Holly. Was she jealous? Couldn't be. She had no right to be. And why wouldn't Jake be interested in a woman as beautiful as Sylvia? Crisp leaves skittered across the brick walkway and brushed her ankles as she made a quick introduction and then excused herself. Jake was a free agent, after all.

Holly turned to walk away, then remembered she hadn't told Jake that Toni was "the backer" or that there was a moocher in Abe's cabin. She spun around and called Jake over.

"Looks like you have a fan," she told him.

"What makes you say that?"

"It might have been her drooling as I introduced you."

Jake shrugged, as though he hadn't noticed.

"Toni is the mystery lender. They're not the smugglers."

"How do you know?"

"I heard them talking."

"Were you snooping?"

"Maybe. Oh, and just FYI, when I checked the loft, it

looked like someone had slept there last night, and not a paying guest."

Jake's face turned ashy. "Any idea who?"

"At first, I thought it could be the smuggler. Then I decided it would be stupid for them to get busted for mooching a room. Then I found the same book Miss Alice was reading the other night. I can't imagine her climbing into the loft to read."

"Probably not, but I'm sure there's more than one copy of the book. How'd they get in?"

"I could have left it unlocked, but a latch is broken on the window. Mackie was supposed to fix it, but—"

"I'll take care of it," Jake said. "No more snooping. Don't leave the house until you talk to me."

He walked away without another word.

The grandfather clock in the hall chimed its distinct half-hour tune. The séance would start at eight o'clock. She scanned the crowd one more time and caught a glimpse of Mr. Dunbar. Miss Alice was talking his ear off, as Grandmother Rose used to say.

The honeymooners hadn't shown up yet. Holly wanted to believe they weren't at the séance because they were "honeymooning." Of course, Holly had barely seen them since she accidentally cursed the bride. And how could she eliminate them, since she hadn't been able to search their room?

The only other person missing was Jake. Burl had suspected him, but she'd dismissed it earlier as jealousy. What if Burl was right?

This would be a perfect time for the smugglers to make their way to the river and back unnoticed by the other guests. She had to know if the honeymooners were in their room. She grabbed a bottle of wine, then scooted out the door.

When Holly reached the honeymoon cottage, the lights were off. She cradled the bottle of wine and knocked on the door. If they answered, she'd offer it as lagniappe. If they didn't, she'd use her master key.

No answer.

She knocked again. "Room service."

Fishing the master key out of her purse, she looked over her shoulder and down the brick path. All clear. If they came back, she'd just say she was leaving the bottle of wine in their room as a surprise.

Holly took one more glance behind her before easing the key in the lock. Her heart thudded so loudly, she wondered if she could hear Mickey and Charlie if they walked up right behind her.

Woman up. You've got to do this. She took small steps through the dark room. She tripped over something on the floor and caught herself on the bedpost. Her heart pounded as she felt for the fake Tiffany lamp she knew was on the bedside table.

With the click of the switch, an amber glow illuminated the room. Holly trained her eyes on the place where she'd tripped. A sleeping bag? Why would honeymooners have a sleeping bag on the floor? A fight?

She stepped over the rumpled sleeping bag and opened the armoire. One of two big duffel bags stacked side by side toppled out and landed on her foot. Pain shot through her toes. "Ouch!" What did they have in there? She kneeled and unzipped the bag.

Her mouth went dry.

CHAPTER 35

"Holy moly." Holly stared at a Rambo gun and enough bullets for a small military coup. Her heart thudded like gunfire as she pulled the mouth of the bag open as wide as she could without touching the gun. Night-vision binoculars, a satellite phone, a GPS, and some other gadgets she had never seen before were stuffed in the corners of the bag.

All this gear would allow them to sneak around at night, when everyone else slept. She had no doubt she'd found the smugglers, but she had to catch them with the dope. If they'd made the trade, they wouldn't hang around Holly Grove with their merchandise. She eyed the other duffel bag and sucked in a big breath. It could be filled with cash for the trade.

Metal teeth moaned as she unzipped the second duffel bag. Her shoulders slumped over the contents. Dirty laundry. She plunged her hand into the clothes, and her fingers brushed against something cold, hard, and angular. Pushing the laundry aside, she spotted a tablet PC. She turned it on. Quickly, she clicked the last used application, a webcam.

A fuzzy image in a distorted blue-green color came
into view. A night-vision webcam? She squinted to
make out the video. Trees, maybe cottonwoods, swayed
in the breeze, and a river rushed by. She blinked. It was
her Mississippi riverbank, just over the levee. Were
they watching for the barge to snug up to the bank?
Why wouldn't the boat captain just call them? Unless
they didn't want a record of the call? Or was the camera
to make sure the area was clear? *Whoa. This is way too
James Bond.*

Movement on the screen caught her eye. *A man?*
Holly searched the screen for a zoom function. She
tapped the magnifying-glass icon three times. She
shook her head, as though that would clear the image.
Mackie?

Voices from outside jarred her from the video.
Blood pumped through her with a whooshing sound
as she slammed the PC shut and stuffed it back in the
duffel, then pushed it in the armoire. The voices neared,
followed by the unmistakable metallic scrape of a key
sliding into a lock.

Oh, crapola. Holly dove under the bed. She needed
Jake. Clutching her phone, she searched for Jake's
number, then pinched her eyes shut. She'd never entered it from the registration card. *Double crapola.*

From under the bed, Holly watched the door swing
open. Feminine feet clad in ballerina flats padded into
the room, followed by a pair of Red Wing boots. Holly
couldn't see anything from the calf up but guessed it
was Mickey and Charlie.

"Ooh." The ballerina flats stopped short, then spun
around. "Keep your hands off my butt," Mickey said.

"We're supposed to be on our honeymoon, aren't
we?" Charlie's boots stood toe-to-toe with Mickey's flats.

"Only when we're in public." Mickey tapped her foot. "This is private."

"Sorry. Guess I got lost in character."

I'll say. They'd acted like they were in heat every time Holly had seen them.

"Get lost in checking the webcam for action," Mickey said, walking to the armoire.

Holly barely breathed for fear they would hear her. She needed Jake. Holly scrolled through her call history to see if his number was still there.

A duffel bag thudded to the floor, and Holly nearly gasped.

"That could have broken my foot," Mickey said. "Be careful how you put the equipment in there."

"Broken your foot? That thing is pointed at me. You could have blown my head off."

"Okay, okay. Cool it," Mickey said. "Jake says it's going down soon. I'm going to gear up."

Jake says. What does Jake have to do with them?

A knock sounded at the door.

The ballerina flats padded to the door.

"Change of plans. I want you both at the séance to keep an eye on Holly. I don't want her messing this up," Jake said. "Put your phones on vibrate, and leave if I call you."

"Sure thing, boss."

Boss?

Her heart tumbled in a free fall.

CHAPTER 36

Holly scooted from under the bed as soon as Mickey and Charlie left. Her legs wobbled a bit when she stood. Disappointment stewed in a toxic brew in her gut. How could Jake have fallen so far?

She steadied herself and made her way back to the main house. Logic told her Jake was nothing like the man she thought she knew, but her heart didn't want to accept it. She'd have to see him make the exchange to believe it, and now she'd have that opportunity.

Minutes later, Holly stood in the candlelit foyer of Holly Grove for a séance, along with the rest of her guests.

"Oh, spirit, come to me so that I may help you find peace," Angel said in a melodious chant, with her eyes closed. She stood with her arms lifted, framed by the massive pocket doors that opened to the dining room. As though on cue, a breeze from nowhere pulsed her black, flowing dress in ripples around her body. Her eyes popped open.

Holly sucked in a breath, along with the rest of the guests, to form a collective gasp.

"The spirit is willing," Angel said, lowering her arms with the grace of a dancer. You may enter." She spun around and paced into the dining room.

Holly and the guests inched their way into the darkened room. Tiny candles hovered in the center of the pitch-black room. Holly's eyes began to acclimate to the dark, and she noticed the tea light candles firmly planted on the dining table, in front of each of the chairs. *Definitely creepy.*

The scent of sulfur and jasmine permeated the room. Holly had never known the room to be so dark. She made her way to the floor-to-ceiling window and touched velvety black cloth. Staging? The dark fabric blocked out moonlight, starlight, and the glow from the gaslights on the porch.

"Allow your eyes to adjust to the darkness, and then sit in silence, please," Angel said.

The darkness faded with time, and the eight tea light candles on the table cast a dim glow over the room. Angel sat at the head of the table. Duke, Toni, Miss Alice, the Fletchers, Mickey, and Charlie filled in the chairs on each side. Jake and Mr. Dunbar were noticeably absent, but Mr. Dunbar had asked for aspirin earlier for his headache. And the reason Jake wasn't there made Holly wish for an antacid.

A small red dot of a video camera glowed in the darkness from the corner of the room. Behind the red light, a dark silhouette moved. Holly glanced around and noticed another red dot and a smaller silhouette in the opposite corner.

"Ready in five," Liz said from behind the camera.

Sylvia held her own candle and sauntered in like a runway model. Her white dress reflected the candlelight, giving her a chic supernatural glow. Anyone else holding a candle under their chin would look like a sixth grader telling a spooky story. *Bless her tiny little heart.*

From behind the other camera, Bob counted down. "Three, two, and action."

As though no one was in the room except Sylvia, she paused and stared into the lens. "Tonight *Inquiring Minds* is going deeper into the supernatural than ever before," Sylvia said in pitch perfection. She glided like a cat to the end of the table opposite Angel. "Join us as we summon the dead at Holly Grove Plantation."

She seated herself, then leaned forward and looked into the red eye of the camera. "*Inquiring Minds* is all about explaining the unexplainable." She cocked a perfectly plucked brow. "Since we haven't seen the reported ghost in the grove, renowned New Orleans psychic and medium Angel Dupree will lead us in a séance to contact the resident ghost."

"Please join hands so we may call the spirit to join us," Angel said, clasping her warm hand around Holly's.

An eerie tension rippled from Angel's fingers through Holly. She repressed a shiver and dismissed the feeling as nerves. Who wouldn't have the heebie-jeebies with cameras watching every move in a room decked out for spooks but harboring criminals?

Holly stole a glance at Mickey and Charlie. *Still there.*

Toni let loose an excited squeal. "Don't you love this, Dukie?"

Duke shrugged. "If you like it, I like it."

"Shh," Angel said, cutting her gaze to Toni, then to the rest of the guests. "We must save our energy for calling the spirit."

Holly caught her lip between her teeth. *There's that energy thing again.* Burl had mentioned how he needed her energy to appear and how it was hard work to be visible to her. Holly slipped her hand in Miss Alice's hand and didn't feel a thing.

"Hogwash," Miss Alice said, dropping Holly's hand.

Angel frowned. "Is there someone beyond whom you wish to contact?"

"I don't need a séance to contact my Harry." Miss Alice straightened in her chair. "I speak to him every day."

Angel lifted her chin and eyed Miss Alice. "But does he answer?"

"Of course not," Miss Alice said. "He's dead."

"If Harry wishes to speak to you tonight, he will, if you focus your energy," Angel said.

Miss Alice huffed and took Holly's hand again. "I'll believe it when I see it."

An odd tingle trickled from Miss Alice's hand to Holly's.

Kate Fletcher patted Miss Alice's other hand and whispered, "He hears you." Then Kate smiled at her husband, Tom. "I'll hear you and the boys, too, if . . ."

Tom's Adam's apple bobbed up and down, as though he were trying to swallow something too big. He cleared his throat and looked at his lap, like he could find a way to hide his sadness there. A wet trail crept from the corner of his eye.

Holly's throat tightened around all the empty words of comfort she could offer Tom.

"Think of nothing, except here and now." Angel closed her eyes, but no one else did. She tilted her creamy white face upward. "Nothing else exists."

Holly scanned the room for Burl. Would he mar Angel's perfect record of ghost calling?

"Oh, spirit, use my body as you will," Angel continued in a melodious chant.

Burl's hazy form appeared behind Angel. "Why couldn't I get a woman to say that when I was alive?"

Holly's hand ached as Angel clamped down her grip. Angel breathed in through her nose, then exhaled slowly. "A spirit is among us."

Holly looked from Angel to Burl.

"Tell me your name," Angel said.

Burl leaned down and whispered in her ear, "Burl Winston Davis the Third."

Angel nodded. "His name is Burl."

Holly's mouth gaped open as she shot Burl a look. "Don't be so gullible, Blondie."

"Burl Winston Davis the Third," Angel whispered.

Burl paced over to Holly, then thumbed toward Angel. "Big whoop. She knows my name and that I'm dead. That doesn't mean she's psychic."

"Does anyone here know Burl? He's speaking to Blondie."

Burl jerked his head around and looked at Angel like she was speaking in tongues. "Holy cow. She can hear me."

Holly's jaw went slack. No one called her Blondie except him, and there was no way Angel could have known that. *Angel is for real.*

"Burl calls me Blondie," Holly said in a small, shaky voice.

Angel nodded. "Burl, how may I help you find your way from this world to the next?"

Holly's brain skittered over the possibility Angel might actually be able to usher Burl into the next world as the guests looked from one to the other. An uneasy hush settled over the dining room. Angel's séance was no dog and pony show.

"What a plant," Duke said as he stood.

Toni yanked him down by his Hawaiian shirt. "Sit down, Dukie. I want to see what happens next."

Bob focused his camera in on Toni.

"We're on TV, and you don't want to look like a barbarian, do you?" Toni asked.

"Better a barbarian than a sucker," Duke shot back.

"If you ruin the séance, you're the one who'll look like an idiot." Toni batted her lashes at Duke. "Come on, Dukie. Be a sport."

Duke settled back into his chair. "Only for you, fly baby."

"Watch this." Burl sauntered to Duke's chair and blew out the candle in front of him.

Duke stared at the spent candle a second, then glanced around at the remaining lit candles. He smirked. "Trick candles. You watch. They'll all go out at different times."

"He is an idiot." Burl blew down Duke's collar. "Can you feel that, big guy?"

Duke shivered and looked over his shoulder.

Angel eyed Duke. "Burl seems to be a prankster."

Burl melted into Duke's body. When Duke opened his mouth, Burl's voice came out. "Joke's on you, Conan." Burl seeped out of Duke and stood behind him.

"I didn't say that," Duke said, jerking his head from side to side.

"If you want to use a body to communicate, use mine," Angel said.

"Gladly." Burl strode to Angel. He hesitated behind her chair; then his gaze drifted to Sylvia. "What about her?"

"Sylvia, the spirit wishes to use your body to communicate. Are you willing?" Angel asked.

"Me?" Sylvia stared, wide-eyed. She quickly recovered

and looked into the camera. "We never back away from a challenge at *Inquiring Minds*."

Burl poured a look over Sylvia. "I'm going to love this."

He seeped into Sylvia's body. She stood and rubbed her hands down her curves.

"Nice." Burl's voice came from her lips.

Duke stared at Sylvia from across the table.

"What are you staring at, Conan?" Burl's voice came from Sylvia's body again.

"Nothing," Duke choked out.

Angel addressed the members of the séance. "Would you all agree the spirit is here, in Sylvia's body?"

Everyone nodded.

"Then we'll proceed." Angel sucked in a breath. "Burl, you don't belong in this world. Can you tell me why you are here?"

"Duh. I died and didn't make the cut for heaven."

Angel nodded. "And why do you suppose you didn't?"

"Unfinished business."

"How can we help you finish this business?" Angel asked.

Holly piped up. "That's not something that he wants to share with everyone." And especially with Mickey and Charlie, if those were even their names.

"That's right. Very personal." Burl winked at Holly with Sylvia's mascara-laden lashes.

"I've helped hundreds find their way, and none of them were ever trapped here because of a business problem. Are you sure you don't have an unresolved personal issue?"

"Positive."

"What about you, Holly? Do you have any unresolved

personal issues with Burl? Honesty is important to his journey."

"Yeah. He didn't live long enough for me to divorce him."

Burl grumbled. "What is this? Marriage counseling?"

"It's whatever you need to find your way," Angel said in a voice as calm as a windless day.

Sylvia looked down at her curves again. "I can't handle this," Burl said from her body. She did a little dance, like ants were crawling on her; then Burl lifted from her body like smog.

Sylvia slumped in her chair. "What happened?"

"Don't worry. I've got it all on camera," Liz said.

Burl leaned between the honeymooners and blew all the candles out, plunging the room into darkness. "I'm out of here."

Angel took her hand from Holly's. "The spirit has left us."

"For good?" Holly said. "Just like that?"

Angel sighed. "I'm sorry. He's not ready to be led to the other side."

Chairs scraped the cypress floor; then light from the chandelier flooded the room just as Mickey and Charlie slipped out the door.

Holly followed, then watched from the back door as they headed toward the river.

"Don't go after them." Burl's chilled breath brushed her ear.

"I don't have a choice."

Holly ducked behind an oak tree as the fake honeymooners disappeared over the levee. She'd lagged behind so they wouldn't see or hear her, but her heart pounded like she'd run a race.

Sucking in a breath, Holly remembered playing hide-and-seek as a kid and how her lungs had burned when she ran for home base. A fallen cypress over the levee. Back then, the race from the top of the levee to the cypress had been the easiest place to get tagged out. Now, there was more riding on getting over the levee without being seen than a child's game.

The wind howled as she mounted the levee and her heels sank into the sod. She groaned. *These are my best stilettos, and they'll never be the same.*

Holly wondered if she'd ever be the same, either. She rubbed her hands over her arms to fight the chill. When she neared the top of the levee, she dropped to her knees. Her black stockings wouldn't survive the crawl, but she dared not stand at the top of the levee, where she could be seen.

She peered over the levee. Two dark silhouettes moved into the wooded bottomland of the river. Beyond the woods, she glimpsed a barge, lights off, snugged against the bank. Her heart pounded double time.

Everything rested on busting the smuggling ring, and it was going down tonight.

This was her chance to dart over the levee and follow them. She stood, then trotted down the levee in a diagonal line to keep her footing and move faster. Her heels helped by digging into the earthen levee, but she'd have to ditch them if she really had to run. She reached the massive fallen cypress and stole a peek around it.

No sign of Mickey or Charlie. If she followed them into the woods, they might hear her crunch through the leaves. She needed help. Holly dug her cell phone out of her pocket, then punched in 9-1-1.

"I need the FBI, the Coast Guard, and the police right now," she whispered. "There's a drug deal going down right in my backyard."

"May I have your name and your location?" the operator asked in a crisp professional tone.

"This is Holly Davis, and I'm over the levee behind my house."

"Holly? This is Melanie." Any trace of crisp professionalism in the operator's voice evaporated into a familiar Southern twang.

Holly remembered Melanie from high school. She'd married right after graduation and had twins lickety-split. "Melanie Breaux?"

"Yeah. God, it's been a long time since I saw you. What are you doing on the levee, and why do you think there's a drug deal going down at Holly Grove?"

"It's a long story," Holly said as she gripped the phone a little tighter. "Just make the calls."

"Didn't we just send an ambulance and the sheriff to your place a couple of weeks ago for a drug overdose?"

"That was all a mistake. This is the real thing. I need you to call this in right away. There's a barge full of dope pushed up on the bank, and I don't know how long it'll be here."

"Are you sure you didn't fall off the wagon, Holly?"

"Huh?" She wanted to reach through the phone and strangle Melanie.

"You know. That little problem you have."

"I never took drugs," Holly said, noticing the pitch of her voice rise. "The Deltas just thought I did."

"I heard you were in rehab."

"Rumor. Are you going to call for help or not?"

Melanie sighed. "It's my sworn duty to act on all 911 calls, but you really need to get in a program and stay there."

"Melanie, I'm stone-cold sober and straight as they come. Please call this in."

"You do know you can be charged for misuse of this service."

"So charge me. Just make the calls."

The phone clicked. Holly held the phone out and stared at it in disbelief. Didn't 911 operators always stay on the line until help arrived?

Leaves rustled nearby, and Holly froze.

CHAPTER 37

Please be a raccoon or an armadillo, Holly prayed as she hid behind the fallen cypress on the riverside of the levee. The wind blustered through the trees, making every shadow jump in the dark. The police had to be here soon. Surely, Melanie had made the calls. But what if she hadn't?

Holly waited motionless, listening and watching. The thud of her heart nearly deafened her. She held her breath and then let it out slowly to quiet her nerves.

Leaves rustled again. A dark figure stepped from the shadows.

Holly's heart rate amped to the max. She studied the figure. Too small for Jake or Charlie.

"Is that you, Mickey?" Holly called, pumping a light tone into her voice, as though she had nothing to hide.

"Couldn't sleep and decided to go for a run," Mickey said as she stepped into view.

A run? In a totally black cat-burglar outfit? Yeah, right. And how did she change clothes?

Holly cupped her phone in her hand, then slipped

it in her pocket. "Just taking in the fall air." Holly yawned. "Maybe I can sleep now. See you in the morning," she said, then turned toward the levee. The pile of dirt stood between her and safety like Mount Everest.

Please, please, please let me get to the other side.

"Wait," Mickey called.

Crapola. Holly looked over her shoulder.

Mickey jogged up the levee. "I'll walk with you." She seemed thicker than usual, and a bulge poked out at her side.

Holly swallowed hard. *A gun?* "Sure," she said, trying to act nonchalant.

Mickey fell in step beside Holly.

She doesn't know I know she's a smuggler. Be cool. All I have to do is get to civilization at Holly Grove.

As they neared the crest, the silhouette of a male figure topped the levee. Holly came to a dead stop. She had nowhere to run. The figure turned, revealing a keg of a gut, one belonging to Sheriff Walker.

Holly's feet jumped into action. Before her brain had a chance to catch up, she stood panting at his side. "Thank God you got here so fast." Holly pointed to Mickey as she joined them. "She's a smuggler. There's two more down at the river."

"Is that right?" he said.

Something about his tone niggled at Holly. "Look, I know what you're thinking, but this is no misunderstanding."

"I think it is," Mickey said, reaching for the bulge in her pocket. "If you'll take a look at my ID—"

Sheriff Walker drew his weapon. "Easy there. If

you don't want a bullet between your pretty eyes, it's best you drop that weapon."

"Yes, sir," Mickey said. She eased a pistol to the ground and then held her hands in the air. "You may want to see my ID, Sheriff. We're on the same side."

"What?" Holly asked, still reeling from it all.

Sheriff Walker jacked his chin up at Holly. "Here." He pitched Holly a flashlight. "Get her ID."

Holly's hands shook so badly she laced her hand through the strap on the flashlight to keep from dropping it. She fumbled through Mickey's jacket pocket and pulled out a leather case. She stepped back to Sheriff Walker and shone the light on the ID. Holly gasped. "Agent Mickey Heart. Immigration and Customs Enforcement." Her throat tightened. Mickey had called Jake boss. "And Jake?"

Mickey lowered her arms and eyed the sheriff. "I told you we were on the same side."

A fire-blue flash. A deafening blast. And Mickey lifted off her feet and tumbled down the riverside of the levee.

Holly's scream caught in her throat. She wanted to rewind what she'd seen. It'd happened so fast, it didn't seem real. It couldn't be. Unless . . .

"Too bad I didn't notice we were on the same side before I shot her," Sheriff Walker said as he turned to Holly.

Dropping the ID, she took a slow step back and then another. She clutched the flashlight, and the beam quivered in the dark as she flashed it on the sheriff. "W-when I called 911, I told Melanie to call the FBI, the Coast Guard, and . . ." She took another backward step. "They'll be here any minute."

"I wouldn't count on that." He pointed his gun her way.

Tiny hairs on her neck pricked to attention. Was this it? She wasn't ready to die. Talk about unfinished business. The smuggling would never end at Holly Grove. Could she end up a ghost like Burl? And what about Jake? He was out there somewhere, trying to bust the smugglers. She had to warn him.

Holly had to do something. Anything. She aimed the bright beam in the sheriff's eyes. Maybe he'd miss.

He squinted but didn't lower his gun.

"Wait! If you shoot me, I'll haunt you for the rest of your miserable life." The beam quivered across his face. "I swear I will."

Her hands trembled, and light streaked across the bank of the levee. Behind the sheriff, she spotted a dark figure crawling up the levee. Mickey.

"You'll be right at home, because after the drug bust here, Holly Grove will be confiscated and sold at the sheriff's sale for a price I can afford."

"Over my dead body."

"Yep." He raised the gun.

She held her hands in the air. "No, no, no. Bad choice of words."

The flashlight dangled from her wrist, and the beam bounced across the ground. Holly's eyes widened as a sliver of light crossed Mickey's body. Only a few more feet and Mickey could grab the sheriff's feet. Then Holly would throw the flashlight at him, jump him, or whatever it took.

"Let's think about this," Holly said, buying time. "How are you going to explain shooting me? I don't have a gun or any dope."

"That's the beauty of it. You will after you're dead."

* * *

Where was she? Jake rapped on Holly's bedroom door again, then paced the hall. Mickey and Charlie had just left her. How could she disappear in the five minutes it had taken him to get to Holly Grove from the staging area?

To hell with it. He dug the duplicate he'd made of the master key out of his pocket, then unlocked her door. He stepped into her pitch-black bedroom and flipped on the light.

Rhett lay curled up in the middle of her bed, alone.

Jake slapped the door facing on the way out. He jogged down the stairs to the kitchen and found it dark. He checked all the downstairs rooms again and then looked out the window at her Tahoe parked in its usual place. *She's got to be here.*

He returned to the big hall at the center of the house. A cool draft dusted his neck and sent a chill down his back. He rubbed a hand over his neck, then glanced behind him. His reflection caught his eye, and he remembered Holly had covered that mirror for the Haunted Pilgrimage. The sheer black cloth lay in a puddle on the chest beneath the mirror. He picked up the cloth and rubbed it between his fingers. It wasn't like Holly to allow even the smallest detail of the Haunted Pilgrimage to veer from what tourists expected.

A small foggy circle formed at eye level in the mirror. He leaned closer. The circle grew to the size of a basketball. *What the . . . ?*

He laughed at himself. *You idiot. You breathed on the mirror.*

Jake took a step back as a word formed in the foggy circle. *Holly.*

Turning in a full circle, Jake chuckled. "Okay, Holly. You got me."

Then another word was scribbled across the mirror. *River.*

And another. *Danger.*

The unmistakable sound of a gun blast reverberated in the distance.

He tore out of the house and across the lawn. Pulling his nine-millimeter from under his coat, he never broke his gait as he neared the levee. His chest burned, but his legs pumped as fast as they could. He spotted two dark figures.

Jake squinted. One figure was smaller than the other. *A female?* She held her hands in the air. With each step, the scene became clearer. A woman stood at gunpoint. *Holly?*

He planted his feet and dropped a bead on the shooter. A black blur rose from the ground and tackled the gunman as twin blasts from Jake and the gunman pierced the night air.

The gunman rolled in a tangle of arms and legs with the shadowy figure to the base of the levee.

But where was Holly?

Jake dashed to the tangled heap of bodies at the foot of the levee. He kicked the gun away from the man, who lay facedown, with a bloody stain on his shoulder.

Mickey struggled to her knees, then stood. "You winged him."

Jake picked up the man's gun and tossed it to Mickey. "Shoot him in the other shoulder if he moves."

"Yes, sir."

Praying Holly was alive, Jake bounded up and over the other side of the levee. "Holly."

He jogged across the base of the levee, scanning the ground. Nothing. Relief trickled over Jake. He must have clipped the gunman before he got his shot off, or he would have found . . . A cold sweat drenched Jake.

He had to find her. And fast. Before she got herself into deadly trouble.

Holly woke to jarring steps that weren't hers. Someone was carrying her. Her vision blurred as she tried to focus on the man's face. A warm trickle slid from her forehead into her eyes, and her head ached like she'd been hit with a hammer.

The last thing she remembered was staring down the barrel of Sheriff Walker's gun. Then it was as though she'd fallen into the black hole of nothing Burl had talked about.

A man huffed as he carried her with quick strides.

She wiped her eyes, and her vision cleared a bit. Mud, smeared like camo paint, striped the man's face. "Mackie?"

"Shh."

"What happened?"

"You got nicked with a bullet. You're gonna be fine, but if we don't find a place to hide, we're both gonna get shot."

Holly wiped her hand over her face, and deep red blood coated her fingers. A wave of nausea flooded her. "I think I'm going to be sick."

Mackie stopped short.

Shouts in Spanish came from ahead. A muscled-up guy wielding a machine gun stepped onto the path in front of them. The wolf tattoo on his bicep swelled as he tightened his grip on his weapon.

Two more guys with big guns joined him, one bald and sporting a dirty-blond goatee and the other with dark hair slicked back into a ponytail. They jabbered to each other in Spanish, and Holly wished she'd paid more attention in Spanish I.

The one with the ponytail pulled a cell phone out of his pocket. After a few words in Spanish, he stuffed the phone back in his pocket, then said something to the wolf man. With a nod, the wolf man headed in her direction.

Mackie's muscles tensed as he hefted her a little higher in his arms.

She watched a hazy version of the wolf man walk around them and then poke Mackie in the back with the gun. Mackie staggered forward a bit.

"Move," the wolf man said, but the word sounded slow and distorted.

Holly tilted her head away from Mackie and puked.

A dull buzz sounded behind Jake as he mounted the levee. He turned and glimpsed a green glow on the ground. A cell phone? He jogged over and picked up the phone but missed the call. He recognized the cell phone as Holly's. Miss Alice's name was scrolled across the screen as a missed call. Likely not relevant.

"Jake," Mickey yelled from the other side of the levee. "Is Holly okay?"

He jogged to the top of the steep incline, then down toward Mickey. "Yeah, but she must have taken off."

Mickey hitched a boot under the gunman and rolled him over.

Handcuffed and muddy, Sheriff Walker moaned. "I thought I shot you."

"You did." Mickey thumped her chest. "Kevlar."

"I never liked that jerk," Jake said, handing Holly's phone to Mickey. "It's not locked. Find the call history. I have a feeling our sheriff here got a call."

"A 911 at 11:04," she said.

"How convenient for you, Sheriff." Holly had unknowingly tipped off Burl's evident replacement. "If Holly hadn't called, you'd have missed getting busted tonight."

The sheriff groaned. "Screw you."

"Did you read the sheriff his rights?" Jake asked.

"Yes, sir," Mickey said.

"I've got some advice for you, Sheriff."

"Keep it," he grunted.

"Your goons heard the shots." Jake took the sheriff's phone from his belt. "I bet your last call was a heads-up for them."

"My phone is locked, kid." the sheriff said, glaring at Jake.

"Is that a fact?" Jake rolled the sheriff over and brushed his thumb over his phone to unlock it. "You tell them you handled the problem. It's called cooperation, and it buys you a lighter sentence, sometimes."

Jake leaned in closer to the handcuffed sheriff and hit REDIAL. "You do know what happens to former lawmen in prison, don't you?"

Sheriff Walker glared at Jake as he held the phone close enough to the sheriff for him to talk.

On speaker, a male voice answered.

"Problem solved," the sheriff said.

"Not quite," said a voice with only a hint of an accent. "My men found two more problems you evidently missed. A gringo and a gringa. No more noise. I'll have them disposed of upriver. You see to it there are no more problems on the bank tonight." The phone clicked off.

"Where are the state troopers and the Coast Guard?" Mickey asked. "Didn't you call them?"

"I'm guessing the sheriff made some calls, too, and diverted them." Jake cast a hard look at the sheriff.

"But there's only two of us," she said. "I counted five on the deck of the barge. Could be more I couldn't see. We need backup."

"Make the call, but I can't wait," Jake said. *Screw procedure. Screw a clean bust.* "They have Holly." He turned and ran up the levee.

"And Charlie. I'm going with you," Mickey yelled.

Seconds later, she jogged behind Jake as she called for backup, reported that they were in pursuit, and that the sheriff was in custody and needed an ambulance.

"Custody?" Jake called over his shoulder.

"He's not going anywhere. I cuffed his hands to his feet."

A rustling came from the brush nearby. "It's me, Charlie."

Mickey rushed over to Charlie and threw her arms around him. "I thought they had you."

Charlie grinned. "I knew you had the hots for me."

"In your dreams," she said, stepping back.

Jake raised his hands. "Hold on a minute. If you're not the gringo, then who is?"

"An old guy in camo. I spotted him on the surveillance camera."

A sickening feeling settled into Jake's gut. He prayed Mackie wasn't trying to play the hero.

CHAPTER 38

Holly's derriere was cold, but what could she expect from sitting on the steel deck of a barge in the wee hours of the morning? She dared not move. The wolf man held a gun on them, and from the icy look in his eyes, he'd used it before. Somehow, she had to get off this barge before it shoved off, or she'd never see Holly Grove again.

Mackie sat beside her, but the wolf man had ordered them to keep quiet. She had so many questions as she studied Mackie. He looked like an aged Rambo with a salt-and-pepper braid down his back. He must have lost fifteen pounds and gained it back in muscle.

She eyed their captor. Could she and a retired Rambo fight their way out of here? Holly blew out a sigh. Where was Jake? The Coast Guard? Anybody? *Sweet baby Jesus, Mary, and Joseph, have mercy.*

The bald guy with the blondish goatee called to the wolf man. He ambled over and handed the bald guy a cigarette.

No way could they take down two bad-to-the-bone

smugglers, but if help didn't arrive soon, she'd have to think of something.

While the smugglers smoked and jawed back and forth in Spanish, Holly leaned over to Mackie and whispered, "What were you doing out here, and where have you been?" She looked him up and down. "Boot camp?"

His worn face cracked into a grin. "Yep. Miss Alice's boot camp."

"Huh?"

He rubbed his neck. "Long story."

Holly glanced at their captors again, then turned to Mackie. "But why are you out here in the middle of the night, mixed up in all this?"

"A couple of weeks before Burl crashed, I was drunk and rode my bicycle home down the levee. I saw Burl and some goons off-loading a barge. They saw me, too, but Burl held them back. He told them I was a drunk and didn't know what was going on. He probably saved my life, but . . ." He looked down and blew out a breath.

"Why didn't you tell me?"

"For all I knew, you were in on it, too." He thumbed his chest. "I fought for this country, and I'm not letting drugs in my back door."

Holly blinked. She'd never seen Mackie climb on a soapbox like that before. Considering his little problem, his reaction surprised her.

"Booze or a little pot is one thing, but that powder is a killer. I saw that in . . ." He gave a sideways glance and rubbed his hand across his mouth.

The smugglers' voices in the background filled the awkward pause as Holly wondered what Mackie had held back.

"So," Mackie said as he looked at Holly again, "I watched the river from the top of the levee for weeks. The next time I saw Burl at the barge, I called Sheriff Walker. That old snake in the grass blew me off. Said I was drunk." Mackie lifted a shoulder. "Which was true . . ." He dropped his gaze to the deck. "But Burl was dead a week later."

"You don't think—"

Mackie shook his head. "I can't prove a thing, but I wouldn't put it past them to sabotage Burl's plane. I thought it was all over after he died, but the shipments kept coming. So, I called Sam, and he called Jake."

"Why didn't you call Jake yourself?"

"Drunk," he said in a matter-of-fact tone. "Besides, he'd never believe me."

"He will now." She patted Mackie on the knee. "If not for you, Jake would have never come to investigate."

"I didn't have proof until you asked me to clean out Burl's container, and I found his stash."

"Quiet," the wolf man shouted.

Holly waited for him to turn around, then whispered to Mackie, "What did you do with it?"

"I figured you didn't know the stash was there, because you asked me to clean the place out. But I couldn't trust you—so I hid it."

"In Eudora?"

"Yeah. Drunk decision. I figured I'd decide what to do about that sober and no one would look in the coffin until October." Mackie gave a hard grin. "Gave me a month to have a dry day."

Holly shook her head. "So why didn't you move it before I hauled Eudora out of the barn?"

"Couldn't." He rubbed the back of his neck and glanced at the guys with the guns. "Remember when you had some suits coming to look at renting the hangar? When they showed up, I recognized one of them from the night I saw Burl at the riverbank. I got on my bike and hauled tail before they pegged me."

Holly's stomach pinched. "They asked if you'd do maintenance if they rented the hangar and how to get in touch with you. I figured you'd want the job." She winced. "Since you don't have a phone, I told them where you lived."

"They found me, all right. They chased me to the river, and I made them think it took me. If I didn't turn up anywhere, they'd think I'd drowned, and that'd be best after what happened to Burl. Couldn't go home or get a drink anywhere. I got the shakes so bad, I went to Miss Alice to get me through. I've been hiding ever since."

"And she came here. . . . It was you who was sleeping in Abe's cabin."

"Sorry. I'll work off the rent."

"Why there?"

"I owed Miss Alice for helping me out, right?"

Holly nodded.

"You know how the Deltas love bridge." Mackie took another look back at the guys with the guns. "Glaucoma is blinding Miss Cora Beth, and she read where smoking pot slows down the disease. Miss Alice thought I might have a connection." Mackie lifted a shoulder. "I didn't, but I told her I knew where I could get enough to last the rest of her life. When it wasn't there, I didn't know whether I'd finally killed my last brain cell or what."

Holly closed her gaping mouth. "So that was you in the barn and in the house, looking for Eudora."

He nodded. "I figured I was drunk and misplaced it,

or you were in on the smuggling. Only way to figure it out was to move in, and Miss Alice didn't trust me alone."

The guy with the ponytail flicked his cigarette into the river and gave the wolf man a nod. They both started walking across the barge, toward Mackie and her.

She leaned into Mackie and whispered, "Can you swim?"

"Like a fish." He winked at her. "Follow my lead. We'll jump on the downriver side, so we don't get sucked under the barge."

"No talk," the wolf man said, jabbing a machine gun at Mackie.

Mackie held his hands in the air. "Hey, man. She's gonna puke again. If you don't let her do it over the side, it'll be all over the place."

Holly followed Mackie's lead and gagged. Then she puffed her cheeks out like she was going to spew.

The bald guy screwed his face up and took a step back. The wolf man waved his weapon toward the side of the barge.

Mackie helped her to the edge of the barge and whispered, "I'll distract him. You jump."

"What about you?"

"I'll be right behind you."

Holly looked at the current below, then back at the big guns. She'd take her chances with Old Man River.

The cold that slapped her took her breath away. Muffled gunshots sounded from above. Then bullets streaked through the water around her. She dove deeper, until the current took her.

Jake, Mickey, and Charlie watched through night-vision binoculars as three men tossed crates in a fire line from the barge pushed up to the bank to a trailer attached to a four-wheeler.

"Fan out," Jake ordered. Together, they didn't have a chance; but separate, they might fool the smugglers into believing there were more of them.

Jake found cover behind a birch in the underbrush. He glanced upriver and spotted Mickey crouched behind a stump and Charlie belly down in a thicket. As long as the barge didn't push off and the situation remained calm, he could wait for backup. They were ten minutes away, but ten minutes ticked by like days.

On deck, two armed men guarded Holly and Mackie. Jake tracked them in his sights. He couldn't take any chances.

Mackie said something to the gunmen, then helped Holly to the edge of the barge. The bald dude backed away, and a muscle-bound monster of a man with black hair trailed them to the side. Holly leaped into the river, and Jake's gut felt like it went overboard, too.

He trained his sights on the gunman at the edge of the barge, but Mackie jumped on the big dude's back and blocked any chance Jake had of getting an accurate shot. Automatic gunfire charged the night as the gunman shot into the water and Mackie rode his back.

"ICE. Freeze where you are," Jake called from behind cover. "Drop your weapons."

Crates crashed to the ground, spilling bags of marijuana. The men on the fire line drew their weapons and some ducked as best they could behind the crates or the trailer. Their heads swiveled as they searched past the riverbank for a hidden target in the dense underbrush of the bottom woods.

"I got one of yours." The big dude pressed the barrel of a pistol to Mackie's head and held him as a shield.

Jake called to Mickey and Charlie, but not loud enough for his voice to reach the barge. "Either of you have a clear shot to take that guy out?"

"Negative," they said in tandem.

"Aim at the fire line," he called back, just above a whisper. Jake kept his weapon on the big dude holding Mackie.

"We could drop five of yours any minute," Jake yelled back to the big dude. An optimistic prediction at best, but the the fire line grunts squirmed.

"So what?" The gunman tightened his grip on Mackie until his feet lifted off the deck.

"I've also got the goods Burl was skimming from you."

"We knew that hombre was stealing. Why you think he's dead?"

"Let my man go, and he'll get the goods."

"No. You get the goods. Then I'll let him go."

Cold steel touched the back of Jake's neck.

"Drop it," Mr. Dunbar said.

Jake turned his head slowly and just enough to glimpse Mickey and Charlie held at gunpoint, too.

Holly gulped air into her lungs as she hauled herself onto the riverbank. "Mackie, you there?"

"Psst," came from the dark.

"Mackie?"

A wrinkled hand motioned to Holly.

She blinked, not believing who she saw. "Miss Alice? What are you doing here?"

Dressed in a black velour jogging suit and tennis shoes and carrying her purse, Miss Alice stepped from behind a cottonwood. "Mackie called me from your cell phone. He said you'd been grazed by a bullet. I came to check your wound, and all hell broke loose."

"I'm okay. It's not even bleeding anymore."

Miss Alice pulled Holly into the bushes, then shined a flashlight on her head. "Just a scratch." She aimed the beam in Holly's eyes.

Holly blocked the light with her hand. "How did you get over the levee?"

"I'm old, not crippled," Miss Alice huffed. "Your pupils are equal. Any nausea?"

"Yes. When I saw the blood."

"Head wounds bleed a lot. Any nausea since?"

"No, but if you don't quit shining that light in my eyes, I'm going to have a headache."

Miss Alice clicked off the flashlight. "You'll be fine, until I can give you a thorough examination."

"Where's Mackie?"

"Back on the barge." Miss Alice stepped over a fallen log with her white tennis shoes. "Let's go."

"You can't go there." Holly grabbed her by the arm. "They've got guns."

"I've got one, too." Miss Alice reached in her purse and pulled out a revolver that looked like the kind used in old westerns. She handed the gun to Holly. "In fact, I have two," Miss Alice said, grabbing a twin revolver from her purse. "This one was my husband's."

"Do you know how to use it?" Holly asked.

Miss Alice cocked a brow. "Want to see my license to carry?"

CHAPTER 39

As Jake watched Mickey and Charlie walking to the barge at gunpoint, a click sounded close behind him. He shut his eyes and waited for the blast.

Then he heard another click.

"Go ahead. Make my day," Miss Alice whispered.

Jake turned his head slowly to the right. In his peripheral view, Miss Alice stood with an old-school revolver pointed at Mr. Dunbar's back. Beside her, Holly held a matching gun. His heart darned near stopped. Never had Holly looked better or had he been happier to see her.

Holly winked at Jake and jump-started his heart.

"I've always wanted to say that," Miss Alice said.

"Have you women ever killed a man?" Mr. Dunbar said with gravel in his voice. He stood perfectly still, with his gun pointed at Jake's side and his back to the women.

"No, but I've watched them die," Miss Alice said.

Holly lifted her gun a little higher, and her brows pinched as she steadied her aim. "Put that gun down, so I don't have to see my first."

Holly looked serious. A shiver of unease danced across Jake's shoulders. *Whoa. If either woman pulls the trigger, they're just as likely to shoot me. But more likely, Dunbar will turn on them and take his chances with me, unarmed.*

He needed to make a move and fast. Before he could twitch a muscle, Dunbar spun around to the women. Instinctively, Jake went for the gun to protect the women. He struggled to force Dunbar's arm toward the ground to keep him from shooting Holly or Miss Alice.

Jake caught sight of them dancing around the scuffle, with their guns tracking Dunbar and sometimes him. "Get back. Don't shoot."

Dunbar squeezed off two rounds into the dirt. Shouts rang out from the barge. If Dunbar didn't respond soon, they'd either shove off with Mackie on board or come to check on Dunbar.

Jake crushed Dunbar's neck in an armlock. "Drop it, or I'll squeeze you till you mess your pants and die," Jake said, straining to get the words out.

Holly took a step closer and leveled a shaky pistol barrel at Dunbar. "At this range, I won't miss."

"Careful, deadeye," Jake said. "You don't want to see two men die."

Realization flashed across Holly's face as she took a sideways step, changing the angle of her aim. "Sorry."

Dunbar's gun hit the soft ground with a thud.

Jake grinned at Holly. "Good job, sweetheart."

Miss Alice dug in her purse and pulled out a ball of what looked like knitting yarn. "It's nylon. You can tie him up with this." She edged over next to Holly and pointed her revolver at Dunbar, too.

Jake nearly chuckled as he yanked Dunbar's hands

behind his back. "If I were you, I wouldn't make any quick moves."

More shouts came from the riverbank, and Dunbar's men closed in. Jake could see Mackie wrestling with two goons on the barge now.

Jake tied Dunbar's hands behind his back and then picked up the man's weapon. Jake pointed the gun between Dunbar's eyes. "Call them off."

Dunbar gave him a steely "go to hell" look.

Jake cocked his gun and matched his stare.

"Put the guns down," Dunbar yelled.

Guns clattered to the ground as Dunbar's men raised their hands over their heads. Mickey and Charlie picked up the guns and herded Dunbar's men in a line, then made them lie facedown on the riverbank.

Out of the corner of his eye, Jake caught Mackie launching the big goon into the river. Jake blew out a breath. Then he shoved Dunbar to the ground and tied his feet. "Make yourself comfortable."

Holly noticed Miss Alice tuck her revolver in her purse, then toddle off toward the barge. Nosy didn't begin to describe the woman. Holly shook her head and nearly grinned.

It's a good thing she stuck her nose in my business and Mackie's. Things could have turned out much worse if she hadn't. And even worse if Jake hadn't been here.

"You're soaked." Jake put his coat around her shoulders. He held her at arm's length, then inspected the nick on her head. "I told you to stay in the house. Do you realize you could have been killed?"

"Jake, I'm so sorry about all this," she said, looking into his eyes. "I thought you were a smuggler, so I called 911, and they called the sheriff. Why didn't you say you were an ICE agent?"

He put his hands on her shoulders and looked into her eyes. "Because you were the prime suspect, and a good agent never breaks his cover."

"Was everything a cover?" she asked.

Jake pulled her close. "Sweetheart, I've been undercover so many times, I'd forgotten who I was, until I came back to Delta Ridge. This is the only place on earth where everything is real."

She caught a glimpse of Miss Alice picking something up from the ground. Holly squinted, not believing what she'd seen. The old gal's oversize purse bulged as she stuffed it with marijuana from a bale that had busted out of its plastic wrap. Sirens blared, and Miss Alice glanced over her shoulder. She caught Holly looking and lifted a finger to her lips.

Holly grabbed Jake's arm and walked him away from Miss Alice. An ICE agent might not be able to turn a blind eye to her medicinal harvest.

The tugboat engine revved up as it towed the barge away from the bank an inch at a time. She spotted Mackie chasing after goatee guy. He must have known he was beat, because goatee guy ran for the wheelhouse. Mackie jogged toward the end of the barge. He hurled himself off the barge and rolled onto the bank.

"That's one tough son of a gun," Jake said.

Holly clasped her arm around Jake's. "You don't know the half of it."

"Tell me something I don't know about Mackie," Jake said, more as a flip comment than a request.

Holly looked up at him and grinned like she knew the secrets of the universe. "I'll let him tell you," she said as she slid her soft hand from around his arm. "I need to check on Miss Alice."

"He's going to tell me where the devil he's been and how he ended up in the middle of a bust," Jake said, marching across the muddy riverbank, toward his dad. The old fart was lucky he hadn't been killed.

A Coast Guard boat zoomed up behind the barge, and a Guardsman on the speaker called, "U.S. Coast Guard. Kill your engines and prepare to be boarded."

Mackie dusted his clothes off and headed toward Jake as approaching voices from the levee carried over the water. The cavalry had finally arrived. Better late than never.

The closer Jake got to his old man, the more he realized how much he'd changed. Yeah, he was older, but that wasn't it. As Jake watched his dad walk a straight path to him, Jake's steps faltered. *Mackie sober?*

Mackie stood in front of Jake and stared for a moment. His dad had always been a handshake kind of guy, but he didn't offer one. Jake extended his hand to get the greeting out of the way before he got down to the business of why Mackie was there. The old man's eyes glistened with tears as he wrapped Jake in a bear hug. An unexpected tightness strangled Jake's vocal cords. He swallowed hard.

His dad patted him on the back, then pushed away. Mackie rubbed his workingman's hand across his eyes. "Oh, man. I haven't shed a tear since your mama left."

"Or been sober after dark." Jake cocked an eye at his dad. "Until now."

"Twenty-one days." He grinned. "Get used to it. I went through hell to dry out, and I'm not goin' there again if I can help it."

"What brought that on?"

"You."

"Me?"

Mackie shrugged. "I needed to call you, and I couldn't."

"Did you lose my number?"

Mackie shook his head. "I know it by heart. You said I could call you when I was sober." He sucked in a breath. "But some things are best done in person."

"You know you've got some explaining to do," Jake said.

"No problem, son."

Flashlights streaked the night sky as more voices neared them. Jake turned as footsteps sounded behind him. A greenhorn trooper approached, gun drawn.

"Hold on." Jake held his hands in the air. "I'm ICE. Agent McCann."

"Show me some ID real slow."

"I've got agents over on the bank, holding six suspects." Jake eased his ID from his pocket and flashed it at the trooper. "Don't shoot them, either." Jake thumbed toward the bank. "They need some cuffs and some muscle."

The trooper shot a look at Mackie. "What about him?"

Jake tossed a look at his dad. "He's one of the good guys."

CHAPTER 40

Back at Holly Grove, Holly sat in the parlor watching the aftermath of the bust. State troopers and ICE agents had swarmed the house and were questioning the guests. Sam had arrived and was scribbling notes like a kid acing an exam. Holly's head ached from a combination of the nick the bullet left on her scalp and answering too many questions. But she was confident the smuggling at Holly Grove was finally over. And she'd seen the last of Burl, she hoped.

Somehow, Miss Alice had locked her loot in her trunk before she met with the agents. She'd held up like a pro under questioning about how she came to be at the river. She'd insisted she'd only done her civic duty.

Mackie and Jake had had a heart-to-heart about Mackie's part in the bust, and it looked like Mackie was going to be one of the star witnesses for the prosecution.

A chill inched over Holly. She pulled the blanket the agents had given her earlier a little tighter, then looked over her shoulder for Burl. He wasn't there. He wasn't supposed to be. His business at Holly Grove was finished. Yet she couldn't shake the feeling he was still in the house.

Don't borrow trouble, Holly. If Burl were here, he'd be smack-dab in the middle of all the excitement.

A little sigh of relief escaped her lips as she slipped upstairs to change out of her damp clothes. Soon everyone would leave or go to bed, and she and Jake would be alone. And then what?

When she opened her bedroom door, she stopped short. All the adrenaline she'd been running on evaporated.

Burl stood staring out her bedroom window.

"Why are you still here?" She slammed the door behind her. "Didn't you notice the house is crawling with law enforcement? We caught the smugglers. You're free."

He didn't turn around. "You know what's out there?" he said in a somber tone and didn't wait for an answer. "Fire and damnation."

A headache throbbed at Holly's temples. "So what?" She marched to Burl. "Didn't you hear me? We caught the smugglers. That was your ticket out of here."

Burl shot a look over his shoulder. "*I* didn't catch them."

"Okay. Technically, Jake did."

"Yeah, right." Burl turned to face her. "Some undercover man. I've known he was an ICE agent for a while."

"And you didn't tell me?"

His pale brow creased in deep folds. "That bozo was up here looking for you, instead of looking for the smugglers." Burl thumbed his chest. "I'm the one who sent him to the river."

"How? He can't hear or see you."

Burl gave her a halfhearted grin. "One of my new tricks."

"See? You helped. Did St. Peter miss that?"

"He doesn't miss anything." Burl shrugged, as though trying to slough off a burden. "I don't know why I'm still here. All I know is I didn't want to leave you." He dropped his gaze to the hardwood floor, "When I was alive, I messed everything up for you. Now I feel responsible. This may sound crazy, but it's like I'm supposed to do something. Watch over you, maybe."

"Great. Just great." Holly paced in front of Burl. "Not only do I have a ghost for my ex, but he's also certifiable. Listen carefully. I don't want you, and I don't need you. Now make your exit, while you've got the chance, please."

He lifted a shoulder. "I think I missed it."

"How did you mess up your chance to weasel your way through the pearly gates?"

"It is what it is." He glanced toward the window. "The only exit I see is out there, and you know if I take one step outside, I roast." He stuffed his hands in his pockets. "Looks like you're stuck with me."

"Oh, no I'm not." She paced in front of Burl. "If Jake asks me to go with him this time, I'm so going."

In my dreams. Jake isn't going to ask and if he did what would become of Holly Grove?

"Really?"

She squared herself, toe-to-toe with Burl. "Really."

"You're booked through Christmas. Who's going to run the place? Nelda?" He laced his hands under his lapels. "I'm not going anywhere, and I seriously doubt she could handle me alone."

Holly glared at Burl. "Nelda has a reputation as the best cook in plantation country. She'd probably rather get a job anywhere else than be in the house with you. I'll sell Holly Grove if I have to." The words tumbled out of her mouth, but she wanted to eat them as soon as they hit her ears. A deep ache settled in her soul.

"You'd sell Holly Grove with me in it, after I saved your life?"

Holly folded her arms over her chest. "Saved my life? Ha! You were stuck here in the house. You didn't do squat."

Burl paced in a slow circle around her. "Jake was up here looking for you, while you were getting your hummingbird heinie in alligator trouble down there." He nodded toward the Mississippi. "I wrote him a message in the mirror, and he hauled tail. If he'd made his shot a second later, you'd be checking in with St. Peter yourself. I didn't send your Romeo to bust the smugglers. I sent him to save you." He stopped in front of her and held her stare like he had nothing to hide. "Ask him if you don't believe me."

Holly jacked her chin up a fraction. "I will." She whirled around and stormed out of her bedroom.

"And by the way," Burl called as she marched down the hall. "He hasn't asked you to go with him, anyway."

Just like when he'd left after high school. Her feet faltered, and she did her best to hide it.

As she descended the stairs, she looked for Jake. In a room crowded with testosterone, he still stood out. Actually, he led the pack. Jake barked orders, and "yes, sirs" rang out. He signed digital clipboards and shook hands with men in uniforms designating their service.

Jake was the man in charge, and it fit him like he'd been born for it.

He pulled his cell phone from his belt and pressed it to his ear, then covered the other ear before slipping out the back door to the porch. Holly made her way across the crowded room. With any luck, they'd be alone on the back porch. She eased the screen door open, and Jake's voice drifted across the night air from the backyard.

If Burl was telling the truth, she owed him her life. But she wasn't about to take his word for it.

Holly stood in the crisp air on the porch. The darkness and shadows hid Jake in the backyard, but she could hear his voice as he talked on the phone.

"Look, I know this operation had a few hiccups, but Dunbar and Sheriff Walker are spilling their guts to save their hides." He paced as he talked. "If you give me a chance, I can follow the food chain all the way to Central America."

Her heart weighed on her like an anvil. She'd seen the news. Central America was a dangerous place, and he'd be dealing with the worst.

"In Guatemala? Yeah. I've read the briefs on them." He stopped. His shoulders rose and fell as he listened. "I know the risk. I want to cut the head off this organization."

He might never come back this time, even if he wanted to.

"Yes, sir." He shoved his phone in his pocket and then fist-pumped.

"Good news, huh?" Holly said, stepping to the edge of the porch.

Jake turned. His silhouette reminded her of a G.I. Joe doll. He was made for his work.

"Yeah." He mounted the steps and joined her on the porch. "That was Chief. He sent me down here because I was the only agent who could fit in as the local boy coming home."

"Worked like a charm."

"I had some help."

Her eyes widened. "Who?"

"Mickey, Charlie, Sam, Mackie, Miss Alice. You."

She raised a delicate hand to her chest. "Me? I thought I nearly ruined the whole thing."

He gave a wry grin. "You do have a nose for trouble."

"So I hear."

His brows took a downward slant. "Well, you nearly got yourself killed."

"How did you know where I was?"

"If I hadn't seen it with my own eyes, I would have never believed it." Jake dragged a hand across his forehead like that would help make sense of what he'd seen. "A foggy patch formed on the mirror near the front door in the wide hall and three words were written on it. *Holly. River. Danger.*" He shook his head. "I was just in time to wing the sheriff before he shot you point-blank."

For once, Burl had told the straight truth. "Looks like I owe my ghost one."

"I have to be honest." He hesitated, as though he were gauging his words. "My career was riding on this bust."

"I was watching you in there." She glanced toward the house. "Your career means a lot to you, doesn't it?"

"I used to think it meant everything."

"And now?"

"It's my job. I'm good at it." He hooked his thumbs in his pockets. "That was my chief on the phone, congratulating me on the bust and giving me my next assignment."

"When do you leave?"

"As soon as I wrap things up tonight."

Holly nodded. What could she say? She had known he'd leave all along, but . . .

"I may not get another chance to see you alone." Jake laced his arms around her waist. "Long-distance relationships are complicated—"

"By all means, don't complicate things. I've had smugglers running drugs through Holly Grove. I brought her back from the brink of bankruptcy and did it all with my ex haunting the place. I can handle complicated. Evidently, you can't."

"You've taken what I said all wrong," Jake pleaded as voices sounded from the other side of the house and car doors slammed. "Look, I've got to go. I probably won't be able to call you or anything. When I get back, we'll work something out."

"Like what? A flight pattern?"

"Come on, sweetheart. What do you want me to do?"

"Don't make promises you can't keep. You said you'd be back last time you left Delta Ridge. It took you fifteen years to come back to me, and I didn't have the added attraction of my ex-husband haunting my house. You may want to drag this out and let it die a natural death, but I can't do that again."

Mickey swung the porch door open. "Boss, we've got a trooper escort to New Orleans ready to roll."

"Good-bye, Jake." Holly turned and ran in the house.

* * *

A week later, on Halloween night, Holly opened a bottle of champagne Toni and Duke had given her as a thank-you gift for the fun they'd had at Holly Grove. With any luck, it would drown her sorrow. Holly missed Jake but reminded herself this was the only way it could end. Jake had outgrown her and small-town life years ago.

She poured a glass of champagne. The purchase offer that had come with the champagne lay next to the bottle on a small mahogany table in the parlor. Toni and Duke had had such a good time, they wanted to buy Holly Grove. Evidently, the Gold Member start-up was doing quite well. She'd been tempted to sign the thing to get away from Burl, but she just couldn't bring herself to do it. She owed him her life, and besides, she couldn't part with Holly Grove or put Nelda out of a job.

Thanks to the success of the Haunted Pilgrimage and a steady flow of reservations, she wouldn't be forced to sell it, at least for now. She'd even set aside money to pay the tax assessment on Holly Grove. She lifted her glass to her lips and took a sip. *Bittersweet success.*

Rhett's ears perked as Nelda walked in from the kitchen. She wrinkled up her nose and fanned the air. "You gonna have to make them Deltas blow dope someplace else. The back porch smells like one of them flophouses or somethin'. I'm gonna have to take the plastic down and air it out 'fore spring."

"Only one Delta is using, and it's medicinal," Holly

said, though she had to admit Miss Cora Beth was a hoot high.

"Yeah. Miss Alice told me Miss Cora Beth can see her cards better after her medicine. Humph. That's what Miss Alice calls it." Nelda grabbed her purse. "Guess if I was goin' blind, I'd puff, too."

Nelda turned to walk away, then spun back to Holly. "Oh, and don't go thinkin' someone stole my big skillet. I'm takin' it to the church circle to show my sisters. And I ain't braggin'."

"You brag all you want. Your gumbo won by a landslide." Holly raised her glass and took another sip.

"That's a fact, but I still ain't braggin'." She flashed her bright white smile. "I'm sharing a blessin'." She hoisted her purse on her shoulder. "Me and my big skillet will be back in the mornin'."

Holly couldn't help but smile. She'd never seen Nelda so happy. She hadn't even complained much about Burl since she won the gumbo contest.

Rhett gave a low growl as Burl rolled into the room like winter fog.

Jeez. She didn't even have to speak of the devil. All she'd done was think of him, and there he was. They'd busted the smugglers and his plane crash had been reclassified as a murder and Sheriff Walker had been indicted for a host of charges. None of it had been enough to get Burl through the pearly gates.

"'Night," Holly called as Nelda headed toward the door. Knowing she'd be alone with Burl now did nothing for Holly's mood.

"I waited for Nelda to leave. Aren't you proud of me?"

Holly sighed. A lifetime was too long with Burl.

He leaned against the mantel and eyed the open

bottle of champagne. "You know you shouldn't drink alone. Allow me to make a toast."

In no mood for Burl, she rolled her eyes. "You can't drink." She topped off her glass of champagne, but not for a toast. It was strictly medicinal.

"I can still make a toast." He pretended to raise a glass. "To my wife. May she forgive me in this lifetime."

Holly set her glass down. "I won't forgive you in a hundred lifetimes. I did everything you said. You aren't supposed to be here."

Burl dug his toe across the hardwood floor. "You can't blame me for trying. All I want is for you to be happy."

"Happy? Ha! How can I be happy? You can't leave the only place on earth I love, and I can't leave Holly Grove."

"You mean won't." Burl pointed to the purchase offer. "One stroke of the pen and you're free of me."

"Don't tempt me."

"No need. You won't do it."

The doorbell chimed, and Holly grabbed a bowl of candy for the trick-or-treaters. She marched to the front door, with Rhett yapping beside her.

"Just because you're mad at me, don't take it out on the little goblins."

Holly huffed, then opened the door.

Jake stood on the porch, holding two suitcases. He sported a tropical tan, a killer smile, and a sparkle in his eyes that would light up any woman's world. "I hear you rent rooms by the month."

"I do," she said, taking a step back.

"How about by the year?" He strode into the foyer and set the suitcases on the floor.

Her heart pounded against her ribs. "What are you saying?"

"ICE liked the work I did here so well, they've re-assigned me to the New Orleans unit."

"Why would you accept that?" She placed the candy on the Empire table. "You never liked Delta Ridge."

Jake shrugged. "Maybe I never knew the place. Look, I've got a few debts to pay here. Sam secretly paid my college tuition." He blew out a heavy breath. "And I missed a lot of years with Mackie. He's sober now, and I want to make sure he stays that way."

So his coming back has nothing to do with me. "Then why not live with him?"

He closed the distance between them. "Because I want to keep an eye on you."

"Me? Why?"

"Should I count the ways?" He put his hands on her shoulders in a brotherly way and looked down at her. "You and all of Delta Ridge know you have a nose for trouble."

She lifted her chin a fraction. "Maybe trouble has a nose for me, starting with you."

"Me?"

"Yeah. You think you can just waltz in and out of my life at will."

"I don't waltz anywhere, and I never made a promise I didn't keep. I promised you I'd keep you safe, and I'm going to. The cartel could move in under your nose, and you'd never know it."

"I can take care of what goes on at Holly Grove. And I thought you wanted to see the world, have adventure, and everything that isn't in Delta Ridge." The only place she wanted to be.

"Oh, I will. I'll still take undercover assignments anywhere ICE sends me. I'll just have a new home base, if we can work out a deal."

Did he just look at my boobs? "A deal?"

"I'll be away more than I'm here. Between assignments, I'll keep this old house from going to rot and ruin. All you have to do is have a room, any room, available for me when I come in."

Holly lifted a shoulder. "But what if the rooms are all rented out?"

"There's always your bed." He laced his hands behind the small of her back. "I'm willing to share if you are."

"Over my dead body," Burl said, glaring at Jake.

"Remember, I have a ghost that may not cotton to that idea." Though she might under the right conditions, which she'd never have with Burl around.

"Holly, he's dead." He leaned his forehead against hers. "What does it matter what he thinks?"

Her resolve was melting faster than the four flakes of snow they got last year. "It's not just what he thinks. He's always here and always will be. The only way out is for me to sell." She grabbed the purchase offer from the Empire table. "Duke and Toni want to buy it. All I have to do is sign this."

"Whoa there." Burl stepped between them. "Let's not rush into anything."

She tried to ignore Burl since Jake didn't know he was there.

Burl stared at Jake for a long moment. "Okay. I get it. You think this guy could make you happy. I couldn't. But I tried." He looked back at Holly. "I meant it when I told you all I wanted was for you to be happy."

Slack jawed, Holly stared at Burl.

"Is your ghost—I mean Burl—here?" Jake asked, following her gaze.

"Afraid so." She folded her arms over her chest.

"I know you can't forgive me." Burl bowed his head. "I deserve to go to hell for what I've put you through, so I'm going to take my punishment." He glanced toward the open front door. "Out there."

"What's he saying?"

"He's babbling on about taking his punishment. If he walks outside, he goes to hell." She shoved a hand on her hip and eyed Burl. "He won't do it. I'm stuck with him, and if you move in, you're stuck with him, too. Complications, you know. Unless I sign this."

Jake took one look at the paper and tore it in half. "I can handle complications. You and Holly Grove belong together."

"That's my cue if I've ever heard one." Burl walked toward the open front door.

Flames licked through the door, and all the outdoors blazed like a raging furnace.

Jake pulled Holly back. "What the hell is going on here?"

"Can you see the fire?" she asked, clinging to Jake.

He nodded.

"Looks like home to me." Burl smiled at Holly. "I know you can't forgive me, Blondie. And that's okay. I don't know why, but I feel good about this. Closure, I guess."

She didn't want to send him to hell. He hadn't deserved her forgiveness at first, but Burl had proved to be a better man dead.

"Don't do it," she screamed. "I forgive you."

And she meant it.

The flames died like a lit match under glass. A bright light shone through the door.

Burl smiled at Holly. "Do you hear that?"

"No," Holly said.

"The angels are calling me. St. Peter says my unfinished business was your forgiveness." He shrugged. "Who knew?"

He looked at Jake. "Take care of Blondie. Believe me, the man upstairs is watching what you do."

"I will," Jake said.

"You can hear Burl?"

Jake nodded and put his arm around her.

"I was going to make a toast." Burl winked. "Thanks for setting me free, Holly."

Burl slipped off his wedding ring and tossed it in the air. It landed on the hardwood floor and spun like a dime as he walked into the light and out of Holly's life forever.

RECIPES

HOLLY GROVE MINT JULEP

As y'all know, I'm not much of a cook. Spirits are my
specialty. Not the ghostly kind. Mercy. I could live without those. Wicked good cocktails make living worth the
effort on some days. In the spirit of Southern hospital-
ity, I welcome every guest with a mint julep in a silver
mint julep cup. You, dear reader, are my virtual
guest at Holly Grove. The least I can do is give you
my mint julep recipe so you can sip and read. I
haven't poisoned anyone yet! Enjoy.

**6–10 fresh mint leaves, plus 1 nice sprig for
garnish** (The small leaves are sweeter. I pluck
the sprig down to three leaves to represent past,
present, and future good times. No one knows
this, but it feels like making luck, and who
doesn't need a little luck?)

1 jigger mint-flavored simple syrup (Since making
simple syrup requires cooking, I use store-bought
mint-flavored simple syrup. The nice man in the
brown uniform delivers it by the case to the
front door of Holly Grove.)

Enough crushed ice to overflow a mint julep cup
(Yes, it must be crushed. If you have to, take a
hammer to cubed ice. Just dump the ice in a
plastic bag, then wrap it in a dish towel and get
after it. Watch your thumbs.)

3 jiggers bourbon (Pick your poison. Any bourbon will do.)

Mixology:

Place the mint leaves in the bottom of a mint julep cup. Y'all above the Mason-Dixon Line may not have a set of julep cups handy, so just use a short, sturdy glass. An old-fashioned or lowball glass works pretty darned good.

Drizzle a little of the simple syrup over the mint. Muddle the mint in the bottom of the cup or glass. If you have a wooden muller, use that. I use a sturdy wooden spoon. Muddling is gentle. Press down gently on the mint and twist. Don't mutilate it. That makes the mint bitter, and all the little shreds of mint can seem like grass clippings when you drink the mint julep. (I learned that the hard way, like everything else. Mercy.) Just work the mint enough to let the oils and the aroma out.

Mound up the crushed ice like a snowball over the mint in the julep cup or glass. Mix the bourbon and the remaining simple syrup in a separate glass and then pour the mixture over the crushed ice. The mound of ice will settle down to the rim of the cup or glass.

Stir the mint julep and garnish with the reserved sprig of mint. Sit back and sip like you're on the front balcony of Holly Grove, in spirit.

Serves 1

* Note: I keep a jug of julep mix in the fridge
to make serving easy when I know I have guests
checking in. If you have a crowd coming for
cocktails, just multiply the bourbon and
mint-flavored simple syrup by the number of
people in your crowd, mix the two ingredients
together, and keep the julep mix in a jug in the
fridge. Mull the mint in the julep cups, then
cover the cups with plastic wrap. Keep them
ready and waiting in the fridge. When your
guests arrive, all you have to do is scoop crushed
ice into the julep cups, shake up the julep mix,
pour it over the ice, garnish, and serve.

NELDA'S BOURBON PECAN PRALINES

I don't know how I let little Miss Hurricane Holly talk
me out of this recipe. I know she can't make 'em,
bless her heart. Maybe you can, but don't spread this
recipe around. My pralines are a special treat just for
Holly Grove and folks I like enough to cook for.

¾ cup granulated sugar (Cane sugar is best, and
don't even think about that fake stuff.)

¾ cup firmly packed light brown sugar (Just pat it
down good and tight in the cup.)

½ cup canned milk (Some folks call this evaporated
milk.)

1 tablespoon bourbon (This is my secret ingredient.
Don't tell Jake. He's a teetotaler.)

1 tablespoon butter (Real butter. No oleo or fake stuff.)

1 teaspoon vanilla extract (The real stuff. If it says imitation, it is.)

1 cup unsalted whole pecans (Get some nice fat ones, fresh, too.)

This is the important part:

Mix together the white sugar and the light brown sugar in a nice-sized pot with a thick bottom (but not in an iron skillet). Pour in the canned milk and the bourbon and mix that up, too.

Then place the pot on a burner, turn the fire up to medium, and start stirring and keep stirring. After the mixture thickens up a bit, scoop some up on a spoon and drop it in a clear glass filled with cold water. If that drop spreads out and looks kinda fuzzy in the water, keep stirring the pot, because the mixture needs to cook some more. If it makes a nice soft ball, take your pot off the fire quick, because the sugar mixture is ready. Don't it smell good! If the mixture makes a hard ball that looks like glass, bless your heart. You've made hard candy. Take a swig of bourbon and start over.

Stir in the butter and the vanilla extract, then the pecans. Stir real good but not for too long, because you don't want the mixture to set up yet. Now get you a spoon, a big one if you want big pralines or a little one if you want lady-size pralines. I make the lady ones for Holly Grove and get a dozen out of the batch.

Spread out a nice sheet of waxed paper. If you don't have any, go buy some. Nothin' else will do. Use your spoon and scoop up a spoonful of the praline mixture and put it on the waxed paper. Repeat until all the pralines have been formed. They may be a little runny at first, but the pralines will start to set up as soon as you spoon them out. The last of the batch will be stiffer. Give 'em a few minutes to set up good, and then peel 'em off the waxed paper and put them on a china plate.

If you did it right, you'll have a sweet taste of Holly Grove and the South that will melt in your mouth.

Love y'all,
Nelda Varnado
First-Prize Winner (The big skillet)
Haunted Pilgrimage Tour of Homes
Holly Grove Plantation Home and B & B
Delta Ridge, Louisiana

* Note from the author: This is the recipe my husband's aunt, Suetee Kopfler, used to make pralines for seventy years. Her pralines were a special treat, and I'm thankful she shared her recipe with me and Nelda. Of course, Nelda had to add a secret ingredient, bourbon, to make them hers. The bourbon is optional but tasty.

Love Holly's adventures?
Keep reading for a sneak peek at the next
B & B Spirits Mystery,

DOWNRIGHT DEAD

Coming soon from
Pamela Kopfler
and
Kensington Books

CHAPTER 1

"I don't see dead people anymore, and that's a good thing." Holly Davis swirled her latest attempt at a Sazerac in a Waterford lowball glass. The ruby color of the cocktail sparkled against the crystal. Maybe this effort would be guest-worthy. She lifted her glass to Nelda, the best cook in St. Agnes Parish, her housekeeper, and the closest thing she had to family. "The only spirit at Holly Grove these days is in this glass."

"You sure 'bout that?" Nelda's brows flattened as she stared up at the steady glow of the milk-glass pendant light in the circa 1928 kitchen, which was modern compared to the rest of Holly's antebellum B & B. Nelda shoved her hands on her generous hips. "That thing's been flickering like a lightning bug off and on all day."

Holly took a sip of the Sazerac and shivered. Her taste buds offered a vague rejection. *Too what? Strong? Sweet? Wrong whiskey?* "It's not flickering now."

"No. But Burl, God rest his soul," Nelda said, making the sign of the cross, "he always messed with me when your back was turned or you weren't around." She snatched a cup towel off her shoulder and folded it into a pad. "You ain't been in here making gumbo and bread pudding all afternoon with that light show."

Holly glanced at her Yorkie, curled up and sleeping in a sliver of what was left of the afternoon sun. "But you know Rhett yapped anytime Burl was around."

Rhett opened one sleepy eye when she said his name, but he didn't budge.

"That pup's been snoring all afternoon long. He wouldn't know if Jesus came in here."

"He hasn't been here, either." Holly strolled across the cypress planks to the deep porcelain sink and dumped her failed Sazerac down the drain. "Hell evidently froze over in south Louisiana last week and bit back all the mint within miles. I always welcome guests with a Holly Grove mint julep, but that's out, and that Sazerac was nowhere near guest-ready."

"I hope all that flickerin' didn't make me mess up my bread puddin', like your Sazerac." Nelda shook her head, then opened the oven. "Is your Jake really coming this time?"

"He's not my Jake by any stretch of the imagination, but he swore he'd be here." *If he cancels this time, I'm done.* Since ICE sent him to Guatemala for a sting on some kid three months ago, he'd called her exactly three times, from three different numbers. Every call had been shorter than the last. *This girl can take a hint.*

"Humph. I'm gonna make it worth his while, even if you don't. You know how he loves my bread puddin'." Nelda grinned and pulled out a pan of golden deliciousness from the oven. The sugary aroma wafted into the room and mixed with the savory bouquet of the gumbo simmering on the stove.

Steam curling from the gumbo pot reminded Holly of one of Burl's more memorable entrances. While it lasted, having a ghost at Holly Grove *had* been good for business, but it wasn't worth keeping the ghost of her sorry excuse of an ex-husband for life.

Nelda's cooking was good for business, too, but Holly doubted it would bring Jake McCann back. It had taken him fifteen years to come back to Delta Ridge after the first time he left.

Nelda picked up her favorite wooden spoon, which looked more like a paddle, and stirred her gumbo. "It's flirtin' with ready."

The pendant light flickered.

Nelda spun around, wide eyed. Gumbo dripped from her wooden spoon and spattered on the cypress floor. "I told you."

Rhett roused and trotted to the spattering of gumbo. Just like a man—selective hearing . . . and sight.

"The bulb is probably loose." Holly shrugged. She'd witnessed her not-so-dearly departed ex's dramatic exit. "Burl is gone for good."

Rhett licked his lips and stared up at the spoon, as though he could will another dribble of gumbo to fall.

"You didn't make up that story for Nelda just so I wouldn't quit on you, did ya?"

"I swear." Holly crossed her heart, then gave the CliffsNotes version of the story she'd told Nelda too many times. "Bright lights. Trumpets on high. Better than any Hollywood movie. And *poof.* Burl was gone."

"And he's at rest 'cause—"

"In the end, he earned it." And she'd found peace in that, too.

"Praise be." Nelda glanced over each shoulder, as if Burl could hear her. "God rest his sorry soul."

"But remember, don't tell anyone our ghost is gone," Holly said. "All the most successful B & Bs have ghosts, and Holly Grove needs that edge to make it."

"I won't tell it, but I won't lie, neither. I'm planning on goin' through those pearly gates one day, too." Nelda stirred her award-winning gumbo, then rapped her big wooden spoon on the side of the pot. She turned and eyed Holly. "The whole world is gonna think Holly Grove is haunted after tonight."

At nine o'clock *Inquiring Minds* would air the episode they'd shot back in the fall all about the haunting at her B & B. Holly ran her finger under the high neck of her black cashmere sweater. She had been on the receiving end of that look practically since birth. Nelda knew her too well. "Technically, Holly Grove *had* a ghost."

"H-a-d." Nelda spelled out the word. "You know you're in for a hurricane of trouble if folks find out you're acting like you got a ghost and you know fool well you don't. That's all I got to say."

Inquiring Minds would air coast-to-coast, full-color proof that Holly Davis's Louisiana B & B was haunted, in less than an hour. *H-a-d a ghost, my foot.* Holly swiped her hair from her face, then backed out into the entrance hall with her cart. *Trouble?* Nelda just couldn't see the value in keeping the ghost—in spirit, anyway.

Holly's basic black stilettos clicked on the cypress planks as she rolled the cart down the twelve-foot-wide entrance hall that ran from her front door to her back door. The wheels wobbled under the weight of the one TV in her entire B & B. She hauled the old thing out of storage only for special occasions, like the

LSU-Alabama game, the Super Bowl, and . . . tonight. Otherwise, she kept her plantation home frozen in 1857, because that was what her guests paid to experience.

That and the ghost.

Holly could live with that lie, but it would be uncomfortable tonight. Her neck and chest heated. She had no doubt red splotches had congregated under her black cashmere sweater like lie detectors.

No one, except Nelda and Jake, could ever know the ghost of her not-so-dearly departed had checked out—permanently. The success of Holly Grove depended on keeping that a secret. She scrubbed a hand over an itchy spot on her neck, then straightened the pearls Burl had given her on their fifth anniversary.

Unfortunately, the ghost had top billing for the show tonight, but Holly Grove would still get nationwide exposure. She liked to think of it as alimony payments from beyond the grave. *Thank you, Burl.*

The steady thud of a hammer sounded from above. Holly and the whole town had done their part to keep Mackie McCann busy and sober until Jake could get back and keep an eye on his dad. She'd hired Mackie to renovate the widow's walk and bring it up to code. Then she'd have an added attraction of stargazing from the top of Holly Grove. She'd even bought a special mounted telescope, which was a little over the top, but she loved it.

After the ghost buzz had died down and winter had set in, business had slowed to a few guests here and there. That was to be expected, so now was a good time to tackle the renovation. After tonight, she hoped she'd be booked for months and Holly Grove's future would be secured.

Portraits of five generations of the women in her

family lined the walls of her entrance hall. She'd never let them down. They'd held on to Holly Grove through wars, epidemics, floods, crop failures, and the Great Depression. Unfortunately, none of them had been able to hold on to a man, either.

A mystery portrait had hung in the entrance hall until she moved it upstairs last week. It had always felt out of place. Mama and Grandma Rose had guessed the portrait was of some relative, but neither had known for sure. With both of them gone, Holly would probably never know. When tourists asked about the portrait, she had little to offer. After replacing the painting with recent ghost memorabilia, she had plenty to say at that stop on the tours. The display clashed with the historical period of the house, but she could live with that infraction for the publicity.

She stopped the cart and straightened a framed glossy magazine article titled "Ghost in the Grove." It was nestled between other articles and a collection of autographed photos of Holly with TV reporters and minor celebrities. The pics on a bulletin board of "supposed" ghost sightings by guests needed tidying, too. Holly stood back and frowned. All the frames hung slightly askew.

She sighed and straightened the *Gazette* article about Nelda's big skillet award for her gumbo. Nelda's housekeeping skills didn't match her cooking skills. It seemed she could never dust and put things back exactly as they had been. But Nelda made up for that one flaw in so many ways, it wasn't worth mentioning.

Nelda busted out of the kitchen and trotted down the hall, waving Holly's cell phone. "Unknown number," she said, panting. "Answer it quick. It might be your Jake."

Holly grabbed the phone, and her heart took an involuntary uptick. "Or a telemarketer." She answered the call with a well-modulated hello.

"Holly Davis?" asked a smooth professional voice on the other end of Holly's cell phone.

Totally a telemarketer. Fifty-fifty chance and I lose. Good reason not to gamble.

"Yes," Holly answered, her voice as flat as her mood. She shook her head at Nelda, and she ambled back toward the kitchen.

"I'm Sylvia Martin's assistant, Megan Long," said the woman on the line.

"Sylvia Martin of *Inquiring Minds*?" Why would she be calling? Did they find out her ghost was gone? Cancel the show? The rash under Holly's sweater resurrected and marched across her collarbones in an organized protest of each scenario.

"Yes," said Morgan or Meagan or whatever her name was. The rat-a-tat of fingers on a keyboard sounded in the background. "I'm certain you're getting ready for a viewing party, but Sylvia asked me to nail this down before you get a flood of reservations after the show."

Holly's internal thermostat kicked up a few degrees. "Nail what down?"

Rhett joined her pacing the hall, as though he sensed something wasn't right.

"She asked me to book Holly Grove for a follow-up, ASAP."

"Book Holly Grove? Follow-up?" Her throat tightened as she spoke. "On what?"

"Your ghost, of course."

Holly practically choked, then stood dead still. *The one that's gone.* "*My* ghost?"

Rhett sat in front of her. He cocked his head to the side, as though he couldn't believe what she'd said. She could hardly believe what she'd heard.

"He was quite a hit with our test audience. They rated 'Ghost in the Grove' the best episode of the season," the assistant continued at an excited clip. "'Return to Ghost in the Grove' will open *Inquiring Minds'* next season."

"But . . ." She rubbed the back of her neck. What could she say? *I don't have a ghost anymore? Oh, hell no.*

"This is quite an opportunity for your establishment. Our viewership is up to three million and growing."

"I'm sure it is." She pinched the bridge of her nose and plopped down on the bottom step of the staircase. "But I'm renovating right now, and after the show, I hope to be booked solid for a while. It's just not a good time." *Ever.*

"We'll work around the renovations and pay you for your trouble. I've booked your available rooms from Wednesday through the weekend for the shoot, as well as the formal rooms downstairs."

A riff from "Sweet Dreams (Are Made of This)" rang out from Holly's computer in the kitchen—her alert for online reservations. The rash on her chest turned to arson to get her attention. Holly launched herself from the steps. "No! You can't."

Rhett's nails tapped the wood planks as he trotted to her side.

Oh, Rhett. This isn't good.

"Excuse me?" what's-her-name said, but she'd surely understood no.

Holly could live with the little lie that Holly Grove

was still haunted, but she would never allow anyone to prove it wasn't. "No offense, but I'm not interested in being on the show again."

"Sylvia will not take this well." The assistant's tone had turned sour. Holly had firsthand experience with Sylvia and didn't need round two. She was a force to be reckoned with.

"Give her my apologies," Holly said. *And tell her to butter my biscuit and take a bite, because that show ain't gonna happen.*

"That won't be necessary. Please hold the line for Sylvia Martin."

Oh, crapola.

Almost instantly Sylvia said, "Holly, my dear friend." She coated her pitch-perfect voice in enough artificial sweetness to clog the line.

Gag me.

"Sylvia," Holly gushed. Not to be outdone, she faked it, too. "Thank you so much for thinking about me and Holly Grove. It would have been so much fun to be on another episode of *Inquiring Minds*." About as much fun as digging up her ex for old times' sake. "Unfortunately, as I told your charming assistant, we're in the middle of renovations. Maybe another time?" *Like next February 30.*

"Holly, dear, I've booked the rooms. This *is* the time."

"Sylvia, dear, no offense, but I just can't make that commitment right now." Holly rubbed muscles knotting in her neck.

"May I be perfectly honest?" Sylvia asked.

If possible. "Always."

"I report on the strange, the unusual," Sylvia said,

repeating the promo line from her show. "I'm very good at what I do."

Modest too.

"It's not all real," Sylvia said. "I report, and the fans decide what's real and what's not."

Holly rolled her eyes. Most of it was questionable, in her opinion, but Nelda and millions of others were true fans of the show.

"The ghost in the grove is *real*," Sylvia said emphatically. "I know it. You know it. And my viewers will know it after tonight, right?"

"Right." The word squeezed through her vocal cords an octave higher than the truth would allow. *H-A-D a ghost.* Nelda's correction looped through Holly's mind. "Tonight's show can speak for itself. Why do another one on the same ghost?"

"Because I can win." Sylvia chopped each word with cool calculation.

"Win what?"

"I'm getting to that."

Lordy. The long way, especially for a New Yorker.

"There's this creeper, a debunker, who's been trolling me ever since the debut season of *Inquiring Minds*," Sylvia said.

"I've had a few trolls on my Web site." Some of them had a creep factor that gave Holly chills. She wouldn't wish trolling on even a frenemy. "Just ignore him and delete his posts."

"I've blocked him several times. He *was* a nobody. Now he's got a huge following on his blog and YouTube channels. He's questioning my credibility. My integrity." An edge crept into Sylvia's voice. "A few hours ago, I was promoting *Inquiring Minds* on a live radio show and that troll had the nerve to call in."

Holly pitied the guy for taking on Sylvia live. "What did you do?"

"He said he could debunk any of my hauntings—anytime, anyplace."

Oh, crapola. "And you called his bluff?"

"Of course. I challenged him to come to Holly Grove to attempt to debunk your ghost on my show, because I know he can't. The whole thing is going viral. My producers are loving it. The sponsors will love it. Plus, your ghost is going to silence him once and for all. That troll is going down."

Holly cringed. *My ghost was real, but he's gone—and I can't tell her or anyone else ever.* A twinge of guilt lulled about in her gut, but so be it.

"There's just one teeny-tiny problem," Holly said in a singsong voice. "Burl and I are, um, going through a rough patch. You know. Marital trouble. To tell you the truth, we're not speaking right now." *A proper lie is always partly true, right?* "He may not even show up if I want him to. He's spiteful like that."

"No problem," Sylvia said. "My undergrad is in theater. I'll act as if he's there, even if he doesn't show up."

"Wouldn't that be lying?" *And if she could actually act, wouldn't Sylvia be acting?*

"No. That would be great television."

"What if that's not enough to convince the debunker?"

"Holly, dear. Cameras fail. Hard drives crash. I wouldn't be the first to lose footage." Sylvia gave an exasperated sigh. "Believe me, nothing will air that makes me look bad."

"But without proof of the ghost, the debunker wins."

"*I* don't have to prove there *is* a ghost at Holly Grove. The show tonight proves that. He has to debunk the ghost on the follow-up show, and he won't. I guarantee it. My career is on the line here."

"Mine too. I just can't chance anything to ruin the publicity Holly Grove will get after the show tonight. I'm sorry. I just can't do another show."

"There's just one tiny problem, Holly," Sylvia said.

Is she mocking me?

Papers rustled. "I'm looking over the contract and releases you signed with *Inquiring Minds* back on October twenty-seventh."

Holly's mouth went dry. She'd been so thrilled for the publicity, she'd barely read the darned things.

"Section six-A," Sylvia said. "It's called an option. An option for us to follow up on the show or retake the episode within one hundred days of the original shoot. You know, in case there was significant public interest or something went wrong, which we know can happen, right?"

Holly plopped back down on the steps. "And if I don't allow the shoot?"

"Legal tells me you'd owe the production cost of the shoot. Megan, can you draft an estimate of the flight costs for the crew, four days' labor, and so on?"

"I'll have my attorney call you." Holly didn't have a lawyer. Delta Ridge hadn't had a lawyer since Leo Perkins went senile, but they had a bail bondsman who'd lost his law license. At least he could read legalese.

"Holly, dear. There's only one choice here. Pay or play."

* * *

"You better have a good reason for messin' up that bed you made this morning." Nelda's brows creased over her brown eyes as she peeked in the bedroom door. "What's the matter? You sick?"

Holly sniffled and shook her head. "I'm so screwed, and it's all my fault."

"Says who?" Nelda crossed the well-worn antique rug and propped a hip on the side of Holly's four-poster bed. As the mattress sagged under Nelda's weight, Rhett slid next to her.

"This." Holly waved the contract.

"A piece of paper made you crawl up in bed and blubber like a baby?" Nelda cocked her head to the side. "Must be some piece of paper."

"It's the contract I signed to have Holly Grove on *Inquiring Minds* back in October."

"And it's making you cry three months later?"

"I would have signed a deal with the devil to get publicity from *Inquiring Minds* back then." She flung the contract across the bed. "Evidently, I did."

"I'm guessing Miss Sylvia Martin is the devil."

"Pretty much." Holly blew her nose, then wiped at her eyes. "There's an option in there that forces me to agree to a follow-up show if they ask, and Sylvia did. She called a while ago to schedule a follow-up show on my ghost."

Nelda scrunched up her brows. "The one you've been telling me is gone?"

"And worse, she's challenged some debunker to try to prove Holly Grove isn't haunted on her show. I can't tell her it's not haunted anymore!" Holly fell back onto the bed and pressed her palms to her skull to ease her brewing headache.

"Don't *option* mean 'optional'?"

"Yeah. For *Inquiring Minds*." Holly rubbed her temples. "Not for me."

"You sure about that?"

"As sure as I can get without hiring a lawyer. I called my old roommate, Sarah. She's a lawyer in New Orleans now. Her 'free'"—Holly drew quotation marks in the air—"legal advice was to comply and buy her a drink next time I'm in the city." Holly blew her nose. "I even asked Purvis."

"That bail bondsman? Purvis Cumpton?"

"He used to be a lawyer, until he got disbarred." She couldn't remember why, but he was the closest thing Delta Ridge had to a lawyer. "He said the same thing and offered his bail services if things got ugly."

"What happens if you don't do the show?"

"Sylvia said I had to play or pay." Holly held her hand up and rubbed her thumb across her fingers. "Paying is not happening. I can't. Then they'll sue and put a lien on Holly Grove."

Nelda shook her head. "There goes your credit, again."

"And maybe Holly Grove, if reservations drop off." *Debt. Taxes. Nonstop maintenance.* "I'm one stumble away from losing her." She paused. "If I play and do the follow-up show, I could be exposed as a fraud." Holly flopped her hands on the bed. "There goes my business and Holly Grove." *Pay or play.* "I'm so screwed."

"You're only screwed if you keep wallerin' and blubberin' in that bed. If you're gonna get screwed, it outta be fun, right?"

"Nelda!" Holly landed a teasing slap on her arm. "I guess that means I've got to play this thing like a boss."

"Now you're talkin'." Nelda picked up Rhett and stood. "What you gonna do?"

Holly eased off the high bed and slipped on her stilettos. The four inches of height always fortified her confidence. False confidence was better than none. "Whatever it takes."

Connect with U s

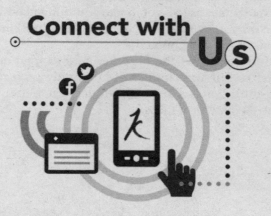

Visit us online at
KensingtonBooks.com
to read more from your favorite authors, see books
by series, view reading group guides, and more.

Join us on social media

for sneak peeks, chances to win books and prize packs,
and to share your thoughts with other readers.

facebook.com/kensingtonpublishing
twitter.com/kensingtonbooks

Tell us what you think!

To share your thoughts, submit a review,
or sign up for our eNewsletters, please visit:
KensingtonBooks.com/TellUs.